"I think you need a real man, Lizzie. Someone who can handle you."

"Do you? I haven't met a man yet who could handle his snuffbox, never mind a woman like me."

"You have now," Jack said.

Lizzie's eyes widened. "Meaning you?" She laughed. "I'd like to see you try."

"Despite all your nonsense, I find you very attractive. And when a man finds a woman attractive, he begins to think certain thoughts. And when he thinks these thoughts, a man is likely to kiss a lady."

"If that man knows what's good for him, he'd think again."

"Are you afraid, Lizzie?"

Lizzie snorted a most unladylike laugh. "Of you? Hardly."

"I think you'd like me to kiss you, but you're afraid you might enjoy it too much . . ."

CAPTIVATED

COLLEEN CORBET

AVON BOOKS ◆ NEW YORK

CAPTIVATED is an original publication of Avon Books. This work has never before appeared in book form. This work is a novel. Any similarity to actual persons or events is purely coincidental.

AVON BOOKS
A division of
The Hearst Corporation
1350 Avenue of the Americas
New York, New York 10019

Copyright © 1996 by Patricia Pellicane
Published by arrangement with the author
Library of Congress Catalog Card Number: 95-94905
ISBN: 0-380-78027-5

First Avon Books Printing: April 1996

AVON TRADEMARK REG. U.S. PAT. OFF. AND IN OTHER COUNTRIES, MARCA REGISTRADA, HECHO EN U.S.A.

Printed in the U.S.A.

RA   10   9   8   7   6   5   4   3   2   1

Prologue

1781, England

S he was naked.

And because naked women were rarely found wandering along England's rocky southern coast, Jack brought his horse to a breakneck stop, scarcely managing to keep his seat. Damn, if she wasn't the most spectacular piece he'd ever seen.

After a year's absence, he'd docked his ship in London this morning, and later met with his man of business for most of the afternoon. Jack knew he wouldn't reach his stepfather's place before dark. It was almost that now. Peering from the wrong side of a huge boulder, hardly able to fathom the scene on the beach below, he wondered if he'd reach it at all.

She stood facing the channel, silent and still as if lost in thought, her golden, hip-length hair curling and lifting from her back as it dried in the warm breeze. Narrowing his gaze, Jack saw she wasn't naked after all. Her far-too-short chemise hugged her body. Wet, it had turned totally transparent.

Gulls screamed and circled overhead, while the sea

1

foamed gently around her ankles. She looked to be a sea nymph, he thought, a goddess. Surrounded by light, she appeared intangible, surreal, an illusion come from the mist or a man's wet dream.

Huge jagged rocks formed a jetty on two sides as they stretched into the channel before her. Nearly meeting at one point, they created a near perfect half circle, ensuring privacy from any passing ship.

The sun, almost set, fought the coming darkness with flaming red light, and the woman at its shimmering center was bathed in ethereal sensuality.

His dark gaze took in the whole of her. Above a round, high bottom, her waist was impossibly small, her hips wide, her legs long. Jack knew he'd have to search far to find better.

Jack ran his hand over Rascal's neck in an unconscious gesture, soothing the nervous animal to stillness, even as he realized some surprise at his unusual interest. It wasn't like him to spy on a woman so obviously disadvantaged. Indeed, he'd seen his share and more of unclothed ladies. Seen and enjoyed their charms, if the truth be told. Jack ridiculed the thought that the mere sight of this one should hold him so enthralled.

He hadn't a notion who she was, but knew he'd soon find out. A piece this lush didn't stand a chance of evading him for long.

Jack supposed had he truly been the gentleman he was raised to be, he would have turned from the sight and allowed the woman her privacy. But Jack never claimed to be a gentleman. Not in the truest form of the word. He was a man first and always. A man who had a normal and healthy interest in women, especially beautiful women, and found it impossible to turn a blind eye to the erotic sight before him.

She turned and stood in profile, smiled, and then, as if she were alone in her bedchamber, raised her chemise and flung it over her head. Jack felt a moan tear itself from his lips, the sound lost in the breeze and foaming sea, for the woman could not only boast of perfection from the rear. Indeed the front of her was even more lovely.

She was small in stature and yet her breasts were large, almost too large for her slight frame. The pale pink tips, hardly distinguishable from this distance, were nevertheless enticing in the extreme. He felt his mouth water at the sight, and felt his groin tighten, as his gaze took in her gently rounded stomach and the golden triangle above long legs.

A woman, a maid no doubt, came suddenly into view, and a clean, dry gown was smoothed down the woman's damp body.

Jack frowned. Obviously she was someone of means and should have known the danger of disrobing in public. Someone should have a talk with her, to warn her of the risk she took. Jack thought he might take the chore upon himself and looked for one of the many paths that would lead him to the sandy beach below. Before he could move, the lady laughed and then suddenly spun on her heels, a gust of wind pressing the gown to her body, her golden hair blowing wildly behind her as she ran out of sight.

Jack sighed, knowing he wouldn't find her, for she could leave this particular cove on a dozen or more paths.

He shifted uncomfortably in his saddle. The woman had been naked for less than the count of three seconds. Judging by the thunder of his heart, and this sudden and foreign inability to breathe, Jack figured three seconds was as much as any man could take. His intention had been to ride directly to his stepfather's home, but Jack reconsidered, knowing a visit with the accommodating Mary Stone was definitely in order.

Chapter 1

The psalm ended just as Jack entered the pew. He sat behind Andrew Thomas, his stepfather. Having learned from servants that Andrew's daughter Margaret and her two daughters had returned from the colonies, Jack thought to find her sitting at her father's side. But Margaret sat farther down the pew, jostling a baby on her lap.

The woman beside Andrew had hair the color of palest gold, with heavy strands of silver entwined. Caught up in some elaborate twist of curls, it was mostly hidden beneath a wide-brimmed hat, its ribbons and ostrich feather dyed to match the blue of her dress. Her skin was unpowdered, a smooth, delicate honey that begged for a man's touch. With features perfectly formed, the gentle smile she shot his stepfather was just about breathtaking in its sweetness. She was a beauty to be sure and shockingly familiar.

She was the beauty he'd seen at the cove. There could be no mistake. What in the world was this wild young woman doing at Andrew's side? Could it be his elderly stepfather had taken leave of his senses and formed an alliance with a woman barely a quarter his age?

Jack silently ridiculed his thoughts. Andrew wasn't the sort to throw convention to the wind, no matter his advancing years. Indeed he'd never embarrass his family by openly flaunting a paramour. Who was she then? And what was she doing in his family's pew?

Jack breathed a sigh as the preacher began his fiery sermon. For the better part of an hour, all within the tiny country church squirmed as he looked down from the pulpit and accused his parishoners of just about every vice known to mankind. The reverend's eyes grew feverish with something close to madness as, caught up in his convictions, he promised, in terrorizing detail, that all would meet in hell's blazing pit should each, in turn, not show a profound change in his or her ungodly ways.

Jack cared little for church, and in particular the less-than-gentle sermons that were far too often and most generously forced upon the faithful. He believed in God, only his beliefs could not conceive of a God filled with hate and vengeance.

It was quite beyond his ability to imagine the majesty of land, water, and sky to have suddenly and for no apparent reason come into being. It was impossible not to believe at least that much while standing behind the wheel of his ship, his gaze focused on the grandeur of a rising sun. No, there had been a creation, he was sure, by some superior supernatural force most referred to as God.

What he did not believe in was the church and its preachers. To his way of thinking, their very existence confirmed God's rich sense of humor. Jack figured the vengeance put to the heavenly being no doubt originated from each man's own sense of guilt, and wondered what a man might have done to levy contrition so extreme.

Which brought to mind some of his own sins. John Black, the Earl of Dover, known to his friends as Jack, had spent the night with Mary Stone, a most obliging lady, trying to no avail to force aside the vision of another.

Now he stood with the congregation, hymn book in hand, as the organist began the closing psalm, listening to the lady before him sing. Her voice was loud, clear, and sweet, and Jack frowned at a stirring where, after last night, there should have been none. He was supposed to be praying in song and yet couldn't bring his gaze to the book he held. Instead it moved helplessly over a long, creamy neck, a slender, gently tapering back, to the smallest waist imaginable.

Jack knew he had a problem. Considering the tender smiles exchanged, she was important to Andrew.

He'd thought at first to stay on a bit and enjoy his stepfather's interesting and lively company before leaving for his manor home and the many properties that had for too long gone without his personal attention. But he wouldn't stay. John Black was a man of principle, of honor. He knew temptation when he saw it and would not put himself to the test.

The service was over and the church beginning to empty, some no doubt in a hurry to shake off the feelings of doom and damnation so lavishly bestowed by their preacher. Jack watched the lady in the pew before him reach for the baby in Margaret's arms. He watched her gather her purse and parasol before again offering his stepfather a smile.

Jack tapped the man before him on the shoulder. Andrew Thomas turned, and Jack grinned as a great smile split the older man's handsome face. "Jack! Good God, man, have you been there all this time?"

"Most of it, I'm afraid."

Andrew laughed. Knowing his stepson's aversion toward preachers on the whole, he guessed correctly the reason behind Jack's pained expression. The two stepped into the aisle and hugged briefly. "It's so good to see you again. I had no idea . . . How long will you be staying?"

"Not long, I think. I've neglected my properties a bit longer than I should have." The lady at Andrew's side turned then, and Jack was hit with the full impact of her loveliness. He'd thought her a beauty from a distance, but none of his imaginings had prepared him for this absolute perfection. Her eyes were blue, surrounded by thick, dark brown lashes; her lips, without the aid of rouge, were pink, her cheeks as well. Jack felt an unwanted tightening in his loins as the picture of her naked came again to mind. If he left on the morrow, it wouldn't be too soon.

"Margaret, Margaret," Andrew called out in a voice that was decidedly less than a whisper as he tried to gain the notice of his daughter, who was talking to the elderly matron at her left. "Look. Jack has come home."

Margaret turned quickly at the news. She whispered something to the old lady and then stepped into the aisle and offered Jack her hand along with her most lovely smile.

Margaret, at eighteen, had married and left for the colonies a year after her father had taken Jack's mother as his second wife. After a twenty-three-year absence, Jack thought her still one of the most beautiful women he'd ever seen. Indeed, the years had only added graceful maturity to sculpted features, creating a remarkably handsome woman.

Margaret recognized Jack as Helen's little boy and was not surprised that the once pretty youngster had grown into an astonishingly handsome man. "I'm happy to see you've come back in one piece. I don't mind telling you Father has been terribly worried."

Jack grinned and, after kissing her offered hand, threw propriety aside and took his stepsister into his arms. For a second it was as if they had never parted. Even now, though he towered over her slight frame, he could remember clearly the love-struck child he had been, trailing after her, watching her every move, his days of joyous pain gaining meaning only when she smiled his way.

Jack wondered if he hadn't, over the years, subconsciously compared all others to this woman. Not that he'd actively searched for a woman to love, for Jack wasn't interested in settling down, at least not yet. Indeed, in a world filled with gardens, there were many flowers to sample, and none so captivating that he might forgo the delightful discovery of yet another beauty.

And speaking of beauties, Jack's gaze moved again to the lady who had held his thoughts from the moment he'd seen her on the beach.

Lizzie, who had been watching this tender reunion with a smile, felt a sudden jolt to her stomach as the young man's dark eyes touched upon her. Lizzie's gaze narrowed. He was family, and even if he were not, a gentleman wouldn't look at a woman in so bold a fashion while in church. She listened to words genuinely spoken. "I was gone longer than I planned," he said, and then, "I didn't know until an hour ago that you had returned."

Margaret nodded as she disengaged herself from his gentle, brotherly embrace. "Jimmy died, and we thought it best to come home for a bit."

Jack's gaze returned to his stepsister, taking in the blue eyes that clouded with pain at the mention of her husband. He frowned, knowing a wave of helplessness, wishing he could take away her sorrow. "You have my condolences," he said with heartfelt sympathy.

"Thank you."

"How long . . . ?"

"A year ago."

"Have you been here a year already?"

"They arrived hardly a month after you left," his stepfather remarked.

A moment later Andrew ushered both his granddaughters forward and introductions were made. "My granddaughter Annie," Andrew informed him proudly.

Lizzie watched Jack press a light kiss to her sister's gloved hand. Annie had only just reached her sixteenth birthday. This was the first time she'd ever been greeted in an adult fashion. Lizzie realized the gesture had endeared the man in her sister's heart forever. She smiled and wondered if Michael, Annie's current flame, wasn't in for some competition.

The man possessed an overabundance of charm, Lizzie thought. Her gaze narrowed slightly at the thought, for she'd never trusted those so generously endowed. Lizzie was well aware that charm could hide a multitude of failings.

"And, of course, her sister, Lizzie," her grandfather explained. The elderly gentleman's grin was filled with love as he added, "You'd best make your offer now, boy. After the ball in two weeks, it will be too late."

Jack felt mildly surprised at the intense degree of relief that flooded his body. So the lady was Andrew's granddaughter, not his paramour. He grinned at this welcoming bit of news, even as he had the audacity to look Lizzie over just as if she were a prime side of beef. "I'm sure. Still," he teased, "she's a little small, I think. You might not ask too high a price."

Lizzie almost gasped at his bold wink, amazed that he might presume such familiarity, no matter that he was part of the family. She wasn't the least bit happy at his look of interest, especially not happy at the words spoken in jest, for they hit far too close to home. His easy remark hinted that she was marketed for sale, which she supposed in a way she was, or at least most assumed her to be.

She frowned, unable to ascertain the cause behind a sudden if slight sense of breathlessness. Confused and finding no reasonable answer for it, she forced her attention back to the man standing before her.

He did not dress with the frills and lace of the upper

class. He wore no wig, but tied his long, dark hair back with a thin string that matched the black velvet collar of his coat. No powder or patch adorned his face. And because he stood closer than what might be deemed proper, thanks to those who pushed at their small group as they made their way toward the two exits of the church, Lizzie grew aware of a light woodsy scent that seemed to emanate from both his skin and clothes. His features were large and his skin tanned, telling of many hours spent under the sun.

He was handsome in the extreme, but Lizzie swore his looks bore no consideration. Her heart fluttered illogically, but that could easily be explained. She'd had one cup of tea too many this morning. And her breathing? Why, anyone would have trouble breathing in a church so small and crowded, wouldn't they?

His dark gaze met hers, and Lizzie knew an unreasonable wave of fear. Fear that his gaze was too intelligent, that the twinkle of humor in dark depths boasted of secrets already gained. *Be careful, Lizzie,* came a warning from the back of her mind. *This one is too handsome, too sure of himself, and far too dangerous.*

"Lizzie," one of two little boys said, interrupting the introductions, as he pulled at her skirt and brought her mind from most peculiar thoughts. "You promised licorice if we were good. Were we?"

Lizzie smiled, looking over her two charges. "You were very good, Joey," she said as she jostled the baby in her arms to extract two pieces of candy from her purse. "And if you continue to be good, you'll have tarts when we get home.

"Wait with Missy at the front door, like little gentlemen." Her voice rose with the last three words, slowing the energetic boys to a walk as they followed their nurse to the church door.

Lizzie turned her attention again to the man before

her as her grandfather said, "Lizzie, this is Jack Black, my stepson, the Earl of Dover."

Lord, she breathed on a silent sigh, *another lord.* Just what England needed. Lizzie wondered if this country did not possess more lords and ladies than common folk. Now she understood her perplexing animosity. He was titled, and some sixth sense must have warned her of the fact, for she hadn't as yet met one of those pompous fools who didn't possess arrogance in the extreme. And if there was one thing Lizzie could not abide, it was arrogance. "Honored, I'm sure, Lord Domer." Lizzie, lost in her own thoughts, had not heard his title correctly.

Jack hardly noticed the misuse of his name, so taken was he with this pretty lady and the fact that she was Andrew's granddaughter. A granddaughter who had three children. But were they hers? The boy had called her Lizzie, not Mother. Could it be that she, too, was a widow? No mention had been made of a husband. Jack glanced at her hand; she wore no ring. And then his gaze moved over her trim form, remembering the sight of her naked on the beach. His mind was filled with questions, but he knew one thing for sure. His properties and business affairs could wait. He would stay on for a bit after all.

She was indeed beautiful, perhaps the most beautiful he'd ever seen, but she was far more than a lovely face and tempting body. Elizabeth Matthews was intriguing, to put it mildly, and hardly the norm when it came to a lady of breeding. For one thing, she was intelligent, Jack thought. And unlike the few of her sex who could claim a degree of gray matter, she showed no prudence in hiding the fact. Far too outspoken, she did not hesitate to speak her mind, while daring any, most especially an ardent admirer, to disagree.

Whether or not any of her suitors agreed with her often outrageous opinions was never clear, for Jack hadn't as yet seen one love-struck gentleman return for a second visit. In fact, only moments ago another had ignored Jack's friendly call and fled the house in a blur of blue satin and lace.

"Was that Chester Marks I saw dashing for the front door?" Jack asked after entering the sitting room to find a grinning Lizzie and her despairing mother. Before them on a low table sat a silver tea service and three china cups and saucers.

Lizzie's blue gaze twinkled with laughter. "Was he dashing?"

Jack grinned at her look of innocence, not for a minute taken in by her guileless smile. He hadn't a doubt that she'd purposely sent another man scurrying. "I don't know. Why don't you tell me? Did you think him dashing?"

Lizzie rolled her blue eyes toward the ceiling. "I meant, was he running?"

Jack shrugged. "Somewhere between a walk and a run. I suppose one might call it a dash."

"Lizzie did it again," Margaret said miserably.

Jack sat in the chair obviously just vacated by their latest guest. His warm gaze moved over Lizzie and her pink gown, noting it fit her form perhaps a bit too closely before flaring out at her tiny waist to a full skirt. Lizzie was a slender woman, small and petite, but fuller than most in certain places.

Jack was a man who had long appreciated the female body. And if this lady suffered some overabundance here and there, it only added to his interest. The truth was, it took some effort not to stare, not to lick his lips, as if faced with a tasty morsel.

He'd been back five days and thought himself mastering the feat quite nicely, especially when another was present. Jack pulled his gaze, his mind as well, from that savory sight and noticed this morning that her hair was piled high into a lustrous mass of golden curls, which pins seemed unable to hold. It was hardly midmorning, and thick tendrils had already fallen against her neck and halfway down her back.

Jack had never met a woman more beautiful, while at the same time less concerned with her looks. He had yet to see her sneak a peek at the mirror over the fireplace mantel. If her hair fell from its pins, she left it. If her skirt wrinkled, she ignored it. If her slippers became stained from damp grass, she never seemed to notice.

She was a confusing mix of elegance and earthiness. Jack never knew what to expect, for at any given time one might find her assisting her mother over high tea, or rolling upon the carpet, laughing with delight, in the company of one, two, or all three of her orphans.

Often disheveled, she brought a lusty, earthy picture to mind, as if she'd just stepped from a man's warm bed.

At the moment she portrayed a vision of delicate femininity, but Jack knew her fragile appearance totally belied a forceful personality. Her color was high. No doubt she'd been arguing again, or was about to, for her cheeks grew deliciously pink every time she began one of her tirades. Jack could not understand why most men seemed to shy away from the lady, for he thought a woman daring enough to have an opinion could only intrigue. His eyes never left the beauty before him, but it was her mother he addressed as he responded to her comment. "Did she? And what did she say this time?"

"She said, since God created both men and women, it's not only a reasonable conclusion, but obvious that He meant a woman to be equal to a man." Margaret breathed a disheartened sigh. "And then she lit her pipe."

Jack's gaze moved slowly over Lizzie. If she considered herself equal to a man, she was doing herself some disservice. Still he grinned as he watched the stem of her pipe slide between two rows of perfect teeth, to be clenched there tightly as she puffed a blue cloud over her head. Jack shifted slightly and crossed his legs, imagining the taste of tobacco on feminine lips, unable to control what that image did to his body. "Lizzie, you should go a bit more easy on men like Chester. His face was quite purple by the time he left."

"I know," she said with undisguised enjoyment as she blew a thin stream of smoke toward the drawing room ceiling. "It was purple before he left."

"Mr. Cross came yesterday and she served tea with Alice."

Any sign of laughter instantly disappeared as Lizzie returned, "The man is a snob and quite detestable, if you must know. Alice is an adorable baby." As if on cue, the orphaned baby appeared in the arms of one of the nursery maids.

Jack had no doubt the baby's appearance was timed for the now absent Chester. He grinned at the thought.

Lizzie put down her pipe and took Alice, cuddling her to her breast. "Look at her. Isn't she beautiful?"

Jack thought she was, but realized, too, that her deformed foot probably made her unadoptable. Lizzie didn't seem to notice her foot, or in any case, didn't seem to care. Obviously she loved the little girl, despite her imperfection.

Within minutes of their first meeting, Jack knew that Lizzie had never married, never had children of her own. Ever the bold spirit, she'd simply claimed for herself two boys and a baby girl from the parish poorhouse. The children were informally adopted. And Lizzie loved them as if they were part of her own flesh and protected them as fiercely as a tiger would her cubs.

"Why, anyone with half a mind can see as much. And Mr. Cross fairly swooned when I bid him to hold her. I couldn't pour tea with a baby in my arms, could I? The little accident should have meant nothing."

"What little accident?" Jack asked.

"The baby spit up on his pink satin coat," Margaret was kind enough to relate, her misery obvious.

Jack laughed. "That must have gone over well."

"It did, actually," Lizzie replied, and then bit her lip in an effort to control her laughter. "It went over his shoulder and down his back."

Jack laughed again. "And you had no idea that she might?"

"What? Spit up? Surely you're not suggesting that I have the power to make a baby spit up on command?"

"Can you?"

Lizzie laughed and then confessed, "The truth is, the man was worse than most. I've never seen contempt directed at a baby. I never thought it possible."

"What did you do?" Jack asked, knowing for a fact she had done something.

Lizzie shrugged. "I might have shaken the baby up a bit while playing."

Lizzie grinned at Jack's obvious enjoyment.

"I hope you hold me in a kinder light."

"I don't think you have anything to fear."

Jack smiled, taking her response in good humor. This was the first time they had actually conversed beyond an occasional good morning or good night. And Jack didn't so much mind what she said, as long as she said something. "Why don't I have anything to fear?" he asked.

"Because you like children. Truly, I cannot abide a man who does not."

"My clothes will be forever grateful, I'm sure."

Lizzie enjoyed his teasing and couldn't resist adding bluntly, "Still, you could do with a bit less starch in your shirts."

"Could I?" Now they were getting down to the meat of it. He'd wondered from the first exactly what she thought of him. "Meaning I'm a bit too stiff?"

Because he was family, because her grandfather obviously loved him, Lizzie was trying to be kind. The truth was, his manners were better than most. He did not curse in the presence of a lady. He did not spit. Yet she found him as arrogant as other aristocrats. Lizzie never realized her prejudice to be unjust. The simple fact that he was an earl was enough to ensure dislike. "Meaning like others of your class, you'll never find dirt under your nails."

"You think I'm too proud to work at hard labor?"

Before Lizzie got a chance to reply, which was probably for the best, Margaret suddenly blurted out, "And then she went riding with Mr. Stanley yesterday afternoon. I thought he was going to faint when she mounted Lightning."

Lizzie was aware that her mother's intervention was timely placed. Jack surely had no interest in what she'd been about yesterday. It was obvious her mother had noticed the growing tension between them.

Lizzie came to her feet and, without asking permission, put the baby in Jack's arms. If she hoped Alice might re-create yesterday's little scene, she did not say as much.

Jack cuddled the infant to his chest, not at all afraid that she might soil his clothes. He tickled her beneath her chin and smiled at her cooing. She was a pretty little girl. Too bad her disfigured foot would render her a cripple.

Lizzie shrugged aside the baby's obvious enjoyment. Alice was too young to know better, and it didn't matter whether this man liked children or not. The fact that he could play with a baby didn't make him any less a blue blood. "I'd rather a brandy than tea, Mother. Would you care for one?" she asked, directing her question to Jack only because manners insisted that she must.

"A small one, thank you."

Lizzie stood before the marble-topped server and poured two snifters of brandy as she responded to her mother's remark. "Why does a woman have to ride side-saddle? Because some man said she must? It's ridiculous."

Lizzie was a lady in the truest sense of the word. Ever mindful of others and their feelings, she never spoke a harsh word to a servant. She was kind, sweet, gentle, and loving to all. Still she was a woman with a mind of her own, and when society's rules proved illogical, she merely ignored them. Her family knew she was head-strong; a stranger might believe her eccentric.

Jack, both family and a stranger, knew only astonishment. "You rode astride?" he asked, obviously flabbergasted at the thought.

"I always ride astride."

Jack had never heard of such a thing. He knew Lizzie to be, if unorthodox, truly a lady. Yes, he was often reminded of the scene at the cove, but she'd thought herself alone then. And except for smoking and drinking strong brew, he hadn't suspected she'd defy society's dictates in the company of others. Obviously this woman did exactly what she pleased, despite the dismay it often caused her family. She threw convention to the wind and dared anyone to tell her otherwise. Oddly enough, he couldn't get the thought of her mounting her horse from his mind. He only wished he'd seen it.

"It's Amelia," her grandfather said upon entering the room, obviously having heard the last of the conversation. He sat beside his daughter. "I'll have to talk to your aunt before there aren't any men left."

Andrew Thomas was a striking elderly gentleman. Lizzie knew him to be three and seventy, and yet he appeared at least fifteen years younger. Tall, lean, and tanned, he had sparkling blue eyes, much like Lizzie and her mother. A shock of thick, pure white hair only added to the man's attraction. And attract, he did, Lizzie thought, just about every female over forty.

Andrew had already buried two wives. But if the anxious ladies in these parts were to have their way, there would surely be another Mrs. Andrew Thomas.

Lizzie laughed at her grandfather's frown as she handed Jack his drink, took the baby back with one arm, and bent to kiss the older man's cheek. "We've been over this before, Gran. It's not Aunt Amelia, and talking to her won't change a thing."

"She wasted her life, Lizzie. I won't see you follow her lead."

"And marriage, of course, must be a woman's ultimate goal?" she asked with a touch of derision.

"It's the natural way of things. How else can a woman find happiness, if not in her husband and children?"

"I already have children, Gran. Besides, I don't see why a woman can't be happy in her own right. Happy doing—"

"Please," Andrew groaned out on a despairing sigh. "Don't start that nonsense again. Happy with charity work?" He gave a humorless laugh, knowing the idea to be ludicrous. "It's not enough and you know it. You won't be happy in the end when you're an old maid."

"I'm already an old maid, Gran. Most women are married by the time they're eighteen."

"You're only twenty-two. I hardly think—"

"She's right, Andrew," Jack said. "Twenty-two is a bit long in the tooth."

Lizzie thought a man so disfavored by arrogance need not remark upon another's inadequacies. She shot Jack a look that clearly told him to keep his opinions to himself.

"What?" Jack asked, strangling on his laughter. "I'm only agreeing with you."

"I never said I was long in the tooth, so you're obviously not agreeing with me." And then turning to her grandfather, she said, "And I never said I wouldn't marry." Lizzie supposed she would marry one day, only if that day ever came, she wouldn't stand at the altar with an Englishman, especially not one of the upper class. She might love her grandfather, but she could hardly say the same of any of the men she'd met so far. No, she'd return to America after the conflict back home was over. And when she married, it most certainly would be to an American.

"You're doing a wonderful job of sending any interested prospects packing."

Jack offered his opinion on the matter. "If they're running, Andrew, you might think it for the best." Jack imagined this woman needed a man a bit more sure of his own worth. One who wouldn't feel threatened by her unorthodox behavior. "Lizzie appears the type that needs a strong hand."

"There has to be one man in the whole of England able to handle her."

"Please, Gran, don't say 'handle her.'" Lizzie couldn't control the revulsion she felt at the very thought that a man might try to handle her. It showed clearly in her eyes and in the small shiver she could not repress. "It's a sorry lot if those that I've met so far are the best that England has to offer. Why, I'd rather the butcher to one of those foppish fools."

"Lizzie," her grandfather warned.

"I know you don't like to hear it, but it's true. Their arrogance is appalling. It's bred into them from birth, and I for one cannot bear their company. Tell me how it is that a man dares to claim superiority over another simply because he was fortunate enough to be born on silk sheets rather than cotton?"

Jack couldn't help but notice her gaze did not leave his during her commentary. Apparently she equated him with all those foppish dandies courting her earlier. He couldn't resist teasing, "You mean to say they aren't superior?"

Lizzie rolled her eyes toward the ceiling in frustration.

"I've noticed a title often confuses a man as to his true worth."

"Meaning what? That you'd prefer a poor man to a rich one?" Jack thought the notion impossible.

"It's not a question of money. It's the arrogance all the noble possess."

"And you claim only the titled to be so disfavored?"

"Are you trying to say that I'm arrogant?" Lizzie thought she'd never admit to so abominable a failing.

"You lump the whole of one class, without exception, into unfavorable light. Can you truly say you're not prejudiced?"

Lizzie thought the accusation hardly fair. Still she wouldn't argue the point, for she didn't care what this man thought of her. "If I am, I have good cause."

"Lizzie," her grandfather interrupted, "all this is beside the point."

"I beg to differ, Gran, it is the point."

Lizzie, despite her former wealth, put on no false airs and hardly took to those who did. The truth was, she'd come to England out of desperation. Still, because of her love for her grandfather, she would enter into society just to please him, even though she thought the elite on the whole an ignorant, pompous lot, who might have invested more in soap and less in suffocating perfumes.

As a rule, the washwomen came to the gentry every six weeks, but if her grandfather could afford to attach such a woman to his staff, so might those of noble birth. Why most did not, Lizzie couldn't fathom.

She knew for a fact the women to be falsely feminine in the extreme. Beneath their powder, rouge, feigned smiles, and ability to swoon at a moment's notice lay a cruelty and coarseness Lizzie had not imagined possible. On more than one occasion she'd witnessed a supposed lady dare to reprimand one of her grandfather's servants, the scoldings delivered in the most vile language imaginable.

The ton all appeared cut of the same cloth, and Lizzie could not find one among the lot who might be considered a friend. Indeed she'd been snubbed by more than one *lady* since coming to these shores. A certain countess explained early on and in no uncertain terms that despite her grandfather's power and influence, a colonialist could never be accepted in polite society.

The lady in question appeared not to realize that if society were indeed polite, Lizzie would never have been reminded of her humble origins. Indeed, she had every reason to dislike the ladies of her acquaintance.

And the men were worse. Almost equally as feminine in their behavior as their counterparts, they seemed to care only about who was sleeping with whom and, of course, the latest tidbit of fashion news from Paris.

Like their ladies, they, too, had obviously been tutored in social niceties. Still, they appeared to think nothing of spitting, even as they bowed and turned a lavish compliment. Their artificial elegance barely veiled a coarseness she had not found at home.

In the colonies the men she'd known wouldn't have thought to swear oaths in the company of a lady. Nor did they speak in riddles of unsavory nature, which made Lizzie unsure if she should be insulted or not.

Smugly she imagined that if this collection of powdered, simpering, wigged fools, every one of whom sported a beauty patch, and held perfumed lace hankies between limp, jeweled fingers, proved to be England's best, she had no doubt that her countrymen would win the war.

"I'd rather a real man, Gran," she said, implying, of course, that those born to title could not qualify as such. "Someone without the trappings of feathers, lace, and satin."

"I have no doubt you will find one at the ball."

They had been over this on more than one occasion.

Lizzie wasn't about to take one of the foppish elite for a husband, and her grandfather knew it. Still, he'd insisted on the ball and Lizzie hadn't the heart to deny him. "No doubt that depends on whom you've invited."

Chapter 2

‟**Y**ou don't mean to say you feel some tenderness for the man?'' Lizzie couldn't help but ask her sister after realizing she'd mentioned Jack's name for the third time. She couldn't name the strange tightening in her breast and wondered vaguely at its cause.

Annie laughed. ''I know you bear him little fondness, Lizzie, although I can't understand why.''

Lizzie did not respond. She knew she was far outnumbered in her opinion and decided to keep her convictions to herself. To her way of thinking, the man was full of himself. Far too sure that every female within a hundred miles would fall at his feet, should he crook his little finger. She'd seen the maids giggle at his smile and watched the wives of army officers, whose husbands came to see her grandfather, goggle at the sight of him. As far as Lizzie was concerned, he was way too confident.

''He is handsome, witty, and a true gentleman, I think. He's dashing and stands out even among the officers that are always here. All the ladies, except for you, are mad for him.''

"Are they?" Again came a jolt that compressed the air in her lungs, and Lizzie thought it might be wise in the future to reduce the number of cups of tea taken with her morning meal.

"Haven't you noticed?" Lizzie watched her sister brush her long black hair. "Yesterday Mrs. Thompson came to tea. She was taken with him, I'm sure."

"Mrs. Thompson has her cap set for grandfather, and she is closer to mother's age than our exalted earl."

"I know, but you should have seen the way she smiled at Jack. She could barely take her gaze from him."

Again Lizzie noticed the familiarity. "Have you taken to calling him Jack now?"

"He's our stepuncle, Lizzie. What should I call him?"

"If he's our stepuncle, then call him Uncle."

"He asked that I call him Jack."

Lizzie sighed.

"He's taking the whole family to Southampton at the end of the week, for a day's outing."

"That sounds lovely, I'm sure," Lizzie said as she opened the closet door, while wondering what excuse she could give to stay at home. Perhaps someone might need her at the parish poorhouse. "Where did you say you put my boots?"

"In the corner. I think I'll wear my white dress. What do you think?"

"I think you look lovely in white," Lizzie said honestly, even as she dismissed the most ridiculous notion that in white her sister could not be mistaken for anything but what she was, a young girl. She had no need to worry on that score, she was sure. No matter the confusing sense of antagonism and attraction she felt toward Mr. Jack Black, she imagined him honorable enough to treat her sister with respect.

"I'm going to ask Mother if I can put my hair up."

"Why?"

"Because I'm sixteen and only young girls wear their hair down."

"Meaning there's a chance you might see Michael?"

Annie giggled girlishly. "Perhaps." Michael being the son of Mr. and Mrs. Thumbolt, the newest tenant in their small community, and the latest cause for Annie's heart to go all aflutter. Lizzie smiled as she watched her sister's eyes take on a soft glow.

"Then by all means ask," Lizzie said. Down on all fours, she stuck her head in the closet. "Finally," she sighed, and then came to her feet. "The next time you borrow these, bring them back."

Lizzie pulled her horse to a stop in an alley behind the Sea Witch Inn, so named after a clipper. Lizzie, hardly the sort prone to romanticizing, nevertheless imagined the name far too exotic for a clipper and thought it more probable the name had been derived from some pirate's ship.

Inside, Mr. Clancy would be polishing his counter, sweeping his floors, and altogether readying his establishment for the usual brisk noonday trade. Millie, his wife, would be working over a hot stove preparing the midday meal.

Southampton, a Channel port city and walled since the time of the Norman Conquest, was less than an hour's ride from her grandfather's mansion. It sat on a peninsula formed by the Test and Itchen rivers. The Sea Witch, a tudor-style inn, faced the Channel, a cobblestone and wood dock stretched out before it. In good weather Mr. Clancy brought a few tables outside so his patrons might enjoy the brisk sea air, along with the sight of ships entering and leaving port on two tides, as they indulged in hearty fare.

It didn't hurt any, Lizzie thought, that his wife was possibly the best cook in all of Europe, or that tales of

her excellent talent brought travelers and townsfolk alike
to feast with some greed on the generous meals served.

Lizzie found her mouth watering at the thought of the
oysters and succulent lobster she'd enjoyed just last
week.

Seagulls screamed overhead as they dove for a piece
of bread on the dock or the shadow of a fish in the
waters. Lizzie dismounted and tied her horse to a post
and hurried into the inn as one daring little beast appeared to think the ostrich plume in her hat a particularly
tasty morsel. She entered the inn by the back door and
headed for the private dining room, reserved as always
on Monday mornings for her and her two friends.

Inside Seth waited. Despite the fact that it wasn't as
yet time for the noonday meal, he nursed a tankard of
ale.

Lizzie blessed the day her gig had lost a wheel and
this man had come to her aid. Had the incident never
occurred, she might never have met Seth and his friend
Red.

It hadn't taken long for the truth to come out. To
Lizzie's delight she soon realized both Seth and Red
equaled her feelings in affection for the Crown. Both
Irish born, they had their own quarrel with the king and
felt no remorse in lending a little rebel, like herself, a
helping hand.

Indeed, over the last six months much had been done
to aid the American cause. Messages were regularly sent
regarding troop movements and times of sailings, while
the two men had teamed up and begun daring raids on
the local elite. At least twice a month, they helped the
cause by relieving those of their excesses.

All was sold, the gold handed over to Lizzie to be
smuggled out to the colonies, marked for those in most
need.

Lizzie found it deliciously gratifying that the very
lords and ladies who held themselves so high above an

ignorant colonist were inadvertently helping those so much more disadvantaged.

The arrival of Jack Black in no way curtailed Lizzie's undertaking. As always, she visited her grandfather's library at night, while all others slept. At his desk she reviewed his papers, noting arms displacements and troop movements. She brought the information weekly to London and her contact, Mr. Kent.

Her grandfather knew well enough where her loyalties lay. Still, nothing was kept under lock and key. Lizzie was never suspected of invading his papers. Because she was his granddaughter, he believed her incapable of treason. Only Lizzie looked at the matter in a completely different light. She wasn't committing treason. She was a spy. Once an active member of Washington's Culpepper ring, she had worked hard to see to the ousting of the British from her land. Now, forced into exile, she worked equally as hard for the cause.

Lizzie knew some guilt at the ease with which she accomplished her subterfuge. However, as much as she loved her grandfather, there was no other way to accomplish her goal. If there were, she would have found it.

Her grandfather had been a high-ranking officer once. And though he had not been an active member of the military for some time, his counsel was constantly sought out by those still in command. The prime minister, Mr. North, often sent aides to confer. Mr. Blake regularly visited to consult on troop maneuvers, strategy, arms displacements, and such.

Lizzie knew that should the worst happen and she one day be found out, Andrew Thomas and his family would not suffer for her action. He was a powerful man, with many a high-ranking friend. At least she could breathe easy, knowing no matter the outcome, her mother and sister would never again be tossed into the street, as they had from their home in America.

It was ridiculously easy to gain the information

needed. Lizzie only hoped that she could tell her grandfather one day of her activities. Most especially she hoped he would not hate her for what she had done. That he might understand that she, too, had to follow her heart.

Eager to keep up their nocturnal jaunts, Seth asked again if she wouldn't care to join him and Red. Seth's crooked-toothed smile was filled with deviltry when he asked, "You looking for a little excitement?"

Lizzie was greatly tempted. Still, she knew better than to put herself in danger so extreme. "I've just about all the excitement I can take, thank you. Is Red coming?"

"He'll be along. His wife thinks he's got himself another woman."

"Bloody hell!" Lizzie gasped without thought, knowing total freedom in her friend's company as she was permitted to act and speak as she pleased. "Does he?" she asked as she reached for one of the three tankards Seth had ordered. She took a long swallow of the cool but bitter brew and then filled and lit her pipe. She blew a cloud of smoke toward the darkened ceiling.

"Nay, the boy is still much taken with his bride. It's the work we're about that has her wondering."

"Do you think I should talk to her?"

Seth laughed. "I doubt Red will take it as a favor. Truth is, every time he's about to leave the farm, she . . ." He hesitated and, to Lizzie's surprise, colored just a bit before finishing with, "Well, to put it politely, she gets a bit friendly."

"Oh." Lizzie colored slightly herself, realizing what the man was about. Most young unmarried women in 1781, of gentle birth and rearing, knew nothing of the happenings between a man and his wife. But Lizzie could hardly be considered the norm. She was a woman of great curiosity. She wouldn't be kept in the dark for long. Years ago she'd questioned her mother, when the girls at school had alluded to the mysteries shared between men and women. Her mother couldn't bring herself to talk of such personal matters, promising Lizzie would know the truth of it in her husband's loving arms. Thankfully, her friend Megan suffered no similar aversion. A week after the girl had married, Lizzie came to know in blushing detail more than she cared to about the marriage bed. She took another long draft of the bitter but refreshing brew.

"Besides, I think it's not likely her mind will rest easy if she knows he's meeting with you."

"Is she one of us?"

"Perhaps, but Red worries for her safety and will not include her."

"Can I not try to explain?"

"Take a look in a mirror, Lizzie. No wife is going to believe you."

"I never thought of this complication. Do you think . . . ?"

"Don't you worry about it, missy. Red isn't complaining any."

He dismissed the subject and went on to another. "With all these robberies of late, word has it the upper crust is getting nervous. Some are getting dogs, others hiring guards."

Lizzie knew a dog could be managed, no matter how vicious, with a chunk of meat and, if all else failed, perhaps a less-than-gentle stroke of a stick, but guards? Guards could prove dangerous indeed. Despite her belief in her cause, Lizzie knew she hadn't the ability to actually kill a man. She wondered if either of these men felt equally inclined. "Are you sure?"

He nodded. "With guns."

"Oh dear."

"Aye, I said something like that the first I heard about it."

Lizzie grinned. Knowing Seth had a vocabulary that could easily rival any sailor's, she could well imagine what he'd really said. "What are we going to do?"

"Be very careful. We'd have a lot of explaining to
do if one of us showed up at the surgeon with a bullet
wound decorating our shirtfront."

"How will you know which one has guards and
which doesn't?"

"They'll be easy enough to see, I hope. In any case
we've got the Penny place staked out for Friday night.
They've gone off to London."

Still dressed in her riding habit, Lizzie stepped into
the breakfast room an hour later and gave a silent sigh
upon spying Jack at the sideboard filling his dish with
eggs and kidney pie. Was it too much to ask to enjoy
one meal in peace? One meal without his perfect napkin,
placed just so, without his perfect smile, his perfectly
asked questions in his perfect voice, his perfect hair, his
perfect tan. The man never dropped a thing, never tipped
over a glass; food wouldn't dare fall from his plate.

Judging from his dress, Jack had been out riding.
Lizzie curved one corner of her mouth down in annoy-
ance, for even the wind had not dared to ruffle his hair.
It was disgusting.

For more than a week now she'd studiously avoided
his lordship at every possible turn. Most every morning
she rode, rather than join her family in the first meal of
the day. Too bad the evening meals weren't as easy to
avoid. Instead they became a study in trying to ignore
him.

The problem was that ignoring him was impossible.
The fact that he seemed more perfect with every passing
day left her in breathless anticipation that he might make
some sort of blunder. Every night she watched, waiting
to see him fail at something, anything. One night she
actually willed a piece of spinach to make itself at home
between his teeth. It didn't, of course. Spinach wouldn't
dare decorate the teeth of this perfect lord.

"Good morning, Lizzie," Jack said as he turned from the sideboard and headed for the table.

Lizzie responded in kind, barely.

Jack sat and watched her fill her plate, knowing, of course, he was the cause of the lady's frown, for she frowned whenever in his company. Jack couldn't understand what he was doing wrong. He'd never met a woman who hadn't responded to his smiles, his gentle teasing, his charm, until this one. She did not like him, and he didn't know why.

They ate for some minutes in silence. Jack had business interests that needed his attention and felt a sudden restlessness to be on his way. He'd only stayed to better know Lizzie. But no matter his efforts, getting to know her proved impossible, especially since she'd somehow erected an invisible wall between them. He'd been charming in the extreme, polite, kind, and as humorous as he knew how to be, and still she remained completely indifferent. What the hell did she want of a man? Jack thought it time to find out. "Would you mind answering a question, Lizzie?"

She did not respond, only lifted her gaze from her plate.

"Have I done something to insult you?"

Lizzie's eyes widened at the question. She hadn't thought that he would have imagined her insulted. "No. Why?"

"Then why don't you like me?"

She frowned. "Everyone in this house likes you. All I ever hear is 'Jack said this' and 'Jack said that.' Your praises are constantly sung."

"By you?"

She shrugged. "You're my stepuncle, aren't you?"

Jack nodded. "And you're very good at evading a direct question."

Lizzie put down her fork and leaned back in her chair.

The man would have the truth. So be it. "What was the question again?"

Jack knew she remembered the question; still he repeated it. "Why don't you like me?"

There was a long moment before Lizzie finally sighed and then said, "My feelings have no direct bearing on you. I find I'm not terribly fond of any who are titled."

"You mean you dislike all of us, without question?"

"I'm afraid so," she said bluntly and with hardly a trace of the regret her words suggested.

"I've mentioned your prejudice before."

"You might be right on that score, but I didn't arrive here filled with intolerance."

"Meaning?"

"Meaning I rather liked the English, even if we failed to see eye to eye on certain subjects. Even those who occupied our home in New York were decent men."

"What caused you to change your mind then?"

"I've found the titled detestable in their arrogance. They sneer at those humbly born, treat human beings less favorably than their animals, and honestly believe it their right."

"I take it you believe me arrogant?"

"A bit, although you do a better job of hiding it than most."

"And how do I hide it?"

"For one, you're kind to the servants. For another, you've been known to share a pint or two with the head groom. And I've seen you with Alice and the boys."

The truth was, Jack had spent a good deal of time with the two boys Lizzie had brought home from the poorhouse. They sought him out every time they managed to escape the nursery. "And I'm only hiding my arrogance by doing so?"

Lizzie shrugged, unwilling to press her point, for in truth he did exhibit far less of that unsavory characteristic than most. Still, she was a stubborn woman and refused to admit an error in grouping him with the others. "With you it's more than arrogance. It's perfection."

"What?" Jack frowned, unsure if he should feel anger or amusement.

"Everything about you is perfect; hadn't you noticed? Your hair, your teeth, the way you smile. Your manners, your speech. The way you walk, your laugh. I'm beginning to wonder if you're real."

"You're talking like a fool."

"Am I? Look at your hair. You were out riding, but is your hair windblown? No, your hair is perfect."

"That's because I cleaned up before coming to eat, and if I'm perfect, then you are possibly the most ridiculous woman I've ever known."

Lizzie laughed without a shred of humor. "And how am I ridiculous?"

"For one thing, you smoke a pipe and drink brandy."

Lizzie fluttered her hand before her face as if she were about to swoon and taunted flatly, "Oh dear me, I'm chagrined."

Jack fought back the need to laugh. "For another, you ride a horse astride." His gaze lowered to her lap. He hadn't missed the fact that her skirt was split at the center and sewn into two wide legs so she might ride with a degree of modesty.

"I should be whipped, surely," she whispered dramatically.

"And you talk about things most men don't even understand."

"Then the men are at fault, aren't they?" she instantly countered.

"You could be arrested for half the things you say."

"Indeed? Arrested because I believe my country should be free of English tyranny? Surely that possibility alone proves me right. In the colonies, before the

British came, one might say anything without fear of repercussions.''

"You're fortunate no one pays you any mind."

Lizzie's mouth thinned with disgust. "No doubt because they haven't a mind to begin with. If they think at all, it's probably 'She's only a woman, poor thing.' "

"Perhaps, but you know what I think, Lizzie?"

"The truth is, Lord Dobber, I don't care what you think."

Jack grinned. This wasn't the first time she'd purposely misused his title. Indeed, he couldn't remember that she'd ever said it correctly. His gaze narrowed as he studied her beautiful face, wondering why her sly insults only seemed to further intrigue. Was it the age-old need for conquest? Certainly he'd like nothing better than to conquer this little spitfire. But that wasn't the whole of it. He couldn't think why, but for some illogical reason he wanted more than to tumble this one into bed. "I think you need a real man, Lizzie. Someone who, as your grandfather says, can handle you."

"Do you? I haven't met a man yet who could handle his snuffbox, never mind a woman like me."

"You have now."

Lizzie's eyes widened. "Meaning you?" She laughed contemptuously. "I'd like to see you try."

"Despite all your nonsense, I find you very attractive." Jack wasn't sure if it was despite her nonsense or because of it. All he knew was, he'd never met a woman like her. And seeing her naked had, in his mind, sealed both their fates.

Lizzie only blinked. His last comment seemed not to fit into their heated conversation at all. Lizzie felt suddenly off balance and struggled for a response. "All my . . . What? You find me what?"

Jack ignored the question. "And when a man finds a woman attractive, he begins to think certain thoughts."

"Bully for him," she said dismissively, hoping that

would end the matter, for she knew well enough by the look in his eyes at what he hinted.

"And when he thinks these thoughts, a man is likely to kiss a lady."

Lizzie came to her feet so suddenly that her chair fell back. She leaned forward slightly as she glared at his smile. Her words were low, the threat behind them clear. "If that man knows what's good for him, he'd think again."

"Are you afraid, Lizzie?" Jack knew fear wasn't exactly the right word here. He thought interest mixed with apprehension closer to the truth. Still, he knew she'd never admit to that or any weakness.

Lizzie snorted a most unladylike laugh. "Of you? Hardly."

"I think you'd like me to kiss you, but you're afraid you might enjoy it too much."

Lizzie felt her heart slam unexpectedly against the wall of her chest, while an unexplained thrill raced over her entire body. She'd never admit to such a thing. Never! She didn't want to kiss him. It was those dreams. She couldn't control dreams. No one could. And in them he not only kissed her, but she kissed him back. Lizzie felt color burn her cheeks. It was all his fault. Everything was his fault. She'd never dreamed of kisses before she met this man. Her words were far weaker than she might have liked. Still, she considered herself fortunate to be able to speak at all. "And I think you're out of your mind."

"Do you? We could try it and see if . . ." Jack didn't bother to go on. He only laughed softly, thinking he'd never seen a woman's back more stiff, nor one who could walk quite so fast.

She was angry. Granted her anger smoldered beneath the surface of cool control, but there was no denying the fact. And Jack knew at last what that anger was about.

As he was quite a bit more worldly than the lady, he

knew sexual attraction when he saw it. She could deny it forever, but he'd seen the emotion flare to life at the mention of a kiss. She was interested; more than interested if the truth be told.

Jack had already admitted to his own attraction. Now all that was needed was for Lizzie to do as much. And Jack had every confidence she would soon.

Chapter 3

⟨⟨⟨◦◦◦⟩⟩⟩

Lizzie sighed and cuddled a sleeping Alice closer as she watched Steven and Joey fidget across from her. "Can neither of you sit still for a minute?"

"Are we almost there?" Steven asked for perhaps the twenty-fifth time.

"We've been to London before, Steven. You know we have a ways to go yet."

"Can we have strawberry tarts when we get there?" Joey asked.

"No doubt," Lizzie returned, "but only if you ask politely."

"You're supposed to say 'may we,' not 'can we,' " Steven corrected. "Don't you know anything?"

"You're the oldest, Steven. Don't you think it would be kind of you to instruct in a gentler tone?"

"But he's so stupid," Steven said, exasperated.

Steven, the older of the two by a year, had been sorely abused by a drunken father. Thankfully he had done the decent thing and died before his son learned to imitate the violence. As it was, the boy was often sullen, suffering in silence from terrifying memories. And when he wasn't sullen he was mean to his adopted brother. Lizzie

37

thought he needed her love the most and expected that it might take a bit of time before he could put aside his defenses and learn to love in return. "I'm sorry you think so. I had in mind today a visit to the park and perhaps a puppet show. The trouble is, only bright little boys could possibly enjoy it. That's too bad, don't you think?"

It took but a second for Steven to see the wisdom in a change of heart. "He's probably not that stupid."

Missy, sitting at Lizzie's side, turned her laughter into a delicate cough.

"Probably not stupid at all, wouldn't you agree?"

Steven nodded, and Joey, much more the even-tempered and good-natured of the two, grinned happily. Apparently he was quite used to the insults his brother threw his way.

"I think such intelligent little boys deserve a treat. Missy, did you remember to bring the candy sticks?"

"I did, miss," the nurse said as she reached into her pocket for hard candies.

After yesterday's visit with Seth and Red, Lizzie had a purse filled with gold that needed to be delivered to Mr. Kent. On such occasions Lizzie often rode to the city alone. Lightning was as fast as his name implied. Usually she could reach the city and make it back before anyone noticed her absence. This time, however, she thought to bring the children as all three needed new clothes. It wouldn't be thought unusual, then, to stop at Mr. Kent's coffeehouse for refreshments after a day spent shopping.

Lizzie's back ached even though she and Missy had shared carrying Alice. Exhausted, she slid into the rickety chair, thankful to have left their many packages with their waiting driver.

At the park, while they'd concentrated their attentions on changing the baby, Joey had wandered off. It had taken the better part of a terrifying half hour to track him down at a stand selling meat pies. Lizzie swore she'd never take all three to the city again. The next time they needed clothes she'd take them one at a time.

"Can I have a strawberry tart?" Joey asked, his bright eyes upon a fellow customer enjoying the tasty treat.

"May I," Lizzie corrected, while wondering how a little boy could eat so much. He'd just finished off two meat pies.

"May I? Huh? May I?" Joey asked enthusiastically.

"You may," Lizzie returned with a tired smile. "And what about you, Steven? Would you like the same?"

Steven nodded just as Mr. Kent approached their table.

Lizzie reached for her napkin. Under it she held the small bag of gold coins. "My napkin is soiled, Mr. Kent. Might I have another?"

Mr. Kent slid both the napkin and bag into his pocket as he said, "Of course, ma'am."

Afterward, while Lizzie sipped at her coffee waiting for the boys to finish huge servings of strawberries, Jack came to suddenly stand in front of them. "I thought I recognized your carriage." He took a chair from an adjoining table and sat uninvited. "Have you spent the whole day in the city?"

"We shopped," Lizzie explained.

"We saw a puppet show," Joey added.

"Joey got lost," Steven added, "and Lizzie started to cry."

Jack frowned, his gaze fixed on the younger boy. "What happened?"

"I was hungry."

Jack's gaze clung to Lizzie's over Joey's head. "You mustn't ever frighten your mother like that again."

"I said I was sorry."

"Good," Jack said, tearing his gaze from blue eyes to empty plates. "Are you ready to go home now?"

"More than ready," Lizzie breathed tiredly.

As if they weighed naught but a feather, Jack took one boy under each arm as they left the coffeehouse. Lizzie was tired. Indeed, more tired than she'd first imagined, for she had a sudden insane wish that Jack's arms were around her.

Lizzie sighed as she folded the last sheet and placed it along with the others upon the shelf. She had worked all afternoon, doing laundry, changing and bathing children; and then, while the babies napped and the older children were outside playing, she'd helped Mrs. Downly with the cooking. Her shoulders ached with the day's effort, but she didn't mind. She loved caring for the children. Besides, anything was better than being forced to bear the earl's company.

The house was dark, the children asleep. All was quiet with the exception of Mrs. Downly's soft snores. Becky stood at the door waiting for her to leave, ready to lock up for the night.

Lizzie took her shawl from its hook and slid it over her shoulders. "Good night, Becky."

Becky gave a little curtsy. "Good night, miss, and thank you."

Lizzie smiled. She couldn't count the times she'd told the woman her thanks weren't necessary, that she truly enjoyed helping out at the orphanage. But Becky thanked her regardless.

With the door locked behind her, Lizzie moved toward the low wooden gate and then smiled when she saw Richard Poole coming to meet her. Lizzie worked two, occasionally three, days a week at the parish poorhouse. Richard often walked her home when she stayed this late. Lizzie wasn't afraid, for the walk to her grandfather's took less than a half hour. Still, she was glad for the company. "Would you like some tea?"

"That would be lovely," Lizzie said, happy for the

chance to sit and talk a bit with her friend. She accompanied the preacher to the rectory next door.

"You look tired," he said as she made herself comfortable in his small parlor. "You shouldn't overdo." He poured a cup of tea already prepared by his housekeeper and handed it to her.

Lizzie smiled. "There was much to do today. The new baby is lovely, isn't he?"

Richard had found the child two days ago just inside the door of the church. No doubt a young girl had found herself in trouble, or perhaps a mother with already too many to feed had thought it the only way for her baby to survive. At least twice a year a newborn was left in his church.

Richard smiled, quite sure of her intent, since over the last year she'd placed three of the parish foundlings with families. "I suppose you'll find him a home soon enough."

"I was thinking about my cousin Jane, my father's niece. She and her husband live just north of London." Lizzie finished her tea and watched as Richard refilled her cup. "They've been married five years, but are still childless." Lizzie smiled as she remembered their last visit. "She was very much taken with Alice. I thought I'd have to wrestle the baby from her arms the last time she left."

"She may not want a boy then."

"I think it wouldn't matter. I'll send off a note in the morning."

"How is Alice coming along?"

"Marvelously."

"And her foot?"

Lizzie shrugged. "It's the same. Dr. Madison said she'll limp, but otherwise she'll be able to walk. I've spoken with the cobbler. When she's ready, he'll make her special shoes."

"No one wants her because of her foot."

"I do. She's a beautiful little girl."

"I can see she's quite stolen your heart."

Lizzie smiled. "She has."

"You're going to keep her then?"

"There's never been a question about it. She was mine from the first moment I saw her."

"What about Joey and Steven? Do you think it wise to keep them at your grandfather's?"

Lizzie frowned. "I can't see why not."

"Well, for one thing, all that pampering is sure to spoil them."

She smiled at the thought of the boys. "All of us need pampering at times, wouldn't you agree?"

"What will happen when they have to come back?"

Lizzie shook her head. "But they won't be coming back. They're taking lessons now, and grandfather told me he's looking into a good school."

"Truly?" Richard asked, obviously surprised by this bit of news. Until this lady came to his parish, the orphans were pretty much ignored. Yes, the good people of the parish saw to their basic needs, barely, and a few ladies, most especially during the Yuletide season, came with gifts, but otherwise the children knew only poverty and deprivation, which would no doubt follow them into adulthood.

"Steven is only eight, and amazing with numbers. Grandfather thinks he should do well in business. First he'll go to school, of course, and then he'll apprentice. Perhaps, after a bit, he could work for Grandfather. And Joey reads everything he can find. I think he's halfway through most of the books in the library."

"And what will he be?"

"A doctor."

Richard smiled. "Is it your hope or his?"

Lizzie only wanted the best for both boys. Still, she knew she wouldn't force either to her way of thinking.

"I planted the seed. We'll see where it goes from there."

"I wonder if you realize how important you've become to the parish."

Lizzie smiled. "No more important than yourself, or Becky or Mrs. Downly."

Richard smiled. "I'm expecting my sister for a visit next week. Would you come for dinner on Sunday?"

Lizzie was surprised at the invitation. Of course, Richard had been invited to her grandfather's for Sunday dinner a number of times, as he had to many of the homes in the area. And her family had been invited back. But Lizzie had never been invited to dine alone, even though they'd worked together for close to a year. Except for an occasional invitation to tea after a hard day's work, there had been no social contact. "That would be lovely," Lizzie returned, and then sighed, "I'd best be getting back before Mother begins to worry."

"Of course," Richard said as he stood with the intention of walking her home as usual. It was then that someone knocked. Richard frowned. "Who could . . . ?" he began as he turned toward the door and opened it.

"Good evening, Parson. Is Lizzie, I mean Miss Matthews, here?" Lizzie heard Jack say.

"Your servant, sir," Richard said with a low bow. He backed up then, and Jack entered the house.

"Here you are," Jack said. "Your mother sent me to fetch you."

"Is everything all right, my Lord?" Richard asked.

Lizzie marveled at the abrupt change in Richard's demeanor. A nervous sort to begin with, he appeared suddenly at a loss as to what to do with his hands. First he clutched them together behind his back and then across his stomach. And as he stood in his own sitting room, he grew slightly bowed, as if naught but the lowest of servants, awaiting permission to raise his gaze to some heavenly host. Lizzie frowned, not at all pleased to see their parson shrivel to something less than a man, while Jack, just as if it were his due, became the recipient of awe. Lizzie thought the class distinction couldn't be more obvious, nor more appalling.

"Everything is fine. Margaret worries when it gets late."

"I was about to walk her home."

"Well then." Jack flashed an appealing smile, unaware of the man's discomfort. "I've arrived just in time to save you the trouble." Jack's gaze moved beyond the preacher and settled on her. "Are you ready, Lizzie?"

Lizzie nodded in response. "Good night, Richard," she said as she offered him her hand, not at all pleased with the parson at the moment. She was annoyed that he should act less than a man simply because an earl was present. "I'll see you Tuesday, if that's all right."

"Tuesday is fine."

"Thank you for the tea. And be sure to tell Mrs. Cunningham the scones were delicious as usual."

Lizzie stepped outside and, without waiting for her escort, began her walk home. Jack murmured a quick good-night and was soon at her side. "In a hurry?" he asked.

"As you said, it's late."

"You don't often work three days a week, do you?"

"Not often."

"Then why did you today?"

Lizzie might have told him she worked only to avoid his company. She might have said that the thought of being forced to endure a family outing with him was far from appealing. She said instead, "A new baby was left at the church."

Jack laughed. "And you couldn't wait to see it?"

"He's beautiful."

"You think all babies are beautiful."

"Aren't they?"

"You should have your own."

"No doubt I will, one day."

"What about you and our righteous parson?"

"Richard?"

Jack nodded. "Richard. Yes, I've noticed you're on a first-name basis."

"Shouldn't I be? He's my friend."

"He's more than a friend. What I can't understand is how you can stand the man. He sees nothing but right and wrong. There is no gray area in his thinking. And his sermons, God, why would anyone want to punish themselves by listening to that rot?"

"What rot?"

"That we'll all find ourselves in a fiery pit of agony for all eternity. How does he dare to judge?"

"I'm sure he doesn't mean to judge. The truth is, some of us may suffer for our wrongdoings."

"Some, meaning you won't be joining the rest of mankind in hell?"

"I don't believe mankind so evil as to end up in hell, Lord Duller." Lizzie frowned and shot him a hard glance. The night was lit only by a half moon, and yet Jack could easily see her annoyance. "And what do you mean he's more than a friend? Exactly what are you hinting at?"

"I'm not hinting, I'm asking. Does his being in love with you make working together difficult?"

"He most certainly is not in love with me."

"He is."

"He is not!"

"He is," Jack continued to insist.

It made no sense to further the argument, for in truth neither could know for sure the man's feelings. Still, it galled Lizzie to let him get the last word. "Reverend Poole has never once given me a reason to believe he's anything other than my friend."

"He will. Has he invited you to dinner yet?"

Lizzie's mouth dropped open with surprise. "How did . . . ?" And then, "You are the most annoying man."

Jack laughed. "Am I? Why? Are my clothes too clean? My smile too perfect, my hair too neat?"

The truth was, his hair wasn't neat at all. He looked as if he'd run his fingers through it several times. Lizzie refused to admit that the sight of his hair mussed was pleasing. It was a ridiculous thought. "Among other things."

"What kind of things?"

"I'm tired; I'd rather not talk, if you don't mind."

"What you mean is, you don't want to admit that I'm right."

"He does not love me! He only asked me to dinner so I might meet his sister."

"He wants you to meet his family and you still refuse to admit that I'm right?"

"If you must talk, would you mind finding another subject?"

Jack laughed softly as if he'd won his point. Lizzie only ground her teeth together. "All right, if you don't want to talk about our parson, we could talk about you."

"What about me?"

"The cowardly way you avoided our outing today."

Lizzie flashed him a smile. "I thought it was quite brilliant myself."

"You missed a delicious luncheon. We made gluttons of ourselves over lobster and oysters."

"Mrs. Clancy is a wonderful cook. Grandfather has been trying for years to convince her to—"

Jack cut her off with, "Why didn't you come?"

"The children needed me."

Jack ignored her response and stated bluntly, "You were afraid, but you shouldn't have been."

"You're being ridiculous again. What would I have to fear?"

"The things you feel. But nothing would have happened. We wouldn't have been alone."

"Are we speaking the same language? I haven't a notion as to what you're talking about. What things do I feel?"

"That you very much want me to kiss you."

Lizzie halted abruptly and eyed the road ahead. He was back to kissing again. "You're not only ridiculous. You're insane." Lizzie wondered if she hadn't made a mistake in stating her thoughts so bluntly. After all, she'd only known this man a short time, which meant she didn't truly know him at all. There was no telling what he was capable of. The moment she realized her words could have easily pushed him over the edge, she began walking again, briskly, her gaze searching for a place that would offer some cover.

Jack ignored her comment and easily kept pace. "But the truth is, no matter how you plead and beg, I won't."

Lizzie stopped again, blinked, and then laughed at the thought that she might beg this man, or any man, to kiss her.

"My moral code would insist on my refusal, I'm afraid."

He was grinning, his dark eyes twinkling with laughter. She realized he was teasing, and knew suddenly she had nothing to fear. "Your moral code? I take it yours does not exclude frightening women."

She was walking again with Jack at her side. "Did I frighten you?" he asked.

"You tried."

"Which is a neat way of avoiding an answer. Why would I want to scare you?"

"Perhaps you thought once I realized you were teasing, I'd relax in your company."

"And have you? Relaxed, I mean?"

"That would be a mistake, wouldn't you agree?"

"I'm practically positive it wouldn't be," he teased.

"Practically positive is a bit inconsistent, wouldn't you say?"

"All right then, positive."

Lizzie grinned and then repeated his words, half to herself, as if mulling them over were a cause of amusement. "No matter how I pleaded or begged?" She laughed again at the thought.

"Not even if you leaned against me and pressed your mouth to mine."

Lizzie only chuckled.

"We're home. You can relax now."

"Thank you for coming to get me. There's no telling whom I might have come across and kissed if you hadn't been there."

"No, it's only me you want to kiss."

"Oh." She laughed again. "Thank you for clearing that up."

"You're welcome."

"Your hair is mussed."

They were both still smiling when she slipped into the house.

"Good God, you're killing me," Lizzie groaned, her slender arms wrapped around a thick bedpost for balance as Mercy pressed her knee to the smaller woman's back and pulled at the corset's ties, effectively compressing three inches from a waist that normally measured no more than fifteen. Lizzie moaned at a wave of dizziness, even as she wondered how she was to manage consciousness while so breathlessly bound.

This was her final fitting for the party in her honor tomorrow night, and she dreaded it with every fiber of her being. Not only because it was impossible to breathe, but because she had no interest in meeting the rest of England's elite, and her grandfather knew it.

Those she'd met so far had been quite enough, thank you.

But Lizzie thought it wouldn't hurt to allow the old man his wishes. After all, he wasn't pressing her into marriage, but offering an opportunity to meet some dashing young fellow. The problem was, Lizzie doubted a dashing young fellow existed in all of England.

"This is the last time, I swear it." Lizzie gasped.

"Stop complaining. Your grandfather went to a great deal of trouble. He has his heart set on all of England falling at your feet," her mother returned while Lizzie silently bemoaned the uselessness of the festivities since she'd made up her mind from the beginning. This little rebel would not be marrying some ostentatious peacock anytime in the foreseeable future. Indeed not ever if she had anything to say about it, and Lizzie thought she had everything to say about it. The moment this war was over, she was going home to take back her properties and live as she pleased, without English interference.

And in order to do as much, she would need to remain unmarried. Her father had given his life for the cause. It would only discredit his memory should Lizzie take one of the enemy as her husband.

Of course, it was one thing to plan a quiet life back home, quite another to see that plan come to fruition. Lizzie was not unaware of her beauty and the great deal of importance men attached to the evanescent attribute. Under normal circumstances she would likely receive many offers. Offers she'd be hard-pressed to refuse, due to her grandfather's urgings. Still, in the end, she would succeed.

So far it had been simple enough to dissuade an eager suitor of his intent by simply being herself. To her way of thinking, there wasn't a man in all of England brave enough to take on a wife so outspoken.

Her mother handed her a gown of ice blue silk. When

it slid into place, Lizzie gasped at the very low neckline. Thanks to her corset, her breasts were forced upward and forward, appearing even larger than they were. The problem was, the bodice of this dress was meager to say the least. It left just about nothing, save the pink tips of her breasts, to the imagination. This was to have been the last of her fittings, and yet the bodice was not nearly ready.

Margaret, realizing her daughter's problem, quickly pressed her lace handkerchief into the daringly cut bodice. "I'll have the seamstress take care of it."

The sleeves were tight almost to the wrist, where a large ruffle covered most of her hand. The gown fit snugly over the bodice and midriff to her waist. At the waist it fell open to the hem, allowing a slip of darker blue ruffled lace to show.

The dress in place, Lizzie stepped into her shoes, only to find the heavily embroidered, jeweled high heels and long, narrow toes made her misery complete. Lizzie had never worn heels so excessively high. It took all of ten seconds for the pain to grow unbearable.

"Lord, someone's bound to fall, but I'm afraid it won't be England. Discounting the fact that I can't breathe, how am I to walk in these?"

"It's only for a few hours."

A few hours or few minutes, what did it matter? The pain was not likely to lessen any until the shoes were off. Lizzie shot her mother a wry sideward glance and took a wobbling step as she let go of the bedpost. "A few hours of misery sounds inviting. In the end, no doubt, my suffering will strengthen my character."

"Heaven help us all if your character grows stronger," her mother said. "You'll need to practice walking in them a bit."

Margaret Matthews sighed as she watched her daughter lurch with something like a drunken gait toward the

center of the room. Her mind was filled with catastrophic pictures of Lizzie tumbling down the great
stairway to the hall below. "Lizzie, you must practice
walking downstairs. Everyone will be watching your
entrance."

Annie giggled at the sight of her sister's inability to
find her balance, even as she wished they could trade
places.

Annie was the opposite of her sister in every way.
She was dark where Lizzie was blond, sweet and obedient where Lizzie usually held to her own way of thinking and acting. Annie would have given much to be in
her sister's place and could hardly wait for next year
and her chance to enter society.

"I can't do it," Lizzie groaned as she felt her ankles
wobble. "Mercy, get my slippers."

"Your slippers will not do," came her mother's response. "The heels aren't high enough and your gown
will wrinkle at the hem."

"Then tell the seamstress to take up the hem," Lizzie
said simply, even knowing as she said the words they
were instantly ignored. Apparently there was a need for
a woman to suffer lest she not look her best. "I won't
be able to dance." Lizzie sighed unhappily, for she did
enjoy dancing. Again her mother ignored the complaint
as she guided Lizzie from her room and said, "Remember, shoulders back. Stand up straight. And for goodness' sake, walk slowly."

Lizzie scowled at the orders. First of all, she thought
it most uncomfortable to keep her shoulders back as they
most definitely needed to be while wearing this dress.
Her spine ached already with the effort. And Lizzie
never walked slowly. It took a determined effort to do
both at the same time.

"Fine, but if I fall and kill myself, don't bury me in
this god-awful contraption."

With her mother at her side, and Annie and Mercy

following close behind, Lizzie leaned one hand against the brocade-covered wall for balance as she made her way toward the great stairway, where tomorrow night she'd make her first appearance before what she secretly ridiculed as *polite* society.

The great hall below was empty. Not even a servant hovered about in its colossal columned midst. Lizzie, being a free-spirited soul, as well as a woman of excellent humor, rarely allowed a prank to pass her by. She grinned as she moved toward the elaborate mahogany railing and in an instant, to her mother's horror, and her sister's laughter, straddled the smooth wood and went sailing down the long, winding length only to fall in a heap at the bottom of the stairs.

This was not the first time Lizzie had descended in such abandoned freedom. Previously she'd been able to bring herself to a stop before chancing injury. In this case two things impeded her intent. One was the fact that the balustrade had been polished to a glass-like finish for tomorrow night's festivities. The other was that her silk underthings offered no friction, no resistance.

Still, all might have ended with no more than a slight gasp and perhaps a bout of laughter at her mother's obvious surprise, had not one of Lizzie's high heels got caught in the folds of her many petticoats. She meant to make her landing on her feet, despite the speed of her descent and the foot pain she would no doubt suffer upon reaching the first floor. But because her foot was completely tangled, she landed first on the twisted appendage and then on her bottom in a flurry of ruffles and lace. Her whalebone petticoat flipped over her head, taking the dress and frilly petticoats with it, leaving long legs and silk drawers exposed for all eyes to see.

Jack had entered the mansion just as Lizzie straddled the railing. He watched with amusement as she, quite stunningly dressed, took the ride to the floor below. But Jack's grin turned into a frown as Lizzie's feet crumpled beneath her and she landed with a small cry of pain on her backside. He rushed forward, ignoring for the moment the long length of leg and silk drawers. "Are you all right?"

Lizzie gasped with pain as she tried to battle frills and lace back into place. She didn't try very hard, since she could barely think beyond the searing agony in her ankle. She pressed the petticoat down for the third time, only to see it pop up again.

"What is it? Is something broken?"

My pride, I think, Lizzie returned in silence, and then, "My ankle. Oh God, it hurts like bloody hell."

Jack bent down and examined the swelling joint as Margaret, Annie, and Mercy came running down the stairs. "Is she all right?" Margaret asked.

Neither seemed to have heard the question, for Jack studied the swelling with a worried frown, while Lizzie only writhed in blind agony. The silent moment was broken by a gruff "That was a damn stupid thing to do."

Lizzie was in excruciating pain and didn't take kindly to his tone nor the damning words. "What the bloody hell is it to you?"

Annie's eyes rounded with surprise at the obscenity, while her mother gasped.

Jack grinned. "I see your tongue hasn't sustained any damage."

At the sight of his smile, Lizzie knew only intense hatred. How could he smile while she was dying from this pain? "Get away from me," she returned unkindly.

Jack ignored her order, and instead of backing away and leaving the woman to her pain, he leaned even closer and, without a *please* or *may I,* took it upon himself to bring her into his arms. With her mother, sister, and Mercy trailing helplessly behind, he walked into the drawing room. Lizzie was shocked into silence and never thought to disobey as he said, "Put your arms around my neck."

Lizzie moaned, for every step he took managed to jar her ankle just enough to bring untold torture. She wondered if it wasn't broken, for the pain was very nearly intolerable.

Jack glanced down at the lady in his arms, his dark eyes widening at the lovely sight before him. He'd seen her naked, but that had been from a distance. And even nakedness could not compare to this intriguing sight. She was beautiful. Indeed the most beautiful he'd ever seen, and Jack couldn't think of anything he wanted at the moment but to see more.

Unbeknownst to Lizzie, the handkerchief her mother had placed at her bodice had somehow become lost during her fall, leaving generous curves very nearly exposed. Somehow, beyond the pain, Lizzie became aware of the man's sudden absorption in one particular portion of her person.

By now they were in the drawing room, heading for the settee. Hopefully nothing stood in their way, for Lizzie hadn't a doubt that this fool would have fallen over a mountain, so engrossed had he become in her bosom.

Pain or no, Lizzie wasn't about to be beholden to this lecher. "Take your hands off me," she said as she thrust herself with a sudden surge of strength from his hold.

Because his mind was otherwise occupied, Lizzie easily made good her escape. The problem was, she landed on her injured foot.

Lizzie cried out, knowing a wave of nausea as the pain intensified a hundredfold, slicing into her brain, into every fiber of her being, leaving her completely off balance. She fell awkwardly against her supposed gallant, actually shouldering him in his middle and causing him some momentary breathlessness. The sudden and unexpected crash of weight into his middle knocked him back a bit; the settee behind his legs managed the rest. An instant later he sat with a hard bounce, and Lizzie ended up between his legs, her face smashed into his chest, her knees stretched far enough behind her to prove useless.

"Oh dear," her mother exclaimed as she rushed forward, she and Mercy dragging her helpless daughter back.

The entire comedy of errors lasted no longer than three seconds. Still, Lizzie's cheeks would burn for some time at their close contact and her less-than-elegant actions.

Lizzie could have escaped her position on her own, she supposed, but that would have involved placing her hands on the man's thighs for balance and pulling her knees forward. And she wasn't about to touch him. No, unless she could have somehow managed with such a tight corset to bend at the waist, and do it the wrong way, she'd have been pretty much stuck in place.

Jack was making strangling sounds as Lizzie was carted from his lap and helped into a chair. She knew he was laughing, though he gave no obvious sign of it. She knew as well if the beast dared to allow the laugh that was choking him, injury or no, she just might do him some serious damage.

"Jack, I've been looking everywhere for you. Where did you take yourself off to?" Lizzie's grandfather asked as he walked into the room hardly a second after Lizzie was pressed into a chair.

Jack smiled and said, "I took Rascal for a ride on the beach again."

Lizzie only vaguely listened to the remark, hardly interested in where the man kept himself. She might have missed the comment altogether had it not been for the fact that she suddenly raised her gaze from her throbbing ankle to the dark, knowing eyes that moved over her.

It didn't take more than that look for Lizzie to realize the truth of it. The beast had been watching her as she swam. Granted she hadn't gone swimming today, but he'd watched her the days she had. She was sure of it. Lizzie forced aside the scathing resentment she felt at his intrusion. If this fool thought his leering conduct might endear himself in her heart, he'd best think again.

Jack hardly noticed her glare, having been the recipient of her frowns on more than one occasion. He put her present scowl to her suffering and moved toward her, pulling a Chippendale chair to her side. "Does it hurt still?"

"What?" Lizzie returned, breathless from the pain. "My foot or your spying?"

Jack's eyes widened at the question; he was unable for a moment to understand, and then he realized her meaning. So she knew he'd seen her. "I've been meaning to talk to you about that." Jack wondered why he hadn't already done so. Surely there had been ample opportunity.

"Of course you were," she interrupted bitterly. "But you haven't had a chance, am I right?" She groaned, "God, this is killing me."

Margaret spoke to her frowning father. "Lizzie has hurt her ankle. We should call for a physician."

"What?" the older man asked as he came toward his granddaughter, concern showing in his blue eyes. "Have you? And with the ball only tomorrow night?"

Ignoring the man at her side as best she could, Lizzie pulled her gown up a fraction to expose an ankle that still throbbed, though it didn't hurt as much as at first. It was swollen to thrice its normal size. Lizzie wondered again if it wasn't broken.

A stool was placed before her and her foot elevated,

while a physician was immediately summoned and servants raced for cool cloths to compress the swelling. A glass of brandy was then pressed into Lizzie's hand. She emptied the glass in a gulp.

Her mother was in the hall looking for the lost hankie, her grandfather calling for the head groom and driver so Lizzie might be carried to her room. Only Annie stood nearby, her expression crushed as if it were her ball in jeopardy.

Lizzie was a beautiful woman and used to men and their tendency to stare. What she wasn't used to was the boldness of this man's stare. Amid her throbbing pain she wondered if his eyes had grown half so large upon spying her on the beach.

She shoved the empty glass into his hand. "If it wouldn't be too much of an imposition, what with all you have occupying your mind, I'd appreciate another drink."

Jack returned with her drink and an apology. "I'm sorry if I was staring."

"If you were staring? What you mean is, you're sorry to be caught staring."

Annie's eyes rounded as she took in her sister's fury and Jack's obvious interest. She could name a dozen women who wished he'd look at them that way, and yet her sister appeared only annoyed at his attention.

Jack also wondered at Lizzie's annoyance. Was it an act? After all, if a woman didn't want a man to look, would she wear a dress half so revealing? "That dress is made for a man's admiration."

"Perhaps I could lend it to you then. So you might admire it at your leisure."

Annie giggled.

Both turned toward the sound, realizing for the first time they were not alone.

"Annie," her mother called, "help me ready Lizzie's bed."

Annie, obviously anxious to hear more, made a face and moved reluctantly from the room.

Jack waited until she turned the corner before asking, "If I borrowed it, would you come with it?" He grinned, for it seemed he'd managed at last to shock the unshockable Miss Lizzie Matthews.

And then Andrew returned to the room just as Jack asked, "How's your ankle?"

"Just dandy," she said tightly. "Thank you."

Chapter 4

❧

Lizzie half reclined upon her bed, her back supported by four thick pillows. According to Dr. Madison, her ankle had not been broken, but had sustained a serious sprain. All Lizzie knew was that it ached something fierce. Propped upon a pillow, it throbbed miserably, especially when Mercy changed the cold, wet wrappings.

Alone with her thoughts, Lizzie fumed, wondering if her annoyance didn't far outweigh her physical discomfort. The man irritated her like no other. Lately it seemed Jack's mission was to seek her out at every turn, with the most unsatisfying results.

Granted he did not act the pompous fool as did others of his class, but to her mind he was the worst of the lot.

Now that she knew the truth of it, she wondered how a man could claim to be a gentleman and yet invade a woman's most private moment. And worse yet, dare to flaunt his insidious actions lest, God forbid, she remain ignorant of his debauchery.

There was but one answer, of course. John Black was hardly the gentleman his title implied.

Lizzie didn't know how yet, but she was going to get

even. There had to be a way to get under the man's skin,
to ruffle his perfect feathers. All she had to do was find
it. Lost in thought, she forgot her ankle and moved it
slightly. She moaned as she was instantly reminded of
her injury.

Mercy, believing her mistress in the midst of agony,
quickly poured a few drops of laudanum into a glass of
water. "The doctor said to take this when the pain grew
intense."

Lizzie shook her head. "Take it away. I don't want
it."

Just that moment, Aunt Amelia entered without knocking. With a crackle of starched petticoats and a rustle of
taffeta, she reached for Lizzie's hand and sat at her side.
"Do be a good girl and take your medicine, Lizzie. It will
ease the pain."

Aunt Amelia was ten years younger than Lizzie's
grandfather and amazingly beautiful despite her advancing years. She lived in a small but lovely house at the
farthest corner of her brother's garden. From the terrace
behind the house, one might sit for hours admiring a
setting sun or the foaming waters of the sea below, all
with the delightful company of this lady. It was Lizzie's
favorite place, and, besides her grandfather, favorite
company as well.

"Dr. Madison said it's only a sprain."

Amelia nodded. "Still, you won't accomplish much
by suffering unduly."

Lizzie, acceding to the two women, choked down the
bitter brew. She shivered in disgust. The drug had an
almost instant effect, no doubt due to the fact that she
never used sleeping drafts of any kind.

Amelia was well aware that she and her niece were
of the same mind, especially when it came to the absurd
trappings of society. She allowed one of her wicked
grins and then nodded toward the injured appendage.

"Andrew can't be pleased. I know he envisioned you making a grand entrance."

Lizzie's mind was not on her grandfather or his wishes at the moment. Lost in her own thoughts, she hardly realized her aunt's remark, and blurted out, "Truly, I cannot abide the man."

Amelia leaned back a bit, her eyes widening with surprise. "Who? Andrew?"

"What?" Lizzie looked confused. "No. Lord Denver or Dover." She shrugged. "Whatever his name is."

Amelia blinked her surprise. She'd never known anyone who didn't love her nephew. As a matter of fact, she was aware of at least two scandalous episodes when women had gone far beyond the norm simply to catch Jack's eye.

"I can see I've shocked you," Lizzie continued, "but you can't possibly know him as I do."

Amelia blinked. "I've known Jack since he was a boy. Exactly what is it that I don't know about him?"

"You're his aunt, so naturally you believe him to be handsome and charming."

"Is he not?"

Lizzie shrugged. "He is, I expect, but you'd be mistaken if you think all the women are mad for him."

"Has he done anything to make you dislike him so?" Amelia might have been a worldly sort who, over the years, had had her share of lovers. Still, she wasn't about to take kindly to someone abusing her niece.

"Nothing if one doesn't count the man's perfection and the misery he brings me in constantly being underfoot, the way he looks at me, the fact that he watched me swim, and his audacity in letting me know he'd been watching."

Amelia's eyes widened with dawning delight. Just as Amelia had suspected, Jack was interested in Lizzie. And if Amelia knew her nephew, Lizzie wouldn't hold out against his charm for long. "You think he's perfect?"

"Didn't you hear me? He watched me swim!"

"Did he? And I take it you weren't decent?" Amelia asked. If her smile of anticipation meant anything, she was obviously hoping Lizzie was not.

"I thought I was alone," Lizzie murmured, her gaze dropping to the coverlet, her cheeks warming to a lovely shade of pink.

"So you weren't decent." Amelia breathed the words almost to herself, and then, with eyes taking on a decided sparkle, she added, "How interesting."

"It wasn't interesting at all," Lizzie whined childishly. "It was awful."

Amelia laughed. "Come now, darling. You mustn't take on so. I've every confidence that Jack came upon you quite by accident."

"Lord help us, can no one see the man for what he is? He has Grandfather bamboozled, Mother, even Annie appears caught in his web. And now you?"

"He's a bit of a rascal, I'm sure, but so charming."

Lizzie breathed a despairing sigh. "I see I've wasted my time complaining to you."

Amelia brought a chair to the side of the bed and made herself comfortable. "Mercy, would you be a dear and ask one of the girls to bring us tea?"

The moment the woman was out of the room, Amelia said with some expectation, "Now, you must tell me everything."

"What do you mean, tell you everything?"

"You said he looks at you. How?"

"Do you know how I hurt my ankle?"

Amelia laughed. "Disgraceful. Imagine a young lady sliding down the railing."

"Yes, well, your charming Jack came to the rescue."

"Did he?"

"I was wearing my ball gown. The seamstress hadn't seen to the neckline yet. It was too low."

"Was it?" Amelia was obviously enthralled by this piece of news.

"And I thought surely some damage would be done to Mr. Charming's eyes."

Amelia laughed again. "Meaning he couldn't take them from you?"

"Meaning he didn't bother to try. And when I suggested he might put some effort into it, he said, 'A woman who wears such a dress is looking for a man's attention.' "

"Isn't she?"

Lizzie only groaned, knowing she'd find no ally on this score. Everyone was smitten by the great Lord Black. Everyone but herself.

The house had been quiet for hours when Jack entered the library hoping to find a book boring enough to lull him to sleep. His eyes widened with surprise to find Lizzie sitting at her grandfather's desk, a small glass of cognac in one hand, a pipe filled with aromatic tobacco in the other. Her spectacles had slid nearly to the end of her nose. She continued to read the day's newspaper, seemingly unaware of his entrance.

The doctor had told her to rest her ankle. Apparently she paid him no mind. "I thought you were asleep for the night, Lizzie."

Lizzie gave a start, and then relaxed once she realized who had interrupted the quiet of the night. She removed her spectacles and glared at his ever-present grin, even as she placed the pipe's bit between her teeth, puffed, and blew a thin stream of smoke in his direction. "I might say the same about you."

"The doctor said to rest your ankle."

"I am resting it."

"By walking downstairs?" he asked incredulously. "Or did you ride the railing again?"

Lizzie ignored the question along with his obvious disapproval and asked instead, "Is there something in particular you want, or have you searched me out simply to annoy me again?"

Jack sat one hip on the corner of the desk. It was a sizable piece of furniture, but Lizzie thought it could have been larger. He leaned forward, not exactly crowding her, but making his presence known. "Have I annoyed you?"

Lizzie wasn't about to back up. She wasn't afraid of him. She wasn't afraid of any man. "You have."

Jack grinned at the admission. He'd made some sort of impression. Perhaps not the one he wanted, but an impression nonetheless. At the very least she no longer ignored him. "And here I've tried to be on my best behavior."

"I take it you consider spying on a woman the best a man can do?"

Jack smiled. She was upset, knowing he'd watched her swim. Too bad. Anyone with half a mind knew the danger of discovery. Indeed, she should have been grateful he hadn't been another. Jack felt a surprising rise of anger as he imagined what might have happened if another had come across her. Would the man have shown half his restraint? Jack thought it unlikely. "One might imagine an intelligent woman to have better sense than to parade along the coast naked."

Lizzie had spent most of the day agonizing over the fact that he had come across her during her swim. Still, she'd managed to convince herself that he hadn't actually watched her, or if he had, it was from such a distance as to have precluded exact scrutiny.

Of course, her hopes had been for naught, for his comment left her without a doubt as to what he'd seen. The beast had watched her, and his eyesight was no doubt as perfect as were his hair and teeth. "I was not parading, nor was I naked." And she wasn't, Lizzie reasoned, except for a second or two.

"You were," he insisted. "And I expect you won't be doing it again." His voice deepened with warning.

Lizzie looked at him as if he'd lost his mind. The day wouldn't come when a man could tell her what she could or couldn't do. "You may, of course, expect anything you wish, but I, as always, will do as I please."

She shrugged aside her misconduct as if it were nothing, quite willing to lay the blame at his feet. "Had you been a gentleman . . ."

Jack's eyes narrowed at her challenge, his words became a raspy whisper. "Had I been anything but a gentleman, I would have done more than watch. And for your information, I was not spying on you. I was riding my horse."

"You didn't turn away," she accused. "A gentleman would have."

The crease always present at the corner of his mouth deepened, and Lizzie forced aside the odd fluttering in her stomach at the flash of white teeth. She didn't trust his smile. For some ridiculous reason it sent chills racing up her spine and caused her breathing to grow a bit choppy. She ran her hand over her robe, needing the assurance that the ends lay demurely pulled together, and then took a drink from her glass.

He laughed a low, wicked sound. "You don't know men very well, if you believe that."

His smile grew strangely innocent, far too innocent for Lizzie's liking. She wasn't fooled. He breathed a sigh, that annoying smile lingering still as he commented with supposed guile, "Of late I've found England's coast to hold some intrigue, wouldn't you agree?"

Lizzie shrugged, knowing, of course, he spoke, not of coastlines, nor of England, but of herself. Still, she was determined to ignore the meaning behind those supposedly innocent words. "Rocks and sand? One can only imagine that you've seen as much before."

Jack grinned. "But there are rocks and then there are rocks."

"Some on beaches and some in heads, you mean?"

He laughed. She was a delightful piece, and oddly enough, only grew more so when insulting him. Jack wondered at the somehow delicious contradiction. "Sometimes a rock can hide a mermaid."

"Indeed? I wouldn't have thought you prone to the fanciful."

"Until I saw you, I would have agreed. But a lady with your charms—"

Jack was cut off with a cold glare. "How long did you watch?"

"Long enough."

"Indeed, sir, you have a most peculiar way of endearing yourself to a lady's heart."

Jack frowned, hesitating, unsure. Even though she often appeared worldly and experienced, there was that indefinable sense of innocence that warned him to be careful. She was his stepfather's granddaughter, and honor should have forbade what was on his mind. Still, she was a woman full grown and as beautiful as one was likely to find. Obviously she was able to make her own decisions. And should she choose to dally with him a bit, he wouldn't be sorry. "Would you have me try?"

Lizzie's glance was incredulous. "You'd have a better chance to keep ice at the equator, I think."

Jack breathed a sigh of relief. Like himself, she wasn't interested in an affair of the heart. Could it be they were then of the same mind? Jack thought there was no way to know unless he asked. "Perhaps you'd prefer a man to put aside flowery speech and come straight to the point?"

Lizzie wondered what he was getting at. Surely he wasn't about to declare himself. Lizzie almost laughed aloud at that thought. "Actually, I'd find speaking straight out most refreshing. I've yet to find a man in this country able to say what was on his mind. In truth it leaves one to draw obvious conclusions."

"And they are?" Jack found himself asking, fully aware that she was about to insult him yet again.

"That not one among you has a mind."

Jack laughed again. She was a spunky little thing to be sure, a woman who did not hesitate to say what she pleased. A far cry from the coy ladies of his acquaintance, who kept their thoughts, if they had any thoughts, private. Ladies who enticed a man to their bed with a practiced look or smile. Jack couldn't remember when simply talking to a woman had felt so good. His warm gaze said as much.

Lizzie had seen that look in a dozen men since reaching these shores, and knew enough to be cautious. Somehow she believed him above the rest. Not the least bit likable, of course, but a man of honor. But now she noted that he'd moved far too close. She forgot her resolve to stay in place and leaned back in her chair. With a nervous gesture she smoothed a perfectly smooth robe and, reconsidering her former response, said, "On second thought, perhaps I don't appreciate it all that much."

Lizzie knew they bordered on the edge of a dangerous chasm that could pull them both into a whirlwind of emotions that might prove quite beyond her realm. She trembled at the thought, for even as it frightened, it was a strangely exciting moment. Still, her fear and good sense won out over the attraction of the unknown and she managed to change the subject with hardly a tremor in her voice. "You didn't answer my question. Is there something in particular you want?"

Jack frowned. He'd felt the tension between them and knew she felt it as well. Still, she shied away from a playful skirmish. One minute the sophisticate, wise to

the ways of men and their wants, then the next she grew
childlike in her innocence. Jack thought her knowledge-
able enough on the subject he had in mind, but innocent
in that she had not so far indulged. The thought only
further intrigued.

He wouldn't push, at least not yet. Something was
happening between them. She was afraid, and he would
have to bide his time until she was ready to take things
further. "Actually I came for a boring book."

"You might try the newspaper, then," she said with
something like disgust.

"What, nothing intriguing?" he asked as he glanced
at the paper.

"Oh, I don't know. Some might think it intriguing
that Mr. Pierson was eighty-nine when he died last Friday, that sixteen hundred rushes weigh one pound, that
farmers often use them instead of candles. That bee wine
is a fermented liquor made from honey."

She puffed again on her pipe and again blew a thin
stream of smoke toward him. A moment later she smiled
sweetly and said, "Truly I intend to astound Mrs. Molston with my mastery of gooseberry cream, the next time
I visit the kitchen."

Jack laughed. "I take it you were looking for
something a bit more newsworthy."

"You might say that." She shrugged and then continued with a nonchalant air, "Of course, one might find
some interest in the fact that there's been another robbery. That Lord and Lady Cambell's home was broken
into and a number of art objects taken."

"But you do not?"

"Not especially. The lord and lady can well afford
the loss, I think."

"What interests you?" he prompted.

"Word about the war raging back home. There's not
a mention of it." Holding the shank of her pipe in hand,
she shoved at the paper with its stem and then returned

the bit to her mouth. She spoke around it as it was clamped between even teeth. "Do the English print nothing but the most mundane? Has your government not informed its people that they are in the midst of a war? Or are you all so arrogant as to believe news of the war to be inconsequential since the outcome can only be victory?"

Jack shrugged. "Some might think us arrogant on that score."

"Only some?"

Jack left the desk to pour himself a glass of cognac. He returned to his original position. "And of course, you're in agreement with those that do."

Lizzie only allowed a glare as a response. She wasn't about to tell his lordship the whole of it. It wouldn't do at all for him to suspect her true feelings on the matter. Especially it wouldn't do for him to wonder of her present activities.

"I know what you think of the titled, but I didn't realize you don't like the English at all."

"Actually, I find some very likable."

"For instance."

She shrugged. "I find the townsfolk lovely on the whole, the shopkeepers most agreeable, Grandfather's gardeners, the servants and stableboys, all very likable."

Jack dismissed the vague sense of disappointment he felt at being obviously excluded from her list. "But not your grandfather's friends."

There was no need to respond, for he knew well enough her thoughts on the matter.

"Then why the ball? Why the desire to enter into society?"

"I promise you, it is not my desire. It's Grandfather's. I've told him I'm not interested."

"And yet he's spending huge sums of money."

"I wish he were not. Grandfather thinks I'll change

my mind, that I'll meet my Prince Charming," she said while puffing again on her pipe.

"And you're sure you will not?"

"I've stopped believing in fantasy a long time ago."

"Surely you're not unaware of your beauty. I'd wager many a man to offer for you."

Lizzie shrugged. "It hardly matters, does it? I won't be taking any offers."

"How can you be sure? Someone might steal your heart."

Lizzie laughed at the inconceivable possibility.

"No? Oh, I see. You'll simply show them that you are a woman of strong will and intelligence. And expect them to run like the others?"

She only chuckled softly. "Poor little Lizzie, she's so very pretty, but have you heard her talk? Lord help us, she'd disgrace a man."

"And your grandfather? Won't he be embarrassed by your actions?"

Lizzie shrugged. "I'll be on my best behavior, for his sake. But the truth is, I am what I am and not likely to grow into a weak, simpering miss anytime soon."

Jack bit his bottom lip as he took in her grin and wondered if she knew how exciting her strength was. The fantasies she caused a man. How she might act when in his bed. He could almost feel the warmth of her breath on his lips as she begged for his kiss, nay, insisted, for this one would demand her share of the pleasure. "Andrew will be disappointed."

"It's not my wish to hurt him, but I've explained I'm not interested in marrying."

"Ever?"

Lizzie shrugged. "Perhaps after the war. After I go home."

"Why wait? Why not go home now?"

"After my father died, soldiers accused him of working for the rebel cause."

Jack interrupted with, "Was he?"

"Perhaps." Lizzie shrugged, unwilling to say more on the subject. "In any case, our home and all personal belongings were confiscated. Until we win the war, I've got nothing to go back to."

"And you're sure you will win the war?"

"Absolutely sure."

"Does your grandfather know you intend to leave?"

"No. I thought I'd wait to tell him."

"Suppose someone else told him."

"No one knows but you, and you won't say anything."

"Won't I?"

"What would you gain by it?"

"The question is, I think, what might I gain by not telling him?"

Lizzie's gaze narrowed as she watched him smile. She felt a shiver run up her spine. The man was too good looking, too tall, and simply too gorgeous if the truth be told. He treated her mother with polite fondness, her grandfather with genuine love, her sister with tender regard. He had obvious good humor and strength of character. The fact that he did not give in to fashion's demands told her that much. He was an earl and she almost liked him, even though she fought a daily battle against his charm, his teasing.

He was dangerous. A man like this one could steal a heart and waylay the best of plans. No, Lizzie reasoned. She must not allow that to happen.

He wanted a dalliance. The meaning behind his dark, intense look was obvious. Lizzie almost laughed aloud as she realized his motives and did not hesitate to ask, "Do you think we might one day become lovers? Is that it?"

Jack's eyes widened with surprise. Aware of her intelligence, he wasn't surprised at her quick understanding of their situation, but at the boldness with which she dared to bluntly state what he'd imagined to be a discreet proposal. "The thought has crossed my mind."

"You mean what little mind you have, of course?"

Jack ignored her sarcasm. "Would that be so bad? I promise you, the ladies that have so far shared my bed have not complained."

"No?" Lizzie grinned quite wickedly as she taunted, "Do they simper and whine, 'Just one more kiss, my lord, please'?"

Damn. Even knowing it was an act, Jack felt his groin stir at her breathless pleading. He swallowed and cleared his throat before saying, "Some do."

"Poor things," she muttered, her disgust liberally tempered with genuine sympathy.

Jack had a time of it keeping his laughter at bay. "You might find yourself saying as much."

Lizzie snorted rudely at the comment. "I doubt that either of us will live so long." A moment of silence followed in which they stared at each other. Jack watched her with that same annoying smile teasing his mouth, while she, in return, glared her resentment. And when her glare proved to have no effect but to cause his smile to deepen and her heart to flutter madly, she broke contact, sighed, and pushed the chair back. "Well, since this conversation has ended, I think it best to acknowledge a standoff."

"A temporary standoff." Jack figured the conversation might have reached its conclusion, but they were far from finished, and she might as well know it.

Lizzie's heart trembled at the promise in his words. He wouldn't be easy to fend off, and for just a second Lizzie wondered if she wanted to try. "It's late. And I'm under orders to look my most beautiful tomorrow night."

Jack came to his feet as he watched her rise and reach for her cane. After knocking the cold tobacco into the fireplace, she pocketed her pipe and then limped toward the door.

But Jack suddenly blocked her path. Without thinking, he reached for a golden, heavy lock that had fallen over her shoulder to her breast. As if it were alive and possessing a mind of its own, he watched it curl around his finger.

Lizzie held her breath, terribly aware of his hand, inches above her breast. She should pull away. She wanted to, but for some insane reason, her feet wouldn't obey the dictates of her mind.

And then he touched her, the back of his hand grazing her robe. And Lizzie felt the shock of fire. She gasped and glanced at the hand, wondering if he hadn't somehow burned her, for the heat spread in rolling waves into her stomach, only to return and fill her chest. Her blue eyes clouded with confusion as they lifted to his. His hand had only touched her hair and lightly grazed her robe, and yet she felt the warmth of that touch grow into an ache in the depths of her belly. She tried for a deep, mind-clearing breath, but only managed a shallow gasp as his scent came to further muddle her senses.

"It happens like that sometimes," Jack said softly, fully aware of her reaction to him and the confusion she was unable to hide. "Sometimes it takes only a touch or a look for both to know."

Lizzie forced aside a shiver as his warm breath brushed over her mouth, her chin, her throat. Her lips tingled, sensitive; they ached as if longing for a kiss. Trembling, every nerve ending suddenly alive and sensitive, she almost leaned into him. He was standing too close. Why didn't she move? "It won't happen to us," Lizzie said without much certainty, for somewhere deep inside, she knew it already had.

Jack thought if he kissed her now, she might very well melt in his arms. He could sense her softness, smell the heat of yearning, feel the thread of excitement, held barely under control. He had to remind himself that this was all new for her, that she was an innocent. It was the only way to keep his sanity. "To deny what we feel only prolongs the pleasure."

She fought back a shiver, her mind in total confusion, unable to understand what was happening. "You're talking in riddles." God in heaven, why hadn't she moved? What could she be thinking to stand here, alone with this man? "I, for one, feel nothing. Now, if you will excuse me," she said, waiting for him to move.

Jack chuckled softly and moved to his side. He sat again on the edge of the desk. "You might deny it, Lizzie, but you won't for long. The next time—"

"I'll lock the door," she said, finishing his sentence. She left the room then, hesitating at the doorway only long enough to say a simple if biting "Good night, Lord Dobber."

Chapter 5

Lizzie was determined, since there was no way she could dance, or even stand, for that matter, what with her foot and ankle wrapped into a mummified position, that there was no need to wear what had been previously planned. The hated corset disappeared along with the gown that could not fit without it.

She sat as if a princess awaiting her admirers' attention, a vision in sparkling gold. The neckline of this dress was not nearly so low; still, it left her shoulders mostly bare, and a man aching to see and touch skin that was only a few shades lighter than her dress.

Her color was high, her eyes sparkling, and Jack thought there wasn't another to compare. He stood just outside the circle of her admirers, content for the moment to simply watch her.

Lizzie smiled stiffly at something Lord Bently said to Lord Billings. Unable to resist, she found herself interrupting. "Nonsense in the colonies? I doubt you'd find one soul there to agree, sir. All believe they're fighting for freedom."

Jack gave a silent groan. Didn't she know any better than to spout her beliefs in public? If the damn woman wasn't arrested for treason, it would be a bloody miracle.

"A rabble of illiterates, I'd say," Billings remarked with a blustering laugh.

"You can't mean to say Franklin, Jefferson, Hamilton, and the rest are not educated, sir, for I assure you they are."

Lord Bently frowned. It took only a look for all to realize his displeasure. "You sound as if you know them."

"I haven't had the honor, I'm sorry to say."

Jack took in her response even as his gaze moved to the man standing almost directly behind the small group.

Lord Summitt leaned against a pillar and listened to the conversation, his dark, knowing gaze moving over Lizzie without a shred of admiration. He was watching her, Jack thought, but not as a man might watch a lovely woman. Instead he seemed to study her words, her every expression, as if searching for some deeper meaning. Jack felt a stab of fear that the man should look upon her with suspicion.

"Do you believe in the rebel cause?" young Adams asked a bit sickly, as if fearful of her answer.

Adams might have been unsure of her answer, but Jack wasn't. Indeed, he had every confidence she was about to make a dreadful mistake. One had only to look into her sparkling eyes to see the light of a fanatic and know the damning response to come. He had to bring a stop to this now, before disaster struck. "Excuse me, Lizzie, but I need to see you for a minute. There's a problem with Alice." He didn't wait for her response, but stepped into the midst of the circle of men and took her arm, bringing her to her feet. A moment later, with his hand still on her arm, she was limping along with her cane. "I promise I'll bring her right back, gentlemen."

The men were still nodding as Lizzie was led to the small, unoccupied sitting room next to the library.

The moment he closed the doors behind them, Jack turned, his rage obvious.

Lizzie looked around the room and frowned to find it empty. "Where is she? What's the matter with Alice? You said there was a problem."

"There is, but the problem does not lie with her."

"What?"

Jack's voice remained low and even. In truth, his lips hardly moved at all. "What the bloody hell do you think you're doing?"

Lizzie frowned, and wondered why his face was growing red. "I don't know what you mean."

"You were just about to tell them your beliefs in your cause."

She scowled at the accusation, and thought to deny it even if it was completely true. Lord, but she truly disliked this man. How dare he scold her on what she was about to say? "You cannot possibly know what I was about to say."

"You're wrong there, Lizzie. I know what the gleam in your eyes meant."

Lizzie justified her stand. "My father died for the cause. Should I deny what I believe?"

Jack breathed a sigh of frustration and ran his fingers through his hair. "Your father should have beat you as a child, I think."

"Beat me for following his beliefs?"

"Lizzie," Jack said in a more agreeable tone, finding most of his anger somehow eased by simply talking to her. "No one asked you to deny your beliefs. Still, there's no need to brag on them."

Lizzie was annoyed. Annoyed that this man should dare to tell her what she should or shouldn't say. "There's every need. I'm proud of my father and all he stood for."

"Then brag on it to someone else. Almost every man

here tonight is a lord of the realm. Where do you think their loyalties lie?''

"I know where they lie."

"Then you should also know they are too powerful for your nonsense."

"Nonsense?" Lizzie gasped at his condescension. "Is it nonsense that men should die for their beliefs?"

"It's nonsense that women should involve themselves in such matters," Jack returned. "Nonsensical and dangerous."

Lizzie had a difficult time controlling her need to rail at the man. "But I'm only a woman, Lord Depraved. Who would listen to me?"

Jack realized their voices were rising. A moment longer and the closed doors would prove useless. He sought a measure of calm and managed at last in a tone far softer than the emotion called for, "Lizzie, most will believe you only a woman, but have you given any consideration to those who will not? Can you imagine how upset your grandfather is going to be when they come to arrest you?"

Lizzie thought about that for a minute and quietly said, "Oh dear, I forgot about Grandfather." Jack could only sigh his relief when she seemed to notice they were standing too close and, with the aid of her cane, limped backward a step or two, creating some distance between them.

"And your promise to be on your best behavior?"

"Yes, that, too, I'm afraid."

"Yes," Jack said as he tried to take his gaze from her lips. "Well, it might be wise not to forget again."

A silent moment went by before Lizzie suddenly realized they were alone. Alone and standing far too close. She took another step back even as she ridiculed an odd sense of anxiousness. She wasn't anxious, of course, but she was wary. This wasn't the first time they had found themselves alone. But something had happened between them last night, in her grandfather's library. She wasn't sure as yet what it was, but she had dreamed of him again last night. He took a half step toward her. "You look beautiful tonight."

Lizzie could have sworn that her stomach jumped at his low, husky words. It hadn't, of course. She had to have imagined it. "Thank you."

A dizzying moment of silence ensued before Lizzie said, "Yes, well, if you're quite finished, I should get back." Was that her voice? Had she sounded half as shaken and breathless as she felt?

Jack wasn't near finished; still, he did not object when she moved around him, returning to her adoring admirers.

In the huge center hall again, Jack watched her laugh at some comment and then laugh again at another. He chatted some with acquaintances, sampled two of the many dishes offered, and sipped from a glass of brandy, all the while watching Lizzie.

At one point he moved close enough to hear, "But she's ruined."

"Indeed, I think not," Lizzie returned. "Some might think of her as a soiled dove, I'm sure, but Sara is only twelve. Surely she's young enough to put her past behind her and begin anew."

Apparently Lizzie had mentioned the newest addition to the parish poorhouse and her crusade to see the youngster change her ways.

"But who would have her?"

Jack almost laughed aloud, for it was easy enough to see Lizzie was fighting down her annoyance at the question. "You mean as a wife, Mr. Kemble?"

Joseph Kemble nodded.

"The truth is, sir, I think no one should dare expect more from his wife than he is willing to give."

Every man there looked confused.

Billings shook his head. "You can't mean that a man

should remain untouched if he expects as much in his wife?''

"Indeed I mean just that."

"But it's accepted that a man should have some experience."

"Accepted by other men, no doubt. Have you ever asked a woman her opinion?" Lizzie asked.

Jack chuckled softly as he moved away from the group. To say she fascinated him was a gross understatement. And if she weren't at this moment surrounded by a band of eager young dandies, Jack might have joined her. Instead, he allowed his gaze to take in a certain young widow. Mrs. Stone was sending him discreet but obvious signals that told him she wouldn't be averse to his company. Jack hadn't visited with her since the day he arrived and saw Lizzie on the beach. He thought he just might take the pretty lady up on her offer and do it in the privacy of his stepfather's gardens.

Jack smiled at Mary Stone and then stepped through the French doors that led to the terrace and the gardens beyond. He lit his pipe and waited for Mary to make her excuses. Hardly a moment later she was at his side. "I truly love the smell of a pipe. I wish Westly had picked up the habit."

Her words filled him with sudden annoyance, and Jack couldn't say why. He might have visited with her only once since his return, but Jack couldn't count the times he'd enjoyed this woman's lush charms before he left England a year ago. Yet the thought of taking her again suddenly brought about as much interest as sipping from a glass of lukewarm water. He felt at odds with her and himself, annoyed knowing the things she wanted from him. Almost used. It was a ridiculous thought, for he gained pleasure at their every encounter. Still, for some reason the thought of taking her tonight seemed most unappealing. He wished to hell he'd never responded to her smiles.

"Mary, you have to come and see this," came a feminine voice from the terrace doors, and Mary Stone whispered, "At the summerhouse. As soon as I can get away."

Jack knew only relief and hoped she might never get away.

Lizzie sighed almost regretfully as she watched the last three admiring dandies, after feeble excuses, make a run for it. Not a challenge among the lot. It took only the last comment of taking Sara under her wing to see the last of them on their way.

Behind her fan she snickered with glee at the unbelievable simplicity. She didn't have to lie, nor exaggerate or pretend. All she had to do was be herself, and as if by magic, they all disappeared one by one. Lizzie chuckled softly, knowing every one of them thought her outrageous and certainly far from wife material.

The great hall dated back some hundreds of years. Originally it consisted of a kitchen at the rear where a fireplace still stood, and doors at the opposite end. Since then, rooms had been added on both sides as well as bedroom suites above, until some distant ancestor merged it all into a magnificent mansion in the style of Charles I. Now the hall was used only for an occasional large gathering. It was enormous. Still, with the amount of people invited, the hall had grown stuffy in the extreme, and Lizzie thought to take advantage of the momentary lull in admirers.

She eyed the library with some longing, knowing her pipe was sitting on the table near the fireplace, but her grandfather and a few military men were sequestered there. She couldn't intrude. Lizzie smiled at the thought. No, tomorrow would be soon enough to find out what they had been about.

Her cane was propped against her chair. Lizzie used it to slip outside. Moving beyond the shadowy figures

on the terrace, she headed for the garden house. Except
for the bathhouse, almost hidden behind a perfectly
trimmed hedge, with its marble walls and a tub almost
big enough to swim in, the garden house, fashioned after
a Greek temple, was her favorite place. Many an
afternoon was spent there, either playing with the children or reading one of the numerous books that lined
her grandfather's library walls.

Lizzie thought it probably too far from the house to
be occupied. Here she might not be found for some time.
With any luck at all, it wouldn't be until the party was
over.

Jack sat on a wide circular bench attached to the summerhouse's thick center column. He leaned back and
stretched his long legs before him as he puffed on his
pipe.

The truth of the matter was, his last visit to Mary had
proved disappointing in the extreme. Not physically perhaps, but mentally, and the fault was not hers. Indeed
she had been most obliging. The problem was with him.
It had taken days to realize the source of that problem.
Mary was lovely, but it wasn't Mary he wanted.

There were no sides to the small building, but narrow
columns that helped to support a domed roof. Still, because of the blackness of the night, he did not see her ap-
proach. It was only the sound of her feet scuffing against
the gravel walkway that alerted him to her presence.

He'd hoped she would not come, but she had. Under
the roof of the garden house, it was almost pitch black,
and Jack thought he'd never find a more perfect place
for a quick, impersonal taking. Mary wasn't the one who
occupied his thoughts, but she was available, and after
days of Lizzie's tantalizing company, he was a man in
desperate need of a woman.

One second she was alone. The next, a man stood at
her side. Lizzie hadn't the time to gasp her surprise when
she heard a low-spoken ''Mary,'' and then found herself

suddenly pulled into his arms. It took her a moment to calm her panic, but once she did, Lizzie realized the man kissing her neck was Jack. No other wore that particular woodsy scent, no other smelled half so clean. And if Jack was kissing her neck, that meant he had mistaken her for another.

Lizzie grew sure of her suspicions when she heard him murmur, "Mary." The best thing to do, the only thing, was to explain that she wasn't this Mary person. That she was ...

Lizzie had never had her neck kissed before, and hadn't till now realized just how lovely neck kissing could be. She made a soft sound of pleasure, and found herself wishing for just a second that she didn't have to bring this moment to an end. It was ridiculous, of course. She didn't like it that much.

After all, the man wasn't even aware of who he was kissing. Lord, they'd probably both have a good laugh once he realized his mistake.

Lizzie tried to pull back. It was time to put a stop to this, perhaps well past time. Only what with his fingers suddenly threaded into her hair, she found pulling back quite impossible. And then his lips no longer brushed deliciously against her shoulder and neck. She didn't have time to say a word before they were suddenly against her mouth.

Lizzie stiffened. This was going too far. She had to say something, do something, only she couldn't seem to get her thoughts together. Instinctively she knew he wasn't about to laugh once his error was discovered. He might very well grow angry instead. It had only been seconds and yet she'd already waited far too long.

"Don't be coy, Mary, not tonight," he said against her mouth.

"But—" was all she managed to say before his mouth stopped any further conversation. This time his gentleness had disappeared and he kissed her with something like aggression.

Lizzie felt nothing less than astonishment. She'd been kissed before and yet hadn't realized until now that a man could kiss a woman in a variety of ways. Oddly enough, she liked it very much. The thought surprised her. How could she like it when she wasn't even sure what he was doing? What in the world was happening here? What could she be thinking?

He sucked her bottom lip into his mouth and ran his tongue over the softness. Lizzie fought back the moan that bubbled up her throat.

Jack frowned. It hadn't been that long and yet he hadn't remembered that Mary had tasted quite this good, or felt this soft. He'd been a damn fool not to have visited her more often, and silently promised himself he wouldn't make that mistake again.

Something dropped to the ground. Jack imagined it was the lady's fan. They'd find it later, he thought; for now, he had something in mind that could not wait.

He couldn't remember the last time the desire for a woman had come upon him with such desperation, and found he had to fight back the need to take her with no further ado. What the hell was the matter with him? Since when did the scent of a woman, the touch of her, send him into a fog of mindless longing? Mary had never inspired such desire before. Being with her had always been pleasant, sometimes erotic, but never wildly passionate.

Jack forced aside his thoughts. It didn't matter the reason. All that mattered was that he'd have her, and as soon as possible.

His arm slipped from her waist, his hand moving between their bodies, tugging slightly at her neckline until a breast was freed for his pleasure. The nipple was slightly stiff. Jack's expert handling only made it more so. He rolled the tip between his fingers and then frowned as the lady stiffened in his arms. Jack wondered at the oddity. He'd never known Mary to play coy. What was wrong with her tonight?

His mouth grew as daring as his hands as he plunged his tongue deep into her heat and then groaned with pleasure as he breathed in her soft sigh and felt her body grow soft against him.

It was then that he pushed the neckline lower, exposing both breasts.

Lizzie had been so engrossed in his kiss that she hadn't at first realized what his hands were doing. Hadn't realized it until it was far too late. She felt his hands gently cup her breasts, and then came a low moan as if weighing the heavy flesh brought about undeniable pleasure. No man had ever touched her like this, and Lizzie couldn't imagine why she felt no shock. Why instead she only wanted more. Much more.

She tried to shake her mind free of its lethargy, but found herself instead only brought deeper into the dreamlike haze. Her arms moved around his neck lest her weakened knees suddenly give way.

His mouth tore itself from her luscious taste and fastened on the tip of her breast. Lizzie couldn't stop the moan this time. Especially when his tongue danced over and around her nipple. Couldn't think beyond the delicious tightening the sucking caused in the depths of her belly.

Her head had fallen back, her knees threatened to collapse, as he pressed his body tightly to hers, grinding his hips against hers. Lizzie groaned again at the feel of his hard body. It was too much; yet it wasn't nearly enough. And she didn't have the strength to stop this lovely, illicit encounter.

Later she'd count herself fortunate indeed that another was not so timidly inclined. "I see you've wasted no time while waiting for me," came the sharp sound of a woman's voice from out of the darkness.

Jack spun around, his intent to guard the lady he'd been kissing from full disclosure. There was no need. Nothing but the darkest shadows could be seen.

It took him a long moment to assimilate the fact that Mary had spoken, but from behind him. Obviously the woman in his arms was not Mary. Jack spun around again only to find the woman gone as mysteriously and as silently as she had somehow appeared.

What the hell was happening? And how was he supposed to explain what he could not understand himself?

"Mary, I . . ."

"Go to hell, Jack," came Mary's angry reply, and Jack watched as she walked off, disappearing into the darkness.

Jack frowned wondering how he could have mistaken the small, lush form for a woman whose curves weren't half so enticing. What had he been thinking to imagine the scent of her and Mary to be one and the same?

Jack knew only relief. That Mary Stone was angry, he had no doubt. Still, he couldn't find it within himself to care. All he could think was, who was the woman he'd held in his arms? He'd have to find her again, he knew, but how when he knew neither her name nor what she looked like?

Jack paced as he tried to think through his problem. As he tried to come to terms with the exceptional emotions this mystery woman had instilled. It was then that his foot hit the cane.

The sun had barely crested the horizon when Lizzie made her way from the bathhouse. An early bath had been a ruse, of course, a reason for being about in the gardens at first light. The last guest had left the house only an hour ago. All inside slept. And had Lizzie not been racked with guilt, she would have been among them.

The truth was, Lizzie knew some desperate need to

find her cane. It was, after all, damning evidence. She would have gone back for it last night had not that fool remained exactly where she'd left him. She'd waited in the shrubbery for close to an hour, watching as he smoked his pipe at leisure. The night had been dark, to be sure, but not so dark that she could have crawled around looking for the cane without notice.

Lizzie shivered at the thought that Jack might have already found it. Of course, he'd know then the identity of the woman in his arms last night. Lizzie breathed a sigh at the thought, wondering how she might avoid disaster. What could she say? How could she explain?

She'd completed her bath in record time. Her hair was still damp, the wet ends trailing down her back as she secured her robe over a nightdress and limped toward the garden house. She'd stop there on the pretext of resting her foot. The cane would be there, she was sure. *Please, God, let it be there.*

Only it wasn't. Lizzie searched the area. It wasn't here. Did that mean he had found it? Oh, please, no!

Lizzie sat for a second, trying to collect herself, trying to push aside the sense of panic that threatened. A panic that grew tenfold as Jack moved from behind the thick center column, holding the very object in question.

Obviously he had been lying in wait for her, for he wore the same clothes as he had last night. He hadn't as yet been to bed. Lizzie qualified her thoughts, not at all sure of his actions after she'd finally left the garden. He hadn't been to bed with her. Of course, there was that Mary creature. Lizzie couldn't be sure . . .

Stop babbling, she silently cried. Her world could be falling apart and all she could think about was what this man might have done after she left him in the garden.

Control, Lizzie. Get some control of yourself. Her reputation and more depended on her complete control.

Lizzie flashed him a brilliant smile and then dared to

look directly into knowing eyes as she said, "Oh, I see you found it. Someone absconded with it last night, and I've had to limp along ever since. I don't mind telling you that my ankle will be forever grateful for your kindness."

Jack handed over the cane. "You're taking your bath early, aren't you?"

"My ankle needed soaking." Lizzie was sure the logical response would satisfy.

"Where did you lose it?"

"I didn't lose it. Someone took it."

"That's odd."

"I thought so." She shrugged, careful not to exaggerate her denial.

Jack thought her very good. Her voice held just the right shade of puzzled indifference. Still, he didn't for a second believe her act.

"The gardens were lovely last night. Did you get a chance to enjoy them?"

Lizzie knew, from years of living in the same house with British officers, the art of appearing the innocent even while she carried on activities for the rebel cause. Grateful for the lessons learned, she put them to the best use possible, while allowing the slightest sigh. "I only wish I had. The hall grew terribly stuffy."

"Does that mean you never met with a man and kissed him here?"

"Met with . . . ?" Lizzie appeared shocked at the thought. She allowed her eyes to widen and her lips to part as she pretended astonishment. "Kiss a man? Before being betrothed? I'm sure I'd never."

"Never what? Kiss a man or lie about kissing him?"

Lizzie allowed the slightest frown, careful not to overdo. "Lord Defect, I'm sure I cannot imagine what you are about?"

"I think you can."

Lizzie breathed a sigh of feigned exasperation. Obviously the man did not believe her story. Too bad, for she wasn't about to admit to the indiscretion should he persist into the next life. "Well, it's been very nice chatting with you, I'm sure, but—" She did not complete her sentence as in the next instance his hand gripped the sleeve of her robe and tugged her back to her seat. "What are you doing?"

"At the moment, nothing. What I intend to do is kiss you."

This time Lizzie did not have to pretend shock. "Lord Denver," she said on a great sigh as if to portray her less-than-enthusiastic participation in this conversation. "I certainly will never give you permission."

"Will you have me steal the kiss then?"

Lizzie's glance was as haughty as a grand duchess's. She, who hated haughtiness and arrogance above all else, never realized she had this ability. "I was under the impression that the English were gentlemen, sir, and no gentleman would—"

Jack's laughter brought her words to a stumbling halt. "I know it was you."

Lizzie felt some surprise as her heart thumped almost painfully in her chest. "You think it was me, but you cannot know for sure."

"How did you disappear? I only turned away for a second."

"I . . ." Lizzie caught herself in time. She'd been about to tell him she wasn't quite sure how she'd managed it, since she hadn't remembered moving at all, and felt her cheeks grow warm at the near slip. "I was not here," she insisted, only her insistence sounded quite a bit weaker than it had at first.

Jack smiled.

Lizzie ignored it, or tried to as she struggled to calm her breathing. Why did he have to smile like that? "I've got to get back to the house." She came to her feet, knowing some relief that Jack had not touched her again.

Her relief was not long lasting, however, as she watched him come to stand before her.

"I remember quite clearly the taste and feel of the lady's mouth. If I kissed you, it would set my mind to rest."

Lizzie laughed and returned sarcastically, "And at all costs, your mind should rest."

Jack shrugged. "If it wasn't you, I see no problem."

"Except for the fact that I don't kiss men in order to ease their minds."

"Why do you kiss them then?"

"This conversation is ridiculous."

"I agree," he said, and a moment later brought his hands to her waist. "I think there's been quite enough talk."

"Jack!" The word came as a startled gasp as his hands lifted her as if she weighed nothing. Without further entreaty, he brought her against him, and again, just like last night, her cane fell to the ground as her hands reached his shoulders for balance. He watched her for a long, silent moment as Lizzie tried to think of a way out. Only deep in her heart she knew there was no way, and Lizzie found herself wondering, if she found one, would she use it? The man was bound and determined to know the truth of last night's encounter. No amount of delicate pleading on her part was apt to sway him in the least. He was bold and absolutely outrageous. He was going to kiss her, and Lizzie couldn't honestly say she was sorry.

It would be over within a few seconds, Lizzie thought, and no need to make a fuss. She had every confidence that it wasn't possible to know a woman by her kiss. Any further resistance would only foster his insistence. It was only a kiss, after all. Only a kiss and they would be done with this nonsense.

Their eyes met and held as his face grew closer. Lizzie's body trembled, her heart pounded, her breathing ceased, as she waited, half in fear, half in anticipation, for his mouth to touch hers. And then the most amazing thing happened. Lizzie felt her lips swell and soften as if a million nerve endings had come achingly alive. And still their mouths did not touch.

He gathered her closer; his arm supporting her weight moved under her bottom and raised her so their eyes were even. His dark gaze moved slowly over her face, studying perfect skin, full pink lips, dark brown lashes, and eyes the color of a morning sky. It was the eyes that had done it, he knew. Eyes, the mirror of her soul. Eyes that could shatter his usual control, his very good sense. Bright with intelligence, or narrowed with anger, and then softened with love. He couldn't get enough of watching them.

He took a long, luscious moment to breathe in her scent, to anticipate her taste, to allow her to slowly invade his senses before he purposely, delicately, touched his mouth to sweet waiting lips.

Lizzie watched the fire dance in his eyes and waited, her heart pounding out of control as he came closer, closer. And then she breathed a soft sound, almost a sigh of relief, as lips brushed gently upon lips. She never realized her moan of pleasure as his mouth took instant and total possession of hers.

Hot, wet, deliciously sweet, her taste threatened to drown him in pleasure. Jack forced gentle lips to part, his mouth, his tongue, savoring the honey-dark sweetness of her, the warmth that grew almost instantly into sizzling heat.

Lizzie was helpless to prevent the low moan. It came from deep in her chest and slipped from her throat almost unnoticed as she grew shaken to the core of her being. She'd thought last night's kisses had made her heart tremble, but even they could not compare with the delicious assault she now greedily endured.

He used his tongue again, gently touching her lips and

then slipping further inside, beyond the barrier of teeth, to tantalize the sensitive flesh of her mouth. Lizzie had been kissed before. She'd been briefly engaged once, but never had she been kissed like this. Lizzie had never imagined one could involve his whole mouth in a kiss.

Jack had known, of course, it was Lizzie he kissed last night. After finding her cane, there could be no doubt. He'd had hours to think on it, to remember her form, her scent. He'd never been more sure of anything in his life. And kissing her now only confirmed his beliefs. Only caused him to want more. A great deal more.

He growled at the taste of her, at the softness against his body, as memories of last night came to flood his mind, his senses. Last night had been a stolen moment, a lapse in her usual good sense, but in fact, only a prelude of what was to come. He would have her, he knew. Despite her ladylike upbringing, she would be his. All he had to do was break down her resistance, and Jack knew of no better way than the constant teasing of her senses.

He nibbled at her lips, loathing to see this pleasure end as he absorbed just a little more of the taste and scent of her. "Tell me it was you, Lizzie," he gasped, their mouths barely an inch apart.

Lizzie blinked trying to clear her mind, trying to tear away the lethargy that had somehow come upon her, even as she wondered how his kisses had managed their nearly disastrous effect. It was all her imagination, of course. The coming together of two sets of lips could not leave a woman weak and somehow aching. It wasn't only impossible. It was ridiculous. "No."

Jack laughed softly, his dark eyes filled with deviltry, his warm, clean breath causing her heart to suddenly throb. "I could make you tell me."

Lizzie knew what he meant. Under his kisses her common sense slipped away. That she allowed the kiss in the first place meant anything was possible. "Perhaps, but would it be the truth?"

His tongue slid over her lips. An inch apart, their mouths weren't touching, but her heart didn't seem to notice. It thundered wildly in her chest.

"It doesn't matter," he said as he slowly lowered her to the ground.

She wouldn't look at him. She couldn't. Not if she hoped to keep her wits about her and resist the most ridiculous need to fall against him. She steadied both her composure and voice and tried for as much elegance as she could muster. "I hope this has settled your mind and we can now put the entire matter behind us."

"I'm afraid it's not that simple."

"Of course it is." Lizzie looked at him then, not at all happy to see that annoying smile once again in place. She pushed aside a feeling of unease, even as her eyes narrowed with suspicion. Obviously the man hinted at something. She only wished she knew what he was thinking.

"When a lady allows a kiss, it means, of course, a betrothal."

Her head snapped back as if she'd actually been slapped. And Lizzie couldn't have known greater shock had the man done the deed. Betrothal! Was he out of his mind? She'd never marry an Englisher. Especially not one of the aristocrats. Especially not this arrogant beast. It took some doing, but Lizzie finally found the control to manage, "I did not allow it, if you remember. And we are most certainly not betrothed."

"I'm afraid we are," came a soft tease, as Jack mulled over the thought and found the holy state of matrimony suddenly most intriguing.

"And I'm afraid you are out of your mind."

"Your grandfather would be greatly upset if—"

"He won't be upset, because he'll never know."

And as if she had not spoken, Jack said, "Yes, he'll

insist upon a marriage, of course, once I tell him about last night.''

''You'll tell . . .'' Lizzie's eyes widened with shock.

Jack allowed the most wicked smile Lizzie had ever seen. The fact that his smile caused her heart to lurch again made not the slightest difference. Lizzie knew this man for the scoundrel he was.

They watched one another for a long moment. Jack obviously enjoying this encounter, while Lizzie only wished she could wipe that smile off his face permanently. Her teeth were clenched with anger as she asked, ''Exactly what is it you want?''

''You.''

''Me?'' Lizzie looked more than a bit puzzled. And in her innocence asked, ''What does that mean?''

She hadn't a clue as to his meaning. If Jack had known a touch of skepticism concerning her innocence before, her question forever put his doubts to rest. ''It means the total and free use of your body.''

Lizzie's hand was caught inches from his cheek. A second later the hand was twisted behind her back as she was tugged against him. Lizzie took a deep breath as she tried to regain control. Lord, had she ever known more confusion? How in the world could she feel attracted to this beast? She hated him! Well, perhaps *hate* was too strong a word. She didn't hate him. She hated his standing, his class, the fact that in his arrogance he thought her willing to succumb to his debauchery.

From the first she'd known no partiality toward those of authority or noble birth. Hadn't their treatment of her and her mother at home proved despicable?

Still, she knew a fondness for her grandfather. Lizzie only wished all Englishmen could be as loving and sweet as that kindly old gentleman. Obviously she might as well have wished for her own personal star. ''I can't remember the last time I've been so insulted.''

''It was not my intent to insult you. Indeed there are

some who would feel complimented knowing they are the object of a man's desire.''

Lizzie shot him a look of disgust. ''No doubt it depends on the man.''

Jack grinned. That she wanted him gone from her was obvious. Too bad, Jack thought, for he had some definite plans for this woman. ''Your answer?''

''My answer is an emphatic and unequivocal no.''

''I think the end of autumn will do nicely,'' he said mildly, as if she were in total agreement with his outrageous suggestion.

''The end of the world sounds better.'' Lizzie's blue eyes narrowed with warning that this man should know his foe was no weak miss. It didn't matter that she grew weak in his arms. That she readily accepted his kisses, his touch, once pressed against him. It didn't matter her dreams, the erotic hours of slumber that caused her to awaken shaken and longing to dream again. He was English, and worst of all, of the aristocracy. She'd never marry him.

Jack grinned. He hadn't expected her to agree to marriage. No doubt she suffered under some shock. The same shock that had kept him pacing the garden for most of the night. She easily denied the passion that had raged between them, but Jack knew better than to try. It didn't take but a kiss for him to know there was no way he was going to allow this woman to slip away. She was going to marry him. She simply didn't know it yet. In the meantime, until she grew used to the idea, he'd play the seduction game.

Lizzie pushed herself free of his hold, reached for her cane, and ignoring him completely, limped toward the house. Jack walked alongside. ''All right, if marriage is out of the question, what about the alternative?''

Jack almost laughed aloud, for her look told of her certainty that the man had lost his mind. ''There is no alternative.''

"I want you."

"My lord, it has always been my belief that every man has a right to his dreams." And if she could find a way to control hers, a giant step might be taken toward righting her world.

Jack chuckled. She was a quick wit. She did not act the sweet, simpering miss, but rather a woman of strong beliefs, and after last night, he knew her to have strong appetites as well. She had a sharp tongue. Jack figured that after some tutoring, she'd know well how to put that tongue to its best advantage. "Perhaps a few more kisses should persuade you."

Lizzie came to an instant stop. "Lord have mercy, why do you insist on pestering me? Surely this Mary person is willing enough to see to your debauchery."

Jack shrugged aside the thought of Mary or any other, knowing that after last night he wanted only this lady. "Perhaps I'm not interested in a woman quite so willing."

"Meaning what? If I were willing, you wouldn't want me either?"

They reached the house and Jack opened the doors to the hall, standing aside so she might enter. Servants were about, polishing and cleaning after last night's festivities. Jack seemed not to notice and continued on with his teasing. "We could try it and see."

Lizzie lowered her voice to a sneering whisper. "You are a despicable creature."

"Actually, I think 'honest' is a more accurate assessment."

"Were I not a lady, I could tell you what to do with your honesty."

"You'll be needing some help here, I think," he said as they stopped at the wide stairway.

"I'll manage, thank—" Lizzie gasped as she was suddenly and without permission taken into his arms again. Curse this man! Would he never stop touching her? Lizzie wasn't about to fight him, especially with servants looking on. No doubt the beast realized as much.

He had almost reached the last step before Lizzie collected her wits enough to ask, "Is something wrong with your hearing?"

Jack smiled, his gaze on her mouth as he mounted the last step. "I don't think so. Why?"

"No reason," Lizzie sighed as Jack deposited her at her bedroom door. "Thank you," she said as she watched his head lower. He was going to kiss her again, or try to; of that, she had no doubt. She blinked at his unbelievable audacity. Hadn't he heard a word she'd said? Did he believe her so weak willed as to accede without opposition to his less-than-decent whims? If so, the poor man was indeed far more demented than she'd first thought.

Lizzie said nothing as her hand reached behind her. An instant later she slid into her room and shut her door.

Jack lay awake for some time thinking about the lady sleeping two rooms from his. Idly he wondered if she realized just how intriguing was her resistance. He felt totally captivated.

She was an innocent. There was no denying that fact, no matter their heated kisses last night and this morning. A young woman barely tried in the art of loving.

Jack hadn't a doubt that he would soon introduce her to the pleasure.

Chapter 6

❦❦❦

"Are you serious!" Lizzie asked. "Two? You received two offers?" The truth of the matter was, Lizzie had not expected even one, and thought both men either deranged or desperate indeed to have made an offer.

In truth, Andrew hadn't expected an abundance of offers either. Still, he'd been shocked at the meager turnout. Were there naught but two men in all of England confident enough in their own manhood, their own ability to control a wife, to want more than a pretty face? Certainly he'd imagined his circle of friends and acquaintances made of sterner stuff.

Despite his granddaughter's expressed disinterest in gaining a title, he thought the glamour of a ball and a deluge of admirers would soon have her seeing things his way. Obviously his plan had worked, for Andrew was sure he heard disappointment in her voice. "I quite understand your dissatisfaction, dear. I was confident of a half dozen offers at least." Andrew shook his head as he thought. "Can't understand what's the matter with the men in these parts."

"Perhaps they're shy," Jack offered from an easy chair across the room.

Surprised, Lizzie turned and glanced in his direction. She hadn't realized until he spoke that he was in the room. Now that she knew, she wished only that he would disappear.

"Or fools," her grandfather returned.

Lizzie was more of a mind to believe the older man's opinion, for she'd never seen a more foolish group of strutting peacocks in her life. And at first sight, *fool* had easily been the first word that came to mind. "It doesn't matter. Truly," Lizzie said, trying to lift her grandfather's spirits. Lizzie knew he wanted only the best for her; still, she wouldn't have thought that he'd look this disappointed. "I know you'd see me marry someone with a title, Gran, but there wasn't one man among the lot I'd seriously consider."

"Wouldn't you like to know who offered?"

To say she didn't give a fig would have been accurate but most unkind, and Lizzie wouldn't have hurt her grandfather for the world. "Of course. Who are they?"

"Lord Bently and Alex Cook."

Lizzie nodded. "Both gentlemen are very nice, but—"

Lizzie's words were cut off as Jack interrupted. "And myself," he said.

Jack had been waiting all morning to make his intentions known. The truth was, he couldn't wait to tell his stepfather his intent.

Lizzie turned again to the awful man, her annoyance forgotten. It was shock, she imagined, that forced her to twice clear her throat before the rusty-sounding word became audible. "What?"

Lizzie knew what was behind the offer. He was trying to upset her again, a pastime he seemed particularly fond of pursuing.

She hadn't considered his offer in the garden seriously, nor would she now. The man wanted her in his bed. It was as simple as that. Still she wondered why her heart should suddenly beat so erratically.

Jack smiled and ignored her question. "Andrew, you may add my offer to the others."

Andrew's smile radiated happiness, while Lizzie wanted only to run. She felt trapped, cornered, her eyes wide as she tried to think of a way out. "I don't think so," Lizzie began weakly. "Thank you, but—"

"I'm not being charitable, Lizzie, if that's what you think."

Charitable? Lizzie doubted the lecher had a charitable bone in his entire body. She wasn't sure what he was up to, but wanted above all else to tell him just what she thought of his supposed offer. But Lizzie glanced at her grandfather's delighted smile and almost groaned aloud, realizing now that she would not be able to voice her thoughts.

Her heart sank to her toes when she heard his heartfelt "That's wonderful." He came to his feet and hugged his granddaughter tightly to his chest. Lizzie felt tears of frustration smart when he said, "I'm so happy." Her gaze moved to the grinning beast lounging across the room. "I couldn't have wished better for you, for either of you."

"Grandfather, do you think we could have a few minutes alone?" She turned toward the confident wretch and directed at him a smile that held not a glimmer of the pleasure a young woman should feel in this particular circumstance. "Jack, would you join me for a walk in the garden, please?" Lizzie, because of her grandfather's presence, had been forced to politely ask, but what she'd meant was to order the man to do her bidding, and the look she shot his way told him surely dire consequences lay in store should he refuse.

Andrew, having no knowledge of Lizzie's animosity toward his stepson, grinned. The truth was, he hadn't dared hope that a union would form between these two strong-willed young people, and was confident things couldn't have turned out better if he'd planned them himself. "Take all the time you want," Andrew said as he anxiously ushered the two outside by way of the library's French doors.

Lizzie limped along with Jack at her side for some minutes before Jack finally said, "You're very quiet, Lizzie. Has my offer shocked you?"

"You might say that," she said through clenched teeth, even as she marveled that her jawbone remained intact with the pressure she exerted.

Jack could hardly suppress his amusement. He didn't love her. A man did not have to love a woman to want to marry her. Still, he couldn't deny that she was adorable, more so as she tried, without much success, to control her building rage. "You shouldn't be, I think. I mentioned marriage this morning, if you remember."

"We both know you weren't serious this morning. And I was quiet because I was trying to think of a way to decline your magnanimous offer and do it without saying the first words that come to mind."

"And we couldn't have that, could we, Lizzie dear?" Jack laughed aloud, knowing quite well the words she might have used.

"Bastard," she muttered.

Jack laughed again. How was it that sharp words from this small woman stirred him more than any come-hither glance from another? "The truth is, my mother and father were married four years before my arrival, so I'm afraid that particular word does not apply in this case."

When one is very angry, it hardly sits well to see another enjoying that anger. Lizzie couldn't hold back the harsh words, "What the bloody hell are you laughing at?"

"Lizzie dear, after we're married, I'm afraid I'll have to insist that you keep a civil tongue." He grinned at her and wondered if she weren't about to burst from her bottled-up rage. "After all, it wouldn't do, I think, for the Countess of Dover . . ."

Lizzie never heard the rest. Her thoughts froze on the word *Countess*. It was silently repeated with dread, the title bringing on a shiver of disgust. It was out of the question, of course, impossible that she should ever become a countess. Lizzie, every bit as much a rebel as those she'd left behind, worked even now for equality among men. It was unthinkable that she should join the aristocracy. "Lord help us."

Jack couldn't hold back his laughter. The sound might have been rich and deliciously pleasing to any feminine ear, but Lizzie found it almost offensive. She frowned knowing the more his obvious enjoyment, the greater her annoyance. That he was having a bit of fun at her expense was undeniable. The trouble was, at the moment Lizzie didn't feel the least inclined toward fun. "One can only wonder if you'll still be laughing as we're both dragged down the aisle."

"Am I laughing?"

She didn't bother to reply, but snapped instead, "Dolt! What in the world could you be thinking to make such an offer?"

"Actually, I thought I made myself quite clear."

"I will not marry you," she said with absolute finality, and then glared, silently daring him to dispute her words.

Jack almost took the dare, but decided it might be prudent not to push her too far at this time. "And I don't want you to." Jack knew this woman would never give in to coercion; therefore he was forced to resort to trickery.

Lizzie blinked, her eyes widening with surprise. "What? Then why . . ."

"Would you rather marry Bently?"

Lizzie frowned. "Of course not. I told you . . ."

"Or Cook?" Jack shrugged. "He's a nice enough fellow, I suppose. Perhaps you'd rather—"

"What are you talking about?" she asked, her voice rising a bit in her frustration.

"I'm talking about the fact that despite your best efforts, you received two offers. What kind of an excuse can you give to refuse either?"

"What kind of excuse can I give to refuse yours? Especially yours. Grandfather is delighted." She shook her head.

"It's very simple, actually. After a few weeks we'll pretend an argument. Irrefutable differences. You can call the engagement off." He shrugged. "Andrew will know some disappointment, but he'll eventually come around." Jack silently congratulated himself on a perfect plan. Of course, she'd never call off the engagement. Within a few weeks' time he planned to know this woman in every sense of the word. And any thoughts of calling off their engagement would be out of the question.

Lizzie watched him for a long moment through narrowed and suspicious eyes. She did feel some relief, for his words made perfect sense. Still, things weren't always as simple as they appeared. She didn't trust his offer of help and didn't hesitate to say as much. "I don't trust you." Her gaze narrowed further. "You're not that kind."

"You hardly know me. Do you think yourself able to judge?"

Lizzie ignored his question and asked, "What have you to gain?"

"What have I done to merit such distrust?"

"Spying on a woman hardly constitutes exemplary principles."

"I told you I wasn't spying, Lizzie. I merely took Rascal for a ride. Could I help it if a beautiful sea nymph suddenly held me spellbound?"

Lizzie knew a wave of embarrassment even as she dismissed his compliment, not believing for a minute either the pretty words or his explanation.

"All I have to gain is the pleasure of your company for a spell," Jack said, though he had every intention of gaining quite a bit more.

"You can't be doing this out of the goodness of your heart." She shook her head and mused almost to herself, "You have something in mind, all right." A moment later she laughed and said, "I've got it! You imagine being engaged will accord you certain liberties."

Jack shrugged. She was close to the truth. Closer than she knew and more clever than even he suspected. Jack thought he'd have to be careful indeed if he hoped to claim this prize. "That's a possibility, of course."

"Possibility," she repeated in disgust.

"Bedding you is a delightful thought, Lizzie"—Lord, but that was an understatement—"but I wasn't thinking along those lines when I made my offer." The truth was, lately she was nearly all he ever thought about. He wanted this woman. Nothing and no one was going to stop him from having her.

"Of course not," she said in disbelief.

"You've nothing to lose. You can break the engagement anytime you wish."

"Good, I'm breaking it now."

"I'd wait just a bit, if I were you."

"Were I made of sterner stuff, I'd marry you just for spite. Marry you and then play you false every chance I got."

Every bit of laughter disappeared from his dark eyes. And then he said softly enough for chills to run down her spine, "There was a woman once who thought along those very lines. She was the wife of my best friend."

Lizzie blinked. "What happened?"

"She died," he said flatly.

Lizzie wasn't at all sure she wanted to hear the answer. Even so, she found herself asking, "How?"

Jack grinned at her look of dread. "I hadn't a hand in it, if that's what you think." He sighed and then said, "No, the lady in question found herself in something of a predicament. She was three months with child when she and Sam married. Obviously she hoped to pass the baby off as his, but Sam thought her an innocent angel and refused to touch her until they married."

"So you found out and killed her?"

Jack laughed at her supposition. "She visited a midwife and hemorrhaged afterward. They couldn't save her.

"I've never seen pain like that in a man's eyes before or since. I wouldn't take kindly to it happening to me."

"Nothing like that could happen to you."

"Why not? It happens all the time."

Despite her threat, Lizzie couldn't imagine that any woman would play this man false. She looked at him a long moment, never realizing the admiration in that look, before stating quite bluntly, "Something would have to be wrong with her." Lizzie never realized her thoughts. Never realized that she was complimenting this man. She was simply being honest and didn't think on her words as she tried to put her thoughts in order.

Jack did not respond. He hadn't missed her look of honest appreciation and felt a wave of lust crash into his belly. A lust so strong, he wondered at his ability to restrain himself.

They reached the garden house, and Jack sat without asking permission. Lizzie scowled at his lack of etiquette and ignored the gesture that she should sit at his side. She remained standing, while leaning most of her weight on her cane. He shrugged as if it were of no consequence as he knocked the cold tobacco from his pipe and then pocketed the object.

"What happened to him? Did he marry again?"

Jack shook his head. "No. There is a lady in his life, but I doubt that he'll marry."

Lizzie wondered how a woman finding herself with child could marry another, hoping to pass off the baby as her husband's. Had she ever heard anything more sordid? After a long, silent moment, she breathed the word "Lord," on a sigh.

"Are you addressing me or the heavenly kind?"

Lizzie laughed softly, realizing all at once that this man could easily poke fun at himself. That much of the arrogance she placed at his feet was but an act. Perhaps a means to protect what could easily be a bit of insecurity. The thought made him ever so much more human. Indeed, almost likable. Still, she wasn't about to let down her guard, and managed to mingle her laughter with a contemptuous glance. "I'd warrant a man of your arrogance believes himself to be one and the same."

"Not at all. I'm sure I have a failing or two."

"Except you can't imagine what they might be?" The question was accompanied by a snort of derision.

"Well, now that you mention it, I'd have to think on it a bit."

Lizzie couldn't hold back her grin. "Your perfection aside, Lord Dover, how are we to manage this subterfuge? My grandfather will expect us to act as if we care for one another."

"And will that be difficult?"

"Impossible, I think."

"The truth is, Lizzie, all you have to do is be nice."

Lizzie's blue eyes darkened with suspicion. "Nice? What does that mean?"

"Nice? Let's see. It means, agreeable, amicable, friendly . . ."

"I know the meaning of the word," she snapped. "What I don't know is degree. Exactly how nice?" she asked, ignoring his teasing. She only wished she could

as easily ignore his grin. Did he realize the effect his
smile had on women? Well, on some women. It didn't
have any effect on her, thank the good Lord . . . the
heavenly kind.

"Actually," he said, and then suddenly laughed, positive of her response, "you have my permission to be
as nice as you please."

His laughter, combined with the bold look that swept
her from toe to frilly mobcap, left her without a doubt
as to his meaning. Lizzie instantly forgot the man's at-
tractiveness. "You are a beast."

"You might have to stop calling me names."

"Indeed? Not an easy chore, I'm sure, since you're
so very deserving," she said prettily.

He chuckled. The woman rarely said a word that did
not bring a smile of some sort. Damn, but she intrigued
like no other, and Jack thought himself absolutely brilliant, for even if she didn't know it yet, she had no
means of ever escaping him. "And every once in a while
you could smile as if you like me."

"Truly that will be hardest of all." Lizzie turned from
his smile, knowing it wouldn't be hard at all. Knowing
even now the corners of her mouth curved when she
wanted them to remain straight and forbidding.

"No, I think the hardest part will be when you kiss me."

Lizzie's gaze snapped back to his. She watched him
for a long moment. The man was obviously having a
time of it controlling his amusement. And amusement,
after a time, proved infectious. She laughed, unable to
help herself. "You might be right there, except for the
fact that I won't be kissing you."

"Your grandfather will expect some show of affection."

Her gaze narrowed again as a thought occurred. "You
did this on purpose."

"Did what on purpose?"

"How much did you offer them?"

"Who?" Jack couldn't keep up. He hadn't a notion as to what she was talking about.

"Bently and Cook, of course. How much?"

Jack's eyes widened as he realized her meaning at last. "You have a deliciously devious mind." He watched her for a moment before asking, "Do you think I paid them to offer for you, just so I could force you to accept me? Interesting."

"And you didn't answer my question."

"Lizzie dear, you are a beautiful woman. There was no need to offer either man anything."

"I don't believe they offered on their own. And don't call me Lizzie dear."

Jack shrugged. "Apparently some men care more for a woman's looks than her mind. And why not?"

"Because I don't like it."

"All right. What about 'darling'?"

"I think I shall kill you," she said very softly as if giving the thought some real deliberation.

" 'Sweetheart'?"

Lizzie took a deep breath and said, "My name is Elizabeth."

Jack shook his head, ignoring the obvious fact that she was close to the end of her patience. "Too formal."

She began to pace, forgetting entirely about the discomfort in her ankle. "When can we tell them it's over?"

Jack figured she had resigned herself to his proposal, at least temporarily, but just to make sure, asked, "You mean between us?"

"No, I mean between Antony and Cleopatra."

He laughed again. God, but she wished he would stop that. A man didn't have the right, especially this man, to sound that appealing. Appealing? Was she losing her mind to imagine this pompous stuffed shirt appealing?

"A few weeks perhaps. A month would probably be better."

Lizzie came to a stop. A month was far too long. In truth a few weeks were too long, but Lizzie thought she had no real option here. "A few weeks." She nodded at the thought. "The sooner the better."

"Your grandfather is watching."

Lizzie turned and then frowned. From where she stood, shrubbery and trees blocked any view from the mansion's first floor. One couldn't even see the library doors. How could he know her grandfather was watching them? "I don't see—"

"We should give the old man a reason to smile, don't you think?"

Lizzie turned back only to find him standing before her. Standing much too close, in fact. She took a sudden ragged breath and a step back. "He was smiling enough." What was the matter with her? Why was she suddenly breathless? "Besides, he can't see . . . Jack," she gasped as he brought her against him. "Stop it."

"We're engaged, remember?"

"That doesn't mean you have the right to . . ." Lizzie felt an unwanted shiver of excitement race through her body. His hands at her waist again lifted her, and for the third time in less than twelve hours her cane clattered to the ground. "Put me down this instant!" she said, knowing her tone lacked conviction.

Jack remembered quite clearly her responses to last night's and this morning's intimacies. "Is that what you truly want?" he asked.

She couldn't insist. Her heart was pounding. He was going to kiss her, and even though she denied it, a tiny part of her wanted to feel his mouth on hers again. "I'm not likely to get what I want. At least not for three weeks."

Jack sat, and Lizzie blinked in astonishment as she found herself upon his lap. "What are you doing?"

"We have three weeks, correct?"

Lizzie nodded.

"So I should be able to teach you how to kiss a man in three weeks, don't you think?"

"Meaning I don't know how?" Lizzie knew some surprise that he should believe her somehow lacking. Some surprise, and as ridiculous as it might seem, some hurt as well.

"Meaning there's room for improvement," he said with his usual arrogance.

"But not on your side, surely."

Jack's eyes widened at the thought. He'd never found a woman dissatisfied with his kisses. "Have you a complaint?"

"As a matter of fact, I do." Lizzie hesitated for a long moment, wondering how she could voice her complaint without being hurtful. And then realized there was no way but to say her objections aloud. "A gentleman wouldn't think to put his tongue in a lady's mouth."

"He wouldn't?"

"Of course not. That isn't a kiss."

Two earlier encounters had convinced Jack of Lizzie's lack of experience. That she didn't know the first thing about kissing was a given. Despite her attempts at sophistication, despite her totally unorthodox behavior, she was truly an innocent. God, but he was going to enjoy initiating her into the art of lovemaking.

He couldn't suppress a tender smile. "What is it then?"

"Truly, I haven't the slightest notion."

He touched a finger to her full lower lip and ran it gently corner to corner. "You should show me, then, the proper way to go about it."

A pulse pounded in her throat and Lizzie's breathing came in erratic gasps, her voice suddenly whispery soft. "It's terribly simple, really. Just press your lips to mine." Had Lizzie a moment to think on her actions, she would surely have known some amazement in how easily he'd managed to trick her into putting aside her usual reserve.

"Like this?" he asked just before touching his mouth to hers.

"Yes, like that." She took a deep breath and then released it slowly as she tried to regain her composure. It was holding her breath that caused this dizziness, not his proximity. Her heart wasn't slamming crazily against the walls of her chest. Well, perhaps it was, but she was positive his kiss hadn't caused it. "Now, wasn't that nice?"

Jack forced back his smile. God, but this woman was delicious. "Very nice. Should we try it again? I want to make sure I have it right."

Lizzie, forgetting her earlier assurance that she would not be kissing this man, was now of a mind that one more kiss wouldn't hurt. She offered her mouth only to find it left untouched. A moment later she opened her eyes and asked, "What are you doing?"

"Since you're doing the teaching, I thought perhaps you should do the kissing."

"Oh." She nodded, somehow finding logic in his suggestion, and then, leaning forward a bit, gently and chastely touched her mouth to his.

"Shouldn't you put your arms around my neck?" he asked against her lips.

Lizzie obeyed without thought and never noticed her lips opened a fraction. It was hard to notice much of anything while being held in this man's arms. He smelled lovely. Lizzie couldn't remember when a man had smelled quite so good. Only that wasn't the best of it. The truth was, he felt easily as good as he smelled.

Lizzie had been kissed before, but she hadn't ever been held so close by a man. Close enough to feel his hardness against her, close enough to know a fraction of the strength in his powerful arms.

He touched her slightly parted lips with his tongue.

Lizzie should have pulled back then, if only to remind him that this wasn't the way it was done, but decided to ignore the gentle probing. He'd stop soon enough, she was sure, especially if she ignored that action. Only he didn't stop, and Lizzie struggled against the absurd need to allow him his wants.

The flower-sweet scents of summer disappeared. The pounding of a distant sea grew faint, lost in the thunder of her heart. Birds no longer chirped, frogs stopped their croaking, bees their buzzing. She could hear only the rush of her own blood, her desperately ragged gasps of air. Her world condensed to the touch, the feel, the taste of his mouth. And as it did, her body softened, her will to fight him forgotten. She leaned into him.

His tongue ran over her lips and then slid inside to tease the sensitive soft flesh. He took her bottom lip and sucked it into his mouth, groaning his pleasure at the taste and feel of her, and Lizzie thought she'd never feel anything half so lovely again.

And then his tongue was there again moving deep into her warmth, stealing her breath, her mind, her senses. Joining their mouths as if they were one. She breathed with him, of him, whimpering her need for even more. Lizzie's lips, her entire body, were relaxed by now. It took almost no pressure at all for his tongue to slide into her warmth again. She didn't think to pull back.

His hand moved from her waist, and Lizzie never thought to object as his palm covered her breast with blazing heat. It wasn't enough. She moaned for more, and Jack opened a few buttons and pushed aside her bodice. Her chemise was easily lowered, and his hand cupped her delicious softness.

"Jack, oh God," she moaned as his finger slipped over a smooth nipple, teasing it to a soft bud of pleasure, and Lizzie felt an ache grow to life, deep in her belly. An ache that increased tenfold as his mouth left hers to suckle the tip to aching hardness. Lost in passion, Lizzie could think of nothing but to have more, to feel all the promises of his mouth.

His mouth was on hers again, his breath coming in hot, delicious gusts. "You taste so good."

Lizzie tried to clear the fog from her mind even as she wondered how he had managed to read her thoughts. Sucked into a haze of need, she found herself tightening her hold, bringing his wicked mouth into closer contact, besieged with a growing need she could not identify.

Jack knew what was needed. His body was rock-hard and throbbing for release. He couldn't remember when he wanted a woman more, and God Almighty, she was so giving. Only this wasn't the time or the place. Her seduction had to be delicately handled. He didn't want her remorseful of her actions. Nay, he wanted her to glory in them, to long for his touch, to meet him halfway and demand her own share of the pleasure. Near the end of his control, Jack knew he'd have to stop, and soon. Idly he wondered if he had the strength it would take to slowly convince this woman to see to his way of thinking.

Dazed by passion, Lizzie frowned as he pulled back, knowing a perplexing degree of loss as her lips reluctantly left his. He was breathing heavily, his head leaning against the thick post behind them, his eyes closed as he fought for control.

"Lord," she breathed, lost in her own trembling need. Indeed she was easily as breathless and found herself leaning weakly against his chest as she spoke into his neck. She never realized the kiss unconsciously bestowed to the side of his throat. "You weren't supposed to use your tongue."

"Did I forget?"

Breathing his warm scent, Lizzie found it impossible to do more than nod.

"I need more practice."

Lizzie forced aside the need to linger, to experience

even more of this fascinating and decidedly wicked encounter, and pulled away. She took a deep breath and
pressed one hand to his chest for balance as she reached
to smooth her hair, perfect beneath her cap, and knocked
the cap askew. "I don't think practice will matter. We
shouldn't do this again."

"Kiss me again. I swear I'll—"

She frowned as she shook her head, in her innocence
never realizing the man's underhanded ways. "You
can't seem to get it right."

Jack slowly opened his eyes, and Lizzie trembled at
the fiery hunger she read there. She felt a chill race up
her spine and fought back the insane need to lean against
him again.

"Have you always kissed this way?" she asked, wondering if it might not be better to simply forget the entire
matter and leave the man to his oddities.

Jack thought this probably wasn't the best time to
mention previous kisses. Instead he said, "I wish you
liked it."

"It's not that I don't like it, exactly. It's just that it's
so unseemly."

"You mean you might like it?" he asked with some
obvious hope.

Lizzie couldn't honestly say if she did or not. All she
knew for sure was that her shock at the unusual intimacy
was somehow fading. "It hardly matters whether I like
it or not, does it? We'll only be engaged for a few
weeks."

"And you can manage to bear up under my kisses for
a few weeks?"

"We won't be kissing all that much."

"I'm sure we won't," he returned, knowing the words
to be an outright lie. The truth was, he was quite sure
of the opposite, for Jack had every intention of kissing
her whenever and wherever possible. Kissing her until
she came to love the taste of his mouth as he did hers,

kissing her until she ached as he did for quite a bit more.

He reached for her gown and pulled the ends together. His hands trembled as he tried to rebutton her dress. He didn't touch her, but his hands were so close, Lizzie could feel the heat of them. "I'll do it," she said, her voice shaken as she remembered the touch of his hand upon her.

Their eyes held as she covered his hands with hers. The slightest pressure. Lizzie knew that was all it would take and he'd touch her again. And she wanted him to touch her. Nothing had ever felt so lovely. But to do so would be to court disaster.

Jack smiled and brought his hands to her waist again. Her fingers were hardly any more steady, but Lizzie managed the chore.

A moment later she turned at the sound of a gasp and found her sister standing there watching, her eyes wide with shock.

"Lizzie has promised to be my wife, Annie," Jack said with surprising ease.

Lizzie thought it most fortunate that Jack remembered the lie, especially since she couldn't for the moment think of a reasonable excuse why she should be found sitting on this man's lap. Indeed, at the sight of her sister, she had somehow forgotten their supposed engagement and knew at first only intense confusion.

Lizzie managed to come to her feet. She smiled a bit vaguely, even as Jack retrieved her cane and stood behind her, his arm wrapped possessively around her waist.

It took a moment, but Annie finally took in the truth of the matter and laughed as she reached for her sister, hugging her tightly. "I can't believe it. I thought . . ." She laughed again. "Well, it doesn't matter what I thought, does it? Are you happy?"

"Very," Lizzie said, somehow saddened at the lie and then knowing still another moment of confusion as she wondered why. A moment later came the thought that if her supposed engagement were an engagement in truth, she might have been happy. And then she nearly gasped aloud at the absurdity. Lord have mercy, what could she be thinking? Granted she nearly melted every time this man took her into his arms, but she did not love him. She couldn't ever love an aristocrat. Her whole life was dedicated to equality, to freedom. Certainly she did not want to marry him. The only reason she felt this wave of sadness was that she'd never lied to her sister before.

"Does Mother know? Does Grandfather?"

"Your grandfather knows," Jack said as Annie dutifully kissed her future brother-in-law's cheek.

"Oh, may I tell Mother?" she asked in girlish delight. "Please, Lizzie, may I?"

"Go ahead. I'll be along directly."

Annie kissed her sister again. A moment later she was gone, disappearing up the path toward the house. Jack and Lizzie were once again left alone. Jack turned Lizzie and then tipped her face back with a finger beneath her chin. "Your mother will suspect something amiss if you don't do a better job of looking happy."

"I've never lied to my family." Lizzie felt a wave of guilt that she not only had lied, but would continue the deception for the next few weeks. "It's all your fault, anyhow. If you hadn't made that ridiculous offer, I wouldn't have had to lie."

"It doesn't have to be a lie. If you want to get married, it's all right with me." Jack knew it was more than all right. It was an absolute. He might not love this woman. In truth, he'd never allow a woman that kind of power. Still, there was something about this woman that intrigued. Intrigued enough to bring him to the holy state.

Lizzie laughed. "That's very considerate. Are you always this obliging when it comes to marriage?"

Jack bit his bottom lip trying to hold back another

grin. "Most think I'm a very obliging fellow."

Lizzie did not respond, but merely turned from him and began the long walk to the house. Her ankle was beginning to throb miserably. Obviously her thoughts had been otherwise occupied and she hadn't realized until now its sore abuse.

Jack couldn't help but notice her struggles. "I should carry you."

Lizzie came to an abrupt stop and shot him a dangerous glare. It was only now that he wasn't touching her that she found herself able to think. And Lizzie wasn't the least bit happy at her thoughts. All her forgotten suspicions rose again to the surface, and Lizzie grew sure of his manipulation. "What I want to know is, how did you manage it?"

"What did I do now?"

"You tricked me into kissing you."

"Did I?" Jack chuckled. She was right about that, of course. He had tricked her. Still, he held little hope that she'd ever admit to her satisfaction. "Well, since you're so prone to truth telling, why don't you admit to the brilliance of my plan?"

"You are contemptible," she said, the words so soft, so lacking in anger, they might have been love words.

Jack grinned as he lifted her into his arms. "I know."

Lizzie laughed again. "Three weeks," she muttered. "I don't know if I have the strength."

Chapter 7

❝**W**hat are you doing here?'' Lizzie asked Jack. He was standing beside his horse at the parsonage gate when he was supposed to be in London meeting with his man of business. "You weren't expected back until tomorrow."

Jack shrugged. "Finished everything in record time."

"How lovely," she said, trying to pretend a coolness she did not feel. In truth Lizzie wasn't sure what it was she felt. Certainly she couldn't look at him without remembering his kisses, the excitement of his touch. And know a longing for more.

The problem was, he was too attractive. He threatened everything she was, everything she believed.

Granted their encounters were lovely, far too lovely if the truth be told. But they had no future together. Nothing could ever come of sweet stolen moments of passion. He was an earl. And to the core of her being she longed for equality, for freedom for all. She'd dedicated her life to the cause, having lost both a father and her first love to it, and chanced death that the dream of freedom might live.

Undoubtedly she no longer lumped him with the rest

of England's elite. He wasn't at all the pompous fool, something she'd suspected from the first but had tried to deny. He was intelligent, caring, and the most dangerous man she'd ever known.

It had taken hours of thinking before Lizzie had finally come to the conclusion that personal feelings could not bear consideration. That she owed at least that much to those who had given their all.

Jack grinned at her less-than-enthusiastic look. "Happy to see me, I take it?"

Lizzie's answer was to pretend a dramatic sigh and then laugh adorably. "Very happy."

He tied her horse to the post and turned, ready to help her from the gig. Lizzie hesitated, knowing the usual familiarity of his hands. "I won't bite."

"Yes, you will," she said as he took her by the waist and swung her smoothly to the ground. Something fluttered in her chest and she knew a sudden sense of exhilaration as he leaned far closer than he should have and whispered, "Only if you ask politely."

Lizzie looked away and smoothed her gloves. "You didn't answer me. What are you doing here?"

"Going to dinner, I expect."

"Are you? Have you been invited as well?"

Jack held his hand to the small of her back as he opened the gate, ushering her down the path that led to the tiny house. "We're engaged, are we not? That means, if you're invited, so am I."

Again the arrogance of the elite, Lizzie thought. He might be far better than the rest; still, he was without a doubt an aristocrat, expecting, as the usual course of events, instant respect. He took it for granted and never gave the homage received a second thought. "But we're not. Not really," Lizzie quickly returned, and wondered why he took every opportunity, even in private, to remind her of their supposed engagement. They both knew it was naught but a sham. "And you weren't invited."

Jack grinned. "I haven't a doubt your parson friend will extend—"

Lizzie came to an abrupt stop and frowned her irritation. "You're being condescending. His name is Richard, Jack, not *my parson friend*. Do you put yourself above us all, simply because you're an earl? Do you truly believe a title makes you the better man?"

Jack's eyes widened at the accusation. "I never thought it did, Lizzie."

"Then why don't you like him?"

"You mean aside from the fact that he's in love with you?"

Lizzie moaned and rolled her eyes toward the heavens. "Don't start that again."

"I don't like him because he's a pompous stuffed shirt who thinks he knows it all."

Lizzie laughed softly and touched a finger to his jaw, trailing it over his white cravat to his chest. "It's like looking into a mirror, I'd warrant."

That she believed him arrogant was a given. Jack had never thought about it much, but he supposed she was right. He grinned and pulled her closer. "I might be arrogant, pompous, and the lot, but I don't pretend to have the ear of the Lord. I don't tell people how they should live or damn them if they don't come up to my standards."

"He's a parson. Who else would have the ear of the Lord?" She gave a small sigh and continued on with, "Perhaps he does get a bit carried away during his sermons, but he's a good man."

Jack grunted, obviously unconvinced.

"Very well," she said, "if you don't like him, don't come."

"Considering his feelings for you, he should know of our betrothal."

"What betrothal?"

Jack nodded as he narrowed his gaze. "I wasn't

wrong, then, in presuming you wouldn't tell him."

Lizzie laughed. "I never thought the subject might come up."

"Don't worry. I'll make sure it does."

The words "Oh, hello" prevented any further conversation as Richard opened the door to his small home. "I'm so happy you've come. My sister is so anxious to meet you." His gaze moved beyond Lizzie then to the tall man just behind her. Richard's mouth dropped open and he seemed to shrink before Lizzie's eyes. "And, your lordship, truly I'm honored."

"He won't be staying," Lizzie teased as she hurried forward and then turned, shooting Jack a wicked grin.

"Oh, but you must. Please, my sister has come for a visit. She'd be disappointed if you didn't stay," Richard returned.

"Your servant, sir," Jack said, shaking hands. And shooting Lizzie a look that promised retaliation in the very near future, he said, "Indeed, I'd be delighted to stay."

Lizzie began her visit in a glorious, lighthearted mood. As the hours progressed, however, the glory slipped into a headache of mammoth proportions.

Dinner became a dreadful affair. The fowl was perfectly cooked, the wine light and fruity, the table beautifully appointed, and still it was dreadful. Except for one comment concerning her work at the poorhouse, Lizzie was completely ignored. All it took, it seemed, was the presence of an earl and she might have disappeared into the woodwork for all the attention she received.

And Jack, never seemed to notice. In fact, he seemed to especially enjoy the attention bestowed by Richard's sister, Mrs. Agatha Pentigast.

Upon stepping over the parsonage threshold, the aversion Jack felt for his host apparently slipped his mind. He conversed in the most friendly manner. In truth one might have assumed he and Richard longtime friends as he flashed that perfect smile.

"I understand you're recently back from the West Indies," Richard remarked. "I hope the trip was comfortable."

"Yes, quite comfortable. Indeed, the sea was so calm, most of us found the crossing quite boring."

"The West Indies?" Mrs. Pentigast breathed softly. "Have you a plantation there?" she asked, her eyes bright with interest.

Jack nodded. "We grow a bit of fruit."

"I'm sure you're being modest."

"Agatha," Richard said in obvious disapproval.

Mrs. Pentigast laughed. "Richard thinks I ask too many questions."

And Richard is right, Lizzie silently mused.

"I can't imagine an earl growing a bit of fruit."

Jack flashed one of his smiles. "The place was left to me by my uncle. He died before producing an heir. And you're right. There's more than a bit."

And so it went from there. Mrs. Pentigast asking questions, Jack answering them. And Lizzie swore she'd never been so bored in her entire life, even if she listened to every word.

The main course was finished and Mrs. Cunningham's helper removed the plates, while the housekeeper brought a beautiful custard to the table.

"Oh, you must try this, my lord," said Mrs. Pentigast. "I made it myself. And not to sound immodest, my poor husband used to say it was the best in all of England."

Jack sampled the dessert, and swearing he hadn't tasted such fare in all his years, added more to his plate. It was during his second helping that he raved, not only was Mrs. Pentigast a beauty (which, to Lizzie's way of thinking, although true, should have been totally beside the point), but an excellent cook. Lizzie thought his compliments a bit much.

Mrs. Agatha Pentigast, although recently widowed, seemed ripe and ready for a new man in her life.

Lizzie had imagined widowed ladies to act with a bit of decorum. But not in this case.

And Richard, Lord, he was the worst of the lot. Never once did he stand or sit up straight. Actually he seemed to grow smaller and more insignificant with each tick of the clock. Lizzie thought if she didn't get Jack out of here, and soon, the poor man might wither down to a melted blob of muscle and bone.

Of course, Richard's subservient attitude wasn't Jack's fault. Still, Lizzie was annoyed.

After a seemingly endless dinner, they adjourned at last to the small sitting room, where Mrs. Pentigast played the spinet and sang. Jack couldn't have looked more pleased and seemed not at all aware of the occasional flat notes. It was then that the beginnings of Lizzie's headache truly took hold.

After a half hour of torture, Mrs. Pentigast left the spinet at last to seat herself close to Jack on the small settee. Far closer than could be deemed proper.

Jack seemed not to mind.

Lizzie, unable to bear the thought of yet another bout of gushing compliments, decided a walk in the church garden just the thing. She ignored Jack's dark look as she invited Richard for an evening stroll. "I've a need for a breath of air, Richard. Would you care to join me?"

"It's getting late, Lizzie. I think we should be on our way."

"Oh, stay, please," Agatha Pentigast implored, almost leaning into him. Lizzie watched Jack come quickly to his feet. "We could have a game of whist."

"Lizzie's mother will begin to worry," Jack said. "We'd best not return too late."

"But you'll come again, won't you?" the disappointed lady purred prettily.

"With your expertise in cooking, how could I stay away?" Jack returned. At the door Jack took Lizzie's hand and announced without preamble, "I'd like you to be the first, outside the family, to congratulate me. Miss Matthews has promised to be my wife."

Brother and sister looked startled at first, but soon managed awkward felicitations. Moments later Lizzie was whisked from their company.

The entire visit lasted no longer than three hours. Still, it felt closer to ten before Jack tied his horse to the back of her gig and sat at Lizzie's side for the ride home.

Brother and sister were still waving and calling out their good-nights as the gig moved out of sight, and Jack remarked, "That went well, don't you think?"

Lizzie only grunted in response.

Jack glanced in her direction, only to find her looking straight ahead, her chin up, her back stiff. She was angry, and Jack hadn't a notion why. "You were very quiet tonight. Is something wrong?"

"It was worse than I expected."

"Truly? I thought Reverend Poole and Mrs. Pentigast very nice indeed."

Lizzie could well believe he thought Mrs. Pentigast very nice indeed. Surely he bestowed enough compliments on the woman. "Mrs. Pentigast most especially, I take it?"

"Do you think I went too far?"

"That depends, I suppose. How far did you want to go?"

"What does that mean? I was only trying to be polite."

Lizzie snorted and then, thinking the subject best laid to rest, remarked, "I was under the impression that you disliked Richard."

"I thought as much myself. It turns out the man isn't quite so abrasive once you get to know him."

"I'm sure."

"Are you annoyed with me? Don't you want me to like him?"

"I'm not annoyed with you, exactly. I'm annoyed with the entire evening. I'm sure I've never seen two people come closer to groveling." Lizzie sighed softly. "Actually, now that I think on it, they were groveling. Yes, my lord, no, my lord. May I kiss your feet, my lord? Can I get you anything else? A second helping? More wine? Tea? Cakes? A sacrificial virgin?"

Jack laughed at her mockery, knowing she wasn't far off the mark. The brother and sister had gone out of their way to make sure he was comfortable. He thought his title was probably the cause. At least it was with the brother. The sister, well, she was another matter entirely. Her direct looks and secret smiles left not a doubt what she had in mind. "Is that what is bothering you? Do you need a bit of attention? Were you feeling ignored?" he teased.

"What I need is air. I have a headache."

"Well then, take all you want." He waved his arm before them. "There's plenty of it, I'd warrant."

Lizzie shot him a glare. "Thank you."

They drove in silence for a moment before Lizzie remarked, "I wonder how her husband died. She's so young."

Jack chuckled. "He died on his wedding night." Jack's chuckle grew louder until hearty laughter filled the silent night. "When you stepped into the kitchen to greet Mrs. Cunningham, Mrs. Pentigast thought to inform me of the details. It seems he was an older gentleman who suffered from a bad heart." Jack wiped his eyes with the back of his hands.

"What's the matter with you?"

"Nothing." The word sounded strangled.

"Something is. You're laughing because a man died."

"I'm laughing because the lady brought up the subject

as if to boast. Apparently she imagines the episode to make her more desirable.''

"I don't understand. How could his dying make her desirable?'' Lizzie knew, of course, the basic happenings between a man and his wife. Still, having no firsthand experience left her somewhat disadvantaged.

"Lizzie,'' he explained, ''remember how your heart pounds when we kiss?''

Lizzie lowered her gaze to her lap. The night was dark and they were alone. She was hardly comfortable with the turn in conversation.

"Well, when a man and woman make love, hearts are bound to beat even more wildly. The experience can't be good for a man with a bad heart.''

Lizzie frowned. ''How does all of this make her more desirable?''

"Except in her own mind, it doesn't. I promise you.''

Jack thought a change of subject to be in order. He snapped the reins and the horse began to trot along the shadowy road. ''Richard took to the news well, don't you think?''

"What news?''

"That we are getting married, of course.''

"Oh, of course.''

"He was disappointed, though. I could tell.''

"Could you? It's amazing that you could see anything beyond Mrs. Pentigast. At one point, I thought she was going to sit on your lap.''

Jack smiled, not at all unhappy with the lady's bold attention, since it had made Lizzie jealous. And she wouldn't be jealous if she didn't care. ''Yes, she was a bit friendly.''

"To you. I don't think she remembered my name.''

"Lizzie, you've absolutely no reason to be jealous.''

Lizzie brought her fingertips to her temples and winced as she began to rub. She, who never suffered headaches, was nearly blinded by the pain. ''Please, I've suffered through hours of nonsense. I don't think I can take a minute more.''

''Are you in pain?''

''No, I have a passion for groaning and rubbing my head.''

Jack pulled the horse to a stop beneath a thickly branched tree. ''Here, let me,'' he said as he reached beneath her chin and untied the ribbon. A moment later her hat lay upon her lap. His fingers were warm and gentle, bringing a moan of pleasure from her lips. And Jack thought she had passion, all right. She simply hadn't learned yet where to direct it.

''This feels too good,'' she said, leaning slightly toward him.

''You're a stubborn woman, Lizzie.'' His hands cupped the sides of her face, his fingers moving gently at her temples. ''Why didn't you mention your headache sooner?''

''And tear you away from such delightful company? I'm sure the lady would have been crushed.''

Sarcastic, nasty, and stubborn to boot, and still Jack knew only delight. She'd told him often enough that he was deranged. Perhaps she was right. Jack could think of no other reason why he should enjoy her so well. ''Come closer.''

She backed away instead. ''It's getting late.''

''I know and I'll have you home in no time. Just relax. It will ease the pain,'' he murmured as his mouth whispered over her cheek, her nose, her eyes. And then he pulled back, knowing this sweet intimacy could only tempt him beyond bearing and lead him to further frustration. She wasn't ready yet, and he couldn't seem to touch her, even in the most casual fashion, without wanting more. Jack thought himself totally captivated and couldn't be happier at the thought. ''Here, lean against me,'' he said, and then cuddled her to his side. ''I'll drive slowly.''

Lizzie said nothing as she leaned her head upon his chest and sighed, never questioning the fact that there was no need, for her headache had mostly disappeared.

"I'm afraid we have a leak."

"Good God, man, are you sure?" Mr. Blake asked, coming instantly from his chair.

Lord Summitt nodded and, motioning for him to sit again, sat opposite him. Both men reached for their cigars. "I've thought as much for a few months. Now that my man has finally infiltrated their ring, there can be no doubt."

"Can you not round the lot up?"

"I could, but they only pass on information, and another would soon come to take their place."

"What are you going to do?"

"I'm going to find the one securing the information and see the bastard hang."

Annie pulled her horse to a stop as the young man who occupied her thoughts lately rode towards her, a wide smile curving his handsome mouth. A moment later Michael Thumbolt dismounted and helped Annie reach the sandy beach. "I can't stay away long. I promised Lizzie I'd ride with her this morning."

"Where will you be riding? Perhaps I could come across you, by accident." He grinned at her look of reprimand. "Your sister and I should get to know one another, don't you think?"

Annie laughed softly. "My grandfather would have an attack of some sort if he knew we were meeting. He has his heart set on my coming out next year."

"And you will," Michael promised even as he boldly took her against him. "And you'll gain countless offers, but mine will be the best."

"Suppose it's not the best."

"Then you'll have to tell your grandfather that you've

lost your heart to this young whelp, and that will end
the matter.''

"Have I?''

"What, lost your heart?''

Annie grinned, feeling very sure of herself.

"You'd best not look at a man like that, Annie, lest
you lose even more.''

"I couldn't lose what no longer belongs to me.''

Michael moaned and then nuzzled her sweet lips. Until now he hadn't touched her but for a hug and kiss. He
wondered if he was strong enough to last out this next
year.

The sound of girlish laughter mingled with the gentle
sounds of lapping water and flowed deliciously sweet
over the rock and sandy beach as Lizzie bent low beside
Lightning's head. Her hat and veil had been torn away;
her hair, plucked free of its pins, flew in a golden cloud
of wild curls swirling behind her. She was a length
ahead, but her sister, almost as expert in horsemanship
as herself, was fast closing in. Beyond that black rock.
Only another hundred yards and she would win.

Lizzie's laughter turned into a shriek of victory as her
horse sped past the mark. She slowed the horse and allowed him to walk a bit. As he cooled down, her sister
pulled up alongside. Both women were breathless.
Lizzie glanced at Annie, knowing they were both disheveled and windblown. "It's getting harder every
time. Before long you'll leave me in your dust.''

Annie laughed. "You've been saying that since I was
ten.''

Lizzie smiled. "Only when you were ten, I didn't
mean it.''

"I'm thirsty.''

"Let's go back then. I could do with something myself.''

The two turned their horses, heading for the basket

and blankets previously left on the beach. Since there was nothing but rock, sand, and a bit of grass about, the horses, perfectly trained, were left untied some yards from their meal. Lizzie and Annie made themselves comfortable on blankets just before reaching for the basket and the cooling drinks waiting inside.

Thirsts were first conquered before meat pies were enjoyed. Lizzie was brushing crumbs from her skirt when Annie bit into an apple and said, "I love it here."

"I know," Lizzie said, knowing, despite her initial hatred of England, a deep fondness for this country and its people.

"Do you still miss New York?"

Lizzie nodded. "Terribly."

"And you want to go back?"

With every fiber of her being. Lizzie thought if she were gone ten years, it wouldn't matter. She'd still long for her home. "I am going back. The moment the war is over."

"What about Jack?"

Lizzie frowned at the mention of the man and the complication he posed. "What about him?"

"Well, he'll be your husband. Will he leave his home, his holdings?"

"A man who loves his wife would naturally want her to be happy." Lizzie thought her statement to be true. She also thought that since Jack did not love her, she had no worry on that score.

"I'd miss you terribly if you left me behind."

"I wouldn't leave you. You and Mother will go with me, of course."

"Suppose I'm married by then."

"What do you mean?" Lizzie felt a jolt of surprise at the thought. She'd never for a minute imagined her sister unable to return to the colonies.

"Well, if I were married, and Mother not likely to

leave Grandfather since he isn't so young, you'd have to go alone.''

Lizzie hadn't imagined this complication, but suddenly realized her sister was right. Annie was no longer a child, but a young beauty who bordered on the threshold of womanhood. No doubt she would receive many offers before the year was out. And her grandfather. Could she leave him behind? Oddly enough, without family, the thought of returning to New York lost much of its glow. Lizzie shrugged aside her thoughts. The war might end tomorrow. She'll think over her options then. ''I hadn't thought about leaving any of you.''

''Perhaps you should reconsider.''

''Perhaps I should.''

A moment of silence went by before Annie said, ''If I told you I let a young man kiss me, would you think it awful of me?''

Lizzie leaned her back against a rock and shifted until she found a place smooth enough for comfort. The sun was warm, the sea breeze delightful. It was the perfect moment for two sisters to tell secrets. Lizzie only wished she could tell her own. ''Michael?''

Annie nodded, a soft blush creeping up her cheeks. ''Do you think I'm terribly fast?''

Lizzie's smile was filled with tenderness. ''Terribly.''

''I know I should have waited until we were betrothed, but he so wanted a kiss.''

Lizzie, well aware of one particular man and his need for kisses, knew exactly what she meant. Still she managed, ''You shouldn't allow him another. It's best, I think, to keep a man in his place.'' That sounded all well and good, but Lizzie hadn't the slightest notion as to where that place might be. Still, she would have very much liked to see Jack go there.

Annie smiled. ''Does Jack kiss you often?''

Far more often than she liked, far more improperly,

if the truth be told. Lizzie kept those thoughts to herself. "Men enjoy kissing, I think."

"I need to ask you something."

"What?" Lizzie asked, her gaze upon the calm waters of the cove. After the morning ride and a tempting meal, she was feeling deliciously drowsy.

"Does he use his tongue?"

Lizzie's gaze moved quickly to her sister. She felt suddenly the fool. If a man as young and obviously inexperienced as Michael kissed that way, then men kissed women with their tongues as a usual course of events, and she had only shown Jack her ignorance by insisting it wasn't done. Her friend Megan had forgotten some pertinent information about kissing when she told Lizzie the details of her wedding night. Lord, how Jack must have laughed at her. "Michael shouldn't kiss you like that. It's most unseemly."

"I know, but it's so lovely. Don't you think?"

The truth was, Lizzie did think it lovely, only she'd rather go to the gallows than tell Jack. There was no telling his response if he knew she liked it.

"He said he wants to marry me."

"Annie, he's only one and twenty. Is he financially able to support a wife?"

"His father is a banker."

Lizzie nodded, aware of Mr. Thumbolt's profession.

"Michael is apprenticing. He'll take over one day."

"Even so . . ." Lizzie's gaze and tone were filled with doubt.

"I know. We'll have to wait. At least until next year and after my season."

"You'll meet many men then."

"I know, but Michael is so special."

"Do you love him?"

Annie's cheeks grew in soft color, and Lizzie thought her the most beautiful creature imaginable. It was mind-boggling to think she had yet to reach her prime. ''I do.''

Lizzie breathed a less-than-happy sigh at this new complication. Annie was in love. Perhaps truly in love. If so, Lizzie would have to rethink her plans. She wouldn't go back alone, but could she live under a king's rule? Would she be happy always longing for a freedom found only at home?

Annie's gaze suddenly moved to her right as the man in question suddenly rode into view. Moments later, after greeting both ladies, he was invited to join them. Michael did so without hesitation, and Lizzie couldn't help but wonder if this meeting had been planned.

By midmorning Lizzie realized Michael Thumbolt was a fine young man, easy to laugh, easier still to laugh at himself. Lizzie thought him quite nice indeed. And the shores of America seemed suddenly to recede even farther away.

Lizzie frowned as she listened to the almost one-sided conversation. She and her mother were in her room looking through Lizzie's clothes, separating those her mother insisted would serve her well during her wedding trip from those that would not. ''Mother, truly, we're wasting our time.''

''What do you mean?'' Margaret stopped in the act of depositing a petticoat into the pile that would not be of use, her blue eyes round with confusion.

''I mean no date has been set. What good does it do to bother with clothes now?''

''Oh, that. Your grandfather and Jack are in the library discussing the particulars even now.''

Lizzie gasped. ''Without me? Will I have no say?''

''Of course you will. But certain matters need to be settled first.''

''What kind of matters?''

"Your dowry, for one. And the new home Jack is buying."

"He is?" Lizzie knew nothing but amazement. "Why?"

"Why, for you and he to live in, of course." Margaret gave a small frown. "Perhaps he meant to surprise you. I shouldn't have said anything. Only I'm so happy you'll be close by."

Lizzie could honestly say she was quite a bit more than surprised. She frowned. Jack was taking this marriage business far too literally. Not only did he take every opportunity, no matter her objections, to kiss her, he was now talking about a dowry. Lizzie figured since there would be no marriage, he certainly did not need to buy a home, nor secure a dowry from her grandfather. It was time, well past time, in fact, to put things to right.

Margaret noticed her daughter's frown. "Don't worry of it, dear. Your grandfather will be generous, I'm sure."

"I'll be right back," Lizzie said as she left her mother looking over her clothes.

"Where are you going?"

Lizzie did not respond. By the time she realized her mother had asked the question she was halfway down the stairs. A moment later she knocked on the library door and peeked inside. "I'm sorry to interrupt, Gran, but may I see Jack for a moment?"

Her grandfather nodded, "Of course." Jack came up from a chair and followed her into the hallway.

Lizzie took his hand and nearly yanked him into a small sitting room. The room was small, but more than small, it was empty. Lizzie should have known better, for of late she made it her business not to be found anywhere alone with this man, lest he give in to the constant need he seemed to have to kiss her. Indeed, she should have known better, and she might have if she weren't so upset. "What do you think you're do—"

Lizzie's words were cut off as he lifted her from the floor and brought his mouth against hers. Very deliberately and quite deliciously, if Lizzie were at all truthful about it, which she usually was not.

It was a long moment before he finally allowed her to breathe, and when he did, Lizzie could only slump weakly against him. A moment later she found herself on the settee, sitting upon his lap. "I wish you would stop doing that," she said without much assertion.

Jack only smiled and boldly ran his hand over the curves of her bodice, an action that, like his kisses, was becoming a common occurrence. She pushed his hand away only to find it instantly returned to where it had no business being. "And I wish you would wear something a bit lower. How am I to reach you when you're dressed like a cloistress?"

Lizzie sat up straighter and again removed his hand from her person, holding it still in her lap. "That is my point exactly. You're not supposed to reach me. We're not getting married, remember? And even if we were, an engagement gives you no right to touch me with such familiarity."

"I'm only touching you, Lizzie. I don't see where that's so bad."

"Of course, you wouldn't," she breathed despairingly. "Let me up."

"In a minute. I didn't kiss you good morning."

"Yes, you did."

"No, that was just hello, this is good morning," he said as his mouth closed over hers again.

He had said they wouldn't be kissing very much, but it hadn't turned out that way. Indeed, she was never in his company that he didn't somehow manage at least one kiss.

Lizzie thought it best that they not kiss, but it didn't seem to matter what she thought. In truth, he never listened to a word she said, while she seemed to nearly melt at every heated encounter. Vaguely she wondered how and when her usual modesty had deserted her. And why she couldn't find the strength to tear herself from this man's arms.

She liked him ever so much better, even if she couldn't figure out exactly why. His teasing had not lessened any, only she seemed no longer prone to anger at every encounter. Still, her likes or dislikes of the man hardly mattered once she was in his arms. And for the life of her she couldn't understand how that could be. Wasn't she supposed to love a man before enjoying his kisses, his touch?

Lizzie thought that should be the case. Still, for some insane reason she forgot everything once he took her against him, and she knew only the deepest sense of yearning.

Though she might not admit the truth to him, Lizzie wasn't the least bit sorry that he wouldn't listen, and did not resist with any intensity the liberties he took. Liberties no decent lady should have allowed.

But was she truly decent? If one took into account the things she was thinking, she was not. Lizzie knew these delicious moments would soon come to an end and secretly wished she had the courage to take them a step further. Until Jack, she'd never thought of herself as that kind of woman. Until Jack, she'd never been tempted.

His hands cupped her breasts, and again Lizzie only moaned as she arched her back, silently pleading for more.

The back of her dress came undone. With his mouth on hers, Lizzie never noticed the material being dragged from her shoulders. Never noticed until she was sucked into blazing heat and almost cried aloud at the pleasure.

He'd touched her many times. And with each encounter, his touch had grown bolder and more possessive. His mouth moved over her breasts, sucking and licking, leaving not a portion of exposed flesh untouched, sending chills up and down her spine, while bringing a tightening to her stomach that both hurt and felt wonderful. Lizzie thought nothing could ever feel this good.

Still she knew it was wrong. Even if she hadn't the strength to fight him, it was wrong. Her head fell back against his arm and her back arched even as she moaned, "Jack, you have to stop this."

His mouth sucked her deep into his heat and held her there for a long moment before he finally groaned in response. "I know. It's killing me."

Lizzie didn't know what he meant and couldn't think to ask. All she could think was, despite her plea, she didn't want him to stop touching her. She arched her back farther, mindlessly offering herself to his praise. And praise, he did. With every luscious openmouthed kiss, he murmured his appreciation of her taste, the silkiness of her skin.

In the end, it wasn't Lizzie who brought a stop to the passionate moment. Jack could feel his control slipping. And this wasn't the time or the place for what he had in mind.

Jack knew they would marry. This woman was going to be his forever. There was no way another would sample her charms. Not as long as he lived.

His mouth brushed along her nose, her cheeks, her jaw, as his hand cupped, weighed, and played with her softness. And then he frowned, wondering what was happening. The ache in his groin now gripped his chest, his heart, in a breathless hold. It wasn't possible, of course, that emotion should enter into this moment. Women were, on the whole, an empty-headed lot, made for a man's pleasure. And if this woman was more intelligent than most, it made no matter, for it wasn't her mind he wanted. Jack bit her chin playfully, trying to make light of this moment, of emotions that left him suddenly and oddly shaken. He groaned and said, "Stop tempting me, woman."

Lizzie sat up, weakened and not entirely herself as she tried to shove his hands from her nakedness. She allowed a wry but somehow wicked smile that was almost Jack's undoing as she said, "I'll try to control myself in the future."

"Wait a minute," he said as she strove to bring her dress back into place. "I'm almost finished."

As long as he wasn't kissing her, she could think. Mercifully he seemed more interested at the moment in using his hands rather than his lips. "You're more than finished," she said, managing at last to bring the material between her body and his hands. "And I'd appreciate some restraint on your part."

"Believe me, you'll never know the degree of my restraint."

Lizzie only frowned. If he thought his actions were restrained, obviously he did not know the meaning of the word. "I want to know what's going on?" she asked, getting back to the reason why she had sought him out.

Jack was satisfied in the fact that Lizzie had not left his lap, seeming perfectly at ease with her present position. "Well, the truth is, I'm trying to break down your resistance."

Lizzie raised wide, knowing eyes to his gaze. She'd suspected as much, of course, for each of their encounters had grown far more heated and daring than the last. She should be angry, for the man's design was cold, purposeful seduction. Still, she was every bit at fault as he. He might be the initiator, but she willingly succumbed. Finally she breathed a sigh and then said, "I already know that. I'm talking about Grandfather."

Jack only stared. Knowing he'd said too much, he'd been fully prepared for her rage.

At his blank look she gave him a little shake. "Your interview."

"Oh, that." He frowned and then asked, "What do you mean you already know?"

"Exactly what I said, of course."

"And you're not upset?"

Lizzie knew she should have been upset and yet couldn't seem to muster the emotion. "I should be very angry."

But she wasn't. Jack gained hope. There was a long hesitation before he dared, "What do you think of my plan?"

"You mean besides it being terribly wicked?"

Jack smiled, and Lizzie couldn't help but smile in return. She'd found herself smiling quite a bit of late. "Well, it's probably a very good plan, but it won't work on me."

"It won't?"

She shook her head and turned just enough to show him her back. "Button me up."

"Why won't it work on you?" he asked, helpless to resist nuzzling his mouth to her back.

"Stop that! Because our engagement will be over by the time anything serious might happen." Lizzie wondered if she spoke the truth. A few more encounters like this one and she thought his plan would work very nicely indeed. "We only have another week or so to go."

"Are you sure you don't want to marry me?"

"Positive. Now, answer my question. What are you doing with Grandfather?"

"Talking."

"About?"

"Well, I was thinking of buying the Stanford place."

"Why?"

Jack shrugged. "Why not?"

"Because we're not getting married and you don't need a place of your own. Besides, you're a lord. Haven't you a manor house or an estate somewhere?"

"I do, but I thought you'd prefer living closer to your family."

"But I won't be living in it. And what about my dowry?"

"We could use it for the down payment. I would put the house in your name."

Lizzie smiled at his comment. "Are you trying to bribe me?"

Jack shrugged. "It's a thought."

"Jack, we are not getting married." Lizzie came to her feet. "And I don't think it's fair of you to make Grandfather believe—"

"What can I do? It was his suggestion."

She tried to smooth back her hair, but her mobcap, along with her pins, lay upon the floor. She retrieved what she could find and began to work her long hair into a knot. "Couldn't you have put it off?"

"I have put it off, Lizzie. This wasn't the first time he suggested we talk about it."

"He's going to be terribly disappointed."

"That's your fault."

Lizzie's gaze narrowed angrily. "This was your idea from the first. And you said he'd get over it."

"I didn't think it would mean this much to him."

"Meaning?"

"Meaning I think we should go through with it."

"Out of the question!"

"You enjoy being with me," he said with his usual arrogance. "What's the problem?"

"The problem? Besides your being an English earl and arrogant in the extreme, the problem is we don't love each other."

Jack wondered if the last of her statement was entirely true. Never having been in love before, he couldn't honestly say he now suffered under that mysterious emotion. Still, something drew him to her. Something beyond the thought of bedding her. He truly liked her. And despite his plan to have her in the end, he enjoyed every minute of her company. "You're not marrying my country, Lizzie, you're marrying me. And love is hardly necessary for a good union. As a matter of fact, it's better that we don't."

"The truth is, if I married you, I'd have to stay in your country, so I might as well be marrying it. And how could it be better that we don't love one another?"

Jack wouldn't have thought that the straightforward, no-nonsense Lizzie would long for romantic love, and imagined she wouldn't believe him if he took this opportunity to explain his growing feelings. Instead he tried another tactic. "Lizzie, love is for poets. It makes for pretty words, but in truth it is followed by endless pain."

Lizzie frowned at his callous reasoning and wondered if the experience with Sam and his wife's infidelity hadn't affected him quite a bit more than he would admit. "That is a ridiculous notion. How can hurt come from loving?"

"Obviously you've never been in love, or you wouldn't have to ask that."

"But I have."

A surprising jolt of jealousy surged through Jack at the thought that she should have loved another.

"He died fighting for the cause. And I loved him very much."

"And you weren't hurt when he died?"

"Of course I was hurt, but he didn't cause the pain. It would be cowardly, don't you agree, to live the rest of my life without love, simply because I was afraid of being hurt again?"

Jack put aside his jealousy and swore the only thing that mattered was that they should marry. And somehow, someway, he would convince her of it. "We could grow to love one another," came his bleak suggestion.

Lizzie smiled at his dismal tone. "I should tell Grandfather it's over."

"Not yet. He'll only say we haven't given it enough time. As a matter of fact, he is insisting on a date. What should I tell him?"

"Tell him Christmas."

Christmas was months away. Jack knew Andrew would never be satisfied at a date set so far in the future. "He's your grandfather; you tell him."

"Tell me what?" Andrew asked. Having grown impatient to settle the business at hand, he had come to find his stepson.

Lizzie spun around, her cheeks warming with guilt, wondering how long he'd been standing there. She hesitated for a moment and then blurted out, "Christmas. That I want to be married on Christmas day."

Andrew was surprised that she should want to wait so long. But then he noticed her disheveled appearance. Her cheeks were high in color, her eyes shining for no apparent reason. Her cap was crooked, while a good-sized piece of hair had fallen down her back. And because her back had been to the door, he'd noticed almost immediately that her dress had not been buttoned up correctly. Andrew shook his head. He hadn't a doubt as to what these two youngsters had been about, and the sooner the words were said between them, the better. "Christmas will not do, I'm afraid. In fact, next month cannot be too soon."

Lizzie glared at her betrothed, silently prodding the dolt to come to her aid. But he did not. Well, she didn't care what her grandfather said. And she didn't care what this fool thought. She wasn't getting married at all, never mind marrying next month.

"Next month is too soon. What about invitations, clothes, planning the wedding trip? I couldn't manage any of it until the month after at the earliest."

"By the end of next month you should have had plenty of time for preparations."

It was settled. There was no way out but to break off the engagement, and she couldn't do that. At least not yet.

Chapter 8

Mary Stone was a spoiled woman. She was a beautiful woman who had been married to an unassuming, generous man some thirty years her senior. Her lifestyle, while married, had been lavish. And Westly, her late husband, had left her financially set. Her style of living suffered no decline after he was gone. She lacked for nothing, if one didn't count the one man she wanted above all others.

Since she had been widowed, Mary had taken many men to her bed. Her only goal was to see her desires met.

It came as something of a shock that, for the first time, Mary had been denied her wants. The brief moment in Andrew's garden had been a mortifying experience. She had never before been spurned, and Mary was very angry at first. But she was not a woman with little experience. She knew anger to be a useless passion and wisely brought the emotion under control.

No, it wasn't anger she needed here, it was a plan of action, something that would ensure her her wants. And she wanted John Black, not as an occasional lover, even though he'd been one of her best. Mary wanted him for her next husband, and she always made sure to get what she wanted.

Mary smiled into her looking glass, admiring the lovely face reflected there. With smooth, unblemished skin, dark eyes that could turn quite mysterious at times, and white, even teeth, she was confident that she looked closer to twenty than her thirty-plus years. Her raven hair, completely out of fashion, was pulled back and up. Since it was far too dark to powder with good results, she often wore a wig. Today the color was nearly as white as her skin. With rouged lips, she knew she looked smashing.

Above her wig, a wide-brimmed Gainsborough hat was pinned in place. Only this hat sported the most spectacular, if outrageous, display imaginable. At its center stood a bluebird, surrounded by a near garden of flowers and ribbons.

She realized that it wouldn't do to boldly state her intentions, despite their previous intimacy. No, Mary understood that a woman had to go about these things in a far more subtle fashion. Margaret Matthews had invited her to tea, and Mary had no intention of refusing the invitation while Jack was in residence.

She hadn't seen or heard from him in weeks. Not that she could have, of course, since she'd gone north to visit with a special friend the morning after the ball and had only yesterday returned. Still, there had been no notes left with her staff, no mention of an apology, no mention of the man at all.

Of course, she hadn't taken Jack's rejection to heart. Indeed, she had no hold on the man. Mary smiled at the thought, for she expected she soon would.

Until Lizzzie heard the sound of feminine laughter, she had been unaware that company had come. She entered the drawing room to find her mother presiding over tea. Jack sat across from the small settee. Mary Stone sat to her mother's right.

Lizzie knew Mrs. Stone, of course, having been her neighbor for close to a year. Still, except for an occasional dinner invitation, she'd rarely visited. And this was the first time she'd come to tea.

Lizzie held Alice firmly upon her hip. Joey and Steven followed her into the room, arguing over who owned the ball they intended to play with. "I marked it. See?" Steven said, trailing behind and holding the ball up for Lizzie's view. "There's an S."

"He put the S on my ball," Joey insisted, tugging on Lizzie's skirt.

Lizzie sighed. "It doesn't matter who it belongs to. Robert is waiting for you." Robert, one of the stable-boys, often played with the boys.

Huge tears welled up in Joey's eyes, and Lizzie's tone softened as she leaned down, combed his hair back with her fingers, and kissed his forehead. "I'll buy you another one the next time I go to town. All right?"

Joey smiled. The argument apparently settled, the two took off at a run, but not before calling out, "You coming, Uncle Jack?"

Jack often played with the boys, too, during the afternoons. He nodded. "I'll be there in a minute."

Lizzie called after them, "Remember to play close to the house. I don't want you near the cliffs."

Lizzie turned then and smiled at Mary Stone's shocked expression. Only then did she realize the sight she no doubt made. Lizzie rarely fared well after feeding the baby, especially since Alice had recently taken to playing with her food. Today Lizzie had been at the center of the baby's play. And although she'd wiped her face, it was still dotted in places with mashed carrots.

"What have you there, Lizzie?"

Lizzie thought to mention the baby wasn't a what, but a who. She strove to keep her annoyance at bay as she said, "Her name is Alice. Isn't she simply lovely?"

"Quite lovely," Mary returned, snubbing both Lizzie and her charge with practiced efficiency. "Now, where were we? Oh, yes, Lady Armstrong's gown. It was the talk of London, I'm told. Some say it wasn't only daringly cut, but that the fabric was dampened and quite transparent. Can you imagine?"

Jack could, having come across a lady here and there bold enough to have deliberately displayed her charms in public. Margaret looked slightly confused. She'd heard of such carryings-on, but had dismissed them as nonsense. It was Lizzie who hadn't a notion as to what the woman was getting at. "What does that mean? Dampened? You mean she was caught in a downpour?"

Mary laughed a full, throaty, superior sound. "The night was unusually dry, I'd wager."

Lizzie frowned in confusion. A titled lady had arrived at a social gathering with her dress purposely wet and transparent. Lizzie had never heard of such a thing and could only wonder what she was doing living among these scandalous elite. "Had she nothing better than her body to display then? No intelligence, no sense of humor, no character? The woman is to be pitied, I think."

"The gentlemen seemed to enjoy her company well enough."

"I've no doubt," Lizzie said as she shot Jack a look of disgust.

Jack figured the look was his reward for having had the temerity to be a man.

"The trouble is, I've yet to find, among the elite, a man worthy of the title gentleman," Lizzie pronounced.

Mary Stone laughed again and said, "You'll have to broaden her horizons, Jack. There must be dozens you could introduce her to."

Jack thought Lizzie's horizons were broad enough. He had no intentions of introducing her to anyone.

Lizzie sat and shifted the baby in her lap until both

were comfortable. It was then that the long dress moved aside and uncovered Alice's deformity. Mary noticed the twisted foot and webbed toes. She shivered her disgust. "What's the matter with her foot?"

"It's nothing," Jack returned quickly, for he couldn't help but see Lizzie stiffen. "The doctor said she'd walk with only a slight limp."

"Disgusting."

Fire came alive in Lizzie's eyes. There was no telling what she might say or do next. And Jack racked his brain trying to think of something that would defuse the situation. He never got the chance.

"You're quite mistaken there, Mrs. Stone," Lizzie said, her lips barely moving as she strove to contain her rage. "Alice is a beautiful baby who happens to have a deformed foot. And since God made that foot, I'd be careful what I referred to as disgusting."

Mary laughed uncomfortably. "I never meant to upset you, dear. After all, she's only an orphan."

"She was an orphan. She's mine now."

Jack had known a mixture of relief and trepidation when Lizzie had finally joined them. For the last half hour he sat in breathless dread, waiting for Mary to drop some hint about their past relationship. He should have claimed a previous appointment, only he hadn't dared. There was no way he was leaving Mary Stone alone with Margaret, and most especially not with Lizzie. Jack might have smiled politely, and acted the perfect host, but in his heart he only wished Mary would go home. Most especially he wished it now. "Lizzie is wonderful with the children."

Mary's smile was as false as the beauty patch that adorned her powdered skin. "How nice," she said, addressing the younger woman. "Since you have such affinity for children, it's a wonder you haven't given some thought to becoming a nurse. Or perhaps you have."

Lizzie blinked at the insult, knowing some surprise at

the animosity directed her way, wondering what she'd ever done that this woman should dislike her so intensely. The truth was, she wouldn't have thought twice about laboring alongside the baby's nurse, or any of the servants, for that matter. Indeed, she often did as much and didn't mind the implication that she might also serve. What she did mind was this woman's condescending tone. Apparently Mary Stone held herself far above her young hostess. *Lord help us, but these aristocrats are hard to tolerate,* Lizzie silently mused.

Lizzie thought to remark upon the older woman's conclusions when Jack said, "She'll make an excellent mother, I've no doubt."

Lizzie glared at Jack. She was certainly able to speak for herself and couldn't imagine what had prompted him to interfere. But then she noted his nervousness, unable to imagine its cause.

Jack was nervous, for Mary never socialized, at least not in the usual fashion. He'd never known her to come to tea. There could be only one answer for her sudden appearance now, and that was to make trouble. And he certainly did not need trouble, not at this delicate stage of his and Lizzie's courtship.

"Perhaps one day, but a lady would need a husband first, wouldn't you agree?"

It was only then that Jack realized Mary was unaware of his and Lizzie's betrothal. He thought to immediately correct the oversight before irrefutable damage was done. "Lizzie and I are to be married, Mary, at the end of this month. The banns were announced at church last week." And then, realizing Mary never went to church, he asked, "Haven't you read the announcements? They were in all the London papers."

There was a long moment of obvious shock before she said softly, "I only just returned from visiting friends up north."

Lizzie felt the absurd need to apologize and then wondered why Mary should suffer so at the mention of Jack marrying. Obviously there was something going on here. And if Jack's desperate, cornered look meant anything, it was something more than friendship. *Mary.* Lizzie remembered, it was the name Jack had whispered against her throat in the garden. Had he been waiting for Mary Stone? Had they formed a liaison?

"Are you all right?" Lizzie asked, for white powder aside, she doubted she'd ever seen a complexion quite so ashen.

"Jack, help her outside. She needs some air," Margaret said as she took the teacup from Mary's limp hands.

Jack silently cursed, but instantly did as his stepsister asked. A moment later Mary sat on one of the garden benches, while Jack stood at her side. "I'm sorry, dear," she said, "I didn't mean to make a fuss."

Jack almost groaned at the endearment. Thank God she hadn't said anything of the kind in Lizzie's presence. "I'm sure you didn't, Mary." He patted her shoulder awkwardly.

Mary frowned at his less-than-genuine concern. "How could you do it, Jack? How could you, after all we've meant to each other?"

Jack stiffened at the admonishment and then became annoyed that she should hint of a relationship to exist between them. "Exactly what the hell is that supposed to mean? There were no promises exchanged between us. You knew what you were doing."

Mary knew the truth of that. Still, she wouldn't give up easily. She batted her lashes and said in a voice far too loud for Jack's liking, "The promises were implied, darling. I never would have allowed you to sate your lust if I didn't think we would eventually marry."

Jack knew that was a lie. Both had gone into the affair with one thing in mind. The woman was experienced in the extreme and knew exactly what he wanted, what they both wanted. "And of course, there was no lust on your part," he mocked.

Mary ignored his sarcasm. "You're a very attractive man, darling," she said, as if that fact had left her incapable of controlling her actions. "How could I resist inviting you to my bed?"

"Are you feeling better?"

Jack almost jumped at the sound of Lizzie's voice behind him and groaned out a barely muffled curse, wondering how long she'd been standing there. How much had she heard?

"Much better, thank you," Mary said. "It's the weather, I think. I can't remember when it's been so warm." Mary turned her attention to Jack, and again batted her eyelashes. Lizzie thought the gesture ridiculously false and wondered if men truly liked that sort of thing. "Would you be a dear and see me home? I'm afraid I'm not feeling terribly well."

Jack took a deep breath, his discomfort obvious. "I promised the boys . . ."

"Oh, do be a dear, Jack," Lizzie said, repeating Mary's words almost verbatim, realizing he was about to refuse the lady. "See the lady home. The boys will understand."

Jack was positive there was sarcasm in those words, but when he looked into her eyes, he couldn't see a thing amiss, unless one counted the fact that she was blinking madly.

"Are you all right?"

"I'm perfectly fine."

"What's the matter with your eyes? Have you gotten something in them?"

Since he hadn't inquired as much of Mrs. Stone, Lizzie imagined her efforts in mockery a miserable failure. "I told you, I'm perfectly fine."

"Good. I'll be right back," he said, and nearly yanked Mrs. Stone from her seat.

"There's no need to hurry, I'm sure. Mrs. Molston can make another pot of tea."

From the front door Lizzie watched in disgust as the two of them moved down the brick path to the waiting carriage. Mary held tightly to Jack's arm, leaning into him as she limped along at his side. Why she should limp, Lizzie hadn't a clue. The woman was supposed to be weak, and as far as she knew, the weakness did not extend to her ankles.

Lizzie turned from the infuriating sight, entered the library, and began to pace the polished oak floors, her mind on the hated snake and the woman he now escorted home. They were lovers. And Lizzie couldn't help but wonder if he touched Mary the same way he touched her. Lizzie shivered at the disgusting thought.

A moment later she vowed she didn't care. Truly she did not. What difference did it make to her if he touched a thousand women? Her anger didn't come from caring. It came from the fact that he dared to invite one of his women to her home.

All right, perhaps he hadn't done the actual inviting, and in truth, this wasn't her home, but her grandfather's, but he certainly hadn't objected to her visit. Indeed he had been most gracious and, Lizzie thought, even more sociable than usual.

Lizzie growled and then suddenly and quite uncharacteristically took a book from the shelf and threw it. It landed in the cold, but blackened fireplace. "Cursed beast!" she said, and then picked up another volume, her obvious intent that it should follow the same path. She never heard her grandfather enter the room.

"Just a minute," Andrew said, and Lizzie jumped at the sound of his voice. "I'd rather you wouldn't burn the book, Lizzie. If you don't like it, simply don't read it."

Lizzie gave him a weak smile and then breathed a long sigh. "I'm sorry. I didn't mean to do that."

Andrew retrieved the book from the fireplace. "What's the matter?" he asked, while dusting its cover.

"Nothing." Lizzie tried for another smile. She didn't quite make it. "Everything is just lovely."

"Something is the matter. Why don't we sit? You can have a puff on your pipe while you tell me all about it."

Lizzie smiled at that, knowing her grandfather's despair concerning her habit. From her skirt pocket she took her pipe and tobacco and lit up before saying, "It's Jack. He's a rotter."

"What do you mean?" Andrew asked as he brought two glasses of port to the settee and sat beside his spirited granddaughter.

Lizzie took the offered glass and downed half of it before saying, "I mean, he and Mary Stone are somehow involved."

Andrew knew Mary Stone to be a beautiful woman. Still, he couldn't imagine Jack involved with her. His stepson obviously loved Lizzie. There could be no doubt of that. One had only to look at the man to know the truth of it. "Oh, I don't think that's possible."

"Nevertheless, he is. I heard them talking."

"Exactly what did you hear?"

"I heard Mary say, 'How could you, Jack, after all we've meant to each other?' "

Lizzie's words were an odd mix of dramatic flare and scathing revulsion. She was obviously jealous, and Andrew wondered if she realized it. "And?"

"She said she allowed him to sate his lust. Jack reminded her that the lust wasn't one sided." Lizzie came suddenly to her feet and began to pace again. "I hate him." She glanced at her grandfather and said, "I know you think Jack is the best England has to offer. But it's a sad state of affairs for this land if he is."

Andrew smiled at his granddaughter. "Lizzie, I think there are things you should know about men."

"What kind of things? That they're all rutting beasts? That they'll bed anyone in skirts?"

He looked suddenly uncomfortable. Sorry he had said anything, he croaked out weakly, "Not all surely. Still, you must know men have certain needs."

Lizzie looked into eyes identical to her own and snapped, "Poor babies. And of course, their needs must be met." She growled a sound. "God, I hate him!"

Andrew cleared his throat, not at all at ease in broaching upon such personal matters, especially with his granddaughter, and found himself taking an unusually long drink of his port, while wishing he were somewhere else.

Lizzie's anger was suddenly replaced with the realization of a perfect opportunity. She and Jack would be breaking this supposed engagement soon. What better time than now? She'd found out about Mary. Wouldn't any young lady break her engagement after finding her fiancé involved with another?

She turned to her grandfather and steeled herself, knowing he would be greatly disappointed. Still, his disappointment would eventually pass. Lizzie clung to that one thought. "You might as well know, I'm breaking it off with Jack."

Andrew started as if receiving a great shock. "My God, Lizzie, you can't do this."

"I can and I shall."

"Lizzie, what the man has done before meeting you is none of your concern."

"I'm not concerned with the past. It's the present and future that worries me. I don't trust him."

"He loves you."

Lizzie breathed a sigh. She hadn't thought it would be this difficult, hadn't imagined he'd take the news so hard. His blue eyes appeared filled with pain. "I know you wish it were so, Gran, but the truth is, he doesn't love me. Thankfully I found out in time."

"You're making a grave mistake."

"I don't think so."

"Please, don't do anything rash. Give yourself time to think this out." And then he finished with a plea, "As a favor to me?"

Lizzie loved her grandfather and rarely went against his wishes. She felt herself weakening at his pleading. "It won't work, Gran."

"It will. You'll see. He loves you."

Lizzie sighed and decided not to insist. She'd planted the thought, at least. When she next brought up the subject, he wouldn't be half so shocked. "I'll think about it."

"Promise me you'll try to understand. Whatever happened with Mary, it meant nothing. You're the one Jack loves. And when a man like Jack loves a woman, he keeps to her and her alone."

Lizzie hugged him tightly. God, she hated to see him so distressed. "I promise, I'll try."

While Lizzie suffered through the encounter with her grandfather, Jack found himself even less satisfied conferring with the lady at his side. Too late he realized he should have ridden Rascal rather than tying the horse to the back of the carriage. "I hope you don't mind accompanying me, Jack. I felt so weak."

Jack glanced at the woman beside him, wishing he were anywhere but here. "Meaning you don't feel weak now?"

"Well, now that you mention it, I do feel quite a bit better."

Jack only grunted in response, hardly surprised.

"You will come in for a minute, won't you, dear?"

"I think it's best if I don't."

Mary wouldn't press. Still, if he refused to stay with her for a bit, she'd best get her questions out in the open, before this little ride was over. "Why did you ask her to marry you?" she asked bluntly.

Jack shrugged. "Why does any man ask?"

"Granted she's a pretty little thing, but so unorthodox. Hardly someone of our class. Surely you could have had your fun without promises of a wedding. I certainly wouldn't have minded."

When Jack did not respond, Mary apparently felt the need to further enlighten him about her rival's character. "Word has it she smokes a pipe and drinks strong spirits."

Mary had forgotten somehow that she enjoyed her own libation on occasion. "Jack," she said frankly, "a lady wouldn't ride her horse astride, nor spend most of her time with orphans."

Jack was looking straight ahead, silently urging the carriage to hurry. "I suppose not."

"And that's what you want? A woman without means, properties, or class? A woman who has no concept of our rules?"

Jack smiled. "She sounds refreshing, doesn't she?"

Mary's eyes widened with surprise and then she laughed. "For a moment there I actually thought you were in love." She chuckled softly, seductively. "It's impossible, of course. I suspect we're too much alike. And people of our station simply do not fall in love. It's so very common, wouldn't you agree?"

Jack wondered on her words. Was she right? Was love a common emotion? Did only the lower class suffer from it? No, his friend Sam had been in love. But Sam's marriage had failed miserably. Something was terribly wrong when there wasn't one couple among his acquaintances who hadn't married for either title, wealth, or to produce an heir. And every one of them searched outside the marriage bed for that elusive something that would bring meaning to their lives.

People of their class had everything they wanted and

yet nothing at all. It hardly made sense and yet it was the greatest of truths.

Jack knew he wasn't like them. He wanted more. Much more. Mary was wrong; it wasn't impossible for him to love.

He cared for Lizzie. He thought about making love to her just about every minute of every day. And knew he was falling in love with her.

Mary smiled sensually and placed her hand on Jack's thigh. ''We're almost there,'' she whispered provocatively. ''Come in for a minute, please?''

Jack watched her hand slide up and down his thigh and knew he could easily give in to her offer. With the need he'd known lately, it would be a relief. But to what end? Yes, his body might know a brief moment of pleasure, but it wouldn't be enough. If he took her a hundred times, he'd find no lasting satisfaction, for she wasn't the one he wanted.

Jack gently removed her hand. There was no need to be cruel. She was a woman of experience and would understand it was over. ''Perhaps another time. I told Lizzie I'd be right back.''

Twenty-five minutes elapsed before Lizzie saw Jack hurry down the path from the library. She figured he must have raced Rascal as hard as the horse was able, for she hadn't expected him for a good ten minutes yet. She was in the garden house reading. From the corner of her eye she watched his footsteps slow to a more casual gait upon spying her.

Jack wasn't any less nervous since accompanying Mary home. Indeed he wondered if he hadn't grown more nervous over the last half hour, almost terrified by the thought of what Lizzie had heard.

He sat beside her and frowned, noting her reading material and knowing for a fact *Tom Jones* was far too risqué for a lady's taste. ''Where did you get that?''

Lizzie looked up and then, after adjusting her spectacles, down at her page. "From grandfather's library, of course."

"Do you think you should read it?"

"I am reading it," Lizzie countered coolly. "After I'm finished, I'll let you know if I should have or not."

Jack couldn't hold back his chuckle. "It's a bit daring."

"Why? Because he's a bastard?"

"No, because he's a rutting . . ." Jack knew when to keep his mouth shut. Too bad he hadn't realized it one word sooner.

And when he didn't finish, Lizzie thought to finish for him, "Beast?"

"Well, yes, I suppose you could say that."

"It's fiction, Jack; people don't really live like this." There was a moment of silence during which she expected his agreement. When it was not forthcoming, she asked, "Well, do they?"

"Not that I know of," he lied weakly.

Lizzie's smile was mysterious as she put down the book and slipped her spectacles into her pocket. "Shall we take a walk?"

Jack felt a wave of relief. She hadn't heard a thing. It was his own guilt causing him this suspicion. Lizzie wasn't the sort to hide her anger, and she'd be angry, he was sure, if she'd heard Mary's candid remarks. But would she? If she cared for him, she would be, but what if she didn't care?

"Do you want to go down to the beach?" Jack asked, noting the direction she'd taken.

"I thought the cliffs," she said, aiming a long, meaningful look in his direction.

Jack laughed. "You wouldn't be thinking of pushing me off, would you?"

"I can't imagine why I should," she said, noncommittally.

"Nor I," he returned.

"I often sit there. I love to watch the sea."

Jack slipped his arm around her waist and smiled when she made no attempt to remove it.

The wind was picking up. The sky was growing dark in the distance. A storm looked to be brewing.

"It seems our little plan is working. Grandfather thinks you're in love with me."

"Does he?" Jack asked surprised. "And he just happened to say so?"

Lizzie shrugged. "I told him I was breaking off our engagement. He tried to talk me out of it."

Jack had no need to ask why. She had heard all she needed of the conversation between Mary and himself. Probably far more than she needed. Something twisted in his chest, something hard and painful, leaving him unable to think of a single word that would change things back to the way they were. All he could manage was a despairing "Did it work?"

"He was very upset. I thought I wouldn't push it for now."

"You mean we're still engaged?"

"Temporarily."

A wave of joy washed out the pain. Still, he knew there were matters that needed settling between them. "You heard her, I take it."

"I did."

"You should know there's nothing between us."

Lizzie didn't believe him for a minute. "It doesn't matter in the least."

"I think it does. You tried to break the engagement because of it."

"I was going to do it soon, in any case." She shrugged. "It just seemed the perfect opportunity."

"Because you were angry?"

"Certainly not," she returned, satisfied at her cool

response. "I've no reason to be angry. You're being ridiculous."

"Am I? You mean you don't care for me, just a little?"

"Of course not."

"I think you do," he said in all confidence.

"And I think you're mad."

Jack chuckled softly.

"And that won't work, so you needn't bother to try."

"What won't work?"

"Your smiles. You think you're irresistible when you smile. No doubt that's why you're always at it."

Jack hadn't imagined such a thing, but was delighted the thought had occurred to her. "Do you think I'm irresistible?"

"I think you are arrogant beyond belief."

"You once said I was perfect." He laughed softly at her frown. "I think perfect people have the right to be arrogant."

"I meant it in the worst sense, of course."

Jack laughed again. "Shall we kiss and make up now?"

"Didn't you get enough kisses from Mrs. Stone?"

Jack frowned, not at all happy to have Mary's name brought up again. "I told you there's nothing between us."

Lizzie laughed, a low, luscious sound. Jack thought it deliciously seductive. He hadn't realized she could laugh like that. "Poor baby, she wouldn't allow you one kiss?"

"I didn't want a kiss."

"Nor to sate your lust?"

"Lizzie, damn it! Don't talk like that."

"You mean, it's all right to do it, but we shouldn't talk about it?"

"The trouble is, you don't know what you're talking about."

Fire flashed in her eyes as they narrowed threateningly. "I know exactly what I'm talking about, thank you. One does not have to actually experience the act to understand the particulars."

"Lizzie," Jack groaned. "I swear there's nothing—"

"And if I find out that you and Mrs. Stone are still involved, I'm going to box your ears."

Jack watched her walk suddenly away. The wind whipped her skirt, blowing it wildly behind her, and Jack knew an ache unlike anything he'd ever known before. He wanted her and felt a desperate need for her kisses. His eyes darkened with the hunger of that wanting, while a smile teased his lips. She was angry. Angry enough to threaten him with bodily harm. And that could only mean that she cared.

Lizzie spent the rest of the afternoon with her aunt Amelia, sipping tea and watching the storm come and go from the little house that bordered the sea. Hours went by as the two enjoyed each other's company. It was almost time to leave, to ready herself for dinner, when Lizzie finally managed the subject paramount in her mind. "Mary Stone came to tea today. She said she was sorry to have missed you."

Amelia laughed. "Did she? And did you believe her?"

"Shouldn't I?"

Amelia chuckled softly. "Mary Stone hates me because she thinks Westly and I were lovers."

Lizzie gasped. "Were you?" The words slipped out before Lizzie had a chance to think.

"His marriage proved to be a grave disappointment. Hardly a month after the vows were said, Mary took her first lover. I imagine she thought Westly too old, or too besotted to care. He was neither."

Lizzie noticed her question went unanswered and decided not to press. "Why didn't he divorce her?"

"Pride. Men are odd creatures, I'd wager, and old men more so. He stayed with her out of fear that some might suspect he wasn't man enough to keep her happy." Amelia sighed. "I like to think I brought a measure of comfort to his last few years."

"She and Jack are having an affair."

It was Amelia's turn to gasp. "You're mistaken, surely. Jack loves you. I'd stake my life on it."

Lizzie wondered at the peculiarity. Everyone, it seemed, was sure of Jack's love. Obviously they had carried on their subterfuge all to well. "I'm not positive about the present tense, but they definitely were involved."

Amelia laughed suddenly, the sound purely wicked. "So it seems two women in this family have won against her. She'll come to hate you now."

"There's no need, I'm sure. Jack and I are finished."

"Because of Mary?"

Lizzie shrugged. "No doubt there have been others."

"Good God, Lizzie, you can't expect that Jack should have remained a virgin. Mary is an unimportant creature. The women in Jack's past are nothing. He loves you."

Lizzie sighed and shook her head. "I hope you won't tell Grandfather. He asked that I wait and think things out."

"And you'd best take his advice. You're not likely to find a better man—"

"In all of England," Lizzie said wearily. "I know."

Lizzie entered the library by way of the garden. Hurrying so as not to be late for dinner, she almost missed Jack sound asleep before the fire. It was all his fault. If he'd never made that ridiculous offer to begin with, she wouldn't be bombarded with his praises and nagged to reconsider. Agreeing to his plan had been a mistake from the first. And now, thanks to her family, breaking off with him was proving almost impossible.

Lizzie decided then that the man looked a bit too comfortable.

It was an awful thing to do. A purely shameful thing. Still, the knot in her stomach had miraculously eased as she closed the library door. The soft sound of her laughter echoed through the massive hall as she ran for the stairs.

Finding her alone in the drawing room just before dinner, Jack came up behind her and asked, "Did you punch me on my head?"

Lizzie sipped from her drink. Not a glimmer of surprise, either from the fact that someone had hit him or the accusation that she might have been the one behind the assault, showed in her dark blue eyes. "What? Me? I can't think why I should do such a thing."

"Perhaps you missed my ears and boxed my head instead. What I want to know is why you did it."

Lizzie gave up all pretense of innocence. "Because I hate you," she said clearly, distinctly, and without a trace of remorse.

She was furious, and Jack was delighted. The only possible reason behind her anger was love, he was sure. She loved him, but hadn't as yet realized the fact. "You're still angry."

"Not in the least." She shrugged, her expression pure indifference. "I couldn't care less whom you sate your lust upon."

Jack laughed at her denial, his voice lowering to a husky pitch as he took a step closer. "I think you're not only angry but insanely jealous that I've yet to sate it on you."

Jack watched her tremble and grinned at her obvious rage. The more furious she grew, the more confident Jack became.

Lizzie decided her only option, short of violence, was

to ignore the beast. She turned as one of her grand-father's dogs ran into the room.

Jack watched her bend toward the dog. She might try to ignore him, he thought, but she wouldn't succeed for long. "If you want to see what you've been missing, we could go upstairs now," he taunted.

"Go to hell. Better yet, go to Mary."

"You know it's not Mary I want."

"You might tell her that," Lizzie returned as she scratched Tyler behind his ear.

"I have." He nodded at Lizzie's look of surprise. "I told you that was over a long time ago."

Lizzie stood again and glared. "Was it? Exactly how long is a long time ago? An hour? Two? Three?"

Jack didn't want to tell her it had only been a few weeks. A lot could happen to a man in a few weeks. For one thing, he could fall in love with a wild-tempered, irrational hellcat. "Lizzie, there was nothing between us then."

"And there isn't still."

"There is."

"There isn't."

"Isn't what?" her grandfather asked, stepping into the room and overhearing the last remark.

"Time to buy my trousseau," Lizzie returned with amazing agility. Jack almost laughed aloud. Every day he found more to like in her. She was a quick wit and never at a loss for biting words. Her intelligence was equal to any man's. Nothing about her was practiced or false, except for, like now, the loving smile sent his way.

"Of course there's time, dear. I have some business in London. You could come with me and visit all the shops.

"Jack, do you still keep your house there?"

Jack nodded.

"Good. We can stay a few days. Perhaps see a play

or two, and Lizzie can get all her shopping done. We'll have a lovely time of it.''

Andrew Thomas was a military man, long since retired. Still, because he was a brilliant strategist, his knowledge and advice were often sought by both the military and the prime minister's staff.

Almost from the first day of her arrival in England, Lizzie had gathered information, sometimes overheard, but more often read from the papers left on her grandfather's desk. That information was then transferred to her contact in London.

Lizzie loved her grandfather, but she loved her country with equal fervor. She knew her cause to be right, and any means needed to gather information, just. But the longer she remained in England, the bigger a quandary she faced. She was betraying her grandfather's trust and entangling herself in a web of intrigue that she would no doubt hang for one day.

Lizzie didn't so much mind giving her life for her country. What she did mind was the disappointment and heartbreak her grandfather would suffer upon discovering a spy in his own family.

She wouldn't be treated as a spy by the authorities, of course, although a spy and a traitor could only know the same end. No, she'd be accused of treason, for England had yet to admit to anything but an uprising in her colonies. An uprising believed initiated by a small, rabble-rousing group of discontents.

Mr. Burke, a member of the prime minister's staff, had come today. He'd spent three hours with her grandfather. Later that night, after all were asleep, Lizzie sat in the library, committing to memory the secret documents her grandfather never thought necessary to lock away.

From the papers she learned that Cornwallis, given command of the South and having already taken

Charleston this last May, was planning to send his left wing, a Tory force under Patrick Ferguson, to sweep the Carolinas' interior. Lizzie thought something surely needed to be done lest the British make impenetrable their grip on the states.

They'd be leaving for London in a few days. Lizzie smiled knowing Mr. Kent wouldn't be averse to obtaining this small piece of information.

Chapter 9

⌒⌒◯◯⌒

L ondon was a city much like New York, except darker, its streets narrower, its buildings dingier from years of coal soot. Still, the city boasted of anything and everything from the finest shops to the best restaurants and coffeehouses, theaters and gardens.

However, Lizzie found the street vendors the best of all. She could spend hours wandering in their midst. She loved the tasty meat pies, the aroma of freshly baked bread, the chunks of cheese, the strawberry tarts—all of which she would top off with a refreshing mug of cool ale.

A walk among these hearty folks was often entertaining as well as filling. Chickens escaped their pens, along with an occasional pig, and crowds would gather to cheer for the frightened animal's salvation. Sometimes a musician would play and sing, sometimes acrobats joined the sport. Once Lizzie saw a monkey dance, while secured on a long chain to its master. The crowd delighted at the little fellow's ability and then cheerfully dropped a penny or two into his hat as he went begging through the audience.

Lizzie thought the sights and smells were the best in

the world. Confusion, noise, and crowds of people were the norm, and Lizzie felt the throb of energy, the surge of excitement.

"What do you want to see first?" Jack asked, watching Lizzie's blue eyes grow wide with excitement as the coach moved slowly through crowded city streets.

"The street hawkers."

A smile touched the corner of his mouth as he asked, "I would have thought a jeweler, or seamstress, perhaps."

"Oh, don't worry about me," she said stiffly, realizing she'd momentarily forgotten her anger and her pledge not to talk to him again. "If you'd like to go to a jeweler, please do. Give me your address and I'll find my way back."

Andrew Thomas frowned at that. Knowing his daughter and granddaughters often came to the city for a day of shopping, he only now wondered if he hadn't been a bit too lax in seeing to their safety. "Margaret, you don't mean to say you and the girls wander about these streets on your own?"

Lizzie avoided Jack's eyes. She hadn't spoken to him in three days. Instead she had spent most of that time remembering Mary Stone's intimate words. It didn't matter in the least that Jack was obviously finished with the woman. She still hated him and thought she always would.

Margaret explained, "Jacob is always with us. You needn't fear for our safety, Father."

"Still, I think more than a driver is needed here. Suppose you were set upon by a gang of toughs?" Andrew said, his voice showing alarm as if he'd only just imagined the possibility.

Lizzie didn't like the look in her grandfather's eyes and thought a word was needed here. "Were it a gang, Gran, another man wouldn't be of much help."

She might have been speaking to her grandfather, but

her gaze moved to Jack, silently warning that he should not interfere.

"Depends upon the size of the gang, wouldn't you agree?" Jack said, obviously ignoring the warning sent his way.

Andrew shook his head. "You aren't familiar with the city. You could easily stray into a rough part and find yourself in trouble. I don't want you to go alone again. Either Jack or myself will accompany you."

All three ladies knew the hopelessness of pleading their cause.

Lizzie could only imagine her grandfather's distress if he'd known of her occasional early morning rides into the city. He was right, of course. It was dangerous, but necessary in her case. As for their shopping trips, Lizzie thought that as long as Jack wasn't their guard, she could bear the situation. After all, her grandfather's presence wouldn't lessen their enjoyment, nor prevent her from meeting with her contact after a day spent shopping.

"Oh, look!" Lizzie said, spying a dark-haired woman in a yellow scarf and red skirt. With her stood a dozen or more people dressed just as colorfully. They were setting up two small tents and a long table to display their wares. "A band of Gypsies. Stop the coach, Gran. I want to see."

Andrew tapped the ceiling with his cane and the coach came to a stop.

"Lizzie, let's get to Jack's place first," her mother said. "I'd like to freshen up a bit."

"I'll meet you there. I don't want to miss this."

"Impossible!" Andrew said, even as Lizzie jumped from the coach, her gaze on the group across the street. "We'll wait here."

Jack thought it fortunate indeed that he was only a step behind her. An arm snaked around her waist and Lizzie was suddenly pulled backward, her feet suspended from the ground as she was whirled out of harm's way. A man on horseback dashed across her path, racing his horse through the crowd and missing her by mere inches. It was a miracle she hadn't been trampled.

Jack's voice was low, his breath warm against her ear as he kept his hold. "Watch where you're going, lest you give your grandfather further reason to worry."

Lizzie tried to shake herself free from his steel vise, but the effort proved useless until she was safely deposited on the cobblestone curb.

Lizzie gasped, less from the fright she'd just taken than from the inability to breathe. Her impulse was to rail at the man, and the ache he had brought to her midsection, but Lizzie held her tongue, well aware of the fact that he'd just saved her life. To show anything but gratitude at this moment would have been beneath her. Lizzie waved at her grandfather. "I'm all right. You can go on. I'll see you later."

Andrew reentered the coach, his face having not yet regained its normal color. Obviously he'd been witness to the near accident.

"That would have been messy, I'm sure. Thank you," she said as she smoothed her skirt and adjusted the ruffle at her cuff.

Jack grinned. She hadn't spoken to him in days. Her words had come stiffly. "That must have hurt."

Lizzie brought her gaze to his and felt her lips curve in response. "Truly, it wasn't easy."

Jack laughed, wondering how much longer he'd have to wait before she realized she loved him.

Lizzie instantly dismissed the lurching of her stomach. It was ridiculous to think a man's smile could cause her stomach to jump and then squeeze as if held within a tight band.

Lizzie looked her most innocent. "If that lady doesn't stop looking at you, there could be trouble."

"What lady?" Jack looked around.

"The one standing next to the man with the knife."

Jack saw them then. The Gypsy woman and the man at her side. The man glanced at Lizzie, to the woman at his side, and then at Lizzie again.

"I don't know her."

"Apparently you don't need to."

Jack shoved Lizzie behind him, only to hear her soft laughter. "I'm teasing. They're my friends." He turned in surprise and reached for her, but grabbed only air, for Lizzie was already moving toward the two. A moment later both the man and woman were laughing, each in turn hugging Lizzie.

Lizzie turned as Jack approached.

After introductions were made, she explained that Nick and Rose were part of the same group who often camped on Andrew's estate. Lizzie had seen them only a few months ago. "And the baby?" Lizzie asked. "Is everything all right?"

"Everything is good," Rose answered.

"Better than good," Nick added, his chest swelling with pride.

"Yes, he has his son. Now he can leave his woman in peace."

Nick only laughed at that, his eyes telling clearly, along with the hand that possessively cupped her hip, that the woman he loved shouldn't look for peace for any appreciable length of time.

Lizzie saw the look and understood its meaning. She felt the most peculiar twinge of envy. "I want to see the baby. Where is he?"

"At camp."

Lizzie was obviously disappointed, until Nick explained where the camp was and Jack promised to bring her there as soon as possible.

Later as they browsed through copper pots and kitchen utensils and silver bowls and candlesticks polished to brilliance, Lizzie found a more private moment to ask, "Did I scare you?"

"Twice. I'm afraid you'll have to pay for that."

Lizzie chuckled softly, the anger she'd known over these last few days forgotten, and found herself teasing as she leaned into him. "There's a fortune-teller in that tent. Perhaps she'll tell me how I should go about it."

Jack allowed Lizzie to lead the way. Inside the tent, they sat at a small table, opposite a wrinkled old woman. Lizzie knew her as Nick's grandmother, Magda. Lizzie winked and hid her grin as the old lady put out her hand, the gnarled fingers twisted into a claw.

She said, "Cross this palm with gold and know the secrets held from you."

Jack dropped a coin into her hand. The fingers, although gnarled and swollen, moved deftly enough as they slid the coin into her skirt pocket.

"I see a long life."

Jack shot Lizzie a look that suggested the old lady might have done a bit better. "Perhaps she gives change."

"Shush," Lizzie said, ready to concentrate on the words she'd hear.

"And many children. You will be happy."

"Who?" Lizzie asked, feeling her body stiffen as she realized Magda's look had encompassed them both.

The old lady smiled almost secretly. "You don't think you love, but you do."

Jack looked at Lizzie. He knew he was in love. Obviously the woman was referring to Lizzie.

"She's talking rubbish," Lizzie said, about to come to her feet, her cheeks coloring with a guilty flush. She found Jack attractive, but that didn't mean she loved him. It didn't mean anything of the kind.

His hand on her arm prevented her escape. "Just listen," Jack said. "I want my money's worth."

"I'll pay you back. Let's go."

Jack kept his hand on Lizzie's arm, the pressure holding her in place. "Go on. What else?"

"Stubborn, but you'll soothe her."

Jack grinned, imagining quite clearly how he might go about such a chore.

Lizzie looked at the tent roof and tapped her foot impatiently. "I'm not listening."

The old woman frowned. "What does it mean, perfect teeth, perfect smile?"

Lizzie's cheeks grew warmer. "I'm sure I couldn't say."

Jack chuckled softly.

And then the Gypsy's frown deepened. "Be careful. There's trouble."

Jack was instantly alert. "What kind of trouble?"

"Danger. Much danger." She looked right at Lizzie and said, "Gran will cry."

Lizzie gasped, for she instantly understood. Her grandfather would cry because she'd be caught. She knew it and terror filled every fiber of her being, even as she knew she wouldn't, couldn't, stop.

"You're frightening her," Jack said angrily. "Let's go." He almost dragged Lizzie out of the tent. Her hands were icy cold. "What's the matter?" he asked. "You don't believe her, do you?"

Lizzie, still ashen from the Gypsy's revelation, said, "She said, 'Gran will cry.'"

"A lucky guess. She's part of this group and knows you and Andrew. She must have heard you refer to him as Gran."

Lizzie didn't respond. She knew Magda wouldn't have scared her on purpose. The Gypsy had seen something, Lizzie was sure, and just as sure she knew she couldn't do a thing to stop what would come. Her father had given his life for the cause. She could do no less.

"You need a drink."

"A cup of coffee," Lizzie said. "There's a coffee-house around the corner."

Jack guided her to the small storefront shop and they sat down as a man came to get their order.

"Two coffees, if you will, my good man. And put something strong in both."

"Better?" he asked later as Lizzie started on her second cup. Her trembling had stopped and her color was returning to normal.

Lizzie nodded and smiled.

"She was a foolish old woman."

Her blue eyes clouded with doubt, with pain. Lizzie was obviously unconvinced even as she agreed. "I know."

"I should have her arrested."

Lizzie shook her head. "Don't. I'm fine now. Let's forget about it, all right?" Lizzie changed the subject. "If you get a paper, we could see what's playing and decide which show we want to see tonight."

Jack smiled. "Good idea. I'll be right back."

Lizzie knew Jack would buy a paper and be back within minutes. She didn't have much time and cursed the fact that Mr. Kent was busy with a customer. It seemed to take forever before he stood at her table.

Lizzie whispered her information to him and then said, "Could I have another napkin, Mr. Kent?"

"Of course, Liz . . . Miss Matthews."

"How does he know your name?"

"Who? Mr. Kent?" Lizzie asked, surprised to see Jack slipping into his chair, a newspaper in hand. "I'm not sure. I've been here before. Perhaps he overheard it during one of my earlier visits."

Jack doubted that. If she came here before, it would have been in the company of her mother and sister. Neither of whom were in the habit of calling her Miss Matthews. Besides, the man had been about to say "Lizzie" until he realized they were no longer alone. Obviously they were on a first-name basis. Equally as obvious, Kent didn't want anyone to know. Jack could only wonder why.

"Oh, I remember." Lizzie couldn't allow a flicker of suspicion to fall on Mr. Kent. It took only a moment before she came up with a logical story. "Mother and I were sitting here one day when she met a friend."

"A friend called her Mrs. Matthews and not Margaret?"

"Well, not a friend exactly. It was one of Grandfather's acquaintances."

Jack nodded, wondering if she was telling the truth. She made all the pieces fall into place. Perhaps a bit too perfectly. Did anyone possess a memory so great as to remember an incident so small?

Jack wasn't happy to admit to a surge of jealousy. It was easy enough to believe they were friends. Close enough, in fact, to call each other by their first names. Did that mean they were more than friends? If not, why were they suddenly going to great lengths to ignore one another?

Damn, he was thinking nonsense. What in hell had come over him today? It was the near accident and the dire prediction from that foolish old woman. Both had shaken him more than he might have liked.

Lizzie finished her second cup, and Jack asked, "Are you ready?"

"For what?"

Jack's dark eyes twinkled with pleasure. "Well, we could do one of two things."

"Only two?"

"We could hire a cab and drive around the city, so I could kiss you until both of us are as weak as newborn babes. Or I could take you to the jeweler and buy you your engagement ring."

Lizzie pressed her lips together, trying to force aside her smile. She'd been so angry. Only an hour or so ago, she wasn't even talking to him. And now she was trying to hide her glee. What was there about this man that caused her to forget? "Are you sure there's only two? I thought perhaps London offered a bit more amusement."

Jack sighed wearily as he said, "Well, I suppose we could hire that cab and I could kiss you until we arrived at the jeweler's."

Lizzie came to her feet and began to slip on her gloves. "The walk will do us good, wouldn't you agree?"

"It's perfect, don't you think?"

"No."

"No?" Jack asked, surprised by her answer. "What's the matter with it?"

"I can hardly lift my hand now. What would happen if I were foolish enough to wear two rings on one hand?"

"Oh, you mean your wedding ring?" Jack frowned. "Is it really that heavy?"

Lizzie laughed. "No. It's just too big."

"I like it."

"Then you wear it." And to the anxious Mr. Simon she said, "May I see that one?"

The jeweler looked disappointed.

Jack snorted at the size of the stone Lizzie had pointed to. "Forget it. It's too small. Let's see that one." He pointed to another, one just as huge as the ring she'd taken off.

Mr. Simon grew happy again.

"Jack, may I talk to you for a minute?"

"Of course."

"Over there?" Lizzie said as she nodded to the far corner of the room.

"What are you doing?" Lizzie asked, once she was sure of privacy.

"Buying you a ring."

"Does it make sense to buy one so expensive? After I give it back you won't get half the original cost."

"I don't want it back. You can keep it."

"Then that would be even worse. I couldn't take something so expensive, knowing I won't be your wife."

"I want you to have a big ring. If you don't want to keep it, give it to charity."

Lizzie's eyes brightened. "Oh, that's a thought, isn't it? All right then, I'll take the big one."

A confused Mr. Simon named an exorbitant price when Lizzie asked, "What would this be worth second-hand?"

Lizzie was amazed. "That's an awful lot, isn't it?"

"Madam, the emerald is a flawless stone, cut into a perfect square, and the diamonds surrounding it are an identical match to each other in both size and quality."

Jack slipped the ring on her finger and then said, "I'd like to see a watch."

"Lady's or a man's, my lord?" Mr. Simon asked as he returned the rings to his safe.

"A lady's watch. Something on a gold chain or maybe a pin."

The jeweler displayed what he had.

Jack asked, "Which do you like, Lizzie?"

Lizzie's gaze grew from suspicious to knowing. "Why?"

"Because you need a wedding gift."

"I have the ring."

"That's for our engagement and you don't have a watch."

The truth was, Lizzie had sold her watch along with her grandmother's brooch to gain passage to England. And although her grandfather was more than generous, she'd never gotten around to replacing it. "This isn't necessary, Jack."

"Pick one or I will."

"This one," Lizzie said as she touched a small watch that hung from a delicate gold bow.

"Shall I wrap it, your lordship?"

Jack shook his head and slipped the watch into his pocket. "Send me the bill, Mr. Simon," he said. And then to Lizzie he whispered, "I think I'll give it to you on the ride home."

Lizzie rolled her eyes toward the ceiling and sighed in weary resignation. Then their eyes met, shining with laughter, as he offered his arm and guided her out of the store.

"We've been here a week. And I've been poked and prodded and stuck by more pins than I can count. I dare not drink a glass of water, lest I spring a leak."

Jack laughed, having overheard her comment as he stepped into the drawing room. "Have you gathered enough clothes then?"

"Enough? I seriously doubt there is a bolt of cloth left in the city. I'll have to change twice or more a day just to wear it all."

"Good."

"Does that mean you're finally satisfied?"

Jack knew he wouldn't be truly satisfied until they both wore a plain gold ring and he had this woman beneath him in bed.

"Can we go home then?"

"Tomorrow, if you like."

"We'll have to return next week for the ball," Margaret reminded. The Blakes, close friends of Andrew, had planned a ball in the young couple's honor.

Lizzie nodded.

"As long as we're staying one more day, what about seeing that show tonight?" Andrew asked. He'd been wanting to see Miss Angel Markham since coming to the city. Everyone was raving over the woman. She was aptly named, her voice said to rival a heavenly being, her face and form magnificent to behold.

Jack had heard the ravings, but was less than enthusiastic. Some two years ago he'd seen all he wanted of Miss Markham, and in a most intimate fashion, and had no desire to see her again. Especially while he acccompanied Lizzie. "It's been sold out for months, Andrew. I checked."

"Yes, but I have a friend who is personally acquainted with the lady. Not only did I get tickets, but all of us are invited to dinner afterwards."

Jack stifled his groan. Every time he was making some sort of headway with Lizzie, another woman from his past showed up. The truth was, there hadn't been all that many women in his life, and yet the list seemed suddenly endless. Damn. All he wanted was to marry Lizzie. Why couldn't the rest of the world, and most especially his past, leave him in peace?

Jack watched her walk down the stairs. God, but she was gorgeous. She'd done her hair up in curls, held in place with pins and two diamond combs. Her eyes were shining and almost exactly matched the blue of her silk gown. The evening gown dipped low off her shoulders and allowed more than a glimpse of creamy soft flesh. Quite a bit too much flesh, Jack thought.

"Is everyone ready?"

"They're waiting in the drawing room."

Lizzie nodded and then said, "Stop staring at me. I feel like I forgot to put something on."

"You have. The top part of your dress."

"Stop teasing. It's a very lovely dress, and you know it."

"I've no doubt every man in London will think as much." Jack sighed in weary resignation. "Just do me a favor and don't take any deep breaths."

Lizzie laughed. "You're being ridiculous. I've worn

gowns lower than this before. I think it's smashing."

The truth was, she might have worn dresses lower, but Jack hadn't cared at the time. He cared now. "Where's your shawl?"

Lizzie ignored his question.

Margaret, Annie, and Andrew joined them in the hall, and Jack thought they made a particularly handsome family.

"I'm so excited," Annie said.

Jack frowned. "Why? You've been to the theater before."

"I've never dined with a star."

"She's only a singer, Annie. No different, I'm sure, from you or I." He held the door as they exited the house.

"Oh, but she must be. I think one would have to be different to be a star."

Jack nodded as he helped her into the coach. "You might be right. One would have to be selfish and arrogant and inconsiderate of others and their feelings."

"You can't mean to say she's a noble," Lizzie asked sweetly, while accepting his assistance.

"One of these days I'm going to change your mind about England's elite."

"You mean you're going to find one who is genuine, perhaps even a decent sort?"

"I'm going to be all wrinkled," Annie complained, her skirts at least as full as her sister's. "Jack, sit up on top."

"There's enough room," Margaret insisted. "Sit by me. My skirts aren't nearly so wide."

It promised to be a lovely affair. The concert hall, filled with elaborately dressed men and women, buzzed with excitement. Jack and Andrew, with Lizzie between them, sat in the back of a box, Margaret and Annie in the first two chairs.

The music was beautiful, and Miss Markham was

truly as talented as everyone claimed. Lizzie was quite
sure she'd never heard anything so lovely. She sat very
still, her eyes closed. Surrounded by darkness, she allowed her entire body to absorb the sweet, melodious
sounds.

Jack watched Lizzie experience the music and
knew she didn't have a clue as to how she fascinated
him. He'd never known a woman more earthy, more
naturally sensual, and marveled at how she delighted
in all of life's offerings. She seemed to take nothing
for granted and treated each day, each happening, as
if it were her first or perhaps her last. Through her he
found every day to be a new and exciting experience.
She didn't merely drink wine or brandy, she savored
it. She didn't eat a dessert, but relished it over her
tongue, taking from it all the scent and flavor possible. And she did that with everything, from her enjoyment of the children to a sunset. He loved her and
couldn't wait for the day when he could tell her as
much.

Jack reached for her hand and slowly removed her
glove. He entwined their fingers, and Lizzie gave him a
breathtaking smile before closing her eyes to the pleasure surrounding them once again.

He felt their souls merge, becoming one in the darkness, as if she were already his, and swore there was no
way that he was going to lose this woman.

When the concert was over, Jack realized there was
but one way out of a possibly catastrophic situation. On
their way backstage to meet Angel, Jack suddenly
groaned and touched his stomach. "I'm afraid I'm not
feeling myself, Andrew. Would you mind if I took a cab
back to my place?"

"Are you all right?"

"I will be, I'm sure. I just need an early night. Some
clear broth should do me fine."

There was a commotion at the end of the hallway.

People were leaving a room and then suddenly Angel appeared at the door. She was saying good-bye to three of her guests when Annie said, "Isn't she beautiful?"

Angel smiled and looked toward the girl, and then just beyond her. Jack's heart sank. He'd almost made it out safely, and now it was too late.

"Jack! I'm so happy you came to see me." She was moving toward him, and Jack looked wildly around, searching for a means of escape. "Oh, darling," Angel gushed as she wrapped her arms around Jack's neck and kissed him full on the lips.

Jack didn't feel a thing. He didn't even know her tongue was trying to get into his mouth. All he could think, all he could feel, was Lizzie. All he could see were her eyes wide with astonishment.

"Hello, Angel," Jack said when she finally allowed him to break free of her hold.

"You must come to dinner, darling. A friend of mine made plans. Oh, please, you must come and save me from a dreadful time of it."

If Lizzie thought she was tense, it was nothing compared to what she felt at the woman's words.

Angel lowered her voice to a stage whisper. "These country folks, you know. I expect they'll bore me to tears." As she spoke she attempted to drag him down the hall.

Jack shook her off as gently as possible, at least as much as he could, for Angel refused to let go of his sleeve. Jack reached for Lizzie's hand, his eyes dark with annoyance, remembering quite clearly why he had broken it off with this woman some two years past. "My fiancée, Angel. I'd like you to meet Miss Lizzie Matthews, the lady I'm to marry."

After managing to put aside most of her shock, Lizzie had a hard time keeping back a groan. *Another one,* she silently mused, and couldn't help but wonder how many more of Jack's women there were.

"And this is her family. Her grandfather, Andrew Thomas, and her mother, Margaret. Her sister, Annie."

Andrew explained a bit stiffly that through a mutual friend, Joseph Mann, it was his family she was to dine with tonight. "I quite understand, madam, if you'd rather not."

Angel laughed, dismissing her hurtful words as nothing. "Oh, do come. Any friend of Jack's is welcome, I'm sure." Never letting go of Jack's arm, she ushered them all into her dressing room. Jack couldn't have looked more unhappy. Obviously he wished he were anywhere else.

It wasn't long before they were all sitting in the large private room just beyond the dressing room, with waiters at the ready to see to the lady's slightest whim.

The table was set, while another held an array of tempting dishes.

Dinner was at least as awful as the concert was lovely. No one but Annie ate. After a time the others didn't bother to pretend. Jack wondered if it were possible to be more tense or more anxious to be on his way home. He had to talk to Lizzie. She hadn't looked his way once during the entire meal. There wasn't a doubt in his mind that she was furious. Jack had every confidence that this woman loved him, but love was a fragile affair. How much anger could it take before it disappeared?

Sooner than expected, dinner was over. Jack wasn't the only one relieved when the lady claimed a previous appointment this evening.

If it weren't for Annie, total silence would have accompanied them the entire drive home. No one dared mention the woman's horrid comment, since she and Jack had obviously once been friends. Jack wished he could apologize for her. Of course, he couldn't. He'd never felt more uncomfortable in his life.

"Oh, it was divine. I knew she'd be wonderful," Annie breathed the moment they entered the coach.

Lizzie frowned. "Who was wonderful?"

"Why, Miss Markham, of course. She was so beautiful. Truly, I don't think I've ever seen a woman so lovely. Do you think I'll be half as pretty when I'm—"

"You're already twice as pretty," Andrew said. Annie didn't seem to hear.

"Didn't you love her voice? Wasn't it the best you've ever heard?"

"It was," Margaret said. "I'm sure one cannot deny the truth of it."

"And her hair. Wasn't the color smashing, Lizzie?"

"It's dyed," Jack said, and then silently cursed himself when he felt Lizzie stiffen at his side. Like a fool he'd just reminded them all of his previous involvement with the woman.

"I decided tonight. I want to be an actress." Obviously Annie was unaware of the reputation accorded actresses. "I haven't the talent to sing like Miss Markham, but someday people will stand up and cheer for me."

There was a long moment of shocked silence until Andrew finally said, "I'm afraid that's not only impossible, Annie, I expressly forbid it."

"Annie, you don't know about actresses," Margaret said. "We'll discuss it in the morning."

"Why can't I? There's nothing wrong in pleasing people. The audience adored her tonight."

"As your mother said, you'll discuss it in the morning," Andrew returned.

Annie sulked for the next few blocks, joining the rest in silence.

Jack felt a desperate need to talk to Lizzie. He had to know what she was thinking. The moment they entered his town house Jack said, "Lizzie, may I have a word with you in my study?"

"Tomorrow, if you don't mind, Jack. I'm feeling a headache coming on."

Jack had no option but to let her go. In a moment he was left alone in his hall as the entire family mounted the stairs in silence, all heading for their respective rooms.

An hour went by and the house quieted for the night. Lizzie sat in one of two chairs facing a small fire. She was dressed for bed, but not the least bit sleepy. She smoked her pipe as she thought about the singer, her amazing talent and her horrid manners.

Angel Markham was a beauty. Lizzie would have had to be blind or a liar not to admit that. And apparently she and Jack had once enjoyed a relationship. Oddly enough, Lizzie felt no anger at the thought. Well, perhaps she did feel a little angry.

But the truth was, the lady wasn't a lady, and Jack knew it. It was easy enough to see why they were no longer together. One couldn't hide for long a disagreeably low nature beneath heavy makeup.

Earlier Jack had remarked that stars, no doubt referring to this particular singer, were arrogant, selfish, and inconsiderate of others and their feelings. In this case, Lizzie couldn't help but agree.

Lizzie was startled from her thoughts by a knock at her door. She knew it was Jack even before she heard his soft call. "Lizzie, are you awake?"

The doorknob turned, but the lock above it held. "Lizzie?"

Lizzie did not respond. She was tired, tired most especially of Jack's women, and thought tomorrow would be soon enough to discuss them.

She heard him walk away. Moments later she jumped at the sight of a man's boot suddenly coming over the windowsill. Before crying out, she recognized the trousers that followed.

Obviously Jack had climbed the tree outside and entered her room by the window. Lord, but he was a stubborn sort, and sure to always get his way. He was in the room staring at the bed, which was deeply shadowed, apparently trying to figure out what to do next.

"You could have given me a terrible scare," Lizzie said.

Jack jumped, and took a step back. The heel of his boot caught on the edge of a rug and he suddenly sat hard on the floor. His head banged against the wall. "Damn!" Rubbing his sore head, he asked, "What are you doing?"

"Sitting here. Thinking. What are you doing?"

"I wanted to talk to you."

"And you thought the best way to go about it would be to climb in the window? Suppose I wasn't dressed?"

"I gave you more than enough time to dress. And why didn't you answer my knock?"

Lizzie ignored the question and asked instead, "What did you want to talk about, Jack?"

"Well, I thought . . . It's just that . . . Did you enjoy the concert?"

He was nervous, Lizzie realized, and probably thought she put the blame for this dreadful night at his feet. "The concert was lovely. Miss Markham has the most amazing voice."

"May I sit over there?" he asked, nodding toward the chair across from Lizzie.

"Of course."

They sat for a long moment in silence before Jack said, "Are you angry?"

"I was. The lady was far from pleasant. Grandfather is too kind. We should have left immediately after the insult."

Jack nodded. "I wanted to whisk all of you away."

"But she was stronger than you thought?" Lizzie asked, a small smile teasing her lips. "And you couldn't break loose?"

Jack breathed a weary sigh. "She means nothing to me."

Lizzie nodded. He'd said as much about Mrs. Stone, and yet he'd been intimate with both women. Lizzie couldn't help but wonder if any woman could mean anything to him. "How many women have you been with, Jack?"

"Not so many. Why?"

She smiled. "They do seem to crop up, don't they?"

"I'm having a run of bad luck. I swear I've gone years without seeing a one."

Lizzie blew a thin cloud of smoke toward the ceiling. "And you're sure she means nothing to you?"

"Absolutely."

"Do you feel like that about all your women?"

"They're not mine, Lizzie, and mostly I can't remember their names."

"Then it's fortunate for me that we won't be marrying, isn't it?"

Jack frowned. "I don't understand."

"A lady hopes that a man feels enough for her to remember her name, especially if she sleeps with him."

Jack sighed. "Lizzie, you don't understand."

"Don't I? Do you mean you don't use women for your pleasure and then discard them without a thought?"

Jack looked distinctly uncomfortable admitting, "Some women perhaps."

"Only some?"

She didn't understand the way of things. "Do you think all men are alike?"

Lizzie frowned at the question. "I don't know all men, so how could I say?"

"They're not. And neither are all women alike. Some are meant to be wives, while others long for the excitement in diversion. For them only a great number of men can satisfy. No one forces them. Indeed they are quite willing to give up the esteem offered to the former to indulge in the pleasure of the latter."

"Are you saying there's no pleasure for those who have chosen to be a wife?"

"I've never been married, Lizzie. Still, I think there's more pleasure than either of us can imagine. Pleasure in the fact that a man and woman belong only to each other. That in all the world, there's one who grows so close that her pain is yours, her happiness as well. So close, you know you couldn't live without her."

"Meaning a wife would be cherished?"

"Without a doubt."

"Taking for granted that the woman is satisfied with one man, what would stop the man from seeking diversion and excitement in others?"

Jack wasn't sure when it began, but slowly over these last few weeks his fascination with this woman had grown into love. He awoke anxious for the sight of her smile, her laughter became more important than food, her teasing more desirable than drink. He loved her more than he'd thought it possible to love. He was a man possessed with the need to always have her at his side.

And still he knew that she was not ready to hear the truth. It was best, Jack thought, to keep these feelings to himself for the time being. She loved him, he was sure, but did she love him enough? She had to put him above love of country, before politics or causes, or her hatred of class distinction. He wanted first place in her heart. He had to have it before he could bare his soul.

"Honor," he finally said. "Once I said the vows, I'd hold to you alone." The truth of the matter being he held to her even now.

"Yes, Gran said as much." Lizzie sighed. "Honor and vows would keep you to me. It sounds terribly cold."

Jack smiled, his dark eyes intense with emotion. "I can promise you one thing. You'll never know cold in my arms."

Lizzie felt a thrill of excitement race throughout her

body at his softly spoken words. His eyes promised sizzling heat. Lizzie trembled remembering the fire in their
previous encounters. Tension filled the small room.
Need, raw and aching, was all there in his eyes, perhaps
in hers as well. It would only take a word and she'd
discover the whole of it. But she wouldn't say the word.
She couldn't. Far too much stood between them, so
much Lizzie doubted even love could win out against
their insurmountable differences.

And he wasn't offering love. He offered honor, and
no matter the riches or prestige that came with it, it
wasn't enough.

Lizzie stood and walked toward the door. Holding it
slightly ajar, she said, "It's late. I have to get up early
and finish my packing."

Chapter 10

It was Tuesday, and as usual, Lizzie trod the uneven road to the church and the orphans awaiting her charge. Today she used the gig. At least once a month she brought food and something special for the children. The packages beside her contained clothing, pillows, and much-needed bedding. Jugs of milk bounced at every bump and gully in the road. Beside the milk sat fresh vegetables, bread, and, wrapped in a towel, a huge roast. Atop it all were Mrs. Molston's delicious strawberry tarts as well as a creamy custard pudding. The children were in for a treat today.

Lizzie frowned as she pulled the gig to a stop. The orphanage was normally quiet, but for a screech or two from playing children, or the crying of a baby. Today the sound of hammers filled the air, along with Jack's thunderous voice shouting orders to a half dozen men.

A man mixed an enormous vat of paint with a stick, another mortar with a shovel. Lumber was being unloaded from a wagon, while a group of men were digging what appeared to be footings behind the small house.

Lizzie jumped from the gig and was soon standing at Jack's side. "Why are you here?"

"Oh, hello," Jack said, and then called to the men unloading the first wagon. "By God, man, at this rate we'll be here forever."

"There's only two of us, sir."

"Then get more men." Jack finished with a frustrated "Damn it!"

"Watch your language." Lizzie glanced at the boys standing close by, watching the goings-on. "Those three are already practicing how to say 'damn it.' Look at their lips."

Following the direction of Lizzie's gaze, Jack laughed. "Come along, lads," he called to the boys, "let's have at it." The three moved toward him and the wagon. "We're short a few men here. I'd be obliged if you'd give these gentlemen a hand."

Jack and Lizzie moved toward her gig. "You're very good," she said as the boys set out to do their share, happy to be included.

"Am I?" His eyes widened at the compliment. "Thank you."

"Is it always that easy to maneuver someone to your will?"

Jack sighed, leaned against the vehicle, and folded his arms over his middle. "It can't be that easy. I haven't maneuvered you, have I?"

An arm snaked suddenly around her middle and brought her close to his side. "I'm to tell you to go to the rectory, the minute you arrive."

"Why?"

"I don't know. It's a surprise, I think. Unless you'd rather stay with me. I could—"

Lizzie pushed herself from his embrace. "You didn't answer my question. Why are you here?"

"A few of the parishioners thought something should be done about the place. After all, it's more than an orphanage. Sometimes whole families have to stay until work can be found. It's hardly fitting that men, women, and children should share the same small room.''

''So you're building on?''

''I thought a new room could be divided into three. One for babies, another for boys, another for girls. Families, since they aren't usually here that long, could share the old one. What do you think?''

Lizzie shot him a puzzled look. ''I think you're being very kind. What I'd like to know is, why the sudden interest?''

Jack knew he'd been a fool. Of course, she'd question his motives. He should have known better than to imagine her all soft and lovely, smiling her appreciation. ''What do you mean?''

''I mean, the poorhouse has been here for years. Why are you fixing it now?''

''Because I've never been inside it until today.''

''Oh? Did Mrs. Pentigast invite you?''

''Mrs. Pentigast went home, I think.''

''Then why?''

Jack could see this wasn't turning out exactly as he'd planned. The woman was determined to know the truth of it. He could tell her he'd do anything for one of her smiles, for a loving look sent his way. But no, it was best that he keep those facts to himself. At least for now.

Jack breathed a sigh and said, ''All right, I came because you're always here and I was curious about what you do. I'm fixing it because the place is falling apart. How in hell are people supposed to live like that?''

Lizzie knew Jack cared about others less fortunate than himself. He showed it in a dozen small ways. Despite her belief that aristocrats never cared about anything or anyone other than themselves, she knew he was different. She couldn't class him with the rest of England's elite. She couldn't even try. A wave of warm emotion suddenly squeezed at her heart, and Lizzie found it impossible to raise her gaze to his.

"Did you imagine I did this so you might see me in a kinder light?"

Lizzie wasn't sure what she'd thought, but soon realized it hardly mattered what his motives were. It only mattered that he was doing something. Not just giving money to charity, but actually physically involving himself. "If you did, I think it's working."

Jack grinned. "Is it?" He laughed as his hand reached for hers, holding it in his warm palm. "Perhaps I shall repeat this, then, with all the poorhouses in England."

"This parish will do for now, I think."

"You know what I think, Lizzie? I think you're generous, kind, and caring of all you come across. With or without a title, that makes you a greater lady than any I've ever known."

Lizzie managed only a blink as a response, never having imagined he thought so highly of her.

"Have I caused you to grow speechless?"

"Very nearly, I'm afraid."

Jack chuckled. "Then this should set you to rights again. You're generous and kind and wonderful to all but me, and I need it the most."

Lizzie giggled. The sound was somehow girlish and at the same time deliciously wicked.

Jack wondered how she managed it. And wondered as well how her laughter could make his chest squeeze tightly. He was mad for her; of that, there could be no doubt. He'd once wanted others, but never with an ache to compare to this. And never before had he known this constant need to shine in a woman's eyes.

"Perhaps you need it most, but the question is, are you deserving?" she asked, a teasing smile softening the words.

Jack managed a dramatic sigh of relief. "That's better. I couldn't live with myself if I thought I'd dulled your sharp tongue.''

Lizzie grinned. ''I doubt you'll have to worry much on that score.''

''Unless you want me to kiss you, I suggest you let me get back to work.''

Lizzie shot him a no-nonsense look and then, shaking her head, left him to be about his business and walked toward the small rectory.

''Miss Matthews, you're here at last,'' Richard said as she stepped inside.

''I'm sorry I'm late. I did some shopping this morning. There are packages in the gig, food and milk as well, and treats for the children.''

Richard nodded. ''I'll give Becky a hand unloading.'' He took two steps down the path and stopped. ''You have visitors waiting inside.''

Lizzie entered the rectory to find her cousin Jane talking sweet nonsense to the newest addition to the small parish, a foundling only a few weeks old. Harry, her husband, hovered nearby. ''So what do you think?'' Lizzie asked.

Jane tore her gaze from the baby and grinned. ''Oh, cousin, he's simply lovely. A perfect little boy.''

''I think he looks like you,'' Harry said to his wife.

Jane's gaze widened with amazement as she looked the little fellow over. ''He does. How could that have happened?''

Lizzie laughed and hugged her cousins. ''I thought you might like him.''

''I think you can safely say that.''

''I've a surprise for you,'' Jane said proudly. ''We're having a baby. That's why it took so long before getting back to you. We saw a doctor in London, just to make sure.''

''Oh,'' Lizzie said, torn between happiness for the couple and disappointment that she'd have to look elsewhere for a home for this baby. "I think that's wonderful. I take it you're happy."

"Ecstatic might be closer to the truth," Jane offered.

"Then you won't be taking this little one?"

"Of course we're taking him. Harry and I decided that the moment your note came."

Lizzie smiled and hugged them both again. "Lovely."

During the next hour, the cousins caught up on family news over tea and scones, thanks to Mrs. Cunningham's generosity. Alice and the boys were discussed, as were Andrew, Margaret, and Annie. And of course, congratulations were extended on Lizzie's coming marriage. "Are you terribly excited?"

"Terribly," Lizzie said.

"It was a bit sudden, don't you think? I hadn't an idea you were in love the last time I was here."

"Lizzie plays things close to her chest," Jack said, entering the cottage without knocking and joining the conversation in midstream. "Hello, Jane. Harry. I hope things are going well for you."

"Very well indeed," Harry said, shaking Jack's hand.

Jack gave Lizzie a long look and had the audacity to say, "The truth is, the woman can't keep her hands off me. She has me bedazzled by her kisses, so I thought it best that we should marry. Save ourselves a scandal that way, you know."

Lizzie gasped and then shot him a glare. "Don't believe a word he says."

Jane giggled.

"She thinks I'm perfect," Jack further informed, his dark eyes twinkling with laughter. "I thought I should catch her up before she finds out the truth."

"She's already found out," Lizzie returned on a weary sigh.

All three laughed at that.

"She must love me then. Why else would she marry me?"

"Because I want to be a countess," Lizzie returned sickly.

They laughed all the harder, for Lizzie's aversion to the upper class was hardly a well-kept secret to her family.

All too soon it was time to leave. Harry stood and took the sleeping baby from Jane's arms. "We'd better be going, darling, lest we find ourselves on the road after dark."

Jane gathered together her shawl and the clothes she'd brought for the baby and promised to return in two weeks for the wedding.

Those words gave Lizzie a nasty start. Two weeks. Of course, she'd been aware that the time was fast approaching. She simply hadn't realized how fast.

Jack stood beside Lizzie at the gate as she waved good-bye. "It's only two weeks away," she said.

"I know."

"We have to do something before it's too late."

"After the Blakes' party should be soon enough." His arm tightened at her waist.

"Jack, the wedding is costing a fortune. You're wasting—"

"A pittance," he returned with careless disregard. "Don't worry about it."

Lizzie frowned. She'd been born to a moderate degree of wealth, and enjoyed even more living beneath her grandfather's roof. But Lizzie did not take kindly to the man's flagrant wasting of money. So much could be done with it. So many were in need, and yet Jack thought nothing at all of spending a near fortune on a wedding that would never come about. His careless attitude showed him for the aristocrat he was.

Lizzie paused in her thoughts, for she knew Jack was far more than simply an aristocrat. Far more and far better, if the truth be told. She'd never found him to be careless before about money or anything else. Surely today's work proved him to be a caring man.

If she didn't know better, she would imagine that he planned on a wedding despite her objections. Lizzie almost laughed at the thought. Jack was arrogant, she knew, but even he wouldn't go that far.

Lizzie leaned into him, and found her tension eased simply by the warmth of his touch. He was right. They had time to set this matter to rights. Plenty of time.

His jacket hung on a gate post. The ties of his shirt lay open, exposing the hard, tanned flesh of his neck and an intriguing shadow of black hair covering his chest. His sleeves were rolled to his elbow. His arms, dusted with hair, thick and tight with sinew and muscle, lifted wood, stacking it for the carpenters.

Lizzie had seen men sweat before. The sight of his damp shirt sticking to his back was no oddity. Muscles straining beneath damp fabric caused her no trembling or shortness of breath. It was ridiculous to think it might. And still her gaze was drawn to him time and again.

The last wagon was almost unloaded. She and Becky stood beside it, dispensing glasses of lemonade. Jack walked toward her, wiping his face and neck with his handkerchief. "Thank you," he said just before reaching for the offered glass and downing the whole of it without stopping to breathe.

Lizzie's gaze was drawn to his throat; she was fascinated even as a frown came to mar her brow. What in the world was the matter with her today? Why couldn't she stop looking at him? What was so special about a man's throat and its movement as he swallowed?

Lizzie was hardly able to breathe as she watched a droplet of lemonade gather with others on his throat and then disappear beneath his shirt.

"What's the matter?" Jack asked. Having finished his

drink, he noticed Lizzie watching him. He scratched the tickle at his throat, leaving a smudge of dirt behind.

Lizzie couldn't have said, for she hadn't a clue as to what had come over her. All she knew was, she'd never felt so strange, so oddly weak. Watching him work and sweat, his muscles rippling, straining beneath his shirt, had caused her stomach to tighten, her skin to grow feverish, and her body to shiver as if she were affected with ague.

"Nothing," she finally managed, tearing her gaze from his throat, ignoring the power and strength in his chest and arms, forcing herself to meet his dark eyes. "It's just warm, is all. I could stand a breeze."

"We all could," Jack said, and then took the pitcher from her hand and placed it on the back of the wagon. His hand on her arm, he guided her toward a tree. "Stand in the shade for a minute. You'll feel better."

Long, silent moments later she said, "This is better. Thank you."

"You were watching me."

Lizzie felt a guilty flush creep up her neck to stain her cheeks. She turned to watch a group of children running in the meadow that bordered the church property. "I was watching everyone."

He took a half step toward her, and she could suddenly smell him. Lord, have mercy, but this was too much. She closed her eyes as his scent filled her senses. He smelled dark and musky from hard work and yet clean with a trace of soap and his cologne. He smelled like Jack Black, only more so.

"Tell me what you're thinking."

"That I should go home." Though her voice trembled, she forced herself to go on. "Mrs. Miller and her daughter are coming for tea."

Jack reached a finger beneath her chin and made her eyes meet his. "Now tell me the truth."

"That I'm probably coming down with something."

"Are you feeling light-headed? Shaken?"

Lizzie nodded.

Jack wasn't surprised. He'd seen the look in her eyes, and knew sexual attraction when he saw it.

"I like the way you smell." Lizzie blinked in shock, unable to explain why she had blurted that out. Surely she couldn't have said such a thing. It didn't matter that it was true.

Jack leaned heavily against the tree beside her and closed his eyes. A moaning sound came from deep in his throat. "You're driving me mad."

"I've got to go."

His hand caught hers and brought it to his damp chest, holding it there against his pounding heart. "Don't. Just stand here for a minute." He looked at her for a long moment, his breathing harsh and labored. "God, I wish we were alone."

Lizzie could hardly breathe herself. There was a ringing in her ears, and her solid world grew strangely out of focus. She didn't know what was happening, but realized she hadn't the strength to fight it. Her voice was shaken, hardly above a whisper when she said, "It's a good thing we're not, I think."

After a long, silent moment, Jack finally nodded. "You're probably right."

Lizzie had no interest in seeing his new house, either with her mother or without, and couldn't imagine why the man had suggested she might. She glanced at her mother and felt suddenly trapped. Margaret's expression told clearly of her eagerness, and Lizzie didn't dare claim yet another headache, for she'd been doing so routinely of late and didn't want her mother to worry unnecessarily. She had no choice but to agree to the outing.

Jack smiled, ignoring the short but potent glare shot his way. "You don't mind if your mother joins us, do you, dear? I mean, you will have the last say, of course, but the house is so large and in such need. I thought Margaret might see something we miss.''

Margaret's blue eyes sparkled with pleasure, for she loved nothing more than decorating and couldn't wait to offer her opinion. "Of course she doesn't mind, do you, Lizzie?''

Lizzie shook her head. "I couldn't do it alone, Mother. Of course I don't mind.''

"I'll be ready momentarily,'' Margaret said as she hurried from the breakfast room, while Lizzie bestowed upon her tormentor yet another glare.

She lowered her voice lest a servant suddenly enter the small room. ''What's the purpose of involving Mother?''

Jack's grin turned as lecherous as any Lizzie had ever seen as he lowered his voice and teased outrageously, ''Now, Lizzie, I know how you get when we find ourselves suddenly alone.'' His sigh was a dramatic telling of hopeless acquiescence. ''I hope you can promise me, especially since your mother will be with us, to keep your hands to yourself?''

Lizzie's lips, at the edge of a teacup, twitched, and from deep within her throat came a soft sound. Jack wasn't sure if it was laughter or a growl. Perhaps it was a bit of both. ''You have my word on it, Lord Deranged.''

''That's a relief since I know you to be a woman of your word.''

''Oh, do be quiet, please!'' she moaned softly, not at all sure what to do about this man and his teasing. It would have been so easy to tease in return, to smile and allow her feelings to soften, but to what avail? No, it was best to keep her distance, to ignore his subtle and intriguing promises, to forget any intimacies they might have shared. ''What do you think to gain by this nonsense? We aren't to marry. Why in the world would you want my opinion, or my mother's for that matter?''

"I can't tell you if I'm to be quiet."

Lizzie sighed and leaned back in her chair. "I wonder if you've said one serious thing since we met."

"The truth is, Lizzie, I need a woman's touch and I trust Margaret. Only I couldn't ask her and not my supposed intended."

"Oh."

Jack chuckled, a low, wicked sound, as his fingers played idly with a fork. Lizzie's gaze was drawn to his hand, to the long, tapered fingers that could be gentle and yet so strong, to the sunbrowned skin, showing in stark relief upon the white cloth, to the clean nails and smudge of dark hair between each knuckle. She couldn't seem to pull her gaze away. "You know what I've discovered recently, Lizzie?"

"Another mermaid on the beach?" she offered hopefully.

Jack smiled at that memory. If he lived a hundred years, he wouldn't forget that day.

Her gaze lifted to his, and it was all there in his eyes. It was as if she could see a picture of herself, every line of her body remembered in detail, and his delight in seeing it. Lizzie felt a thrill of emotion smack hard into her stomach. She swallowed and forced her feelings under control.

"I've discovered that nasty-mouthed women are exciting."

"Are they?"

"Indeed they are. Shall I tell you the erotic thoughts a woman like that brings to a man?"

Lizzie knew the wisdom in ending this conversation. She was aware of where he was leading them, and knew that to allow it could only court danger. "No, but I should make it a point, then, to find you one. Perhaps you could tell her."

"Come over here."

"I don't think so."

"Why not?"

"Because if I came over there, I'd end up sitting on your lap again, and we both know where that leads."

"You promised you'd keep your hands to yourself today. I trust you."

Lizzie laughed. "A shame I cannot return the compliment."

"We're getting married. No one would think it unusual."

"But we are not getting married, we're *supposed* to be getting married. There's a big difference."

"No, there isn't," he said as he came to his feet and casually dropped his napkin near his plate. Moving quickly so as to give her no warning, he was suddenly at her side. A second later Lizzie was lifted from her seat and deposited on his lap as he took possession of her chair. His arms moved around her waist, holding her in place. "Now, isn't that better?"

"No."

"Are you peeved at me? Would you rather I hadn't asked your mother?" His dark eyes shone with laughter at her frustration. Jack didn't wait for Lizzie's answer before saying, "The truth is, I would have preferred it, but I doubt your grandfather would have seen the merit in an unchaperoned outing. One that is sure to last most of the day."

There was a time only a few short weeks ago that Lizzie might have known some anger at his flagrant disregard of her wishes. She breathed a soft sigh at the thought and, realizing her lack of anger, imagined she was growing used to this man and his tendency to do exactly as he pleased. "Do you always get what you want?"

His gaze grew dark and hungry. Lizzie felt a chill run down her back. "I haven't gotten anything I want from you yet."

Lizzie decided to ignore his comment, and more important, the look in his eyes. She reminded him, "I'm sitting on your lap, aren't I?"

"A mere pittance."

"It's more than I've gotten," she said with a touch of weariness.

Jack's gaze moved to her bodice and the small watch pinned there. "Let me see what time it is."

Lizzie slapped his hand away. "You can see it without touching me. I think the only reason you bought this watch was so you might touch me at will."

"I wouldn't think of touching you," Jack lied. "I was just trying to bring it closer."

"You have your own watch."

Without a twinge of conscience he added one more lie. "It's broken."

Lizzie reached into his vest pocket and popped the lid on his watch. Just as she suspected, it was working perfectly. She breathed a hopeless sigh as she dropped it back into place. "You're impossible. Let me up. I have to get ready."

"First kiss me good morning."

"We already kissed good morning, remember? The truth is, we kiss every time we meet, and you said we wouldn't be kissing much."

"Actually you said that."

"You agreed."

"I would have agreed to anything to get you where I wanted . . ."

Lizzie's eyes widened and then came a low, deliciously erotic chuckle. "You beast."

He said, "You should do it again. I'll remember this time."

"What else have you promised that you didn't mean?"

"Nothing that I know of."

"Jack," she said seriously, "I understand you think

this is all great fun, but wouldn't it be wise to stop all this kissing?''

"You're mistaken if you think kissing you is fun." He watched her for a short moment before continuing on. "It's far more than fun, it's misery and ecstasy, it's agony and delirium." And if he didn't have her soon, he wasn't sure he could hold on to his sanity.

Lizzie's eyes grew puzzled; obviously she didn't understand. "Do you know the feelings you sometimes get here, when I kiss you?" He placed his palm on the lower part of her stomach and smiled at her small jump.

"How did you know?"

"Because I feel the same just thinking about kissing you."

Lizzie wasn't sure what she could say. She had no firsthand knowledge of sexual attraction and couldn't imagine why either of them suffered as they did. After a moment she offered, "Maybe we should stop then."

Jack's only response was to lower his mouth to a hairsbreadth from hers.

"Are you ready?" Margaret asked from the doorway, her eyes soft with happiness at seeing her daughter and the man she was to marry so harmoniously involved. The two of them together reminded her of herself and James.

"Almost, Margaret. I'm just trying to pry a little kiss from my fiancée."

"Lizzie, give him his kiss and let's go. The coach is waiting," she said matter-of-factly as she smoothed her gloves into place and walked away.

Lizzie could hear her heels on the parquet floors moving toward the front door. "I have to get my hat," she whispered softly almost against his lips, just before closing her eyes.

Jack lowered his hand from her waist to her backside and gave her a quick if far too intimate squeeze. "Hurry, then." A moment later she stood leaning against the table, slightly dizzy from their encounter, watching as he followed her mother down the long hall, knowing a sense of utter bewilderment.

They sat across from one another, with her mother at her side, and Lizzie wondered at the slight sense of irritation she knew. Of course, she wasn't annoyed because he hadn't kissed her. She didn't want this man's kisses and had, from the first, gone out of her way to avoid them. Then why couldn't she find her usual good humor? No doubt she was tired. And the more she thought of it, the more she was sure of it.

It had only been a few days since they had returned from London. No doubt she hadn't as yet recovered from the sight-seeing and shopping. The wedding preparations were proving to be exhausting. Every day there was more to do, be it a fitting, a list to see to, well-wishing visitors to entertain, and a hundred particulars concerning the party that would follow the wedding.

Lizzie sighed again at the waste of money. She couldn't wait to put this entire matter behind her. Her grandfather wouldn't be half so disappointed, she thought, since she had brought the subject up once before. And even if he was, he'd get over it. She was sure he would.

But would she? Lizzie started at the thought. What in the world could she be thinking? And why did the thought of breaking it off with Jack suddenly fill her with dread?

Andrew Thomas owned a number of two- and four-wheeled vehicles. Because the morning was particularly lovely, it was decided they would use an open carriage. Larger than a phaeton, this one consisted of wide seats that faced each other, a door, and steps that allowed the ladies easier access.

An hour from her grandfather's estate, Lizzie watched as the carriage moved beyond a tower or gatehouse, mostly in ruin, and pulled into a long drive. "This isn't the Stanford place."

"I know. I've found us something better."

Ahead was a wide avenue, bordered by tall, leafy trees casting it in cool shadow. Beyond the trees stood a gray, cold, and forbidding building devoid of all shrubbery with the exception of ivy, which grew almost to the fourth-floor windows. The place was twice as large as her grandfather's home.

This wasn't a country estate at all, she realized, it was a castle complete with turrets, battlements, stained-glass windows, and gargoyles. All that was needed to complete the picture was a moat.

The carriage rolled to a stop, and Lizzie glanced at her mother, who was looking a bit sickly, obviously amazed at the size of the place. Lizzie laughed. "Never fear, Mother, my betrothed is known for his wicked sense of humor."

Jack frowned, wondering what Lizzie was talking about.

And then she turned to him and asked, "Where is it, really?"

"Where is what?"

"The house you bought."

"You're looking at it." Jack felt his spirits sink. She didn't like it. Damn! A moment of silence went by before he dared to ask, "Is something wrong?"

"This is a country estate?" Lizzie couldn't have looked more amazed.

"Well, actually it was once a castle owned by—"

Lizzie shook her head and interrupted with, "Jack, this wasn't once a castle. This *is* a castle. How can anyone live in something like that?"

"What's wrong with it?"

"It's too big." And again Lizzie was reminded of the man's careless disregard of money. Even if they had truly planned on marrying, they didn't need a place this large.

Jack felt a wave of relief. If it was only the size of the place that bothered her, he knew she'd soon get used to it. "Well, there's the gatekeeper's house back by the tower. Would you rather that?" he teased.

She shot him one of her delicious glares. "Very amusing."

Jack grinned, jumped from the carriage, and helped Margaret down. His stepsister was already inspecting the massive front door as he assisted Lizzie.

She closed her frilly parasol and allowed Jack to lift her down. "It's a good thing we're not really getting married. We'd never find each other in this place."

Jack looked down at her, a tender smile curving his lips. "Yes, it's a very good thing. If we were married, I'd definitely want to find you." He kissed her then, unable to resist the sweetness of her.

Strangely enough, Lizzie found her good humor instantly restored. It wasn't his kiss that had done it, she thought. No, she was simply growing used to this man's company, and Jack was wonderfully sweet and accommodating. Truly it was a marvelous day.

"Children could be lost forever," she said, as she moved with him to the door, her head back as she strained to see the top floor.

"I'd have to find you first, of course." And at her puzzled look he added, "You know, in order to have children."

Lizzie felt her cheeks grow warm with color.

Her mother opened the door, and all three entered a huge vestibule. The floor was white and black marble squares, the walls dark oak paneling. To the left and right stood doors. And beyond the doors stood two huge stairways leading to the floors above. A thick coating of dust covered everything.

"As soon as I saw the stairways and their railings, I

thought of you," Jack said, his dark eyes shining with laughter.

Lizzie poked his side with an elbow.

"This could be lovely," Margaret said. "The walls would have to be cleaned." And then almost to herself she remarked, "I wonder if Burns could find something that would lighten this wood."

"How long has it been since this place was used?" Lizzie asked.

"I'm not sure. Fifty years, maybe."

"It's probably filled with mice," she said, backing slowly toward the door.

"I'll make sure they're gone before we move in. Don't worry."

Lizzie wasn't worried, she was scared. There wasn't anything she hated more than mice, unless it was spiders. And webs hung from every corner.

Jack, noticing her retreat, took her arm. "Don't be afraid. All you have to do is make a lot of noise and they'll run."

"They can't run faster than me."

Jack laughed. "I've no doubt they wouldn't make as much noise either."

They went through the entire downstairs, every cupboard, every hallway, every closet. There was a pantry and then a butler's pantry, and three small rooms beyond, no doubt sitting rooms meant for the household staff. There were four sitting rooms in the main part of the house as well as a library, study, and billiards room. But most surprising was the chapel. Lizzie couldn't imagine any home boasting of its own chapel. There was a dining room, a breakfast room, and of course, a kitchen. While in the kitchen Lizzie found one of the fireplace bricks protruding slightly from the others. She touched it and, finding it loose, was about to comment on it when the wall seemed suddenly to give way. Lizzie gasped and backed quickly away, fearful that the bricks were about to topple.

But the wall hadn't given way, a doorway had opened instead. Lizzie pushed a bit against the brick. "Look," she said to Jack, "there's a hidden room." She stepped inside. "I wonder what it was used for."

"Storage perhaps," Jack said, stepping into the vault-like room behind her. "But more likely it was built to hide a priest."

"Hide a priest?" she repeated, her eyes wide with interest. "Do you mean this place is that old?"

"Older probably. The main hall is dated somewhere around 1400. Like your grandfather's home, the rest of the rooms were added later."

Lizzie chuckled softly, "Only one can't compare this place to my grandfather's."

"It could be made just as comfortable."

Lizzie supposed it could, except she wouldn't be the one to make it so. Somehow the thought saddened her.

Lizzie had lost count of the number of rooms. She was exhausted and didn't want to think about climbing those stairs.

"Don't you want to see upstairs?" Jack asked, seeing that she'd taken her handkerchief, and cleaned off a small space on the second step to sit on.

"I'm too tired."

"Your mother's already up there."

"My mother's stronger than I."

"They're all suites."

"What's sweet? That reminds me, I'm starving. We left our basket in the carriage, and Mrs. Molston made a cherry pie."

"Roger brought it in. I was talking about the bedrooms. They're suites. Each of them has a sitting room, walk-through closets, and bathing chambers. This place might be old, but it's luxurious."

"I'll take your word for it."

"The nurseries are on the third floor."

"There's more than one?"

"I think I can safely say, a house this size was made for a large family." She made no response. "We could have a large family if you married me."

"You could have a large family with anyone who married you." Lizzie's smile was unsure. Had he meant that? Was he simply teasing her again? "Can we eat now?"

"How about the library? There's wood. We can eat before a fire."

"The wood is probably petrified. It's been here fifty years."

"I brought it the last time I was here."

Lizzie cleaned another spot, this time in front of the fireplace, while Jack dug into the nearby pile of wood. She was emptying the picnic basket when she saw it. It was only from the corner of her eye, but something flew or jumped from out of the pile and landed on her head.

In an instant she was a woman gone berserk. She tore at her cap and pins, running her fingers through her hair, all the while emitting a terrified scream.

Jack jumped, dropped the wood, and spun around. "What happened? What are you doing?" he asked as she continued to tear at her hair.

"A spider jumped on my head." Talking didn't stop her from shaking her head. "Get it out! Get it out!" Her hair was flying over her face and down her back as she ruffled it wildly.

"I don't see anything."

Lizzie grabbed him by the shirtfront and with the strength of two men yanked him to within an inch of her face. Her eyes were wild with fear. "That's because you didn't look." And between clenched teeth she gritted, "Get it out."

"You're choking me."

"I hate spiders."

Jack looked at her hair. "There's nothing there."

"What's the matter?" Margaret asked, seeing as her daughter held her fiancé in a choke hold.

Gently he pried her fingers apart. "Lizzie thinks there's a spider on her head."

Margaret moved closer, looked her daughter over, and then glanced at the floor. "It was a piece of bark."

It took a moment for the information to sink in. A moment longer for Lizzie to fall into Jack's arms with a sigh of relief. "I can't move in here, Jack. I hate spiders," she moaned against his throat.

And Jack knew she'd forgotten, at least for the moment, that their engagement was a sham. He wished only that she might continue to forget.

"Don't worry, sweetheart, the place will be clean by then, I swear."

Margaret was emptying the basket of food upon a blanket brought for that purpose, and Jack took the opportunity to hold Lizzie against him. He nuzzled his mouth briefly against her temple, unable to resist, even knowing the intimacy would make her leave his arms. It did.

After she repaired her hair, they ate a meal of bread, cheese, and cold chicken. Finishing it off with a light wine, Lizzie felt relaxed, her spirits high. She didn't object this time when Jack asked, "Would you like to see the upstairs now?"

Lizzie smiled and allowed him to help her to her feet. She turned to her mother, imagining she'd join them, only Margaret had already seen the rooms above.

"You two go along," Margaret said tiredly. "I'll wait here."

It was dark upstairs; the hallway windows were large but grimy and dull. The thick coating of dirt allowed only a small portion of the light needed. Lizzie shivered imagining the place full of mice, and dreading with every step that one might dash under her skirts.

Jack led her down a long hall to the master suite. Inside the huge double doors, Lizzie moved closer to his side. "It's dark in here."

"It won't be after the windows are cleaned." Jack moved toward one of the two and opened it. Sunshine streamed in, brightening the cool, dark interior.

The room was far more pleasant than Lizzie had first supposed. It was obviously a man's room, paneled in wood much like that of the hall and library below. Still, Lizzie imagined it could be quite charming and comfortable with rugs, a fire burning in the grate, and the right pieces of furniture in place.

"Do you like it?"

"I do." She glanced up and smiled. "But your wife will probably redo it."

"Why?"

"It's a bit too masculine. A man lived here, alone, I think."

"There's another room through that door. Perhaps his wife slept there."

Jack opened the door, and before Lizzie had a chance to do more than give a startled gasp, he pulled her inside with him. The door shut behind them.

"You mean he kept her in a closet?" It was totally black. Lizzie couldn't see a thing.

Jack gathered her into his arms. "This is a hallway. There's another room behind us."

"I don't see it."

"I haven't opened the door yet."

"Open it."

"I will, in a minute."

"Did you plan this all along?" she asked as his mouth moved over her cheek and down her neck, his fingers at the back of her dress quickly undoing the buttons.

"How could I? Your mother is here."

His mouth was on her shoulder now, her neck; Lord,

but she did enjoy the feel of his lips on her neck. "Exactly," she said a bit breathlessly, "and she could walk through this door any second. Stop that." She tried to twist away. The narrow hallway allowed her not an inch of space. "How do you always manage to get me half-undressed?" She pushed his hands away, but it didn't seem to matter. Despite her protests, and Lizzie supposed she didn't protest quite as hard as she might have, her dress came undone, her chemise was lowered, and her breasts were exposed to his pleasure. "Are you sure you have only two hands?"

Jack chuckled. "Right now I wish I had a half dozen."

His mouth moved down her chest, and then along the outside curve of one breast. Lizzie felt a groan bubble to life in her throat. Her body tensed waiting for him to find the already hardening tip, every nerve ending suddenly alive and aching for the heat of his mouth, even as she heard herself murmur, "Jack, this really isn't . . . God!"

She moaned as he sucked her deeper into the blazing heat of his mouth. Her hands reached for his head, her fingers moving through the thick, crisp hair, pulling him closer despite her words. And then her back arched and her head fell back; her body offered him all he could take.

"Even if she looked for us, she wouldn't find us in here. I locked the door."

His hands moved over her, memorizing her sweet nakedness, loving her flesh, molding it to aching pleasure. "Marry me, Lizzie. Marry me true."

"What?" she asked, hardly hearing his words above the roar of pounding blood in her ears.

"Marry me," he repeated.

Oh, sweet ecstasy, if she could only say yes. "I can't" came on a low groan.

"We could have babies, Lizzie. I know how much

you love babies. Marry me and I'll give you as many as you want.'' He touched her flat stomach. "Here, Lizzie. You'd grow round with my baby here.''

Lizzie couldn't concentrate. Not when his mouth touched her like this. Not when his hands brought moans from her throat. How did he expect her to talk, to think, when she was barely able to breathe? She loved it, loved it more than she could say.

His hands were on her breasts now, cupping her fullness, gently twisting the hardened tips of her to throbbing need. And she did need. She needed him to never stop.

"Marry me," he said again, his mouth a hairsbreadth from her own. His tongue licked her lips and licked again as they parted to the pleasure.

"Kiss me," she pleaded when he seemed unwilling to do more than tease her to madness with his tongue.

"Marry me and I promise to never stop kissing you."

She couldn't marry him, even if she wished it with every fiber of her being. And Lizzie thought it possible that she did. *The war won't last forever* came a small voice from the far recesses of her mind. But Lizzie knew it would. It would for them. She'd dedicated her life to equality, to freedom. It was what she was. Could she forsake it all and marry into the aristocracy? "Oh God, this can't be happening.''

Jack knew she was wavering and pressed his advantage. His hands caressed her flesh and his mouth drove her mad, moving over her, tickling with featherlight kisses, causing her to gasp with a nibble, and then to groan as his tongue came to soothe the injury. "It is happening. Promise to marry me.''

"You're an earl. I can't.''

"Tell me what you want. I'll do anything." And Jack knew, even after this moment was over, he would. It didn't matter what she asked of him. He'd do anything to have her.

"You're an earl," she repeated. It was impossible. From the beginning she'd thought only to fight all he stood for. She couldn't marry him. She couldn't love him. Lizzie almost gasped at the thought. She couldn't love him, but she did. Oh God, why now?

Lizzie wondered where the fire had gone. How had her resolve to see right win out slipped away? How had she misplaced her zeal, the desperate love she'd once known for her country? It was still there, she promised herself, the emotions softer now that she loved, but there.

"We have to talk," he said.

"We are talking."

"No, I mean seriously. Walk with me in the garden tonight."

And then suddenly from beyond the door, they heard Margaret's voice call out, "Lizzie, Jack. Where are you?"

Lizzie stiffened with dread, expecting the door to open any second. A hand closed over her mouth and Jack whispered, near her ear, "Quiet."

They heard the bedroom door close and both breathed a sigh of relief. "How long have we been in here?"

"A few minutes."

"Oh God, I can't do this in the dark," Lizzie said, trying to find the sleeves of her dress.

"I'll open the door."

Something clicked under the pressure of his hand. Neither realized that the sound was the lock jamming permanently into place. Jack shook the doorknob and tried again. Nothing.

"What's the matter?"

"Don't panic, but I can't open the door."

"Open the other one."

"There isn't another one. I lied. This is a closet."

"Jack!" She shoved his hand aside and reached for the knob herself. Lizzie gave not a thought to the fact

that she was still half-naked as she twisted and turned
and yanked to no avail. Finally she kicked the solid oak
door and groaned as pain sliced up her foot and leg,
straight into her brain. "What kind of fool puts a lock
on a closet door?"

"I don't know. I didn't build it."

"We could die in here," she gasped, panic setting in
at the thought. If her mother didn't come back, they
might never be found. No one could hear their cries
through walls so thick. "I'm growing light-headed."
Her breathing grew heavy, strained. "There's not
enough air."

"You're letting your imagination run away with
you."

"No, truly, I can't breathe."

"Lizzie, there's space under the door. Calm down."

Lizzie looked at the floor then. Jack was right. There
was at least an inch between the door and the floor.
"Thank God," she breathed on a deep sigh. "Help me
with this dress."

The moment her clothing was in order again, Jack
began to thrust his full weight against the door. The
doorjamb splintered after three tries.

After the evening meal, the family gathered in the
drawing room. Margaret and Annie sipped their tea,
while Jack and Andrew enjoyed glasses of port. The two
boys played a game of cards on the floor, while Alice
found nothing in the room more interesting than her
mother's frilly cap. After some tugging, she managed to
pull it from Lizzie's hair, and with stubby fingers tried
to put it on her own head. Lizzie came to her aid. Holding the too large cap over the baby's head, she exclaimed, "What a pretty little girl," and then hugged
the little one to her breast. Loud smacking kisses were
shared.

Soon enough Missy arrived, ready to see to the children. The boys protested that it wasn't time for bed, but smiled again when reminded of Lizzie's plans for the following day, a picnic at the beach. Moments after the room quieted, Jack asked Lizzie to join him in the garden.

His arm slid around her waist as they moved down one of the paths. "We have to talk."

Lizzie nodded but said nothing further until they reached a bench surrounded by flowering bushes.

Lizzie stood before him. Jack nodded toward the bench. "Wouldn't we be more comfortable if we sat?"

"No." Lizzie smiled. "I have to tell you something." Lizzie had had most of the day to think on her words, and still she wasn't at all sure what she was going to say. He'd asked her to marry him, and she desperately wanted to say yes. But there were obstacles, things that, as a husband, he had every right to know. She couldn't tell him about her subversive activities, of course, lest she involve others, but he should know her mind, her heart. Perhaps together they could think of a way to put aside their differences.

"I take it you want to tell me that you're madly in love and will marry me," he teased.

Lizzie smiled. "Do you love me, Jack?"

"I do. And you love me, too." Lizzie didn't deny the last of his statement, and Jack's heart threatened to choke him with its pounding. He couldn't stand the suspense of it. He had to know the truth. "You do, don't you?"

"Aye."

Jack laughed and brought her hard against him. "You do?" He hugged her tightly, his face buried in the warmth of her neck. "You truly do?"

"Jack, this isn't about love. There's something I must tell you. Something you should know. Perhaps you'd better sit. I find I can't think as well as I might when standing this close to you."

Jack grinned and did as she asked.

There was a long moment of silence before Lizzie finally began with, "Remember I told you once that there is nothing left in New York, that the English had confiscated everything because my father was suspected of treason?"

"I do."

"Well, they were right to suspect him. In truth most of the colonists should be held suspect, for most believe in equality and freedom for all. Some have even dedicated their lives to this cause."

Jack frowned as fear stabbed into his belly. "Are you trying to tell me you've done as much?"

Lizzie knew she could trust this man with her life and didn't hesitate to answer honestly. "I have."

Jack was unsure as to whether he believed her or not. "You mean you were a spy?"

Lizzie's silence was an affirmation in itself.

"Goddamn it!" Jack became instantly enraged. He stood and began to pace. "You mean you chanced your life?"

"The point is, I think, that my beliefs and yours hardly mesh. For years I've worked, thought, lived, and breathed nothing but freedom."

"What does that mean? You'd rather be free than married to me?"

"It means, you're an aristocrat. It means, despite the fact that you're nothing like the rest of your kind, I can't imagine living my life as a countess."

"Well, imagine it, woman," he grated, hardly able to control his anger, "because that's exactly what you'll be."

"Didn't you hear anything I've said? I hate class distinction. I consider the upper class a repulsive, selfish lot of arrogant ignoramuses."

"Why? Because we have titles? A title means nothing. It's a word."

Lizzie frowned. Could he be right? Was she making the biggest decision of her life based on a word? No, he was wrong. It wasn't only a word. It was a way of life. "It's the ruling class."

"Tell me there's no ruling class in the colonies. Tell me everyone is absolutely equal. And you'd be lying." Jack took a deep breath and forced aside his need to rage. It didn't matter what she had done in the past. She was safe now and always would be. "Your ideals are wonderful, Lizzie, and I love you all the more for them, but the truth is, it doesn't matter where a man lives. There's always going to be someone richer, someone who thinks he's better. I don't care if it's England, the colonies, China, or the moon. No one is ever going to be exactly equal to another."

"Perhaps not in money, but what about consideration? That's what the patriots want. Thomas Jefferson said, 'All men are *created* equal.' It means all men should have equal say in their government, that a duke and a butcher should be treated the same. It will come to that, Jack. One day it will."

Jack shrugged in disbelief. "In heaven, perhaps. But on earth, the rich will always have it better. And they will govern, because power comes to those who have money." He let her think on his words for a minute before continuing on with, "After the war is over, Lizzie, I'm afraid things will go back to much the way they were. They have to, because people haven't changed since Adam and Eve. In the end, rulers, their friends and families, will still get priority treatment. Granted you may not find a titled duke or an earl in your country, but otherwise there'll be little difference."

"You can't be right, Jack, or we have fought for nothing."

"It depends how you look at it, I suppose. Your country might very well achieve independence. But independent from England or not, taxes will still be paid and someone will rule. What it comes down to, Lizzie, is that all reasonably free countries are pretty much the same.''

Lizzie had given too much and worked far too long to be swayed from her beliefs with a few words. It couldn't be that simple, she thought, and yet deep down she knew an uncomfortable truth. Jack's logic held some merit. ''I have to think about this.''

''While you're at it, add this to your thoughts. I'm a very rich man, Lizzie. Once we marry, you could bring about a lot of change.''

''What do you mean?''

''I mean you'll have money, a lot of money. Can you imagine what your help could mean to the poorhouses and orphanages, Lizzie? Can you imagine your influence concerning child labor?'' He let that sink in before adding, ''There's much to be done, I'd wager, and a woman as smart as yourself could leave a lasting mark.''

Lizzie's eyes widened as she realized he spoke the truth. She could be of help, and as a countess, perhaps of great help. Why hadn't she thought of it before?

''Let me think a minute. Take a walk around the garden and leave me to my thoughts.''

Jack wasn't sure the wisest move would be to leave her now. She was about to make a decision that would forever affect both their lives. ''I'll let you think, but if you don't mind, I'll stay right here,'' he said, sitting again and reaching for his pipe and tobacco.

Lizzie blotted his presence from her thoughts and began to think over his words. She believed in her cause, believed in it with all her heart. Her father and a thousand others had given their lives for it. It hadn't been in vain. She'd been naive perhaps to imagine freedom would mean perfection. No doubt they'd never find perfection in this lifetime. Still, it would be better.

Jack was right about taxes. Even if the people were free, someone would have to shoulder the cost of running a government. Could it be that he was right about the rest? Was a title only a word, a form of address? Lizzie thought it was not. Indeed it couldn't be if she was going to make any real difference. And suddenly Lizzie had every intention of doing just that.

She giggled softly, imagining the problems she was sure to cause some. She stopped her pacing and stood directly before him. "Are you sure you want to marry me?"

"Absolutely sure. I have been from the first."

"From the first? Swine. You tricked me into loving you."

Jack laughed and pulled her forward, setting her on his lap, her knees on each side of his thighs. "It just took a little time for you to see the brilliance of my plan."

"I shouldn't sit like this."

"You should always sit like this," he corrected, his mouth brushing over her throat, his hands freeing her breasts from confinement.

Lizzie moaned her pleasure. "Your friends are bound to hate me."

"They'll love you."

"They won't after I shame them into doing good deeds."

Jack grinned and brought her more tightly against him. "Even then. How could they help but love you?" He pulled back a bit. "And I don't want to talk about my friends now."

"What do you want to talk . . . ? Oh God, Jack, that feels good."

"Tell me again that you love me."

She laughed, a low, throaty sound. "I never said that."

"Yes, you did. You said, 'Swine, you tricked me into loving you.' "

Lizzie laughed again.

"I love you, Lizzie."

"I'm glad."

Jack chuckled softly and gave her a little squeeze. "Wretch."

"Earl," she returned as if the title were an insult. And then whispered softly, "I love you, Jack," as her lips lifted to his for a kiss.

Chapter 11

A glimmer of light glowed on the horizon when Lizzie mounted Lightning and headed north toward London. She'd be back long before noon, as always, her message delivered to Kent with no one the wiser.

A brief look at her grandfather's notes last night and Lizzie realized the end was near. Cornwallis was ordered north to establish himself at Old Point Comfort, on the north shore of Hampton Roads. If possible, he was to occupy Yorktown as well. Lizzie knew the area, having visited there with a friend while in school. Could it be Cornwallis didn't know he was boxing himself in, his back to the sea? The outcome appeared, even to her untrained eye, inevitable. Lizzie hadn't a doubt that by the time she next heard, the Americans would claim victory over England.

This was the last time, she knew. She was done with spying. Lizzie had once thought it impossible, but a man, Jack Black, the Earl of Dover, was now first in her life. First before country, before politics, first but for God. And Lizzie was counting the days to when she could call herself his wife.

From his bedroom window, Jack watched her leave the house. Always one to sleep lightly, he'd been having trouble accomplishing even that of late. Most every night he tossed and turned, unable to put aside the constant ache he knew, satisfied if he was able to catch an hour or two of rest. He'd heard her footsteps as she moved down the hall. He dressed quickly and reached the front door only to see her speeding down the drive. She turned north at the road.

Lizzie often rode her horse this early, but never in the direction just taken. Her grandfather's property stretched into acre upon acre of paths through woodland. When tiring of woods, Lizzie would race through fields or along the beach. The direction she took this morning led to London. And after the knowledge gained last night, Jack feared she was up to no good.

Lest she discover she was not alone, Jack managed some distance between them, while keeping her in view most of the time.

An hour and a half later, they were in the city, the horses' hooves clanging loudly upon the cobblestone streets. It was early, the shops only now opening for business. And Jack's heart sank as she headed directly for the coffee shop.

Obviously Kent was her contact. Jack was sure of it. She'd told him last night she had been spying for her cause. What she had neglected to tell him was, she was still at it.

There could be no other reason for this early morning visit. Yes, he'd first suspected something between them, but if that were so, her grandfather would not have stood in her way. Granted he might want quite a bit more for his granddaughter than to marry a shopkeeper, but Jack was positive Andrew would not have forbade the union.

Besides, she'd told him she loved him. And Jack knew it was the truth. He and Lizzie had shared too many intimacies. She couldn't have responded as she had in his arms if she were in love with another. No, it wasn't love that drew Lizzie to the coffee shop. At least it wasn't love for a man.

Jack felt torn between grudging admiration and the need to throttle the woman. How much information had he unwittingly given her? he wondered. How much had she stolen from her grandfather's study, overheard during dinner parties, gained by a careless word spoken in her presence? And all reported back to her compatriots. She was a spy. Of all the women in England, how in God's name had he come to love a spy?

Less than ten minutes went by before she left the shop and remounted her horse. She turned her horse and headed south, moving quickly over the road that would bring her home. Jack followed with one thought in mind. This was her last tryst with danger. From this day forward she would put aside all thoughts of country and politics and think only of him.

With her aunt at her side, the boys running ahead, and a baby in her arms, Lizzie trod the last steps to the beach. Amelia spread a blanket over the grass, while Lizzie took a rest and put the baby down. Alice sat on the grass and played with it.

"Where's Uncle Jack?" Joey asked, already digging into the picnic basket.

"Joey," Lizzie said, pulling his hand from the basket and smoothing the towel over the chicken again, "it's not time to eat yet. And your uncle went into the city today. He'll be back this evening."

"But I'm hungry."

"You're always hungry." Lizzie reached into the basket. "Here's a cookie. That should hold you for a bit."

"He's getting fat," Steven announced.

"Am not."

"Are so."

"Stop fighting with your brother," Amelia said.

"He's not my brother."

"Am so," Joey returned.

"I don't want him to be my brother," Steven whined. "Does he have to be?"

"Did we come here to argue or swim?" Lizzie asked as she released the tabs of her skirt and pushed the material down her legs. Next came her shoes, and sitting on the blanket, Lizzie pressed her toes into the cool grass.

"Is that your drawers?" Joey asked, never having seen a lady without her skirt before.

"No, I had Mrs. Sutton make this for me. It's a swimming costume."

"And a wonderful idea. I think I'll have one made," Amelia said.

"You're so stupid," Steven growled to Joey. "Can't you see it's just like ours?"

Lizzie frowned. Steven had been in a temper for days. She rarely came across him that he wasn't fighting or getting himself into some sort of trouble. "What's the matter, Steven?"

Steven shrugged, his mouth tight, the look in his eyes desperately unhappy. "Nothing."

"Something is. You keep picking on Joey, and Missy told me you've been calling out in your sleep."

Steven shrugged.

"Can't you tell me?"

"Do I have to walk down the aisle?"

Lizzie sighed. She wouldn't force him if he truly hated the thought, but Lizzie thought there was more behind his actions than the fear of walking down a church aisle. "I was hoping my two best chaps could help me out. Don't you want to?"

"I don't want you to go away."

"But I'm not. Your uncle bought a big house only an hour away." Lizzie had every intention of bringing the children with her.

"I won't see you anymore."

"You would if you came to live with us," came a familiar voice directly behind her.

Steven's eyes grew bright with dawning happiness.

"Would you like that?" Jack asked the suddenly radiant boy.

"Bloody hell!"

Amelia grinned.

Joey gasped and then covered his mouth with his hand, stifling a giggle, his delight undeniable.

"A simple yes would have done nicely, Steven."

Steven was missing two of his front teeth. Lizzie thought his smile was the most adorable she'd ever seen. She tackled him suddenly to the ground and tickled him to screeching cries of mercy. "Silly boy. You should have known I wouldn't leave you."

And then as Steven scrambled from her hold, she asked Jack, "Is there something in particular about London you don't like?"

"Why?"

"You never seem to stay there."

"The man is mad for you," Amelia explained.

Jack laughed and made himself comfortable on the blanket. "Truth is, I never went. Mr. Morgan came here. And we finished our business an hour ago." His gaze moved over her dark, loose shirt and trousers, noting the fit and imagining what she'd look like when wet. "I like that."

"It's for swimming," Joey said. "I thought it was her drawers."

"I can see how you might be mistaken."

Lizzie frowned. "You can go into the water now. But stay close to the edge."

Jack watched the boys run to the water. He'd had hours to think. Lizzie was a spy, actively working for her cause. It had taken most of the morning to sort that fact from his anger, his feelings of betrayal, his horror over the possibility of her getting caught. And in the end it came down to one simple fact. He loved this woman more than country, more than God, and because he did, he was just as much a traitor as she.

His one purpose, he vowed, would be to keep her safe from this day forward. And there was only one way. He wasn't going to let her out of his sight. He had no choice in the matter, and neither did she.

She wouldn't be happy with his solution, but Jack cared less for her happiness than her safety. If need be, he'd tell her what he knew. If need be, he'd threaten to expose her. It didn't matter what he was forced to do. In the end he'd have her with him always.

Amelia dozed on the blanket while Lizzie sat at the water's edge with Alice in her arms. The baby splashed happily once she'd grown used to the chilly temperature. Jack stood behind her and watched the boys play. "Come in, Uncle Jack. The water is lovely."

"I haven't a suit."

"Oh, do come in, please," Steven called.

"What do you think?" Jack asked Lizzie.

Lizzie shrugged. "You could wear your breeches."

"They're white."

"Soap and water will clean them again." Lizzie thought she sounded terribly urbane and sophisticated. She only wished she felt as much. She'd never seen him without a shirt and could only imagine what he'd look like. Her heart trembled at the thought.

"You won't be shocked?" he asked.

Lizzie's thoughts were a bit more innocent than those of her betrothed. Still she swallowed, fighting back a shiver of excitement. Would she be shocked to see him half-naked? Lizzie tore her mind from the enticing thought. "If it makes you feel any better, I won't look."

Jack laughed. "You're very brave with Amelia and the boys around."

Lizzie chuckled softly and then directed all of her attention to the baby in her arms.

Lizzie averted her gaze while Jack shed all but his trousers. She didn't look as he splashed his way toward the two boys. Didn't look again until the water came to his neck.

Jack and the two boys played roughly, splashing and dunking one another, until Lizzie thought they were drifting a bit too far out and called, "Jack, don't take them so deep."

It was then that Joey splashed Jack's face and Jack rose from a kneeling position, sputtering and growling threateningly. The water barely reached his thighs. The boys cried out, their squeals of supposed terror abruptly ending as they dove beneath the surface for cover. They came up gasping.

But they didn't gasp as hard as Lizzie. She couldn't seem to catch her breath at all. She knew she shouldn't look and yet couldn't tear her gaze from his body. He was covered, of course; well, from his waist down he was covered. In truth his trousers were modest enough and might have been perfectly acceptable had they not been white and at this moment nearly totally transparent. They clung to thighs that were thick with muscle, to a belly that was flat. Lizzie swallowed, hardly able to breathe as her gaze took in the dark, mysterious, and intriguing bulge below.

He stood glaring at the boys, his arms held wide from his body, in a threatening pose. His broad chest, generously matted with dark hair, narrowed to a waist and slender hips without an ounce of excess flesh.

A pulse throbbed in her throat, almost closing off her ability to breathe. And Lizzie shivered, unable to tear her gaze away. He was beautiful, the most beautiful man she'd ever seen.

And then with a great splash he was beneath the water again. Minutes passed and she'd yet to relax, or breathe normally. She touched her cheeks, hoping the cool water would ease their heat.

A moment later she was back at the blanket, drying the fussing baby, waiting for her heart to stop its painful pounding. She hardly managed the feat when Amelia said, "He's magnificent, isn't he?"

Lizzie felt her cheeks grow warmer. She paid quite a bit of attention to the baby, unable to raise her gaze to Amelia's knowing expression.

Amelia rolled to a sitting position to make room for Lizzie and the baby. "When I was very young, I knew a man who looked like him."

Lizzie glanced up. Amelia's tone had softened; her gaze seemed filled with distance-sweet memories. Lizzie couldn't resist asking, "Did you love him?"

Amelia smiled, her gaze coming back to the present. "I did. Very much."

"What happened?"

"My father refused to allow the match. He was poor, you see, and far beneath us socially."

Lizzie's eyes widened with surprise. "Have you changed so much then? I'd have thought you wouldn't have given up so easily."

Amelia grinned. "I haven't changed. Indeed, I've no doubt my father prayed I would."

"What happened?"

"We became lovers."

Lizzie gasped softly.

"Yes, I was determined to have him, you see. Truly I was a spoiled young girl. And because he was forbidden, I wanted him all the more."

Lizzie thought she could never love someone so much as to become his lover. "And?" she coaxed, her blue eyes wide with interest.

"And we made plans to elope."

Lizzie thought that was the most romantic thing she'd ever heard. "But I thought you never married."

"I didn't. When I told him I was to have his baby, I never saw him again."

Lizzie gasped. "What? Oh, the rotter!"

"Yes, I thought so.

"Once my condition grew obvious, Father searched him out. I'm not sure if it was to kill him or force him to marry me." Amelia chuckled. "Perhaps first the one and then the other. In the end, he was found to have joined the army. Word came that he died in India of fever."

"How awful," Lizzie said. "What did you do?"

"Cried mostly. Too late I realized the disgrace I brought upon my father's name. And then I lost the baby."

"How sad."

"Yes, that was very sad." Even after all these years there was pain in the old woman's eyes. "So you see, there are times when even the most gently raised can be very silly. I should have listened to those who knew better."

Lizzie knew that piece of good sense was a warning directed at her. Of course, Amelia couldn't know that Lizzie had finally admitted her love, that she'd forgotten all about her threats to break it off with Jack. "Is that why you never married?"

Amelia laughed. "Don't imagine me so emotionally damaged as to turn from men. The truth is, after that youthful escapade, I simply never found one I wanted to marry."

Suddenly Lizzie saw a rider coming towards her. It was Red. No doubt he had either information or money for her to deliver to Mr. Kent. Only Lizzie wouldn't be delivering either. She was done with her subversive activities. She knew Red wouldn't stop now that others were about. They'd meet tonight, after the house was dark and all within slept. She'd tell him then that she was done with the business.

Lizzie glanced at the water and the three rollicking within and then at her friend.

"Morning, ma'am, mistress," Red said, slowing his horse to a walk. "A lovely day, isn't it?" He tipped his hat and a moment later continued on down the beach.

Jack was coming up from the water, the boys behind him. Lizzie breathed a sigh of relief as he tied a towel around his waist, but knew only dread that he was coming toward her. Did he suspect the seemingly innocent exchange to be more than a friendly hello? "Who was that?"

"One of the villagers. His name is Red, I think."

"What did he want?"

Lizzie forced her gaze to perfect innocence. "To wish us good morning. Why?"

Jack looked at her for a long moment, realizing for the first time the possibility that she might not have acted alone for her cause. There could be a dozen others in this with her. "No reason. I was surprised to see him on the beach, is all."

"No doubt his intent was to swim. Grandfather doesn't mind the villagers using the beach."

But the man hadn't stopped. If swimming had been his intent, then why hadn't he? Jack thought better of saying anything more on the subject. He wondered, now that he knew the truth, if he'd question everything she did, everyone she spoke to. Jack shrugged, knowing it didn't matter. She was done with her business. She simply didn't know it yet.

"I'm hungry," Joey said, the words breaking the long look between them. "When are we going to eat?"

Except for the night of her ball, Mary Stone had never seen her at her best, Lizzie realized. Indeed, she seemed forever with a baby on her hip, her hair a mess, her skin smeared with mashed food, her dress smudged and wrinkled beyond repair. And now, having just returned from the beach, she knew she looked even worse. Her dress, because of the wet suit beneath, clung where it shouldn't. Her hair was knotted, hanging over her shoulders and blown every which way, her cap long since snatched from her head by a foaming sea. And her skin, hardly in fashion at any time, for Lizzie never wore powder, no doubt glowed a brilliant shade of pink from the sun.

Lizzie sighed and then smiled as warmly as she was able. "Hello, Mrs. Stone. How nice to see you again."

Mary had just arrived for tea, and having given over her gloves and shawl to one of the servants, turned, glanced at Lizzie, and laughed. "What happened?"

"I look a sight, I'm sure. I spent the day with the children at the beach and ended up looking the worse for it, I'm afraid."

"She looks beautiful," Jack said, coming into the hall behind her, his arm reaching possessively around her waist.

Both were wrinkled and damp. It was easy enough to see they had taken advantage of a warm day to do a bit of swimming.

Mary's gaze, filled with interest, moved over Jack. His shirt was only half-buttoned. Lizzie positioned herself directly before him, knowing by her look that the woman imagined a bit too clearly the sight of Jack in wet white pants.

It was clear Mary wanted Jack for herself, and Lizzie could only wonder how far the woman would go to see her goals met.

"Will you be joining us for tea?" Mary asked, her question directed to the man behind Lizzie.

Lizzie ignored the slight and returned as if the question had been asked of her, "I don't think so. Right now I need to clean up."

Missy, the children's nurse, hearing the boys' entrance, came down the stairs and took the baby from her. "Thank you, Missy," Lizzie said. "Could you ask Mrs. Molston to send something to my room?"

"Of course, miss," the nurse returned.

And since he did not respond, Mary asked directly, "What about you, Jack?" Her voice dropped to a low huskiness, filled with meaning, her lashes fluttering madly again. "It's been a while since we shared a warm afternoon."

Jack muffled a curse, feeling color flood his cheeks. "Sorry, not today. I've some business that needs tending."

Lizzie grinned at Jack's discomfort, and leaving the man to follow or fend for himself, she ran up the stairs.

He followed.

Jack managed at last to escape the woman below and, in searching out his lady, heard the ruckus coming from the floor above her room. As he approached the nursery, he heard Steven insisting, "I won't. I don't need a nurse."

Steven stood beside a tub of water, still dressed in soggy clothes. "Come on, Steven," Joey whined, already in the tub. "I want the cake Mummy promised." Jack noticed Joey, the younger of the two, had taken to addressing Lizzie as his mother. He thought Steven would do as much one day. But for the present, Steven wasn't quite ready to trust.

"What's the problem?" Jack asked.

"Steven won't take his bath," Lizzie said, and couldn't resist asking, "Have you finished tending your business?"

Jack's grin was sheepish. "I couldn't think of anything else to say." And then he asked Steven, "Do you think you're clean enough? Is that it?"

Lizzie didn't wait for his answer, but said instead,

"He's not. He's sticky from seawater and sand, and bound to get a rash if he doesn't wash off."

"What's your problem, Steven?"

Steven bit his lip, eyed Lizzie and Missy, and then said softly, "They're girls."

"Oh," Jack said, understanding at once the problem. "And you'd be wanting a bit of privacy, is that it?"

Steven's only response was to look down at the floor.

Lizzie sighed. "Fine. Missy and I will leave, but you cannot bathe alone. Jack will have to stay."

Steven only shrugged. He was pulling off his shirt as Jack shot Lizzie a bold look and topped it off with an even bolder wink. "Don't worry, his modesty won't last."

Lizzie laughed as the baby splashed water everywhere. "I think she's part mermaid," she said to the nurse. "I've never seen a child love the water so. You should have seen the fuss she made today when I dried her at the beach."

"The boys are dry, in their nightshirts, and waiting in the nursery for their treats," Jack said from the doorway.

Missy nodded and left the room to see to the boys and their never-ending appetites. Jack smiled as he watched Lizzie pamper the baby. "Do you do this every night?"

"When there are no guests for dinner, and I don't have to dress."

Her hair had fallen from its pins again, and water stains splashed over the bodice of her dress as she moved a soapy cloth over the gurgling baby.

"Some people think bathing too often can cause one to take a chill."

Lizzie glanced up from her chore at the huskiness of his words. "I don't believe it." She frowned. "Are you all right? You aren't coming down with something, are you?"

"I'm fine," he said, after clearing his voice.

"I've read the Japanese do it every day. Entire families bathe together, and to my knowledge, they haven't died off yet.

"Indeed, I think we could take a lesson from our Oriental cousins. I doubt they wait five weeks before washing their clothes as do most whites."

"Do they get into the tub all at once?" Jack brought the subject back to bathing. He'd visited Japan during his youthful travels and knew firsthand the luxury of a bathhouse.

"It's not a tub so much as a pool. I think they wash first."

"That sounds intriguing."

Lizzie frowned, and in her innocence wondered what he was getting at.

"I mean, all of them being naked, men and women together."

Lizzie shot him a wry glance. "I haven't a doubt you'd imagine as much."

"What do you suppose they do in those pools?"

"I *suppose* we could change the subject. I'm sorry I said anything."

Jack laughed. "Why? Don't you like the Japanese?"

"The Japanese are probably lovely people. It's you I don't like."

"You owe me a kiss for that. Perhaps I shall demand one every time you lie."

"Will you?" Lizzie grinned wickedly. "In that case you have a wart on your nose."

Jack ran his hand over his nose and smiled. "Two."

"And your ears are crooked."

"Three. It couldn't be that you want me to kiss you, could it?"

"Certainly not." Lizzie laughed delightedly and shot him her most saucy look. "And in case you're still counting, that's four."

Jack's heart melted.

Lizzie took the baby from her tub, cuddled her into a fluffy towel, and then nuzzled her face into Alice's neck. "Babies smell so good when they're fresh from their baths."

Jack moved behind her and took both woman and child into his arms. "Let me find Missy and have her finish this. Mrs. Stone is staying for dinner. You'll want to get ready."

Lizzie moaned and then dropped her head back to Jack's shoulder. "Lord, why?" she asked, her gaze moving to the ceiling.

Jack took it upon himself to answer. "Because your mother invited her."

"Because there are only a few more days to the wedding and she's hoping you'll change your mind," Lizzie corrected.

"She knows I won't. I think she's hoping you will." Jack sighed. "She'll be up to no good, I know it."

"Don't worry. We'll act the loving couple."

"We are a loving couple."

"So what can she do?"

"She could say things."

"I'll ignore them."

"You probably won't," Jack sighed. "And then you'll be angry with me again."

Lizzie turned and kissed him. Jack was stunned into immobility, his heart thundering in his chest, for she'd kissed him for the first time, and with feeling. Kissed him without being tricked or coerced into it.

"Just act as if you're mad for me," she said.

Jack grabbed her around her waist and brought her tightly against him, almost squashing the baby between them. He buried his face in her hair, breathing in the clean, lemony scent. "God, I don't have to act it. I already am."

Lizzie thrilled at his words and totally forgot what

she'd been about to say. "You have a shocking effect on a lady's concentration. There's something I have to do, and I've quite forgotten what it was."

"Dinner. You have to dress."

"Oh," she said softly, while nuzzling her mouth to his throat. "Yes."

"Everyone is busy, either with the children or the company downstairs. I'll help you."

Lizzie giggled softly. "Here," she said, handing the baby over. "Watch Alice until Missy gets back."

Lizzie dressed carefully. In a gown of emerald green silk, with her hair piled high into a mass of golden curls, she quite stole his breath. Jack watched her descend the stairs, realizing it hardly mattered what she wore, for each sighting of her only brought him closer to the brink of desperation. He had to have her.

Standing before him, Lizzie shot him a bold wink. "So what do you think?"

It was the saucy wink that did it. Jack was totally lost and held no hope to ever again be in control of his own mind. If she asked him to break into the palace and kidnap King George, Jack thought he wouldn't have been able to refuse. "I think I wouldn't mind if you lied to me six or seven more times."

Lizzie's girlish laughter only reminded him that she didn't look anything like a girl. "You already owe me four. And I look smashing, thank you."

"Actually, I was thinking closer to gorgeous."

"Good, I need to be gorgeous for a change. Mrs. Stone never sees me but with a child crawling over me."

"You're gorgeous then, too."

Lizzie smiled at the compliment and fluttered her lashes outrageously.

"What's the matter with your eyes?"

"How is it you don't ask as much of Mrs. Stone when she does that?"

"Does she do that?" Jack asked, unable to remember if she did or not.

Lizzie laughed again, satisfied that Mrs. Stone made far less of an impression than she thought. "Are you ready?"

Jack thought it was time for one more gift. "Almost. I thought you'd like to wear this tonight." He took a velvet box from his pocket.

Inside, on a bed of black satin, sat a diamond necklace. At its center was an enormous square-cut emerald. It was the most extravagant thing Lizzie had ever seen. "You didn't buy this for me, did you?"

Jack had, of course. Indeed, his intent was to buy her dozens more. "Don't you like it?"

"It's beautiful, but it's . . ."

"Too expensive," they said in unison.

Lizzie laughed. "Well, it is."

"It belonged to my mother," he lied. "Will you wear it tonight?"

She shook her head. "I'd die if something happened to it."

"Nothing will happen. I want to see it on you."

Lizzie hesitated for only a moment. She couldn't resist. The necklace was simply too lovely. She turned her back to him. "Fasten it for me."

Jack locked the necklace in place, and after sampling a taste of her neck and a little of her shoulder, and delighting in her soft sigh of enjoyment, he slid her dress back into place and turned her to face him. "I can't imagine a woman more beautiful."

The tips of her fingers touched the necklace, fingering the huge stone. "Everyone will think you bought it." She glanced at her hand, and then narrowed her gaze as she said, "It matches my ring."

"A bit of good luck, wouldn't you say?"

Lizzie didn't believe him. How could it be that his

mother's necklace just happened to exactly match her ring? "Are you telling me the truth?"

"What? That you're the most beautiful woman I've ever seen? Of course."

"Did you buy it?"

"Yes."

"Oh, Lord."

"Now, don't get upset. It's only a little trinket."

"Little trinket," Lizzie repeated in disbelief. "If you keep this up, I'll be permanently weighed down by these little trinkets."

"Oh there you are," Mary Stone said, coming from the sitting room and sliding her hand in a most familiar fashion up Jack's arm. She didn't miss the spectacular necklace at Lizzie's throat, even as she directed her attention to Jack. "We were waiting for you."

Lizzie forgot about the necklace. Indeed she couldn't think of anything beyond Mrs. Stone touching Jack. The woman was bold to be sure and dead set upon getting what she wanted: Jack. Well, that was too bad, wasn't it? The man belonged to her.

Lizzie managed to move between them, effectively shoving Mrs. Stone aside with a well-placed elbow to the woman's midsection. "Oh, sorry," she said, and then turned to Jack. "Thank you, darling." She kissed him until Mary Stone breathed a disappointed sigh and walked back into the drawing room.

"I got rid of her. Tell me I'm brilliant."

"You are," Jack said. And then, fitting her more closely against him, he murmured, "If we do it again, do you think she'll go home?"

Lizzie laughed and took his arm. "Let's go."

Jack didn't miss the look in Lizzie's eyes. "I'm beginning to feel sorry for her."

"Yes, poor thing," Lizzie returned, without a glimmer of the emotion her words implied.

"Oh, Lizzie, it's beautiful," Margaret said the moment the young couple entered the drawing room.

"Jack just gave it to me," Lizzie returned, her fingers brushing again over the huge stone. "You don't think it's too big, do you?"

"A bit," Mary Stone said waspishly. "You're such a tiny creature. Too small, I think, to wear jewelry so large."

"I think it's perfect," Margaret said.

"As do I," Amelia said, shooting Mrs. Stone a hard look.

"I think it needs earrings to match," Jack added.

"They had better be small earrings," Lizzie warned, and Jack thought he'd take back the set he'd already bought.

Andrew beamed, and Lizzie felt her good mood increase tenfold. He took her aside and whispered, "I'm so pleased. I couldn't have asked more for you."

Lizzie, too, was pleased. Her engagement, a sham in the beginning, was now true. Her blue eyes sparkled with happiness, with love. Love for all God's creatures, and her family most especially.

"I love you, Gran," she said, reaching up to kiss his cheek. "I truly do."

Lizzie soon realized there wasn't one guest for dinner, but a party. Lord Manning, from the prime minister's staff, had come earlier that day. And after conferring with her grandfather for most of the afternoon, he'd stayed on, his intent to leave in the morning.

Lizzie was pleasantly surprised to find the Thumbolts and Michael also invited. Michael prowled the room awaiting Annie's arrival. Margaret sat with Katherine Thumbolt on the settee. Lizzie and Amelia sat in chairs opposite them, while Mary Stone flirted outrageously with all the men in the room.

Conversation between the ladies soon turned to the orphanage and its fine addition.

"Everyone is talking about your nice young man,"

Mrs. Thumbolt said. "No one expected that he would shoulder the entire cost."

Lizzie's eyes widened, for she hadn't expected as much herself.

"Mr. Thumbolt tells me a fund has been set up. And that most every youngster at the orphanage will now have an opportunity to go to school."

Lizzie was astonished. No one had to tell her that Jack was the benefactor. Lizzie knew the man had money. Still, she hadn't expected he had that much. A moment later she excused herself and joined Jack at the far end of the room. Apparently it was his turn to be the recipient of Mary's attention.

"Would you excuse us for a minute, Mrs. Stone? I'd like a word in private with my fiancé."

Mary Stone was obviously unhappy, having no choice but to leave the two alone. She shot Lizzie a condescending glance, smiled provocatively at Jack, and then walked away.

Jack sighed his relief. "Thank you, and I'd appreciate it if you wouldn't leave me alone with her again."

"Why? What did she say?"

Jack thought Lizzie was probably better off not knowing that Mary had just invited him to walk with her in the garden, boldly stating the things she could do for him if he'd be so kind. He looked almost desperate when he asked, "Can't we forget about her?"

Lizzie smiled and said simply, "Done."

"Good. Now, what did you want to talk to me about?"

"How much money do you have?"

Jack laughed in surprise at the straightforward question. "I don't know for sure. Why?"

"Because you're spending it like you've an endless supply."

"Am I?"

"Why didn't you take the offers of help?"

Jack looked confused for a moment and then said, "Oh, you mean the orphanage? I did take them. We created a fund for the children's schooling."

"The impression is you are the sole benefactor."

"I'm not. Mr. Thumbolt contributed quite a bit, as did some of the others in the parish."

"At your urging, no doubt."

Jack smiled. "I might have said a word or two."

"And you didn't tell me any of it?"

"I wasn't keeping secrets, Lizzie." Jack looked at her for several seconds longer before shrugging. "I didn't think to tell you."

Lizzie felt a chill race up her spine at his long look and could only wonder at its cause. He wasn't keeping secrets, he said. Could it mean, then, that he knew she was? That he knew she hadn't told him all of it? No, he couldn't know, she silently countered. He would have said something, done something, if he knew.

Lizzie smiled and sipped from her drink as she watched Mrs. Stone bat her lashes at Lord Manning. "It seems our guest has found other prey."

"Only temporarily, I'm sure," Jack said with a touch of despair.

Lizzie's eyes widened with surprise. "Are you that assured of your worth?"

"No, only sure that she's spoiled. And spoiled women rarely give up that easily."

Lizzie tapped his chin with one finger. And then without thinking, ran her finger over his lips. She felt her fingertip tingle, and then her entire body suffered under the suddenly tremendous sensation. Her heart stumbled and she found she had to force her hand to her side, her breathing back to normal. "Poor baby," she managed at last, in a voice she hardly recognized.

Jack had a time of it keeping his hands to himself, his needs under control, his body from displaying those needs. She hadn't meant for it to happen. No doubt she hadn't totally understood the emotion that had passed between them, but he knew the tiny glimpse of passion had nearly rocked him to the core of his being. He cleared his throat. How much longer could he hold out? How much longer must he wait? "You might laugh, Lizzie, but it's not the least bit amusing. If she has a notion, she could ruin our lives."

"Don't worry, Jack. I'll protect you."

Jack smiled at that. "You'd best stop your teasing or I'm afraid I won't have a choice but to take you into the garden after dinner and kiss you senseless."

"You won't?" Lizzie laughed, not only at his shocking conclusion, but the very proper way the most improper intentions were said. "But suppose it doesn't work. Suppose I tease you still. What will you do then?"

"You're a very wicked lady, Lizzie."

"Am I?"

"And wicked ladies make me think of tubs."

"Tubs?" she asked, surprised, and then frowned in confusion. "How odd. Do they always?"

Jack grinned. "And it just so happens that your grandfather's bathhouse has one big enough for two."

Lizzie only blinked.

"Perhaps I should take you there instead of the garden."

Lizzie waved her fan before her face, feeling it warm with color, and exclaimed, "And I'm wicked? Truthfully, I've never imagined such a thing."

"Perhaps, but you won't stop thinking about it now that I've mentioned it."

"Beast," Lizzie said, knowing it was the truth. "You did that on purpose."

Jack's laughter was cut short at the sound of Lord Manning sputtering and then choking on his drink. All eyes followed his gaze to the doorway.

Annie said not a word. She didn't have to. She looked

at first to be wearing a bunch of carrots. Wild and burnt, orange hair stuck out in all directions from her head.

"Good Lord, what have you done to your hair?" Margaret gasped, coming instantly from the settee and spilling her wine down the front of her dress. "My God, your beautiful hair. Annie, how could you?"

Annie touched her hair and said a bit sheepishly, "It didn't turn out exactly as I planned."

"It was that damn actress," Andrew bellowed. "We should never have gone."

"What actress?" Mary asked.

"Angel Markham," Annie said. "We saw her in London. She has the most beautiful hair."

Lizzie realized her sister had yet to put aside her admiration of the lovely Miss Markham.

"Damn it, Margaret!" Andrew growled, moving close to his daughter. "I thought you were going to talk to her."

"I did!" Margaret said, and then to her daughter she said, "Come along, Annie, we'll have to do something with it. At the very least it can be brought under some sort of control and covered by one of your pretty caps."

Michael didn't seem to mind the color of Annie's hair. Lizzie wondered if it would have made any difference had her sister shaved it off. Indeed the young man was smitten.

Lizzie thought by next year her sister would have a dozen or more beaus to choose from. Hopefully by then she would have put aside her absurd need to be an actress.

Jack did not take her into the garden after dinner. The men stayed at the table and smoked their pipes and cigars, while the women moved to the terrace for a breath of air. A side table had been set up. On it stood a tea service as well as cognac, port, and appropriate glasses. Lizzie sipped from a snifter of brandy. Mary, despite her vows that a lady would not partake of strong spirits, joined her hostess. Margaret and the rest had tea.

Margaret, still upset with her younger daughter, soon went off in search of something that could bring Annie's hair to a more natural shade. She returned empty-handed. "We'll have to go to London. No one here knows what to do."

"It might not look too bad if it were darkened a bit," Katherine Thumbolt said.

"I can't believe this happened. The ball is only a few days away. What are we going to do?" she asked, desperate to see the damage undone. Despite the fact that Annie had not yet made her coming out, she was to attend the ball as part of Lizzie's wedding party.

"I'm sure we'll find something in London, Mother. Don't fret so."

"I could wear a wig," Annie offered.

Margaret only moaned.

Michael stood suddenly among the women and said to Annie, "You said you wanted to show me your new horse."

Annie jumped to her feet. "Oh yes, I forgot." The two disappeared into the garden, heading for the stables to the rear of the house.

Lizzie thought they were probably going to the barn, but doubted, most especially upon realizing the look in Michael's eyes, that his intent was to see Annie's new horse.

"Oh yes, the ball," Mary said after Annie and Michael had gone off. "It should be a lovely affair, wouldn't you agree?"

Lizzie smiled. "Quite lovely, I'm sure."

"Odd, but you don't seem excited. Aren't you thrilled to be marrying Jack?"

Lizzie responded with a low, deliciously secret laugh.

Mary glared at her. "And you'll honeymoon, I expect. Have you decided where?"

"Jack wants to surprise me."

"How sweet," Mary said, her tone pure condescension.

It was then that the men joined them, and conversation soon turned to the robberies that were suddenly plaguing the area. "The Petersons were robbed last week," Andrew said. "It's the sixth in nearly as many months."

"No one was hurt, thank God," Margaret said.

Mr. Thumbolt remarked, "Obviously they know when the houses are empty. They only break in then."

"Do you think we're being watched?" Amelia asked.

"I don't think we have anything to fear. It's only the very wealthy that are bothered," Lizzie said, trying to ease her aunt's worry.

"I've hired guards, I don't mind telling you." Mary shivered delicately. "It's terrifying to think a woman isn't safe in her own home."

"Perhaps you should marry again," Margaret proposed. "You're bound to feel safer with a man in the house."

Mary was of the opinion that she needn't marry to keep a man in her house, and everyone present knew it. Still, she looked directly at Jack, her voice filled with bold suggestion, as she said, "Yes, perhaps I might."

Tension was suddenly thick. Just about everyone stared at the woman, amazed at her daring. And then their gazes moved to Lizzie as they waited for her to say something. But Lizzie decided not to allow this woman to draw her into open hostilities.

"I hope you do, Mrs. Stone," Lizzie said as she stood from her chair and walked to Jack. She leaned into him, and he slipped an arm around her waist. "And I hope you'll be as happy as we are."

*   *   *

It was late. Amelia had returned to her small house, and the Thumbolts had bid all good night some time ago. Lord Manning had retired for the night, as had her grandfather. Margaret and Annie were also upstairs, no doubt trying to find a solution to orange hair, while Lizzie wondered when Mary would leave. She'd yawned a few times, but the woman seemed oblivious to her subtle hints.

Lizzie planned to talk to Red that evening, but knew he wouldn't come near the house until well after all were settled for the night. What was the matter with Mrs. Stone? Why wouldn't she leave?

Jack had yet to return from walking Aunt Amelia home. Lizzie was alone with Mrs. Stone. She had just finished what had to be her sixth glass of brandy and she finally stood.

At last, Lizzie mused in silent relief. The woman was going home. Only it appeared she wasn't, at least not before saying her piece.

"As you've no doubt assumed, Jack and I are close friends. Of course, there was a time when we discussed marriage—"

Overhearing the woman's words, Jack stopped just short of the terrace and stood in shadows, marveling at the lie. Firstly, they were hardly friends, and secondly, he couldn't remember discussing a damn thing with the woman unless one counted their preferences once in bed.

"—but I never imagined he'd choose someone so young, so inexperienced and unsophisticated."

"I take it you imagined his tastes ran more towards older women?" Lizzie knew it was a cutting low blow, but she'd had enough of Mrs. Stone, her snide comments, her barely veiled mockery. Most of all, she'd had enough of her touching Jack. And if she knew what was good for her, she wouldn't touch him again. "As you can see, Jack might have dallied with that sort for a time, but he's marrying me.''

Mary laughed. ''No doubt, dear, but after the marriage, a little girl like you can't hope to keep a man like Jack. I only hope you won't be too hurt upon discovering his little indulgences.''

Lizzie stiffened at the thought. It had never entered her mind that Jack might dally with another. ''Jack has vowed loyalty. Do you imagine him to be a liar?''

''Certainly not. But men are weak. Sometimes they can't help a roving eye. You know how it is, I'm sure.''

''Actually, Mrs. Stone, I haven't a clue.''

Mary laughed. ''I can see what he admires in you. Still, innocence can only go so far toward keeping a man. He's bound to grow bored eventually.''

''I don't think so, Mary,'' Jack said suddenly, appearing from the shadows and walking to Lizzie's side. His arm circled her waist and brought her against him in a loving embrace. ''In truth, I'd say innocence can be most refreshing.''

Mary was obviously sorry that Jack had heard her comments. She looked suddenly trapped and then shrugged. ''You'll tire of her soon enough, darling, I've no doubt.''

''Nor I,'' Jack said in agreement, while looking down into Lizzie's wide blue eyes. ''I can guarantee it won't last beyond forty or fifty years.''

Later, on the ride home, Mary thought over her problem. She'd been a bit too bold, too outspoken. And things hadn't worked out exactly as she'd planned. She shrugged, knowing it didn't matter. She'd planted a seed of doubt that would take hold soon enough.

It didn't matter that Jack had declared himself tonight. Such nonsense wasn't about to influence her thinking.

He was besotted, to be sure, but certainly not in love. Men like Jack simply did not fall in love.

Lizzie was different from most. An innocent. Still, Mary knew men and their preferences. She had every confidence that Jack would soon tire of her. And when he did, she'd be there, perfectly willing to share him with his wife.

Chapter 12

~~~⌒⌒⌒~~~

Jack stood within the shadows of a huge elm, studying the dark sky and the smattering of stars that glittered between low-hanging clouds. Tonight, like most nights, he found it impossible to sleep. His problems were twofold. One was desire, a constant and aching need that had grown to mammoth proportions these last weeks. The other was the terror he knew at Lizzie's involvement in traitorous dealings. Jack hadn't a doubt what would become of her should she be found out. Traitors to the Crown were hung, without exception. The fact that this one was a woman would bear no consideration.

Jack knew there was but one solution. He had to confront her and force a promise from her—make her swear she was done with spying forever. She might fight him on that score, but she wouldn't win. He didn't care what he had to do, what he had to threaten.

The wedding was a few days away. As he puffed on his pipe, Jack smiled at the thought of sharing his life with a rebel. She was trouble to be sure. Trouble that was bound to last him a lifetime, and he could hardly wait for it to begin.

His gaze moved over the large house, noting her window and the dim light that flickered within. She wasn't asleep. Jack had hardly had a moment alone with her all day and certainly hadn't had the chance to bring up the subject of spying. Perhaps he could do it now. And just maybe, if he heard the things he needed to hear, he could sleep.

Jack pushed himself from the tree, anxious to set his mind at ease. It was then that he noticed candlelight in the library. Someone had just entered that room and he wondered who could be about at this hour.

Lizzie moved silently into the room. The house was quiet. Everyone slept.

She sat at her grandfather's desk, watching through the library doors, waiting for Red's arrival. A folder rested at the top of a pile. It hadn't been put away. The most recent ones never were.

Lizzie felt a surge of excitement and then shook off the emotion. She wouldn't look at it. She'd sworn she was done with that part of her life, that there were others who could take her place, that the war was nearly over in any case. She ignored the folder. She wasn't interested. There could be a dozen folders and she still wouldn't be interested. Her gaze moved to the doors again. The clock on the mantel seemed to tick loudly. Where was Red? Again she glanced at the folder and looked away. And then, almost as if it had a will of its own, her hand lifted the cover. She simply couldn't resist. Just a little look, she thought. Surely at this late date, it hardly mattered.

Lizzie frowned, her heart quickening as her gaze scanned the first paper. She'd been so sure that the end was near. Lord, but she hadn't expected this last-ditch effort. A low groan escaped her throat, for she knew Washington wouldn't expect it either.

She had to get this information to Mr. Kent. And there wasn't a second to lose.

Jack watched through the library window. His heart thundered in his chest as he fought back a wave of terror, of rage, that she dared to chance her life. Damn her! Damn her to hell! Lord Manning was still here. Suppose he, too, hadn't been able to sleep. Suppose he stepped into the library, for a book, only to catch her going through confidential documents.

Jack almost groaned aloud at the thought. He'd die if she were discovered. His mouth tightened as he vowed that she wouldn't be. At least not on this day, and if he had anything to say about it, not ever.

Approaching the library doors, ready to confront her with his knowledge, he saw her line up Andrew's papers and slip them back into the folder. A moment later she pocketed her spectacles and was moving toward him, obviously about to step outside. Jack dove into the shrubbery, knowing something to be afoot. Hidden among the greenery, he watched as she walked to the corner of the house.

Now what the hell was she up to?

Jack hadn't long to think on his silent question, for within seconds a man turned the corner on horseback.

Jack's gaze narrowed as he peered through the bush. She could only be up to no good.

"Did everything go well?"

A man's voice returned, "As always, missy."

Jack strained to hear but caught only a word here and there. And then he heard the name Peterson, and an accompanying murmur of laughter. It was all he needed to realize what she was about. The man handed her a small pouch. Lizzie seemed to weigh it in her hand before handing it back. They moved off to a small grove of trees a few feet from the house. Jack couldn't see them. He slithered along the outer walls, moving toward the corner, until he could hear.

"I need you to go to London tomorrow, first thing," Lizzie said. She wasn't due to leave until the day after. Lizzie thought she wouldn't push her luck by going two days in a row. And what with Annie's hair problems and the coming ball, Lizzie wasn't sure when she'd be able to find a spare minute.

Her information was urgent. Mr. Kent should know about this new turn of events as soon as possible. Lizzie gave him directions to the coffeehouse, told him who he was to ask for, and said, "Tell him the English are about to make one last-ditch effort, that public opinion is going against the war, that they have to finish it quickly. Word has it sixty thousand are to be called up."

A moment later Red nodded and then moved off into the darkness.

Lizzie returned to the library again, locked the door, and pulled the heavy curtains into place. She turned and almost screamed until she realized it was Jack standing there. "Oh my God," she gasped, her hand coming to her throat. "You gave me such a fright."

His words were grated through clenched teeth as he said, "Nothing, I'm sure, to compare to the one you gave me." Jack knew he'd given her a terrible scare, but it was his own fright that still sent shivers of horror up his spine. That she'd met with a man in the dark of night. That a woman as small and defenseless as herself had put herself in untold danger. That she chanced death for her miserable cause.

He was furious. No doubt this wasn't the time to confront her, and yet he seemed to have no choice. He'd confront her or explode.

Lizzie said weakly, "Were you about to step outside?"

Jack thought he'd never seen anyone look so guilty. "I've been outside."

"Were you?" Her eyes widened and she glanced to

her left and right, anywhere but at him. "I didn't see—"

"You weren't supposed to." Jack took a menacing step forward and knew some satisfaction when Lizzie quickly backed up. "It seems you forgot to tell me something."

She did not respond.

"Perhaps the fact that you are still working for your wretched cause."

"It's not wretched," Lizzie returned, and then breathed a sigh. "I knew I shouldn't have said anything. You wouldn't have suspected a thing if—"

"That's your answer?" Jack was practically shaking with rage. "That you shouldn't have told me?" His gaze filled with disgust. "Only a spy could imagine that secrets are the way to begin a marriage."

"Lower your voice; you'll awaken the entire house."

Jack knew they were far enough away from the rest of the house to ensure privacy. The others couldn't hear them unless they were already downstairs, and even then they'd have to be close to the library doors. "And we couldn't have that," he grated, taking another step forward. "Could we, Lizzie? Spies are at their best sneaking around in the dark while decent people sleep."

"You needn't try to make what I do sound filthy."

"It is filthy, goddamn it! What could be lower than a spy?"

"Perhaps an aristocrat who couldn't care less that hundreds are dying every day. At least I'm trying to shorten this godforsaken war."

"Bloody goddamn liar!" he bellowed. "What you mean is, you're trying to win the war. You couldn't care less how long it takes, or how many men have to die. Just as long as you win.

"And don't try to twist the facts, to lay the blame at my feet. Your contemptible acts are yours alone."

Lizzie didn't have any excuses except for love of country, only love hadn't been the driving force behind what she'd done tonight. It was like a drug, an exhilaration unlike any other. She'd sworn she was done with it, but had given in to the first temptation. Was it possible that she couldn't stop? "You knew what I was," she returned defensively.

" 'Was' being the crucial word here, Lizzie. I knew what you were, not what you are. Damn me for a fool, for holding you above all others."

Lizzie reached for his arm. Jack shook off her touch, walked toward the fireplace, and sat in a nearby chair. He couldn't be near her now. He couldn't allow her to touch him.

"Jack, I've done with it."

Jack laughed. "And I'm supposed to believe that? What was this morning then? Your little meeting with Kent." Lizzie's eyes widened. "Yes, I followed you. And the man you met with tonight. What has he to do with it all?"

"What man?"

"I saw you, Lizzie. I saw you walk to the edge of the house and talk to him."

Silence.

"Fine," Jack said, coming instantly from his chair. Lizzie jumped back. He shot her a hard grin and then walked to the library door, locked it, and pocketed the key. "But you will tell me."

"What does that mean?"

Jack knew no matter what she was, he hadn't the strength to let this woman go. He didn't care if she was a spy, a murderer, a thief, or worse. Nothing she did mattered. He wanted her, loved her, no matter what she was or perhaps because of what she was. He felt his heart squeeze with terror at the power she held over him, at the pain she could cause him, at what she'd been involved in tonight, at the chances she'd taken with her safety, and remembered how he'd felt nearly frozen with terror. He suffered and, because of that suffering, had to fight to hold his control. Purposely avoiding her, he returned to the chair. "It means you will tell me, Lizzie, exactly what you've been doing. Now!" he said, louder than she might have liked.

"Jack, we can talk about this tomorrow. We're both tired and upset. We shouldn't—"

"We'll talk about it now," he snapped. "I'm not giving you the chance to think up another lie."

"I haven't lied to you." She hesitated and then went on with, "Except perhaps by omission."

"Perhaps?" he mocked. "Then I'd say it's time to take care of that little oversight, wouldn't you agree? You can start with the fact that you're gathering information for your sorry cause from your grandfather's papers, and go on from there."

Lizzie dropped into the seat opposite him and sighed. "You already know the truth. I report every piece of information I come across. What more can I say?"

"God Almighty," Jack whispered on a sigh. "How long have you been at it?"

"Almost since I first came here."

"Why? Why the bloody hell would you chance your life?" Jack saw she was about to respond, saw the fanatical look come again into her eyes, and said, "Forget it. I've already heard your pathetic monologue. What about the man tonight? Who is he?"

"He's a friend."

For the first time Jack's anger was displaced by a wave of jealousy. "A close friend?"

Lizzie scowled, understanding the question behind the question. "Of course not. You're being ridiculous."

"I'm ridiculous? You're the spy and *I'm* ridiculous?"

"Calm down."

"Who is he, Lizzie?"

Silence.

"All right, if you won't tell me, perhaps I can tell you. Let's see, Red and Seth are robbing the local estates, selling the merchandise and giving the money to you. You smuggle the gold out, probably by way of Mr. Kent. How close am I to the truth?"

He wasn't close; he was exactly right. Lizzie's jaw dropped open. "Good God! How could you know?"

"Lizzie, you aren't the only one able to put a few facts together. First of all, I thought something was afoot during our first visit to the coffee shop." Jack remembered her attempts to cover the familiarity between herself and Kent. His gaze narrowed accusingly. "And in case you aren't sure, your response to my questions then were lies." He sighed and slowly shook his head, wondering how he could have been so foolish as to lose his heart to this woman. England abounded in lovely women. Why did it have to be this one? "And this morning, after your meeting with Kent, everything fell into place."

"Because I told you what I was doing in New York. I shouldn't have."

Jack thought she was probably right. If she hadn't told him, he never would have become suspicious in the first place.

"How long have you been watching me?"

"You might not believe it, but everyone is not equally inclined toward spying. I was outside tonight, thinking about this morning and your ride to London and what I was going to do about it, when I saw you enter the library. A few minutes later your friend arrived. He mentioned the Petersons as he jingled a bag of coins. We spoke about the robbery tonight, if you remember." He looked at her hands. "By the way, where's the money?"

"I gave it back. I told you I was done with my work. That was one of the reasons . . . I mean, I told Mr. Kent today."

"One of the reasons? You mean you told him after you gave him another piece of information."

Lizzie did not deny the truth. She lowered her gaze to her lap, and Jack sighed.

After a long moment she asked, "How could you have known about Red and Seth?"

"Even in moonlight one cannot miss the color of his hair, and Seth is his best friend." Jack waited a second before continuing. "I doubt one would be involved and not the other." Jack poured himself a drink and downed it in one gulp. "By the way, you might mention the possibility that he wear something over his head during his next mission. But you'll have to do it in a note, I'm afraid. You won't be seeing either of them again."

"God, you're insufferably arrogant." This was the first time anyone had ever told her whom she might or might not see.

"Surely no more than you."

"We're not discussing me at the moment." There was another moment of silence before she said, "Jack, I've told you it's over. And I swear it is. But if you want to call off the engagement, I quite understand."

"It's not that easy, Lizzie. You might as well know, you'll never get away from me. What I don't understand is why, if you're through with this business, did you look through your grandfather's papers tonight?"

"I don't know. Curiosity, I suppose." Lizzie shrugged. "Habit perhaps."

"Apparently you never gave a thought to the pain you would have caused your grandfather and mother if you had been caught." Jack didn't mention his own pain had that catastrophe occurred. "Andrew might lose everything."

Lizzie shook her head. "He would have been disappointed, Mother, too, but Gran is a powerful man. No one would hold him accountable for his granddaughter's actions."

"The soldiers made you accountable for your father's."

"They took my father's belongings. He was the one they blamed. Mother, Annie, and I were merely caught in the middle."

"I see you've thought it out."

"Some."

He watched her for some time before saying, "After we're married, for my own sanity, I just might keep you under lock and key."

"Might you?" Lizzie smiled. "Hardly a lovely thought. Perhaps I won't marry you after all."

Jack said nothing. There was no need, for their marriage wasn't in question. It was an absolute.

"We might not have an easy time of it. I've been told I'm a bit stubborn."

"I expect it won't be easy." He sighed heavily. "Living with you is bound to be difficult at best."

Lizzie laughed at that. "And yet you seem so eager."

A smile touched the corners of his mouth. "Apparently there's a defect in my character. Of late I find myself inclined toward pain."

Lizzie laughed again and then said, "I'm sorry to have caused you worry, Jack. Truly I am.

"Are you still angry?" she asked.

"Are you still a spy?" he responded.

Lizzie thought on his question. The war was almost over. There was little left to be done. Little that she could do, in any event. The thrill of working for her cause had somehow slipped away, the urgency to return home along with it. Lizzie wasn't sorry. She was tired of carrying on her private crusade and quite ready to live life as this man's wife. "No."

"Can I trust you?"

"I swear it." And after a moment she asked, "Will you unlock the door now?"

"Are you sure you want that?" he teased. "For the first time today we're finally alone."

Lizzie knew only that she wanted more than kisses. She wanted all of this man. Her cheeks burned at her daring, but she forced herself to say, "We could be alone in my room."

Jack was startled by her comment and then breathed the name "Jesus," as if her words were an answer to a prayer. He knew an invitation when he heard one, and he'd waited a long time to hear it from this woman.

Lizzie wasn't sure how she managed it, but within seconds the candle was extinguished, the door unlocked, and with his hand on hers, she was nearly dragged up the stairs. "You wouldn't be anxious, would you?"

Jack laughed softly. He was more than anxious. He was damn near hysterical with the need he knew for her.

A candle, always lit at the top of the stairs, illuminated a few feet of the hallway beyond. It was enough for Lizzie to see his dark gaze smoldering with hunger. "You aren't going to change your mind, are you?"

Lizzie opened her door and they both entered her room. It smelled of her, clean, sweet, with a touch of lemon. Jack closed his eyes and leaned against the door, breathing her scent, trying to bring his emotions, his desire, under control.

Lizzie stood before him, unsure of what to do next. She'd left a candle burning on the mantel and saw his eyes were closed. Perhaps he had changed his mind, perhaps he didn't want to stay. She bit her bottom lip. "Are you all right?"

"I will be in a minute." A moment later he breathed in deeply and watched her closely, knowing he was pushing, but aching for her seduction. "You invited me in here. Tell me what you want."

Lizzie couldn't tell him, couldn't say the things he obviously needed to hear. "Jack, it's the first time for me," she said weakly.

"I know, and unless you surrender, unless we both do, it can't be what it should."

The room grew silent except for the pounding of their hearts.

Lizzie knew he was asking that she make the next move. She might not be able to tell him what she wanted, but she could show him. Her fingers trembled, but she forced them to open the buttons running down her back. The gown slipped from her shoulders. The tabs of her petticoats came easily undone. Material billowed around her ankles, leaving her standing before him in her corset and chemise.

A pulse leaped to life in Jack's throat. He thought he might die if she refused him now, and still he asked, "Lizzie, are you sure?"

Lizzie's eyes were wide, filled with desire and perhaps a touch of fear. "I'm only sure of one thing. I love you."

Jack closed his eyes and groaned. Heaven. It felt as if he'd waited forever to hear those words.

He watched her smile at his reaction, knowing she was well aware of the power she held over him. "More than . . . ?" he prompted.

"More than freedom or equality. More than countries and their politics." Her corset dropped to the floor.

"My God," he moaned. Only the thinnest piece of fabric hid her from his gaze. "I'm shaking so hard, I'm afraid to touch you."

Lizzie wished she had the courage to take off her chemise, but she couldn't. Lord, she just couldn't. He had to make the next move.

Jack reached for her hair, making the pins fall to the carpet as his fingers gloried in the heavy mass. And then, with her hand in his, he led her toward the bed, sat down, and positioned her between his legs. His arms moved around her hips, holding her close as he buried his face against her soft belly. "I love you, Lizzie. God, I'm not sure you'll ever know how much."

She moaned at the sensation of his breath, hot and moist, penetrating the thin fabric, and any doubts that this wasn't right vanished forever.

His hands slid from her hips to her waist, up her midriff to cup her breasts. A moment later the chemise lay on the floor and Lizzie moaned. "I love it when you touch me."

"Then come down here," he said, pulling her forward and rolling her beneath him. "So I can do it right."

Above her, with most of his weight supported by one arm, he touched her again. "So you like this, do you?"

"I thought I did," she teased. "But just to make sure, you might have to do it again."

Jack chuckled. "We'll never get on with this if you make me laugh." He rolled forward, his arms on each side of her, his weight pressing her into the mattress. His hands cupped her face. "Now make your lips very soft, Lizzie." His tongue slipped over them, between them, tempting them to part. "Softer."

Lizzie's eyes fluttered closed.

"Softer," he repeated. "Let me kiss you the way you should be kissed."

Lizzie loved his kisses. From the first, even believing them highly unusual, she hadn't the power to fight them. And this kiss went on forever. And forever wasn't long enough. His lips, soft against hers, grew hard and harder still as he demanded that she give over her soul. And helplessly she did.

Their tongues tangled, hungry to rediscover each other. Both were gasping for breath when he finally tore his mouth away.

"I love the way you kiss me," Lizzie said.

"I know. We're both getting better at it, aren't we?"

Lizzie laughed softly, knowing he referred to the time she had insisted that tongues weren't used in kissing. "Did you think me terribly foolish?"

"I thought you were adorable."

"Shall I tell you a secret?"

"Yes. Tell me all your secrets," he said, his teeth nibbling at her neck and ear.

"I've dreamed of this."

"Have you? Tell me."

"Almost from the first day we met, and the dream was always the same. It was of shadows and darkness, of the feel of your mouth, your body. Your kisses. Especially your kisses. I wanted to touch you, but my hands wouldn't move."

"God," Jack groaned. "Don't move." He rolled away from her. On his knees he tore the shirt from his back. It fell ruined to the floor. His voice was a low gasp of emotion when he said, "Touch me, Lizzie. I can't tell you how long I've waited for you to touch me."

Lizzie watched his chest rise and fall as he strained for each breath. But Jack did not struggle alone. She was having at least as hard a time breathing. And then, unable to resist the temptation set before her, she reached for the hard, warm flesh.

Jack shivered and moaned at her touch. It was heaven; it was torture. He closed his eyes at the pleasure and then opened them again, unwilling to miss a second of this magical moment.

The temptation to take her quickly was great, but he forced his body to go slow, very slow.

"My fingers tremble when I touch you," she said, mystified that such a thing could happen.

Jack could hardly talk for his own trembling. "Like tonight, when you touched my lips?"

She nodded and looked up from her hands to hungry eyes. "Why?"

"It happens like that sometimes. Sometimes when the need to touch is too great."

"But I didn't know I wanted to touch you."

"You knew it in your dreams. You knew it here," Jack said, placing one hand over her breast, her pounding heart.

Lizzie thought he was right. And thought as well that it was time to put aside girlish modesty forever and move forward into the unknown with total abandon. She would learn for herself tonight the pleasure shared between a man and a woman. "Would it be all right if I kissed you?"

Jack moaned helplessly as she reversed their positions and touched her lips to his collarbone, his neck. "You don't have to ask. You can touch me and kiss me wherever you want."

"I should shock Grandfather, I think, if I touched you wherever I want."

"Would you?" Jack asked, his eyes widening at the thought. "That sounds interesting. Where were you thinking of touching me?"

Lizzie laughed at his hopeful look. "Well, a wayward thought did occur to me once that my grandfather's desk could be put to better use."

"God Almighty," Jack said somewhere between a groan and a gasp. "You're fortunate indeed that I can't read minds."

Lizzie chuckled into the hairs of his chest. "Had you no notion that ladies could have wicked thoughts?"

She rubbed her chest against his, and Jack groaned. "I'm about to lose my mind."

"Good. Because I've already lost mine," she said as she ran a hand down his side and then up under his arm and over his chest. "I like touching you."

"Tell me why," Jack asked.

"Because you feel so warm and hard."

"No, I mean, tell me why you've lost your mind."

"Well, that's obvious, don't you think? Had I all my faculties, I wouldn't be in bed with you."

"And you wouldn't allow me to do this, would you?" Jack asked as he pushed her drawers to her hips.

"Stop! Wait," she said, trying to hold his hands.

But Jack did neither. He pushed her drawers to her knees and then brought her to lie upon his length.

She was naked, and Lizzie wasn't quite sure she was comfortable with the notion.

She'd been more than willing to see this deed done, and to feel him warm and hard beneath her. But she'd never lain naked with a man before. And the experience was strangely discomforting.

Lizzie had stopped kissing him, and Jack asked, "You're not nervous, are you?"

"Just a little, I think."

"We won't do anything, I promise. Not until you're comfortable."

Jack ached to roll her to her back, to look his fill, indeed could hardly bear the thought of not looking, and yet he cupped her bottom and held her tightly against his body instead. There'd be time soon for slow, purposeful discovery. He didn't want to frighten her. And looking too close, too soon, would surely do just that.

He sighed at the touch of her, the silk of her skin, the firmness of muscle beneath, unable to believe his good fortune as she accepted the gentle grinding thrust of his hips. His mouth lowered to the top of her head and he breathed in the lemony clean scent of her hair. "I can't believe this is happening, that I'm finally touching you, loving you."

As he spoke, his hands moved over her back and bottom, down her thighs, only to return and cup her softness again.

Lizzie grew relaxed against him. Cloaked in shadows, pressed tightly to his body, she gained confidence at his words. She raised herself a bit. "Why? You've touched me before."

"Not like this, not the way I intend to touch you." He shuddered knowing the pleasure in store, wondering if he had the strength to make it last, to make it good for her.

Lizzie smiled and kissed his lips. Jack felt his heart tremble. "How do you intend to touch me?"

"With my eyes, my hands, my body, everywhere."

"I've been told lovemaking is quite lovely." Lizzie leaned farther back, her gaze moving as if in fascination slowly from where her breasts grazed his chest to his throat, his jaw and lips. And then her gaze reached his eyes and she whispered softly, clearly, and with heart-stopping certainty, "Show me, Jack."

He kissed her then, kissed her as if she were his lifeline, his sole reason for living. Her breath became his own; her heat, his warmth. He kissed her as if the world would end should he dare to stop. She was dizzy and gasping when he tore his mouth from hers at last.

He rolled her to her side and reached down, pushing her drawers and shoes away. And his body was upon hers, his weight pressing her deep into her mattress, legs apart.

And then his hands were touching her where no one had ever touched before, and Lizzie only wanted more. More of his kisses, more of his touch. She thought she might die if he didn't give her more. It went on for hours, or felt as if it did, and still it wasn't enough.

It was finally happening. After months of wanting her, his hands were free at last to touch, his eyes to see, his body to feel the pliable silky softness, and Jack couldn't get enough. He wondered if he ever would.

Breathing harshly, he pulled back, knelt, and quickly

opened the tabs of his trousers. Hardly giving her a
chance to look, he lay upon her again. And it began
again, the kissing, the touching, until heat spread across
her stomach, and her body shook with an unnamed
need.

His mouth suddenly took the tip of her breast deep
into its blazing heat, and Lizzie gasped at the force of
the suction, at the ache it brought to her stomach. He
shifted as his hand moved down her side, her leg and
back, to linger at the juncture of her thighs.

There, inside the folds of her flesh, his finger tenderly
caressed. Lizzie wasn't shocked, even though some distant thought told her she should have been. It felt too
good. Far too good. She moaned her delight as her hands
pressed into her mattress and her hips strained upward,
her body needy, so terribly needy.

"Do you like that?"

Lizzie groaned, unable to answer, her lips growing
tight, her breathing hardly existent. Legs parted farther,
knees bent as she allowed him greater access.

And then desire came in earnest, almost painful as it
grabbed at her belly and she murmured anxious, inco-
herent words, blindly searching for appeasement. Her
belly tightened, her body stiffened, hardened, her heart
pounded, her blood thundered in her ears. She couldn't
breathe and didn't want to. She couldn't think and didn't
care. She had to feel this to the end. Whatever that end
might be.

"Jack," she managed as she strove toward some elusive pleasure.

"Let it come, sweetheart. Let it come." Jack trembled
as he watched her climax.

He said to let it, as if she had the power to stop it.
She didn't. She was dying and still she couldn't stop it.
And then just as it threatened to suck her life away, the
ecstasy came at last, crashing upon her, tearing at her
insides with painful intensity. Agony. Torment. Bliss. In

wave after incredible wave until Lizzie thought she couldn't bear any more. His mouth was there to absorb her cries, and cry she did at the pure wondrous sensation that soon drifted into the glory of sweet, aching aftershocks.

Jack kissed her mouth, her damp cheeks, her softly glazed eyes, and Lizzie sighed knowing nothing on earth could compare to the wonder of this moment.

Jack smiled as he looked down into her face and thought he'd never feel more a man. "What do you think?"

"I think you're wonderful," she said dreamily, totally relaxed, totally replete, unable to imagine anything could have felt so good. "I think everything is wonderful."

Jack smiled. "Wonderful?" he questioned. "You're not even close to what I think."

"What do you think then?" she asked as he positioned himself between her relaxed legs.

"I think you're incredibly perfect."

Lizzie chuckled. "I've already told you that."

"I know, but *I* mean it."

She smiled. "We're not finished, are we?"

"Not quite." He moved forward a bit. "This might hurt a little."

His body, hard, throbbing with need, thickened with pulsating blood, pressed into her scorching heat. Jack closed his eyes, wondering if a man could live through pleasure so great. And then he pushed beyond the slight obstruction and Lizzie winced in pain.

He lay perfectly still. "Was it bad?" Jack asked, knowing if he didn't keep talking, he was bound to end this moment before it hardly began.

"No. Is it supposed to be bad?"

"I don't know." He was waiting for her body to accommodate his length, his width, struggling to remain still. God, he'd never felt anything so tight. It was enough to make a man lose his mind. "I've heard the first time is bad for some."

He stayed in place so long that Lizzie finally asked, "Are we finished now?"

"No. I'm waiting a bit so I won't hurt you."

"It doesn't hurt."

Jack smiled. "Are you in a hurry?"

Lizzie laughed, and Jack groaned, for in laughing, her muscles tightened around him.

"You're killing me. Stop laughing."

She only laughed harder.

Jack groaned, "God."

"Sorry," she said. "I'm trying not to . . ."

Jack couldn't take any more. He couldn't hold back. It was too much to bear. His body drove deep into hers.

The movement effectively brought her laughter under control. She gasped. "Lord," and then some moments later, between gasps, she managed, "this is lovely, don't you think?"

She was a master of understatement.

Jack took her hips in his hands and guided her into the right movements as he drove deep, deeper into the heat of her. Heaven. Jack knew this woman, this pleasure, was as close to heaven as he'd ever find in this lifetime.

He kissed her again and felt her body grow soft once more, pliable, allowing him to drive deeper yet. "Lizzie, sweet Jesus," he groaned, "I can't believe how good you feel."

Her hands moved over his chest, and then down, boldly, touching him where their bodies met. "And you. How good you feel."

The end was near. Too near. Her touch had done it, nearly driving him over the edge. "We have to stop."

"No," she moaned, finding herself lost again in the magic of his mouth, the touch of his body against hers. She strained forward, driving him beyond madness.

"We have to," he gasped, coming to his knees, trying to break free for just a moment. He only needed a moment.

But Lizzie wasn't about to allow him to stop. Not now. Not when he'd teased her body into aching for the pleasure again. She came up with him, her arms wrapped tightly around his shoulders, their bodies still joined, her legs around his hips. She brushed her breasts seductively against his chest. "No."

"Lizzie, damn, you don't know. It won't be good for you."

"It will. I can feel the pleasure coming again. It will."

He was helpless against her demands, her allure; his body, no longer his to control, became an obedient servant to her will. His sex, throbbing with desire and scalding heat, thickened toward the coming explosion as he drove hungrily into her, his mouth taking and giving in a furnace of urgent, demanding fire. He felt her soft cry beneath his mouth, felt her body stiffen to the pleasure and tighten in aching, surging spasms around his sex, and with a cry of his own, gave over all that he was, all that she wanted, wondering if she knew she took his very soul.

Lost in a world of maddening pleasure, two desperate hearts stood poised on the brink of paradise. Heaven beckoned as the tiny death came and then together they fell mindlessly into the ecstasy, knowing nothing could ever be the same again, that they could never go back.

They collapsed at last upon the bed. Endless moments of silence came, when only ragged breathing could be heard above pounding hearts. Their arms holding tightly to each other, each wondering if they had the courage to ever let go.

Later, long after they gained control of their senses, Jack touched her breasts, her belly, her thighs, unable to believe she was finally and forever his. "I'm sorry I hurt you."

"It was only a pinch," she said, and then asked, "How come it didn't hurt you?"

His hand played with one breast. "In case you haven't noticed, we're made a little different."

"Now, that's fair, isn't it? Women get hurt when making love. Women suffer through childbirth. And all the man gets out of it is pleasure."

Jack chuckled. "It won't hurt the next time."

"How do you know?"

"You're not a virgin any longer, so you'll only feel the pleasure."

"Truly?" she asked with undisguised interest. "Let's try it and see."

Jack laughed as he snuggled his face into her neck. "I can't make love to you again."

"Why not?" she asked, breaking free of his hold and coming to lean on her elbow, looking down at him in the dim light of one lone candle.

"Because loving you again will make you sore. I promise, we'll do it twice tomorrow."

"I want to do it twice tonight."

Jack was adamant. At least he thought he was. But he hadn't counted on the passion he'd awakened in Lizzie. It was almost light before he begged for pity. "Lizzie, I've got to sleep, please."

"Are you sure that's what you want?" she asked, rubbing her body against his.

Jack groaned his delight, even as his body trembled with exhaustion. "I swear to God, there isn't a man alive who could do it again."

Lizzie chuckled softly. "All right, I'll let you sleep. Just hold me."

"You said that before, twice before. You know, I can't just hold you. I hate to say it, but after we marry, we'll have to keep separate bedrooms. You're bound to kill me otherwise.''

Lizzie laughed as he rose from the bed and searched the floor for his clothes. Completely at ease in her nakedness, she knelt on the bed and watched him dress. ''Are you leaving then?''

''I have to.''

''I see. You got what you came for, so it's time to leave.''

Jack, in the midst of pulling up his trousers, glanced behind him. ''You don't believe that, do you?''

Lizzie giggled. ''No. The truth is, I'm the one who got what you came for.''

Jack shook his head. In his wildest dreams, he hadn't imagined it would take but one night to awaken in her a woman of voracious appetites, as lusty as he for further samplings and so comfortable in her nakedness, it was enough to drive a man wild. He loved it. ''You're a wicked lady, Lizzie. Now be good and kiss me good night.''

''First you want me bad and obviously like it when I am, and then you want me to be good. Very confusing.'' She grinned at his frown, having not a notion as to how her words were affecting him. ''And I can't kiss you good night when the sun is almost up.''

''Kiss me good morning then. And hurry up about it.''

Lizzie chuckled as she came naked from the bed. But instead of standing on tiptoe to reach his mouth, she offered him her hand. ''Good night, Lord Dover. I must say, I've had a lovely time of it. I do hope we meet again soon.''

The words hardly fit the sight she made, standing naked, her hair curling wildly around her face and over her shoulders, her body pink from his loving. Jack was positive he'd never shaken hands with a naked lady before and thought he couldn't have enjoyed the sight more. ''Good night, Miss Matthews,'' he returned, joining in her play. ''I expect we *will* meet again, and very soon.'' And with that he pulled her against him and left her with one last shattering kiss.

Lizzie recovered her senses before he reached the door. She grinned and offered him a silly little wave. Jack almost returned for another kiss, but knew where that would lead them. He smiled as he backed out of her room. He was still smiling as he fell across his bed in a dead sleep.

Chapter 13

It was almost dawn, the candle long since burned out. Lizzie lit another and, after searching the bed linen, found her nightgown had fallen to the floor. She picked up her clothes and threw them on a corner chair.

She returned to bed, wanting only to think about this long night and the magic she had discovered. But once the covers were drawn up, her head comfortably nestled upon her pillow, Lizzie couldn't manage a single thought.

She slept almost till noon and awakened to find the cup of chocolate Mercy always left on her bedside table, cold. A soft knock sounded on her door. "Lizzie, are you all right, dear?"

"Come in, Mother," Lizzie said, and then prayed Jack had taken with him all incriminating evidence of his visit. Like a fool, she'd forgotten to look when she'd had the chance.

"Are you ill?" Margaret asked, touching her daughter's forehead.

"No, just tired this morning." Lizzie felt her cheeks flush with guilt. She had every reason to be tired, every deliciously scandalous reason she could imagine.

Margaret looked alarmed. "You don't feel warm, and yet you're flushed. Are you sure you're all right?"

Lizzie smiled. "I'm fine, truly," she said. "It's a little warm in here, is all."

"We've decided to leave tomorrow for the city. We have to go a day early to find something for your sister's hair. Perhaps you should stay in bed today. What with your work at the orphanage and these hectic plans for the wedding, I think you could use the rest."

Lizzie almost gave in to her mother's suggestion, for she was tired still, but the thought of seeing Jack gave her a burst of energy. She threw the covers aside. "I'm perfectly fine, I promise."

Margaret smiled and then shrugged. "If you're sure. I'll have Mercy bring you something to eat."

Lizzie washed, dressed, and ate a light meal before leaving her room. It was after one. She wondered where Jack was and then suddenly thought of the boys and her promise to spend some time with them today. Lizzie headed for the nursery. Steven and Joey were fighting over the last piece of cake. "If you can't share, then I shall eat it," Missy said.

"He already had two," Steven said. "He's a glutton."

"Did you?" Missy asked the younger of the two.

Joey nodded.

Lizzie knocked upon the opened door. "Does anyone in here want to play ball?"

"I thought I'd take them riding," Jack said, standing suddenly close behind her.

Lizzie turned at the sound of his voice and smiled. She'd wondered how long it would take before he searched her out. And then she grinned as he whispered for her ears alone, "What? No maidenly blushes? I was sure I'd find you shy this morning."

"Actually, I thought you'd be the shy one."

Jack circled her waist and brought her close to his

side. "Bring them down when they finish, will you, Missy? We'll be in the garden."

They reached the garden before Jack spoke again. "You slept late."

"Yes, I thought you needed time to recover," Lizzie teased.

"That was very kind of you, sleeping so I might recover."

"I thought it was wonderfully kind myself."

Jack had wondered all morning if he hadn't been too hard on her last night. He'd tried to be gentle, but God, she'd driven him so wild. She'd been a virgin and they'd made love so many times. He was the man, the one with experience, the one who should have been in control, only there had been no control. Once in her arms, he was helpless but to see to her wants. Damn, if she was in pain, it was all his fault. "You're all right, aren't you? I mean, you're not sore anywhere."

"I'm fine, thank you."

They watched each other for a long moment, their eyes sparkling with the pure joy of living, of loving, while less-than-innocent smiles teased their lips. "We'd best get ourselves under control, don't you think?" he asked. "Or the family will suspect something."

"I thought we were supposed to be happy."

"Not this happy."

Lizzie laughed. "What do you suppose will happen after tonight? We might be near hysterical by morning."

Jack's heart swelled with love as he hugged her tightly against him. "We'll be good tonight." His hand slid from her waist to cup her bottom. He gave her a squeeze and they both groaned with pleasure. "We'll stay in our own rooms."

Lizzie controlled the need to giggle, knowing by the look in his eyes he had no intention of following through on his own words. "That might be best. Besides, I was thinking I'd take a long bath tonight."

Jack's gaze moved to the bathhouse and back to her supposedly innocent expression. "You little wretch. Now I'll be thinking about that all day."

Lizzie smiled her delight. It was impossible not to. Just then a ball whistled through the air and bounced off Jack's head. He screwed up his features and rubbed the sore spot. "Now say thank you."

"Thank you," Lizzie repeated dutifully. And then asked, "Why did I say that?"

"Because if I hadn't been standing here, the ball would have hit you."

"If you hadn't been standing there, I would have caught it."

Unable to resist, Jack kissed her.

"Are you two kissing again?" Steven asked, exasperated. "I thought we were going to play ball."

At eight Steven obviously hadn't as yet discovered the pleasure gained in kissing. Jack thought he needed a few years. "Who threw the ball at my head?"

"Joey was supposed to catch it. He missed."

Jack, with a twinkle in his eyes, instantly returned, "He's on your team."

"Which one?" Lizzie countered. "The one who can't throw or the one who can't catch?"

After a time, the boys, Steven most especially, appeared to gain some control over their throwing, but groaned in pain every time they caught the ball. Lizzie instructed, "Soft hands, Steven. If you use soft hands, you won't get hurt. Watch how I catch the ball."

Jack threw it and Lizzie caught the ball, following its arc into a downward motion. "See? That's called soft hands, and my palm didn't sting at all."

Later they rode their horses along the beach and returned in time for tea.

"Clean up," Lizzie instructed, eyeing Steven in particular and wondering how the boy managed to get so dirty. All four had participated in exactly the same activities, and yet Steven looked as if he'd rolled in dirt. "If there's no company, you can come down for tea."

The boys ran ahead. Lizzie called, "And, Steven, use soap this time."

"Are you tired?" Jack asked, his arm slipping around her waist. Lizzie shot him a questioning look. "I was thinking you might want a nap."

Lizzie laughed. "You mean you want a nap. And I quite understand. After all, last night's late hour had to be hard on a man your age."

"What do you mean, my age? I'm only eight years older than you."

"Eight years? Good God, that much?"

Jack pinched her bottom, and Lizzie yelped and then ran up the stairs, slamming the door to her room behind her, lest he entertain ideas of joining her. And by the look in his eyes, Lizzie thought he did.

Lizzie washed her hands and face, brushed her hair and tied it with a dark green ribbon, then changed into a lightweight dress of diagonal pale green stripes before joining her family in the drawing room. Jack was already there.

A few minutes later Steven and Joey entered the room. Obviously they hadn't come across Missy upstairs, for the center of Steven's face was white, surrounded by a perfectly undisturbed circle of dirt. And Joey's cowlick stood almost straight into the air. They hadn't changed out of their play clothes. And their hands weren't near to being clean.

Lizzie took Alice from one of the servants and sat the baby on her lap. "Find Missy and ask her to help you," she said, and both boys left the room, while eyeing delicious little cakes and making whining sounds of discontent.

The family spent the rest of the afternoon and early evening together. Lizzie played with the baby, amazed that she was already attempting to crawl. On her stomach beside the baby, she showered Alice with praise, never realizing that she raised her feet and exposed part of her legs and all of her ankles to Jack's view.

"Lizzie, watch your skirt," Margaret said, to Jack's disappointment.

"She'll be running all over the house soon," Andrew remarked, watching his granddaughter and the baby play.

Lizzie smiled. "Won't that be wonderful? I'll have to speak with the cobbler soon. Alice will have to be measured for shoes."

Jack wrestled with the boys. Later, after Alice was put down for a nap, the four of them played cards until it was time for the boys' dinner.

While everyone dressed for the evening meal, Lizzie prepared a bag for the coming night. Into it she placed stemmed glasses and wine, carefully wrapped in thick, fluffy towels, candles and flint, scent, and at the last minute the roses from the hallway table.

The moment dinner was finished, Lizzie explained that tomorrow would be a hectic day and she thought she should get some rest.

Apparently her family felt much the same, for the house quieted soon after.

Lizzie put the bag down upon a bench built into the far wall, lit a candle from the lantern she carried, and locked the bathhouse door. Within a few minutes candles glowed, surrounding the huge marble tub with soft light.

Jack knocked.

"Who is it?" Lizzie asked.

"Let me in," Jack returned.

"Wait, I'm not ready yet."

Sparkling glasses filled with ruby red wine stood on the tub's thick marble rim. She sprinkled scent into the water and tested it for temperature.

"Lizzie, hurry up," he said anxiously, "before someone sees me out here."

"Wait, I'll be ready in a minute," she said, dropping crushed rose petals over the water.

Her cloak was hung on a hook. She wore only her robe and slippers as she unlocked the door.

Jack quickly stepped inside and secured the door behind him. He turned, his gaze taking in the room, the soft light, the wine. He breathed in the scent of her. And then smiled as his gaze studied the loveliness of her hair, the softness in her eyes, the beauty of her smile. And at the sight of her robe, he teased, "I see you're still not ready."

Lizzie kicked off her slippers, untied her belt, and allowed the silk robe to slither to the floor. "I think you're the one who's not ready."

Jack sucked in his breath at the sight of her. Last night he'd only caught glimpses, for beneath a canopy, with one distant candle to lend light, she'd been mostly hidden in shadows. Even this morning, there had only been a hint of light as she kissed him good-bye.

For the longest moment he said nothing, unable to take his gaze from her, unable to master a thought beyond taking her now, this very minute.

"Are you surprised?" Lizzie asked, slightly unsure of herself and growing more so at his prolonged silence. It was one thing to stand naked before a man, mostly naked himself, after a night of unbearable pleasure. It was quite another to do it while Jack remained dressed. Dressed and totally silent. "Jack, you're not saying anything."

"That's because I can't."

"Why?"

"Because you're too beautiful."

Lizzie laughed softly. With both hands she shook her hair until it was a wild mess of curls. "Does that help?"

Jack swallowed. "No, you just made it worse."

Lizzie moved toward him. "I was under the assumption that a gentleman, upon seeing a naked lady, would do the right thing."

"Right thing?" Jack repeated, unable to concentrate on her words. He knew he sounded like an idiot, but he was presently putting every effort into getting his emotions under control, most especially the emotions affecting one particular part of his body. She was a seductress, and he hadn't even guessed it until last night. She was going to kill him, he was sure.

"Yes. For instance, wouldn't he take off his clothes?" Lizzie asked while she unbuttoned his shirt.

"It's a good thing I have a strong heart," Jack murmured, watching her breasts move as she hung his shirt beside her cloak.

"Did I shock you?" she asked as she reached for the tabs of his trousers, noticing he appeared in somewhat of a daze.

"You're always shocking me," he managed weakly. She chuckled, fully aware of her effect on him, but Jack hardly heard, since all his attention was focused on her fingers as they skimmed across his stomach and then down his sides, pushing his trousers away. "I think you're trying to seduce me." He prayed she'd never stop.

"Seduce you?" Lizzie teased, her laugh soft, low, and deliciously wicked. "I'm afraid I wouldn't know how."

"Oh God," Jack moaned as her hand brushed over the bulge in his trousers. "You're doing a remarkable job for a woman who doesn't know how."

"I only thought you'd like a glass of wine."

His trousers fell to his feet. He kicked them aside and stepped out of his shoes. The marble floor was cold beneath his feet, a drastic contrast to the heat swirling through his trembling body, and yet Jack was hardly aware of anything but this woman and his need for her to touch him again. "And it looks delicious, but right now I want you more."

Lizzie's gaze moved to his lengthening, hardening sex and back again. She couldn't resist, and Jack closed his eyes on a groan as her fingers closed boldly around him.

Jack guided her hand, showing her what he needed. His hand dropped away as she came to master the movement. "I hope you know, now that you've touched him, I'll never get him to stop."

Lizzie smiled at the personal pronoun. "He's a brazen little character, don't you think? Standing up straight like he is and silently insisting on all the attention."

"No more brazen than the lady holding him, I'm sure." He opened his eyes and narrowed his gaze. "What do you mean little?"

Lizzie circled his neck with her free arm, pressing her body against his. "You're warm."

"I'm burning up."

Jack reached for her, almost moaning his delight to find her hot and moist. And then with one hand on her hip and the other guiding his sex, he rubbed the tip into the sweet folds of her, against hot, moist, sensitive flesh.

Lizzie dropped her head to his shoulder with a shudder. "I can't tell you how good that feels."

"You don't have to tell me. I know."

She was slippery wet and burning for him. Jack reversed their positions so that she leaned against the wall. And then he raised her, positioning her legs around his hips, and slowly lowered her upon his engorged member.

They both moaned at the pleasure and their whole world became only the touch, scent, and feel of the other, to end all too soon in mind-shattering ecstasy.

Lizzie closed her eyes, gasping for breath, her head falling back weakly, her body contracting still, squeezing him with sweet, aching waves of pleasure.

It was over too soon, far too soon. Jack cursed that he hadn't been able to make it last longer. "Damn it!"

Lizzie giggled. "Love words? How sweet."

"I was thinking about this all day." Jack pressed his hips forward, rotating them slightly. "And when I saw you naked, there was no hope that I could stop."

He carried her to the tub and they both slid beneath the warm, scented water.

Jack sipped at his wine after positioning Lizzie before him. With one hand under the water he touched her as he pleased.

Lizzie snuggled the side of her face to his chest. "This feels too good."

"Umm," Jack returned, leaning back, his eyes closed, his mind and body absorbing her. "How many children do you want?" he asked, his hand moving over her gently rounded stomach. He wondered if they hadn't already begun their family.

She put down her wine, turned and kissed his jaw, his cheek, his eyes and nose. "We have a lot of rooms to fill. I think we'll manage with whatever God gives us."

Jack smiled, his gaze upon her breasts. He moved forward, his mouth catching one tip as his fingers slid between her legs. "When we go back to the house, remind me to show you something."

Lizzie moved closer, obviously eager to learn all. "Show me here."

"I'm likely to drown if I do. We'll need to lie down."

"Let's go then."

"Not yet. I think we could both use a good washing first."

Lizzie sat back and laughed at the wicked look in his eyes. "Do you mean a thorough washing?"

Jack worked up a lather with a bar of soap and nodded. "A very thorough washing."

Starting at her neck and working in downward strokes, it took forever before he finally came near

to where she wanted him most. She could hardly
breathe, so great was her anticipation, and then he went
right by it. "You missed a spot."

"Where?"

"Up a little." She raised her leg, hooking her foot
upon the tub's rim.

His hand moved up her thigh. "There?"

"No. A little higher."

Jack brought his fingers to exactly where she wanted
them.

"Yes," she gasped. "Right there."

It took a while before Lizzie was able to talk again.
"Am I still alive?"

"Did you think you had gone to heaven?" Jack
teased. "With all that moaning and sighing, I suppose
you liked that well enough."

Lizzie shrugged, once again in control. "You might
say I liked it."

"I might say you loved it, but I won't push." He
grinned. "Are you too tired now to return the favor?"

It didn't take more than a glance for Jack to know he
was about to suffer equal pleasure.

She soaped her hands in a lather. Jack closed his eyes
as she moved them over his throat and shoulders. When
she was quite sure he was clean enough she soaped her
hands again, and his arms and chest gained similar attention. Her hands moved so slowly, the moment became more a body massage than a washing.

"I can't tell you how relaxing this is." He opened
one eye and tried to glare through his euphoria. "Have
you done this before?"

Lizzie accepted his question as a compliment. "Thank
you."

Her hands moved to his stomach next, circling in tantalizing strokes to his hips, his waist, and then pressed
hard against his back. "I'm sorry I have to lean on you
to do this; my arms aren't as long as yours."

"I don't mind," he breathed.

Lizzie chuckled, her breasts grazing his chest. "Somehow I thought you wouldn't."

And then she pulled back and soaped her hands again. Neither mentioned the fact that the last lather had been washed from her hands the moment they reached under the water, and this lather was bound to follow the same course. "Do you know you have a beautiful body?" Lizzie asked. Having left off at his hip, she began there and moved slowly over a taut belly down thickly muscled thighs.

"Thank you. It's yours to enjoy."

"And you wouldn't mind if I enjoyed it often, I take it?"

"I have every hope that you will." Jack gasped as her hand brushed over his groin and then began to stroke the inside and back of both thighs. Down to his knees and then up again until Jack thought he'd lose his mind. "Lizzie, please."

"Am I hurting you?"

"No." His breath was coming in short, harsh gasps. "You're killing me."

The instant she relented and touched him at last, Jack's hips strained forward and up, his body nearly as hard as the marble tub in which they sat. He guided her closer until the hard shaft rubbed against her softness. Then he thrust forward into the sweet, hot magic of her.

Lizzie was about to say something, but her words, her thoughts, were already lost to the pounding of two hearts.

The kitchen door shut behind them. And there, in the dim light cast by the glow of a banked fire, the lovers, damp still from their tub, reached for each other, unable to resist a moment of touching, kissing, whispering words of endless love.

They stood there for a long time, lost in a kiss, unwilling to break apart even for the short time it would take to climb the stairs to her room.

Andrew could not put aside his need for another tasting of Mrs. Molston's cherry pie. The candlelight wavered as he descended the steps and walked through the dining room. He never expected anyone to be about. Therefore, he was completely surprised upon finding his granddaughter and stepson lost in a stolen moment of passion.

He cleared his throat. Guilt was written over both their faces as Lizzie and Jack jumped apart.

"Are you coming or going?" Andrew asked.

"We went for a walk," Jack returned, clearing his throat a time or two, feeling once again a youngster caught in a shady act. "I was just about to see Lizzie to her room."

Andrew managed to avoid the obvious by saying, "I haven't a doubt you mean to see her to her *door*."

Lizzie knew it was her grandfather's way of saying he expected them to put aside their needs for a few more days, or at the very least, act as if they had.

"Of course," Jack returned.

"I take it you couldn't sleep?" Andrew asked, his blue gaze taking in Lizzie's dishevelment. She knew her lips were swollen, her eyes probably glazed, her hair most definitely damp.

"Yes, Gran."

"The servants have enough to talk about, Jack. I expect you won't be giving them more."

"I quite understand, sir."

And with that, Andrew turned and retraced his steps to his bed, his need for cherry pie forgotten.

"Wonderful. Just wonderful," Lizzie said softly as they mounted the stairs moments later. "He knows what we were doing," she said bleakly.

Jack laughed and tightened his hold around her waist.

"I'm afraid wet hair is always a dead giveaway, sweet-heart."

They were at her door. "Are you going to invite me in?" Judging by the look in her eyes, Jack thought she would not.

"Perhaps you should come back later," Lizzie said, her grandfather's discovery having left her less than passion filled. "No, tomorrow." She nodded. "Yes, tomorrow would be much better."

"Right now is much better," Jack said as he reached behind her, opened her door, and backed her into her room.

"Gran will hear," she whispered, half-afraid he would, but more afraid Jack would agree.

"His room is at the end of the hall. Even if his hearing were perfect, which it is not, and his room next door, he wouldn't hear a thing." He moved to her mantel and lit a candle, guided only by moonlight. A moment later he was backing her to the bed. "Especially if you can keep some control."

"Me? Are you saying I lose control?"

"You cry out."

"I most certainly do not," she said, knowing full well she did. Knowing if his mouth hadn't been on hers last night, she might have awakened the entire household with her cries. "I can't remember crying out even once."

"They were lovely cries, Lizzie. And I did especially enjoy quieting them." Jack thought the degree of his enjoyment had nearly done him in. "Still, I had in mind to show you a bit more, but since my mouth wouldn't be there to muffle yours, perhaps that could wait until our honeymoon."

"It wouldn't?" she asked, her eyes widening with interest. "Where would it be?"

Jack shook his head. "It's better if I show you."

The temptation was too great. There was no way she

was going to miss out on the promise of pleasure that glowed in his eyes. Her mouth curved into a wicked smile as she suggested, "I could use a pillow."

Jack bit his bottom lip, enthralled, knowing a woman didn't live to compare to this one. "Take off your cloak."

She did as he asked and teased, "One can only hope it's worth the effort."

Jack allowed a slow, lazy smile. Both of them knew there was no need to boast. "The rest of it now. I want to see you."

"Naked?" she whispered, feigning shock at the thought. As if she hadn't been naked for the last few hours. "You want to see me naked, while you stand there fully clothed?"

"God, I love you, Lizzie," Jack whispered on a helpless sigh, knowing he had no choice in the matter, knowing the power he gave over with that love.

Lizzie knew the time for teasing was done. Her heart twisted painfully in her chest at his softly spoken words and she flew into his arms.

"It's scary, isn't it?" she asked after a long, sizzling kiss. "To love this much."

"I can't help it," he said as his hands pushed her robe from her shoulders. A moment later he lifted her to the bed.

"Do you think the time might come when we could get on this bed without shoes or slippers?"

Jack smiled. "Someday perhaps, when we're not nearly so anxious."

"Are you anxious?" She pulled his shirt from his trousers and ran her hand over the warmth of his chest.

Jack groaned and, despite his need for her touch, took her hand in his.

"Don't make me lose control, Lizzie. I need to keep my wits about me, if I'm to show you."

"You could lose control now," she taunted as she

slid her other hand to the bulge below his waist. "And show me later."

He trapped that hand as well and brought both to rest at her sides. "Be good."

"If I were good, you wouldn't be here."

Jack came to his knees and began to pull away his clothes. Lizzie watched, her gaze telling clearly her admiration. She frowned slightly as he settled himself at her feet and took off her slippers. "What are you"— she gasped softly as he took her foot and kissed the instep—"doing?"

"Easy," he said, holding on as she tried to pull away. "Relax."

"I can't. You're tickling me."

"Pay attention now," he said while dragging his lips over her soft, giving mouth. "It will be your turn next."

Lizzie tried to pay attention. She tried when his mouth moved over her shoulder. She tried when his teeth caught the tips of her breasts. She was still trying when his mouth lowered to her waist, his lips and tongue running in circles over her smooth belly. But when his mouth moved lower still, Lizzie realized this was one of those times when paying attention simply wasn't possible.

Jack felt her body stiffen slightly beneath him and realized even though she'd been unashamed, and totally at ease in her nakedness, this was an entirely new experience for her. He was positive she'd take to it after a time, but for the present he'd have to go easy, perhaps take a far slower route. He kissed her thigh, her knees, her shin and feet. She didn't pull away this time.

He heard her soft sigh as he buried his mouth at last into her sweet warmth and knew, even if it were killing him, he'd been right to take this slow.

She was sweetness beyond measure, love almost impossible to bear. He'd never get enough of her.

Her body softened under his kisses, under the loving

mastery of his mouth and tongue, until it grew hard again, needy of the release only he could bring.

Her moans grew louder as the ache spread across her belly, and louder still as the wanting grew to desperate strength.

It was like last night, Lizzie thought, only better. Ever so much better. Her heart pounded, her pulse throbbed in her ears. She never heard the words muffled against her moist flesh, a warning to be quiet. Lost in passion, she never felt the pillow as he reached up and flung it over her face.

It fell to the floor as a groan began deep in her throat. Her body tightened and strained toward his mouth, her breathing shallow and erratic, desperate that he should ease the torment.

Jack knew she was going to cry out. Her mother's room was two doors away. She'd awaken, lest he soften the sound. Jack reached up and placed his hand over her mouth.

Lizzie wasn't breathing at the moment release suddenly crashed upon her. Overtaking mind, body, and senses, it shimmered in a gale of wrenching delight.

Jack waited for the contractions to ease and then, moving up her length, slipped his body into her luscious wet heat. ''Damn,'' he grunted as the last of the surgings caught him in a mindless hold. It took a moment as he fought back the need to finish this coupling with a few mindless thrusts and said at last, ''We'll have to sound-proof our bedroom.''

Lizzie didn't hear him, for she hadn't recuperated from one wave of desire before another was thrust upon her. Jack loomed over her, filling her to overflowing, and moved with steady, smooth force. She thought she couldn't help him, that she hadn't the strength to do her part. But she did.

''Jack,'' she gasped, moving with him.

And he understood. ''I know. It's too good.''

And for a mindless, heart-stopping moment, it was.

His mouth was on hers, this time absorbing her cries, breathing her breath as his body emptied its hot seed into her warmth.

Jack collapsed heavily upon her, unable to move an inch if it meant his life.

"Lord," Lizzie groaned weakly once the world began to right itself again. "I hope you're not going to ask questions."

"About what?" Jack asked, suffering still the aftershocks of loving her, and unable to think what she was talking about.

"You said to pay attention. You know," she said, shaking an unshakable arm. "The lesson you just gave me."

Jack smiled as he remembered his last comment before entering with her into a world of madness. He rested his weight on his arms and smoothed her hair from her face. "One can only hope you learn your lessons well."

"The truth is, Jack, I'm not as bright as I sometimes appear," she said, her eyes wide and innocent. And then she wrapped her arms around his neck and pulled him down again. "It's a failing I'm not happy to admit to."

Jack buried his face in her neck. "Meaning I'll have to show you again?" He rolled to his side, bringing her with him.

"There's no telling how many times, I'm afraid." Lizzie found it impossible to hide her enthusiasm.

"God, you're so wicked."

Chapter 14

~~~◡◠~~~

"We've got all we need to convict her," came the confident announcement as Lord Summitt entered Mr. Blake's office. His face was flushed with excitement as he dropped the file to the desk.

"Her?" Mr. Blake asked, knowing his colleague referred to the traitor among them, for Lord Summitt rarely spoke about anything else these past few months. Still, to imagine the culprit to be a woman went beyond the realm of reason. Had Lord Summitt become so consumed with their problem that he now resorted to wild accusations? "You cannot mean to imply that the traitor is a woman?"

Lord Summitt's gray eyes gleamed with satisfaction; indeed, the informant was a woman. And who better than a member of the gentler sex? Who among them would suspect the turncoat to be a woman? Had it not been for his superior intelligence, she might never have been discovered. "Most assuredly, I mean just that. Our traitor is Elizabeth Matthews."

Mr. Blake looked stunned and then slowly shook his head. Elizabeth Matthews was the granddaughter of one of his closest friends. It was impossible that she was the traitor. "Good God man, there has to be a mistake. She's only a young girl."

Lord Summitt knew that he would have found her sooner if he'd allowed himself to see this supposed innocent for what she truly was. "In point of fact, sir, she's a woman, and a most intelligent woman, I've no doubt."

Lord Summitt sat and reached for the folder. "I met her some time back at a ball held in her honor. You were there, weren't you? She'd injured her leg, if I'm not mistaken."

"Her ankle."

"Yes," Lord Summitt said, nodding at the memory. "She was a daring little thing, I thought then, but dismissed the possibility that she could be anything more. She was, after all, only a woman.

"My mistake, of course. For she made no pretense, even then, for her love of country."

Mr. Blake was hardly interested in the silly chatter of a young girl. Females were known to speak nonsense. "What proof have you? We dare not accuse unless we're absolutely sure."

Lord Summitt took five sheets of paper from the folder and spread them over Mr. Blake's desk. "I'm more than sure.

"Her grandfather is a man of superior knowledge and has often advised the prime minister and his staff. The old man loves her. No doubt he trusts her as well. And she takes every advantage of that trust."

Mr. Blake frowned. Elizabeth was about to marry. He and Mrs. Blake were giving the couple a party in two days. This information couldn't have come at a worst time.

Mr. Blake shook his head. "There has to be a great deal more than suppositions. We'll need solid evidence before bringing the matter to Lord North."

"And I've got it." Lord Summitt nodded toward his

papers. "I created five false proposals and made sure each of them was leaked through different channels of the ministry. My plant picked up only one. The one in Mr. Andrew Thomas's possession."

"Good God, man, you're not accusing Mr. Thomas." Mr. Blake's objection was vehement.

"Certainly not. His integrity is above suspicion. And that leaves us with only one other. His granddaughter."

Mr. Blake shook his head. "I see only supposition and conjecture here, Robert. The traitor could be Elizabeth, but then again, it could be anyone in Andrew's home, anyone with the ability to get into his papers."

"It's her, I tell you."

"I need more than this. I need absolute proof," Mr. Blake said.

"What would you like, her confession? Give me a few hours with the woman and I'll get it."

Mr. Blake shot his lordship a sharp glance. "I hope I don't have to remind you that Mr. Thomas is a confidant of the prime minister himself. Until we find more evidence, we've no choice but to tread very lightly indeed."

"I quite understand."

"I trust there'll be no extraordinary measures taken, then?"

Summitt had no choice but to agree. "Yes, sir."

Mr. Blake nodded, satisfied. "We'll need something that connects her directly."

"Consider it done," Lord Summitt said as he came to his feet and left the room as abruptly as he'd entered.

After arriving in London, Jack's man of business kept Lizzie in the town house library for the remainder of the morning, explaining the extent of Jack's affairs, his investments and properties. Lizzie was at first surprised. She hadn't realized Jack's interests were so large, nor so diversified. Still, she soon grew obviously bored, wondering why Jack had summoned her to this meeting. More than once she shot Jack a puzzled look, only to see him smile in return.

Nearly two hours went by before Mr. Morgan, having apparently concluded his explanations, said, "I have the paper ready for your signatures."

Lizzie frowned. "What paper?"

"Perhaps you should read it," Jack said, expectantly.

Lizzie took her spectacles from her pocket and quickly scanned the paper. She knew only shock as she finished, for the document stated all of Jack's interests would, upon their marriage, carry her name as an equal owner. "This isn't necessary, Jack." Lizzie shook her head. "Please, I don't want your property."

"Our property," Jack returned. "Once we marry, everything I have will be yours."

"And here's the will," Mr. Morgan said, sliding the document forward. "You'll need to sign that as well."

Lizzie came to her feet. It was too much. She understood the need to be practical, but they weren't married yet. And she didn't want to think about a will. "No!"

"Excuse me?" Mr. Morgan asked, obviously puzzled by the lady's refusal.

"I won't sign it."

"Mr. Morgan, do you think you could give us a minute?" Jack asked.

"Of course, your lordship." Mr. Morgan nodded and left the library.

The moment the door closed behind him, Lizzie said, "Jack, this is ridiculous. I don't want your money. I don't need it."

"I'm not giving you money. As my wife, everything I have is rightfully yours."

"Then this isn't necessary," she said shoving the papers from her.

"England's inheritance laws are a horror, Lizzie. I'm just making sure nothing can go wrong."

Lizzie sighed. "Are you planning on dying anytime soon?"

Jack chuckled as he took her in his arms. "Signing a will won't cause either of us an early demise. It's only a precaution. If something should happen, I want you and our children protected."

She leaned into him, her mouth brushing along the side of his neck, her hold slightly tighter than usual, unable to shake her misgivings. A dream last night had left her anxious, and even though she couldn't recall the exact reason why, she had the most eerie feeling that something terrible was about to happen. "You said nothing will happen."

"And nothing will. I promise it won't be easy to get rid of me."

"I know. When you want something, there's no stopping you."

"And I want you." His arms tightened around her. "We're going to grow old together, Lizzie. One day we'll watch our grandchildren play, and then our great-grandchildren."

Lizzie shot him a playful scowl and teased, "That long?"

He pinched her bottom and she laughed.

"Now let's sign the papers. I've something I want to show you." His eyes twinkled with deviltry.

"One might imagine it quite scandalous the things you've already shown me.

"Mother is terribly anxious to see that something is done with Annie's hair by tomorrow night. I promised I'd accompany her and my sister to Lady Summitt's. The lady has a French maid who is said to be brilliant with all matters pertaining to hair."

Jack sighed. "Too bad. I have a small bathhouse out back," he said. "Nothing, of course, to rival your grandfather's marble excellence, but I thought the tub would fit us nicely."

Lizzie's eyes grew wide with interest. "Us?" She kissed his jaw. "Doesn't that sound lovely?"

"I thought so."

Lizzie sighed and leaned back. "I can't get out of this afternoon. I promised, and Mother is so upset."

"Tonight then? After everyone is asleep. I'll come to your room."

"Will you come through the window again?"

Jack chuckled remembering his misgivings that night and the need he felt to explain. "I thought this time I could use the door."

Lady Summitt, a close friend of Mrs. Blake, their respective husbands both high-ranking officials of the government, enjoyed a beautiful three-story home in London's West End. In gold-trimmed, red livery with white gloves and whiter wigs, footmen stood near most every door, inside and out, ready to see them open and close.

At first Lizzie found the atmosphere stilted and pretentious and couldn't help but wonder if King George's palace boasted of as many footmen.

But Lizzie's dread of the coming afternoon quickly evaporated when Lady Summitt came rushing down the stairs with a baby tucked under one arm. She was slightly flustered, but otherwise happy to greet her guests. "Hello, I'm delighted you've come. Mrs. Blake sent a note. I'm afraid she won't be able to join us."

"There's nothing wrong, I hope," Margaret said.

"Oh no. Just last-minute details. She wants everything perfect for tomorrow night."

Margaret nodded. "Mrs. Blake told you of our problem?"

"She has, and I've no doubt Marie will set your mind at ease."

Belle Summitt forced aside her shock as Annie's cap

was whisked from her head. "It is an interesting color, isn't it?" she said with kindness.

"If she were a bunch of carrots, it should be perfect, I think," Margaret said.

Belle laughed, and Lizzie, who thought she liked her on sight, grew positive.

The baby was left with a nurse while the women adjourned to a large bedchamber upstairs. As the afternoon progressed, Annie suffered under the maid's ministrations. Meantime, the three ladies sat at the opposite end of the same bedchamber enjoying tea and delicate pastries.

From the onset Belle Summitt spoke candidly of her own humble beginnings. The daughter of a poor farmer, it turned out, she'd caught her husband's eye at a street festival some ten years past. It was the scandal of the century, that a duke should marry so far beneath him, Belle claimed, but Robert had quite made up his mind to have her.

After that, Belle went on to poke fun at the supposed elite and was soon exhibiting a wicked sense of humor that, to Lizzie's amusement, bordered on the risqué. She was five years or so older than herself, and Lizzie wished she might have made her acquaintance sooner.

"Robert told me Lord Dover has bought the old Anderson place."

"He has," Lizzie admitted. "It's bound to take a bit of work to change a stark, forbidding castle into a comfortable home. It's so big."

"You'll do it," Belle said, as if the two had known each other for years and she had every confidence of Lizzie's ability.

Just then something crashed. A moment later something else banged hard against a distant wall and a young girl screamed, "Mother, he's bothering me again!"

Belle came from her seat and, while heading for the

bedroom door, sighed, "After the children come along, you'll wish it were bigger still."

Lizzie wondered how the footman outside the door knew when his mistress was in need of his service, for even though he stood outside the room, the door opened as she approached it, exactly when it should have.

Lizzie sat alone in Lord and Lady Summitt's bedroom, her mother and sister having gone off with the maid to rinse Annie's hair free of some special, horrid-smelling concoction. Bored with her own company, she wished she had asked permission to smoke.

Waiting for her hostess's return, she walked to the window. It was the first she realized that the house overlooked Hyde Park. Lizzie watched couples stroll the paths, families picnic, nurses push their charges in buggies, while the more active rode their horses through distant bridle paths. It was a sunny day, and Lizzie wished she were among those enjoying the fresh air. Better still, she wished she were with Jack, held close in his arms as warm, soapy water surrounded their naked bodies.

Her hand brushed against a thick folder protruding from the edge of a small nearby table. Lizzie thought she hardly touched it and was surprised to see it suddenly fall to the floor. Papers flew every which way.

"Oh dear," she mumbled as she knelt to collect the folder's contents.

Lizzie glanced at the papers, her gaze drawn to a list of names. Agents. Lord help us, there had to be a dozen or more. And then there were memos, notes, and documents marked "secret," some signed by the prime minister himself. Lizzie knew a surge of excitement. A word said to the right people could deal the War Ministry a final deadly blow. A moment later she dismissed the thought from her mind. She was done with her work.

She'd given her word. The war would have to end without further intervention on her part.

Lizzie was in the midst of replacing the papers when a man asked, "What are you doing?"

She looked up to find a tall, attractive, but stern-faced man with the darkest eyes she'd ever seen staring down at her.

"I'm sorry. I was looking out the window and my hand hit the folder," Lizzie said, hoping she didn't look as guilty as she felt.

"Those are private documents."

"I know. I mean, I didn't *know* exactly. I just . . . I didn't look."

"What are you doing here?" Lord Summitt asked unnecessarily, for he knew exactly who she was and why she was here. In truth he'd left these papers behind in the hopes that she'd read them. The papers were false, of course, but that hardly mattered. The moment a hint of the information in them surfaced, he'd have his proof.

"I'm Elizabeth Matthews. My mother and I are here at Mrs. Blake's suggestion. My sister, Annie, needs your maid's assistance with her hair." Lizzie silently cursed the trembling in her voice.

At her nervous tone, Lord Summitt narrowed his gaze. If she wasn't guilty, if she hadn't been reading those papers, why was her voice trembling? What would she have to fear?

Lizzie's explanation was the truth. Still, she knew that she sounded anything but truthful. Why had her voice wavered? Lord, she couldn't imagine what had come over her. Granted she'd glanced at the papers, but she had no intentions of doing anything about the information learned.

She hadn't fooled him, of course. Robert knew a lie when he heard one. Still, he dared not accuse her again until she leaked the information in his folder. "It's your party we're going to tomorrow night?'' Robert thought it best to play along with her act. It wouldn't do, of course, to scare her off.

"Yes," Lizzie said, almost overcome with relief. "Lord Dover and I are betrothed. Mr. and Mrs. Blake are having a party in our honor."

Lizzie slid the last paper back into place and handed the folder to Robert Summitt.

"Thank you," he said, and then without another word, turned and left the room.

Lizzie couldn't explain her odd reaction to the strangely forbidding man. He had not accused her of anything, at least not openly, and yet she felt as if he suspected her of something. She frowned, unable to find a reason as to why the man had acted so strangely.

Two hours later, Summitt, unwilling to wait for what might take weeks in coming, armed with an official search warrant, arrived at Andrew Thomas's home. Later that night he entered Prime Minister North's office with an uncomfortable Mr. Blake at his side.

In Jack's drawing room, Lizzie and Jack waited for the family to join them. And while they waited, they talked about her afternoon visit and the new friend she'd made. "I like her. She's nothing at all like the rest of the aristocracy."

"What did you talk about?"

"Sex."

Jack looked startled and then narrowed his gaze at her grin and said, "You're getting worse every day."

Lizzie laughed. "I can't help it. It's on my mind every day."

"Thank you," Jack said, taking her words as a compliment.

"You needn't puff up your chest, Jack. Now that I've

discovered the way of things, I've no doubt I'd feel the same with another. I just happen to love you.''

"You might as well understand this, Lizzie. Not only wouldn't you feel the same with another, there will never be another, for either of us.''

"Deal," she said as she stuck out her hand, waiting for it to be shaken.

Only he didn't shake it. He took it in his and pulled her instead to sit on his lap. "Shake hands with me later, when you're naked.'' Lizzie giggled. "Now tell me what you talked about.''

"Well, we talked about the house you bought and the best recipe for tarts and children.''

Jack nuzzled his nose into the warmth of her neck. "You already know the recipe for children.''

Lizzie smiled and then sighed as his fingers moved over her breast. "I know, but I couldn't tell her that, could I?''

"What else?''

"We talked about her work with the poor.'' Lizzie sat straighter and turned to face him. "Jack, I've been thinking we might work together, she and I, for the poor, I mean. She knows all the right people, and through her, so would I.''

"Have you concluded, then, that gaining a title would not be a disadvantage?''

"I concluded that some time back.'' She snuggled closer. "Especially if the title is yours.''

"You never told me exactly what you are looking to accomplish.''

"I thought I'd work with children, especially orphans.''

"God, England won't know what hit her.''

Lizzie giggled. "You're not saying my personality is a bit too forceful, are you?''

"Certainly not.''

Lizzie only laughed in response, came to her feet, and poured them both a drink. A moment later she sat at his side and asked, "Do you know Lord Summitt? Belle said they were at my ball, but I can't remember him at all."

"I've met him. Why? Was he there?"

"For a few minutes. Oh, it was so embarrassing. I was alone in the bedroom, looking out the window, thinking about us and tonight, when my hand hit a folder. All of a sudden papers had fallen everywhere."

Jack watched her carefully.

"I know what you're thinking, but I hardly looked at them. And even if I had, it wouldn't have mattered. I gave you my word."

"That's a relief."

"I was picking them up when Robert Summitt came in."

"And?"

"He accused me of reading them."

"Did he?"

"Well, not in so many words, but I could tell he was thinking I had. What an odd man."

Jack frowned, knowing Summitt's reputation as a fanatical hothead. Still, he wondered what had gotten into the man. Granted Jack had figured out what Lizzie had been up to, but that was only because she'd told him about her activities while living in the colonies. And he'd seen her with Kent. No one else would think to hold her in suspicion. "That is odd. Did you tell him he was mistaken?"

"No, I thought it best to ignore the whole matter."

"What was the outcome?"

"I don't know. After the papers were back in place, I handed him the folder and he left."

"Just like that?"

"He said, 'thank you.' " Lizzie breathed a sigh. "It was the most unusual thing. I wasn't guilty, but he made me feel guilty. I know I acted like a fool, but the longer I was in his company, the more flustered I grew."

Jack smiled. "Don't worry on it. Robert is a bit stiff at first. He's bound to come around once he knows you."

"Do you realize what you're saying?" Prime Minister North asked.

"I do, sir. She was found reading top secret documents. You have my word on it."

"Couldn't it be as she said? Couldn't the papers have fallen and she was merely replacing them in the folder?"

"Of course, and that alone means nothing, but look at the total picture. The girl was raised in the colonies. Reports have it her father died fighting for the rebel cause. She does not hide where her sympathies lie. There's been a leak; we all know that. She's had ample opportunity to look into her grandfather's papers."

Lord North shook his head. "Circumstantial at best."

"I've checked back, sir. Most every time one of your staff has consulted with Andrew Thomas, information has leaked out.

"And now this." Lord Summitt pointed to his papers. "No one but Thomas knew that additional troops were being called up."

"They're not."

"I know. I planted the information."

"Are you implying Mr. Thomas is—"

Lord Summitt shook his head. "I don't think the gentleman has a clue that his granddaughter is a traitor to the Crown."

Prime Minister North watched both men for a long moment. The evidence appeared damning indeed. Still, there was a possibility that another was involved. "Have you given any thought to the possibility that it's not Elizabeth Matthews at all, but someone who works for Andrew? What about his servants? His friends?"

"Mr. Blake pointed out that possibility, sir, but after

watching her scan those secret documents, there can be no doubt.''

"And no one else was present?"

"She was alone when I came upon her."

"It's your word, then, against hers."

"Like you, I'm a lord of the realm, sir. I think my word will stand."

"And within a week she'll be the wife of an earl. Her word will carry weight as well."

Lord Summitt did not respond as he touched the small book in his breast pocket. It was best, he thought, to keep this last piece of information to himself for a bit. Besides, he wanted to see her expression when he placed it before her.

Lord North sighed again. "All right, ask her to come in for an interview." The prime minister reached for his watch, and after noting the lateness of the hour, slid it back into his pocket. "Tomorrow will be soon enough. And be discreet about it. There's no need to upset Mr. Thomas and his family."

"Yes, sir."

Later that same night, just after the dinner hour, the family gathered in Jack's drawing room. Margaret was pouring tea, while Andrew, Lizzie, and Jack enjoyed a smoke. Annie, looking lovely since her hair had been restored close to its original color, suggested a game of cards, just as a knock sounded at Jack's door.

A terrified-looking Mr. Parker came into the room. "Lord Dover? There are soldiers to see you, sir."

"Soldiers?" Jack asked, looking puzzled.

And then, without waiting for permission, the small group suddenly entered the room and stood among Jack and his family. "What is the meaning of this, Major?"

Jack felt his stomach twist into a knot of fear, for he

need not have asked. It took only a glance and he knew.

The major was staring at Lizzie. A major, she realized, who looked almost exactly like one she knew in the colonies.

Suddenly Lizzie was once again back in New York, facing English soldiers who were about to accuse them of treason and throw them out into the street. The dreadful scene that had haunted her for months after its happening.

The major spoke to Jack. "My Lord, the prime minister would like a word with Miss Matthews."

"Would he?" Andrew said, puzzled. "You may tell Lord North that we'll be in his office first thing in the morning."

"I'm afraid it must be now, sir. My orders are to bring Miss Matthews in tonight."

Andrew scowled. "What is this nonsense? Do you mean to say you've come to arrest my granddaughter?"

"I was told only that Lord North would like a word with her, sir."

Major Humphrey presented Andrew with an official document, signed by Lord Summitt. It was an arrest warrant. Apparently the duke was taking no chances that the invitation might be refused. Andrew quickly scanned the paper and then gasped, "Treason! Are you mad?"

Lizzie trembled and forced her wobbly knees to hold her weight. She wouldn't faint. She wouldn't. From a great distance she heard her grandfather shout for the men to get out. Heard her mother's soft cry, her sister's gasp, and Aunt Amelia's plea, "Andrew, do something!"

But it was Jack she looked at. She thought his look to be accusing. It was shock. Shock and her own guilt that tore the breath from her lungs.

Lizzie shook her head and whispered, "I didn't."

And Jack believed her. Only then did his heart start beating again.

Lizzie believed in the cause with all her heart. She'd worked for it, lived for it, until nothing but freedom mattered. She'd been selfish, she thought as she glanced at her mother's white face, her grandfather's trembling hands. Young, foolish, and arrogant, she'd deceived herself into believing her day of reckoning would never come. Yes, the possibility had flickered through her mind, but she'd never truly believed it, never truly imagined the pain she'd cause. She'd thought herself smarter than the English, smarter and more wily. It had taken the love of a man before she realized the possible consequences of her actions. His love had changed her, but the change had come too late.

Lizzie felt her heart crumple. A few more days and she would have been married. No one would have dared to accuse the Countess of Dover. Lizzie smiled. She'd almost made it safely through. Almost.

"She'll have to come with us, sir."

Jack nodded, unable to take his gaze from her, willing his strength to flow into her, knowing she was going to need all she could gather. "I'm going too."

"That won't be possible, sir. You can follow if you like."

Jack nodded again. "You'll take care with her, man, or answer to me for it."

"Yes, sir," the major said as he ushered Lizzie out the front door.

Lizzie's family watched in stunned amazement as she was led out the front door and into the back of a wooden prisoner's wagon. It drove away surrounded by four soldiers on horseback.

Lizzie had left the house so quickly, she hadn't thought to take her cloak. A half hour later she shivered alone in a cold, windowless room. A young soldier brought in a pot of tea and one cup, but left without saying a word. Lizzie shivered so badly she thought she shouldn't chance lifting the pot. Instead, she warmed her hands on its hot round belly and waited in dread for the horror to begin.

Chapter 15

Jack thought the pain he suffered could not have been worse if had he taken a bullet to his chest. Every breath was torture. He believed her when she told him she was done with spying. Whatever Summitt might have come up with had to be conjecture. Still, it didn't seem to matter. She was in custody, and Jack couldn't find her.

It had been hours since they'd taken her away, hours since he'd left off his search for her and turned instead to seeking out his friend Samuel Livingston.

Sam would know what to do. He worked for the government and had contacts that would set things right. Jack was sure of it.

Jack was not a brutal sort. But tonight, in his search, he wasn't sorry to find a fight along the way. In truth, he'd already found two.

Jack entered White's, one of the many clubs Sam was known to visit. Oblivious to the swelling of his left eye and the cuts and bruises on both hands, he singled out David Adams, a longtime acquaintance. "Have you seen Livingston tonight?"

"In the back room," Adams returned, never taking

his gaze from the table and the huge pile of pound notes at its center.

Sam Livingston glanced up from the cards in his hands as his friend entered the room. It didn't take more than that to know Jack was in trouble. "We'll finish this another time, Mason," he said, standing and reaching for the coat hanging over the back of his chair. "I'll pick up my winnings in the morning."

Minutes later Sam and Jack stood outside the club. "Where's your horse?" Sam asked.

"Someone stole it."

The two men sat in Sam's coach as it moved through London's streets, heading for Sam's brownstone. "I feel like I've taken on half of London," Jack said while slowly moving his jaw to the left and right. "I need a drink."

"How many have you had?"

"Not enough. Where are we going?"

"I thought we could finish drinking at my place."

"I hope you've stocked up. I intend to get very drunk."

"You want to talk about it?"

There was a long moment of silence during which Jack thought over his options. Sam was his closest friend, but Sam worked for the government. He couldn't tell him the whole of it. It was bad enough he had gone against his own beliefs for a woman. He couldn't expect Sam to do the same. Finally he blurted out, "Lizzie is in trouble."

Sam said nothing, knowing his friend would explain.

"A squad of soldiers came to my house tonight. They had orders signed by the prime minister, to bring her in for questioning."

"Why?"

"The warrant said treason."

"Treason! Good God, man, how could they have made such a mistake?"

"It's Lord Summitt. Lizzie was in his room today."
Jack dismissed Sam's shocked look with a wave of his
hand. "I'll explain later. It was innocent enough.

"While she was waiting for her mother and Lady
Summitt's return, her hand hit a folder marked 'secret.'
The papers inside fell to the floor. As luck would have
it, she was picking them up when Summitt entered the
room. He accused her of reading them."

Sam knew Summitt as a rash individual, a man never
satisfied to watch government work at a slow, steady
pace. He didn't like the sound of this. The coach rolled
to a stop before his house. Sam opened the door and
jumped out. "Come in. I have a supply of brandy on
hand. Then you can start at the beginning."

Jack was on his third drink by the time he finished
his story, leaving out the most glaring truth of all, that
he had only recently confronted her with his suspicions
himself, and Lizzie had admitted to spying.

"And you think Summitt's behind it?"

"Who else could it be? After her arrest, word came
from Andrew's home that Summitt had been there,
searching Lizzie's room."

"Did the major say where they were taking her?"

"They said the prime minister wanted a word with
her. I assumed that meant his office. But when I got
there I was told Lord North had retired for the night and
couldn't be disturbed."

Sam cursed. "What did you do?"

"I went to Mr. Blake's home. He was hardly thrilled
to find his sleep interrupted, especially since his late
night visitor appeared on the verge of madness. It took
a while before I calmed down. He told me then that
Lizzie wasn't supposed to be brought in until tomorrow.
And he hadn't a notion as to where she might be."

"Did you try Summitt's place?"

Jack nodded. "He said the same thing."

"I didn't know what to do next, so I set out to find you."

"Obviously you came across a tough or two on the way."

Jack followed the direction of his friend's gaze. He looked at his hands and then touched the swelling under his left eye and the bump on the back of his head. "It was after the club on White Hall Street, I think. There were two of them. Now that I think of it, probably three. I was doing a fair job of defending myself when somebody hit me from the back. When I woke up, my horse was gone as well as my watch and the few pounds in my pocket."

"Summitt has her," Sam said. "No one else would have dared. He's always been fanatical in his beliefs. Almost came to blows once when I hinted our illustrious king could be a bit more balanced in the commonsense department." Sam sighed and shook his head. "I wouldn't be surprised to find he did this on his own.

"No doubt he's put her somewhere alone, so as to frighten her. He wouldn't hurt her, of course, but she'd be easier to question if she's scared."

"The bastard," Jack said, coming to unsteady feet.

"We'll find her. Take it easy."

"I can't wait. I have to do something. I have to find her, now! And that son of a bitch Summitt is going to tell me where she is."

Sam glanced at the sitting room clock. "It's already six o'clock. By ten we'll have an audience with Lord North. You're going to need the next few hours to pull yourself together."

It was nine forty-five when Jack and Sam stood in Westminster. By ten they were sitting across a massive cluttered desk from Lord North.

"What?" the prime minister asked, after being told the reason behind their visit. "I said she was to be brought in in the morning. Who authorized . . . ?" Lord North didn't have to think long on the matter to know the truth. Lord Summitt was anxious enough; no doubt he hadn't waited.

A knock sounded before Lord North could further comment, and Lord Summitt entered the room with a small envelope in hand, a satisfied smirk curving his lips.

"If there was any doubt, this should take care of it," he said as he placed the envelope before the prime minister.

Inside was a piece of paper from Andrew Thomas's desk. On it was written "Lord Germain: systematic occupation beginning in the south."

"Where did you find this?" Jack asked.

"A few men and myself visited Mr. Thomas's home late yesterday. It was in Miss Matthews's room, found on the floor behind her headboard. Apparently it fell unnoticed from a folder taken from Mr. Thomas's library."

Jack jumped from his chair. In an instant he held Lord Summitt by the throat against the wall. "If you don't tell me where she is right now, I'm going to kill you."

"In the brig, in the army barracks," came the strangled words.

"Take it easy, Jack. No one is going to hurt her," Sam said, suddenly at his side, pulling Jack's hands from Lord Summitt's throat.

Jack wanted to smash this man's face, wanted it more than he wanted anything in the world. And if Lizzie was somehow hurt, he swore he'd do just that. Slowly he eased his hold. "If she's hurt, there's no place you can hide."

Lord Summitt cleared his throat, smoothed his wrinkled cravat, and adjusted the ruffles at his cuffs. He moved then to stand behind the desk, lest Jack Black once again lose control. "Miss Elizabeth Matthews is a traitor to the Crown. There can be no other reason for her to be reading her grandfather's papers,'' Lord Summitt returned, backing up yet another step as Lord Dover glared his hatred. ''We have enough to bring her to trial.''

As it turned out, the prime minister was hardly pleased that Summitt had taken it upon himself to arrest Lizzie. He ordered Summitt to bring her to his office immediately and promised to get to the root of the matter before this morning was done. Jack and Sam were alone for a minute, Lord North having left the room for a quick word with one of his ministers.

''It looks bad,'' Sam said. ''Summitt's like a dog gnawing at a bone. He's not about to let this one go.''

''What am I going to do?''

''Is she guilty?''

''Yes,'' Jack admitted. There was no way out. If he wanted his help, he had to tell his friend the truth. ''I found her out some time back, but she's stopped.''

At Sam's skeptical look, he said, ''I swear it. She's stopped. Can something be done?''

Sam sighed, knowing from personal experience the power some women had over their men. He could only pray his friend was right. ''Summitt's right about a trial. The evidence so far is circumstantial, but he'll push for it.''

''She often reads in the library. She could have picked it up by accident with a book.''

Sam nodded. ''I'm sure they realize the possibility, but I think Summitt has more than the paper. We'll have to wait and see.''

Lizzie thought she'd never been so cold. She'd suffered through the night without a shawl or cover, and toward the early hours of the morning, exhausted from fear, she lay for a time upon the hardwood floor. She awoke from a short nap with her teeth chattering, her body stiff and aching. It was all over, she knew. No one would dare hold her here if she hadn't been found out.

She resigned herself to the truth of it, to the fact that she'd die. It was a chance she'd taken, one she'd lived with for years. It should have come as no surprise. Even the Gypsy had told her as much.

She thought of Jack, and her spirits sank at the loss. And in order to block out the pain, she found comfort in despair. She would die for what she'd done, but her suffering would end with a quick and final snap of the hangman's noose. Her family's pain would go on for some time. And Jack; remembering the agony in his eyes, she wondered if he'd ever get over it.

She was alone and frightened, cold and hungry; it was the longest night of her life. And by the time the soldiers came, Lizzie was convinced there was no sense in fighting the inevitable. Almost in relief, she welcomed the thought that it was over at last.

Lizzie preceded Lord Summitt into the prime minister's office. Over the next few minutes all of the evidence gathered against her was plainly stated. She never looked at Jack, except for a quick glance upon entering the room, but kept her steady gaze on Lord Summitt, who seemed to take particular delight in his accusations. "So, Miss Matthews, considering the fact that information known only to your grandfather has leaked out, that this paper was found behind your bed, that I caught you in the midst of reading secret files, you won't be surprised if we believe we have a good case against you. Have you anything to say to the charges?"

"Exactly what are the charges, sir?"

She was calm, far too calm, as if she'd already given up, as if the fight had been torn from her. There was no telling what she was thinking, nor what she might do next. Jack trembled. He'd never known such fear.

"Treason." And then Summitt added with gloating confidence, "You will hang."

"If I hang, sir, it won't be for treason."

"Don't say anything, Lizzie," Jack said. "I'll hire the best barristers. They'll straighten out this mess."

Lord North ignored the interruption. Having caught her words, he sought further clarification. "Does that mean you're innocent?" There was no doubting the hope in the prime minister's voice.

"Absolutely innocent, sir," Lizzie returned.

Lord North smiled and then leaned back in his chair with a sigh. He shot Lord Summitt a look that spoke clearly of his disgust. "If you tell me you haven't been gathering information for the colonists, I will take your word for it, Miss Matthews."

"But I have, sir."

Jack moaned. She denied the charge of treason, for she honestly believed it to be so, but she wouldn't deny spying for her cause. There hadn't been a doubt in his mind from the moment she'd entered the room. His world was coming to an end. He had to talk to her alone.

"The lady is in dire distress, my lord," Sam said, coming from his chair. "Can you not see that last night's abuse has left its mark?"

"Is that true, Miss Matthews? Were you abused last night?"

"I was very cold, very frightened."

"Has the experience done something to your mind?"

"Do you mean am I now insane? I think not."

She might not be insane, but she was as close to it as she was ever likely to get. She was about to throw away all they had. It was his future as well as hers, and damn her, she didn't have that right. "Lizzie, I'd like to talk to you for a minute," Jack said, and then turned toward the prime minister. "May I, my lord?"

Lord North nodded, and Jack escorted her from the

room. The moment the door closed behind them, Jack whisked her down the hall and into an empty room. He fought for control, fought to keep the panic from his voice as he closed the door behind them. "Don't do this, Lizzie."

"It's over, Jack. Can't you see that they know what I've been up to? Fool that I was, I never truly thought this day would come, but it has."

"Deny it! Lord North is giving you the chance to deny it."

"I'm not ashamed of what I did."

Jack dropped his hand from her arm and took a step back. "And I didn't ask for you to be ashamed. I don't know you. The woman I love would fight to the death to stay at my side. She'd never give up." He breathed a deep sigh as his words appeared to have no effect. Jack couldn't imagine what they had done to her. How had they managed to break her spirit in one night? He didn't understand that it was her own fears speaking. All he could see was a woman devoid of any spark of life. "I'll hate you forever. I swear I will." Jack was beyond desperation; it showed in his eyes, in his tone of voice. He was nearly beside himself with terror. His voice broke when he added, "When they kill you, they'll kill me as well."

Lizzie blinked at the pain in his voice. "But I did it. Jack, you know what I've done."

"Have you convinced yourself you must suffer now? Can't you understand that if you suffer, you won't be alone?"

Lizzie frowned. Did he mean she could somehow find a way out? "I don't understand. What can I do?"

"Tell them they're wrong."

"But I've already told them—"

Jack cut her off with, "You were confused. You didn't understand. You definitely didn't mean it."

And the last of her lethargy evaporated. Tears blurred

her vision. She loved him more than any cause, any country. What in God's name could she have been thinking to simply give up? How could one night of fear have robbed her of her determination, broken her spirit? It couldn't have. She was made of sterner stuff. "I'm sorry." She rushed into his arms. "Oh, Jack, God, I'm so sorry. I didn't mean for you to suffer like this. I wasn't thinking straight. What can I do?"

"Will you deny it?"

"Yes, God, yes."

He kissed her then, crushing her against him, daring heaven or hell to take her from his arms. And thought he'd kill anyone who tried.

Moments later they faced the prime minister again. Lizzie smiled and, feeling the warmth of Jack's arm around her, said, "I'm sorry, sir. I'm a bit upset, you see. Last night was particularly difficult. I didn't sleep or eat."

"Do you mean to deny the charges then?"

"Indeed I do, sir."

"You haven't been gathering information for the colonists?"

"No, sir. I have not."

"Haven't you, Miss Matthews?" Lord Summitt asked, all too silkily. "What say you, then, about this?" From his pocket he took a small book. It was her journal, and Lizzie knew all was lost.

"Found beneath the floorboards in your room. It's in your own hand."

Lizzie had forgotten about her journal. She hadn't written in it in months. Consisting mostly of her everyday comings and goings, it was innocent enough. But it wasn't a girl's private thoughts that would damn her, it was the coded words. A confusing mix that often made no sense but to her. In it she referred to Mr. Kent as brother. Messages became a thought she brought to brother. Red and Seth were the twins; their work, play;

the money gained from their work, grace; and so on. It was damming evidence, for no one would write in code unless she was doing something wrong, something against the law.

"I want her arrested, sir," Lord Summitt said. "The journal is undeniable proof of her guilt."

Jack took the book from the desk. "A young girl's doodling? Is this the best you can do?"

"Each item alone means little, but lumped together, I think the evidence is impressive."

"Can you explain why this looks as if it's a code?" Lord North asked. "Have you a brother?"

Lizzie smiled. "No. The truth is, I was thinking about a story. I often write a note here or there, lest I forget my thoughts."

Lord Summitt laughed. "Indeed. Are you a novelist?"

"One day perhaps. Right now I'm only gathering my thoughts."

"It was under the floorboard in your room. Why would you hide it?"

"I didn't want anyone to know until the story was complete." Lizzie knew her story was weak; still, it was the best she could do at a moment's notice.

Summitt sneered at her explanation. "She's lying."

"Why haven't you written in it these last few months?" Lord North asked.

"I was busy. The children need my attention. And then I forgot the book was there." Lizzie almost winced at the last of it, knowing she'd made a mistake. She should have said she was too tired at night, not that she'd forgotten.

"She's lying," Summitt repeated. "Had she wanted to be a writer, she wouldn't have suddenly forgotten all about it."

Lord North, hardly pleased with the whole business, agreed to further the investigation. In the meantime the

evidence looked damning, and it was necessary that
Lizzie be held. Lord North tried to ease the shock of the
moment by promising it wouldn't be for long, that the
truth would come out soon.

And as she was taken away, Jack could only pray it
would not.

Fleet Prison was a damnable hole spewed from the
bowels of hell. Beneath it ran a sewer that coated the
stone fortress in an ungodly stench. Below street level,
the floors of the dungeon rooms pitched from the outside
walls to form a gully at the building's center. Through
this narrow hallway, water as well as human excrement
collected into a stream of odious sludge, beckoning disease.

There were rooms that held only one or two inmates,
but Lizzie shared a common cell. The walls of thick
stone were covered with slime. The floors were wetter
still, and Lizzie didn't want to think why as she was
made to share a pile of filthy, lice-infested hay with
twenty other women.

Lizzie knew it was a common occurrence that dozens
at a time came down with prison fever, or smallpox. In
truth many a magistrate or barrister caught the vile dis-
eases once the accused were brought to trial. She could
only pray that the disease would somehow pass her by.

There were no windows, no fresh air. And her fears
seemed only to magnify as she suffered the stench of
unwashed bodies, rotting food, and human excrement.
Lizzie knew she'd never forget the smell, but worst of
all, she'd never forget the sounds of suffering, the wails
of pain, of fear, that filled the night. She might have
been in hell, for Lizzie imagined hell could not be worse.

A lone lamp hung on a nail to the right of the cell.
There was no other light, but for the lamps carried by
the turnkeys.

Down the corridor a woman constantly prayed. Lizzie

heard the guard yell for her to shut up. Lizzie moved to the bars and watched as he kicked the bars of her cell, but still she didn't stop. Next he unlocked the door and went in. And then came the dull thuds of fisted hands smashing flesh and the accompanying soft moans of agony. Still the woman didn't stop.

Later, when their meals came, Lizzie watched as he spit into the woman's soup before passing the bowl under the cell door. And Lizzie knew the hangman's noose would come far too late, for she'd be dead from starvation long before she'd hang.

The entire system ran on one's ability to pay the turnkeys for food or favors. It hardly fared well for those imprisoned for being unable to pay their debts. Lizzie thought the woman Molly held in the same cell as herself had little chance of gaining comfort. The rest were prostitutes. Women of stout hearts and courage. Even in this place of horrors they seemed able to keep their humor about them and accepted their fate with ease.

Wooden bowls of near-rotting soup were slid under their cell doors, and one woman, turning her nose up in disgust at the concoction, moved to the bars and brought her skirt high, exposing herself to his view. "I've got something for a piece of meat, Harry."

The guard looked over the offering with some appreciation and grinned as he rubbed the bulge in his pants. "Aye, and I've got the meat you'd be needing, Mary."

"A piece to sink our teeth into first, mate."

The guard nodded and moved away. The prostitute dropped her skirt, turned from the bars, and shrugged. "That one thinks 'e's got somethin' special between 'is legs."

Another woman laughed. "It's the ones who got the least that think they got the best."

"Makes it easier when they want it the other way," another thought to inform.

"If 'e knew how to use it, it might not matter."

The women laughed and lurid comments were made by a few concerning the general lack of physical endowments enjoyed by the turnkeys. A leg of lamb was cut into four chunks and delivered to their cell. Seconds after the last of it was eaten, five guards came for their reward.

Lizzie's cell mates cared little, knowing what was expected of them. Some obviously enjoyed it. Lying back on dirty straw, they raised their skirts with ease and opened their legs as the men in turn brought swollen rods from their trousers.

Lizzie, unable to bear the debauchery, turned from the sight and thought the place a living nightmare. Only now, as she watched the men force the willing and unwilling alike to do their bidding, did she realize the cause behind the distant screams and wails of suffering that had shaken her very soul.

Lizzie backed against the wall as one of the men approached her. "Leave that one," his comrade said, and Lizzie breathed a sigh of relief as the man turned toward another.

But the other was Molly, a woman hardly older than herself and obviously not a prostitute. She fought the turnkey with all her strength. Lizzie could not stand by and watch as Molly was abused. In a second she was on the man, shouting that he must stop his evil deed. She was ignored.

Even knowing she might suffer for her interference, Lizzie couldn't hold back. She cried out, damning those who dared to take what was not theirs. She threatened to see them all rot forever in jail. And then she had the temerity to hit the man forcing Molly.

He came from the sobbing woman to stand before her, his grin sporting a mouthful of gaping spaces and rotting teeth. "Shut the bloody hell up!" he said a second before backhanding her.

Lizzie fell to the floor, dazed from the blow, her eyes

smarting from pain, her lip already beginning to swell. The man was on Molly again, but thankfully another far more willing realized her desperation.

"Come on, mate," she said, standing at his side as she raised her skirt, enticing him with her offering. "No need to fight for it. I can show you a good time."

Lizzie sat on the dirty straw, shivering with fear, believing the world had gone mad. She closed her eyes to the varied sexual acts performed around her and never saw Molly, forgotten by the guard, crawl to her side and pull her knees up to her chin as she sobbed out her terror.

Hours later, a century later, after the narrow walkways had ceased their traffic, Lizzie caught the eye of the woman who had saved Molly from abuse. "Are you all right?"

The woman shrugged. "No need to worry, miss. The turnkeys were just having themselves a bit of fun."

"They won't be bothering a lady like you." The woman nodded toward those surrounding her. "We'll be out of here soon. Sentenced to the colonies, we are. Out of this hellhole on the next ship."

Molly whimpered.

Sometime later the cell door was opened. But for Molly and herself, those inside were lined up in the corridor. Molly had yet to come to trial, but her fate was a foregone conclusion. She, too, would be sent to the colonies, for she hadn't the means to pay her husband's debts.

Soon other cells were opened and a line of perhaps a hundred women were marching off to a new life. Lizzie offered a prayer that the new would be far better than the old.

"How much do you owe?" Lizzie asked.

"Ten pounds. My husband got sick. He couldn't pay. And then he died. The landlord wanted his money."

Molly shook her head. "I was sewing day and night, but he didn't care . . ."

Lizzie removed her watch from her dress. "Here," she said. "Take this."

"Oh, miss, I couldn't."

"Take it. Tell the guard to bring you to the magistrate so you can pay off your debt."

She shook her head again. "I can't pay you back."

"Call him," Lizzie said, pressing the watch into the woman's hand. "Do it now. And when you're free, go to Southampton, to Rocky Point, the Thomas house, and tell Mrs. Molston, Lizzie said to give you work." Lizzie smiled. "It's a large home and always in need of another seamstress."

"Oh, miss, I'll never forget you," Molly said.

Moments later, Lizzie's watch was offered in payment. Papers were signed and Molly left the horror of Fleet Prison behind.

She was thirsty, but eyed the water bucket with both longing and disgust, for beside it sat an identical pail, used for relieving oneself and filled to overflowing. Either could be mistaken for the other, and no doubt were occasionally.

Lizzie paced, sat, and paced again, and while listening to the woman's prayers, wondered how her family fared. Her mother would be beside herself with fear, and her grandfather, God, how could she have done this to him?

Lizzie was filled with remorse, wondering how she'd ever face him again. What could she say? Would he ever forgive her?

Her thoughts were interrupted by footsteps. Lizzie slipped into the cell's darkest corner. Had the turnkeys decided she was fair game after all? Now that the others had been shipped out, would she be made to pay for her interference? Lizzie closed her eyes in terror and then opened them to find her grandfather and Jack standing

outside her cell. The guard with them unlocked the door.
Jack and her grandfather stepped inside.

Jack stopped short. Thanks to the turnkeys' lamp,
there was no denying her bruised and swollen lip. There
wasn't a doubt in his mind that she'd been abused. "Are
you all right?"

Lizzie folded her arms over her stomach and nodded.

"Who did it?"

"Johnson," she said without hesitation. Lizzie felt no
need for retaliation. The punishment Johnson would receive was for Molly's sake. And Lizzie hadn't a doubt
Jack would offer the man a generous supply.

Jack's gaze moved quickly over the dirty straw, the
overflowed pail, the slimy floor and walls, and turned to
the guard. He grabbed the turnkey by his filthy collar
and shook him like a rag doll. The man was lifted from
the floor. "Is this what I'm paying for?"

The man choked, and gurgled out an incomprehensi-
ble word.

"I want to see the master turnkey, now!"

Jack and the guard went off without another word,
leaving Lizzie to face her grandfather alone.

Lizzie's heart pounded. Did she have the courage to
face his wrath? She loved her grandfather and hated that
he knew his trust had been misplaced. And now that she
faced him, Lizzie thought she couldn't feel more shame
for what she'd done. "Gran," she said, afraid to move
closer. "Is Mother all right?"

"She's fine, dear. Worried a bit about you, but fine."

"Oh, Gran," she said again as he opened his arms in
a loving, welcoming gesture. She moved toward him.
The lantern's light glowed behind his head. She couldn't
see his face. There was no need.

"I didn't think you'd come," she said as she slipped
into his embrace.

"What? Not come? Silly girl, of course I'd come."

"I'm so sorry, Gran," she murmured, her face pressed

into his jacket, breathing in the clean scent of him, knowing she'd remember this moment for as long as she lived, knowing his love was absolute, unconditional.

"Are you?" he asked. And knowing his granddaughter better than she thought, he asked, "Sorry for doing what you did, or sorry for getting caught at it?"

"Both," she answered honestly. Her arms around his waist hugged him tightly.

"But you'd do it again, I'd wager."

"I don't think so." She shook her head.

"Now, don't disappoint me, Lizzie; of course you would. You're a courageous lady, and I'm proud to say my blood runs through your veins."

Lizzie started to cry.

Andrew's large hand cupped the back of her head, pressing it to his heart. "It is a foolish war, and most of the country is well aware of the fact. Imagine the shame of brother against brother, Englishmen fighting Englishmen." He shook his head as if unable to believe such a catastrophe.

A soft sob escaped her throat. "Can you forgive me?"

"There would be nothing to forgive had I not been so lax."

"I abused your trust."

"The truth is, dear, had our positions been reversed, I would have done the same. There's no help for our beliefs, I'm afraid, therefore no fault found in them. Did you think I could love you less because our politics differ?"

"Oh God," she choked, wondering if she'd ever love another human being more than she loved this man.

"Now dry your tears, Lizzie." Andrew reached into his pocket for a handkerchief. "Jack will think I've abused you. I hear him coming."

"Damn greedy imbeciles," Jack said, swinging open the cell door, ignoring the grunt of pain as it hit hard into the turnkey's face behind him. "They took the money fast enough, but no one has gotten around to seeing to even one of the things I've ordered."

"What have you ordered?"

Jack shook his head. "It doesn't matter. You're not staying in this hellhole."

Lizzie blinked her surprise, for at that very moment two guards came and stood silently outside the cell, waiting for her to join them.

Jack walked at her side. "Where are they taking me?" she asked.

"Upstairs. The air is better there. And you'll have a window."

Lizzie climbed the stone steps. Jack was right; the higher they went, the less the stench of human sewage. The walls were drier here, as were the floors.

Lizzie was escorted to a cell that proved, if drier, no cleaner than the one she'd just left, empty but for the mound of dirty straw at its center and two pails much like those she'd left below. Lizzie nevertheless felt her spirits rise. The barred window was too high to see outside, but it allowed light, and to her mind the air smelled as sweet as heather.

"I'll have everything brought from home. Parker will be here mornings and evenings with your food." Jack sighed as she walked into his arms. "At least you'll be moderately comfortable until we can get you out of here."

"Can you? Get me out of here, I mean."

"We're working on it."

"Will I have to go to trial?"

"They won't hang you, if that's what you think," her grandfather said. "They'll have to get through us first."

Lizzie smiled. "Thank God for the two of you."

An hour after he left, Jack returned with his butler and three servants. The cell was swept clean of lice-covered straw and then walls and floor scrubbed with lye soap. Marrying into the aristocracy had some obvious good points, Lizzie thought. It wasn't only money, she knew. Those with money fared better, but she'd know luxury because Jack was an earl.

Next a cot and mattress were brought in, and clean bed linens placed upon it. And then a table, a chair, a small chest filled with her clothes, candlesticks and candles, her own teapot, cups and dishes, and jugs of fresh water.

Lizzie drank from one jug as she watched the room set to order. "I can't believe you've done so much."

Jack frowned, knowing there was nothing he wouldn't do for her. It didn't matter that that damn thief of a turnkey was demanding a fortune. Jack would have paid all he owned before seeing Lizzie sleep on a dirty pile of hay.

Chapter 16

~~~ OC ~~~

"**D**arling," Mary Stone said, as she entered Jack's library with the usual flourish of swishing skirts and overpowering perfume. She wore a pink and white striped poplin dress with an elaborate quilted skirt. At the center of a far-too-low neckline sat a small bow, obviously meant to bring to notice her generous bosom. The tight bodice caused Jack to wonder if those milky white breasts mightn't pop out at her first deep breath. "I've just heard what happened. Surely they can't believe your paramour guilty?"

"Lizzie is about to become my wife, Mary. She is not my paramour," Jack returned, hoping to set her thoughts straight once and for all. He finished off his drink and poured himself another, never inviting Mary to join him. Jack was fully aware of his rude behavior. Far from civil at the moment, he was hardly about to entertain this woman. "She's in Fleet Prison."

Mary pressed her palm to her generous curves and shuddered. "Good God, you must be quite beside yourself."

Jack thought she played the concerned friend particularly well. "And of course, you give a bloody damn."

"Don't be silly. Of course I care." And when Jack did not respond, Mary said, "You need your friends now, Jack."

"Can you help?" Jack thought he'd asked that question dozens of times over the last week and hadn't as yet found the right answer.

"I can bring you comfort."

Jack smiled, quite sure of her meaning, especially since she accompanied her words with a deep breath. Her dress was cut low enough to set a man's blood to humming. There was a time when he might have been interested. A time before a high-spirited, beautiful young woman had come to possess his every thought. Now her attempts at seduction struck him as sadly pathetic. He didn't want her, hadn't ever wanted her, and had only used her body because he was a man and she was so very free with her charms. Being with her had been a mistake. A mistake he wasn't about to make again. "I owe you an apology, Mary. Somehow I gave you the impression that more could come of our brief liaison than sexual satisfaction. I didn't mean for that to happen."

"I thought we were friends, Jack. Marriage does not preclude friendship."

His gaze moved to her nearly exposed breasts and then rose to her beautiful smile. Jack's next comment was interrupted by a knock at the library door and Parker announcing Mr. Livingston's arrival. "If you'll excuse me."

Mary nodded. "You're busy. Perhaps another time."

Jack did not respond as she drew her shawl around her shoulders, but before she quit the room he said, "Truly, I hope this is the last time, Mary."

Eager to see his friend, Jack felt his exhaustion evaporate on a wave of hope. When he wasn't trying to elicit the help of high-ranking colleagues, he spent his days at the prison. At night, unable to sleep, he prowled his rooms trying to think of something, anything, that would see Lizzie out of this mess.

He was about to lose his mind with worry. If Sam didn't bring good news today, Jack thought it time to resort to means that were somewhat less than legal.

Sam entered the room and headed directly for the table by the window, reaching for a glass and the brandy decanter.

Jack said nothing as his heart sank. If the news were good, Sam would have said as much the moment he entered the room.

Sam poured himself a drink and downed it before saying, "Word just came that de Grasse's fleet closed off an escape route at Yorktown, and Cornwallis had no choice but to surrender to Washington."

"Thank God," Jack whispered. He was beyond caring who won or lost this damnable war. All he wanted was Lizzie's freedom, and if hostilities came to an end, it could only further his cause.

"I wouldn't be thanking him just yet."

"Why?"

"Clinton still has New York." Sam shrugged and sipped at his second drink. "Perhaps nothing will come of it, but he's readying his troops for an attack."

"Why might nothing come of it?"

"There are rumors that both sides might press for peace."

Jack whispered a silent prayer of thanks. "And Summitt?"

"Is enraged."

"Jesus Christ! Meaning what? That Lizzie will be made to suffer for it? What's wrong with the man? Why can't he let this go?"

"Because it's a blow to our English pride," Sam said, coming to sit by the fireplace. "A ragtag band of illiterate colonists have damn near beaten us, man. They were weaker, by far, than the mighty Lion. They hadn't the funds, the expertise, the supplies or manpower. At times, not even shoes, and yet we were done in by hardly more than spirit."

"Spirit and France," Jack reminded.

Sam laughed. "Aye, and France."

"I've done with waiting. The man's not about to let go of his prejudices. I want her out and I don't care what the cost."

"You're talking nonsense, man. They haven't enough proof. She'll be tried and set free."

"Can you guarantee that?"

With a bang, the double doors hit suddenly against the wall as Margaret entered the room. Jack knew she'd been visiting with her daughter. His body stiffened with dread to find her white to her lips. "Lizzie is sick."

Margaret stood at the end of the narrow bed. Jack sat at Lizzie's side. His hand brushed a golden curl from her burning forehead. Her skin was like fire, her eyes glassy with fever. Jack forced the fear from his voice. "How are you feeling?"

"I'll be all right. You mustn't worry."

"I wouldn't think of worrying."

The doctor had just finished his examination. He was packing his small bag and nodded for Jack to meet him outside the tiny room.

"I'm going to talk to the doctor. In the meantime, I forbid you to dance."

Lizzie smiled. They both knew she hadn't the strength to lift her head from the pillow. "I'll try to control myself."

He took her hand and brought it to his mouth, knowing he loved her more than his own life. Nothing was going to happen to this woman.

"We never danced, did we, Jack? I should hate to die without one dance."

"Die? What kind of nonsense have you been thinking? We will dance, Lizzie. I promise you that.''

In the dingy hallway, lit only by a lantern at each end, Dr. Madison spoke the words Jack hoped never to hear. ''Typhus, prison fever. We can't be sure until the rash develops, and that will take about six days, but she has every symptom. She told me she had a headache yesterday, no appetite, and was generally feeling poorly. And today the fever and chills.''

''Does it always come on so fast?''

The doctor nodded. ''Always. Once it runs its course, it will end just as fast.''

''How long?''

''Twelve, at the most, fourteen days.''

Jack couldn't bring himself to ask if she'd make it. He couldn't bear to hear she might not.

The doctor touched his shoulder. ''She's a strong lady.''

Which told Jack nothing.

The doctor took a bottle from his bag. ''This will keep her comfortable. Give her a few drops three times a day.''

Jack reentered the room. The small table had been brought close to the cot. Upon it stood a water jug, a bowl, folded toweling, a glass. Jack added the bottle the doctor had left with him. Margaret had pulled the chair close to the bed. Jack sat opposite her.

''What did he say?'' Lizzie asked.

''He said you were ill.''

''One can only imagine the hours of study necessary for such a diagnosis.''

Jack chuckled softly at the droll comment. ''He said you'll be well again soon.'' And she would be, he swore. If it meant bargaining with the devil himself, she would.

Jack gathered her into a half-sitting position and pressed a spoon holding laudanum to her lips. Lizzie swallowed the medicine and shuddered at its bitter taste, only to be comforted by Jack running his hand down her back. "Are you going to nurse me?"

Jack smiled. "Your mother and I together."

Lizzie rested once again upon her pillow and sighed, "I wish I were well enough to enjoy this pampering."

"If you hurry and get well, I promise I'll pamper you after we marry."

She was ill, terribly ill. Burning up even as shivers attacked, leaving her weaker than she'd ever dreamed possible. It was an effort to breathe, to swallow, even to sleep. "I feel bloody awful."

"I know, dear," Margaret said as she replaced the dry cloth with a wet one. "You'll be well soon."

But would she? Jack wondered. The fever burned for five days and nights, and if the doctor was right, she had at least seven more to go. Did she have the strength to get through this? Every day the fever rose higher, while she grew weaker. God, how could anyone live through something like this?

"Gran wasn't angry," she murmured, and Jack held back his groan, for she was rambling again. The higher the fever, the more she talked. They had to cool her down. She'd die if she had to suffer much more.

Jack came to a decision, uncaring of propriety. Nothing mattered but that Lizzie become well again, and Jack was going to do everything in his power to make sure of it. "Take off her clothes."

Margaret gasped at the order. "What?"

"Margaret, the illness will run its course no matter what we do. In the meantime we must lower the fever. It stands to reason, if a cool rag helps her head, then a cool sheet should help the rest of her. Take off her clothes."

"Jack, I can't . . ." Margaret shook her head. His suggestion was impossible. She couldn't allow her daughter to lie naked in his presence. She shook her head again and repeated, "I can't."

"Do you think she has the strength to take seven more days of raging fever? If you won't help me, then move aside and I'll do it myself."

Lizzie muttered unhappily, "He always gets what he wants. God, he can't find out about . . ."

Jack reached for the hem of Lizzie's nightdress and began to pull it up. Margaret stopped him. "I'll do it. Step out of the room."

Lizzie, once again clearly out of her head with fever, suddenly and precisely said, "He's always taking off my clothes."

A small moan caught in Jack's throat and he turned suddenly scarlet, unable to meet his stepsister's questioning gaze. "She doesn't know what she's saying."

Margaret thought that was probably true. Still, thanks to Jack's guilty flush, she hadn't a doubt as to what these two had been up to. Considering that he'd no doubt already seen all there was to see, forcing him to leave the room seemed a bit ludicrous. Margaret said, "Turn around."

A few moments later, with Lizzie's naked body covered by a sheet, she said, "All right. Now what?"

Jack turned and reached for two more sheets. He pushed both into a bowl of water and then wrung them out. "I'll hold her while you spread this one over the bed. Then cover her with the other."

"She'll fight me."

"The fever has already sapped her strength. She won't fight hard."

Jack reached under Lizzie and brought her into his arms, while her mother placed the wet sheet over the bed. A moment later her body was completely encased in wet sheets. Lizzie fought against the discomfort. But just as Jack predicted, she was easily controlled. "It hurts!" she moaned. "God, what are you doing?"

"I know, sweetheart. I know," was murmured over and over.

The rash came on the sixth day and the fever stayed, a bit lower, but always there. Day after day Margaret and Jack tended to her care. Another bed was brought to the cell, and Margaret gave up her worries for Lizzie's modesty. Their strength draining, they took turns working with her, as one day stretched into another and another and then another.

And just as the doctor had predicted, on the twelfth day Lizzie awakened, weak but otherwise totally recovered. Her eyes were no longer glassy, her skin, clear again, was cool to the touch. "Have you been watching me sleep?"

Jack laughed, his heart so filled with happiness, it was a wonder he could keep from shouting. "How do you feel?"

"Exhausted. I was terribly sick."

"I know, but it's over now."

"You have a beard."

Jack smiled. There hadn't been time to shave, for he hadn't left her side longer than it took to grab a bite to eat, wash up, and change his clothes. "Do you like it?"

"You look wicked and mysterious, like a pirate, I think."

"Do I? Perhaps I shall keep it then.

"I've been saving a bit of good news for you. Cornwallis surrendered to Washington at Yorktown."

Lizzie's smile was brilliant. "I knew it. When?"

"October nineteenth."

Lizzie frowned. "October nineteenth?" She tried to think. "That's too soon, isn't it? I only sent the message three weeks ago. They can't have received it, won the battle, and the results have come back already."

"It appears your help wasn't necessary this time. No doubt Mr. Washington was up to handling Cornwallis."

Lizzie breathed a sigh of relief. "Is it over then?"

"It will be soon, I think. Rumor has it both sides are about to press for peace."

"But the English haven't conceded?"

Jack shook his head. "Lizzie, you should know first-hand, we English never give up when we want something."

Lizzie acknowledged the truth of his words. "It was the only time I loved losing."

Jack shook his head and sighed at the effort expended. "It was long and hard fought, Lizzie, but having you was worth the effort."

She glanced around the room, spying her mother asleep on another cot, remembering only then where she was. "I must remember to pen a note to our darling king and tell him how much I enjoyed his lovely accommodations. I shall the minute I leave here. Would tomorrow be too soon?"

Tomorrow would be just about right, Jack thought, what with Lizzie's trial set for the day after. "Summitt swears to see this matter to its end, especially now that it seems we've lost the war. You struck a blow to the man's pride. He won't forgive you quickly."

Lizzie thought she'd never understand how so self-righteous a man could have married a woman like Belle.

"Is the date for the trial set?"

"I don't want you to worry about that. All I want is for you to be ready."

"For what?"

"For whatever it takes. You're getting out of here."

"Jack, I haven't the strength to get out of bed. I'll never make it."

"You'll make it, if I have to carry you. I want you to rest now; I have things to do."

Jack turned then to see Margaret sitting on the cot. Their gazes held for a long moment before she asked, "Must it be this way?"

Jack nodded. "I've tried everyone but the king himself."

"When will I see her again?"

"In a year, perhaps less. I'll have people working to clear her name."

Later that night, while Lizzie bade her family a tearful farewell, Jack set about seeing his ends met.

It was near to midnight before he sat in Sam's drawing room, sipping at a glass of port and smoking his pipe. "Everything is in order."

"Meaning?"

"Meaning, I don't know how long I'll be gone, so I've arranged for my man of business to handle my affairs. I've notified the captain to ready the *Black Gold*, had Mercy pack Lizzie's things, and arranged for a parson to meet us on the ship tomorrow night. I need one favor."

Sam grinned. "You dog. And you waited a full five minutes to tell me this? Who signed her release papers?"

"Sam, I've tried every avenue. No one has the power or guts to go against Summitt, and I've done with begging and pleading. Lizzie is going to escape."

"Good God, man, you can't be serious!"

Jack puffed on his pipe. "I'm perfectly serious, actually. It can't be done through legal means, so that leaves me with but one recourse."

"If they find out you helped her escape, you could lose everything you own."

"They won't find out. The doctor will sign her death certificate tomorrow night."

Sam croaked out his shock. "What?"

"It's the only way. They have to believe she died, or I'll never have a minute's peace."

"They'll want proof."

"A half dozen or more die every day. There'll be a body."

"And when they examine it and find it's not Lizzie? What then?"

"They won't. Lizzie has had typhus, remember? The cause of death a direct result of jail fever. How many prisoners have infected their judges when brought to court? The magistrates are terrified and keep every one of them at a distance." Jack shook his head. "No one will dare go near the coffin, and chance coming down with it themselves."

"You'll never be able to come back."

"And that's the favor I need. After a bit of time, I want you to start working with her grandfather on clearing her name. Mr. Morgan will be at your disposal, of course. There's enough money in the account, if need be, to bribe the King himself. Once that's done we can return."

"Suppose it never happens?"

Jack shrugged at the thought, knowing it didn't matter if he never came back. As long as he had Lizzie, he'd be happy wherever they lived. But knowing the hearts of men better than most, he said, "I suspect attitudes will change once peace is signed."

Lizzie thought she'd never in her life spent a longer day. She'd never known such fear, nor felt more alone. She knew Jack was working on her release, but anything could go wrong. A guard might stop them. Someone could be killed. Jack could get hurt.

Lizzie blocked that thought from her mind. She couldn't lose him now, not when she'd finally come to love him.

Her thoughts moved on to equally dark matters. Suppose she could never come back. Suppose she'd never see her family again. Steven needed her. He'd think she'd abandoned him. Alice would forget her within a month. Would her grandfather keep them? Would he abide by his promise to send the boys to school?

Oh God, she needed Jack. Where was he? What was taking so long? She thought until she was exhausted and then slept only to awaken to the fear again.

And as Lizzie worried, three floors below, Jack stood in a small room lit by only one candle. He wanted to strangle the bastard across from him, but asked instead, "What are you talking about?"

"Just as I said, my lord. The coffins are counted and then matched to the death certificates. It's my head if I come up short on one side or the other."

Huge sums of money had already changed hands. There was no way that Jack was going to let this piece of filth cheat him of more, or Lizzie's freedom. He knew well enough at what the man hinted. "What you mean, of course, is that you want more money."

Charlie Cones instantly saw the error of his ways. The man across from him was big enough to do him some harm, and considering the look of murder in his eyes, an attack on his person was not an impossibility. He'd thought to milk the man of a few more pounds, but imagined staying alive might be the best way to go. "You misunderstand, my lord. I only meant that she'll have to go out in the box."

Jack shuddered at the thought, unable to imagine the extent of Lizzie's horror. She'd been terrified in a closet big enough to hold five. How could she stand a box? Perhaps he could drug her. Jack wondered if there was any laudanum left.

On the stroke of twelve, a man dressed in a hooded dark robe, cinched at the waist with rope, and holding a prayer book, raised the knocker upon the prison's front door. Beside him stood a man dressed as a laborer.

A turnkey, holding a lamp high, edged the door open a crack as if fearful that someone would break into the place. Were it not for the jingle of keys, one might have mistook him for an inmate. His clothes were little more than rags, and his greasy hair hung long and unkempt to his shoulders. Certainly he was no cleaner.

"What? Another one," the man muttered softly, knowing a priest only came when an inmate had died. Why they always died at night, he hadn't a clue. All he knew was, watching these men come and go, praying their secret prayers in Latin, gave him the shivers. "Which one you 'ere for?"

"Elizabeth Matthews. We'll be taking the body."

The turnkey shrugged. "This way," he said, after consulting a chart. He lead the priest and the man with him to the upper level of the prison.

"Shouldn't 'ave come down with the fever, methinks. She wasn't with the rest."

Jack had sent money along with specific orders that Lizzie should have the best of care. And because those orders had been ignored, Lizzie had grown sick. Jack wished he could get his hands on the fool responsible. He said nothing.

There was a plain wooden coffin already in place outside Lizzie's door. The guard unlocked the door and asked, "You need help? I could get someone." They didn't pay him enough to touch the ones who died of fever.

"No. We'll manage. First a few minutes of privacy, if you please. There are prayers that must be said."

The turnkey shrugged. "I'll be back when you're ready."

Jack closed the door behind him just as he murmured, *"E nomine Patre, e . . ."*

Lizzie came quickly from her bed. Her knees buckled beneath her weight. "What are you doing?" Jack asked, reaching for her and bringing her against him. "Don't get up."

"I'm all right. I moved too fast, is all."

Jack knew that wasn't all. She was well again but terribly weakened from her ordeal.

"God, I waited so long. I thought you'd never come."
She breathed a sigh and then leaned back and frowned.
"What are you wearing?"

"Listen carefully, Lizzie. I don't want you to be
afraid. I'll be with you every second. You're to have
died of typhus and I'm here to collect the body."

"I'm not afraid. I'm terrified. What if something goes
wrong?" There was an instant of silence and Lizzie
asked, "I what?"

"Lizzie, I couldn't think of any other way."

"What does that mean? I died?"

"Have you any laudanum left?"

"Why?"

"You should take a bit."

Lizzie realized then his meaning. If she were dead,
she'd leave the prison in a box. She shuddered at the
thought, her fear of small, dark places causing her to
hyperventilate. "Oh Lord," she gasped, and trembled
violently as she asked, "Jack, please, isn't there another
way?"

"It will only be for a few minutes."

"Suppose there's a mix-up and I get buried?"

"Good God, don't even think something like that.
You won't be out of my sight for an instant."

Lizzie knew she didn't have a choice. If she didn't go
along with the scheme, she faced the hangman's noose.
"It's on the table."

Jack handed her the bottle. "Here take a sip."

Lizzie took three.

"Easy with that," Jack said, taking the bottle from
her lips.

"You're not getting into a coffin. I need it."

Lizzie lay down again just as the guard opened the
door and called, "You finished?"

Jack leaned low and whispered, "No matter what,
don't make a sound." Then he took Lizzie into his arms
and turned.

The guard jumped back, even though ten feet separated him from the body. "Jesus, don't touch her! We roll the sick ones into their boxes with sticks."

"God will protect me, my son."

In the midst of terror, Lizzie found herself fighting back the urge to giggle. The scene seemed suddenly ridiculous. Jack, of all people, posed as a priest, while the turnkey trembled in fear of the dead, only she wasn't dead. Lizzie tried to think. Jack had obviously paid a bribe. Then why this elaborate charade?

The urge to laugh didn't last long. The minute the top of the box slid into place, Lizzie knew an almost overpowering need to scream. She bit her hand, needing the pain, needing anything that would take her mind from this horror.

Could she make it? She couldn't breathe. She'd die before they got her out. She knew she would. Terror gripped her soul, and then as fast as it had come upon her, it began to ease. Lizzie knew the laudanum was beginning its work and found she could breathe after all.

"She can't 'ave been dead long. She ain't stiff yet."

"She died just before I got here, I think. She's still warm."

The guard shuddered. "Warm and diseased." He wasn't about to touch either her or the box.

The box was lifted and jostled a bit as it was carried down the stone steps. Doors creaked open and then slammed shut behind her. At last Lizzie recognized the sounds of the street. A horse's hooves on cobblestone, the creaking of wheels as a cab passed by. Lizzie could feel the box being slipped onto something. It was a wagon, she thought, she hoped. Any second now, Jack would tear the top off this wretched thing. Only he didn't. His voice faded instead as he returned to the jail.

Someone moved beside the box. Lizzie held her breath and prayed.

The top lifted a bit, just enough to allow a draft of

delicious fresh air. "Easy, miss. He's signing papers."

"Parker," she whispered, recognizing the voice of Jack's butler and never more grateful for the sound of a familiar voice.

It was an eternity. Even with the cover partially lifted, it was longer than a lifetime. And then Jack was back and the wagon was moving. He waited only until they turned a corner before ripping the top of the coffin away. "Are you all right?" he asked, bringing her from the box and into his arms.

Lizzie gasped again and again. She couldn't get enough air.

"I can't tell you how brave you are."

"Try."

"You're the bravest woman I've ever known. And I love you."

Lizzie watched as they passed by an inn. Inside came a roar of laughter and high-pitched whistles. "I was beginning to doubt I'd ever get out."

"I told you I'd take care of it, and I did."

"Who did you bribe?"

"The master turnkey."

Lizzie frowned. "Then what was this all about? Why did I have to get into a box? Why couldn't I have walked out?"

"Apparently the son of a bitch wasn't willing to share his newfound fortune with any of the guards. I couldn't insist or bribe them myself. I wasn't sure which one I could trust."

"You couldn't have trusted any of them, I think.

"God, I'm so glad it's over. I need a bath, a whole bottle of brandy, my pipe, and you." Lizzie said the words on a slurring breath and then laughed softly, the laudanum having taken full effect. "Not neshessarily in that order."

Parker grinned as he hurried the horse toward the docks and the *Black Gold,* waiting to leave on the next tide.

''Parker, stop the wagon and throw this thing into an alley, will you?''

''Yes, sir.''

''I have a surprise for you.''

''What?'' she asked, laughing softly again. ''You're not an earl, you're a prince. Right?'' She shook her head and grew dizzy. ''No, no, no. You're the bloody King of England.''

''And you're drunk.''

She shook her head again, this time more slowly. ''Never touched a drop.''

''On laudanum.''

''Oh, but that doesn't make you drunk,'' she said, leaning comfortably into his chest. ''It makes you . . .''

''Sleep,'' Jack said softly as he realized why she hadn't finished her sentence.

Chapter 17

Lizzie slumped in Jack's arms. The ship was tied to its moorings, its decks motionless, and still she couldn't seem to find her balance.

The *Black Gold* was set to sail down the Thames in less than a quarter of an hour. There wasn't enough time for her to recover from the overdose of laudanum. They had to do it now.

Jack faced the preacher. "You can start."

"My lord, she's drunk. I cannot—"

"No, sir," Jack interrupted. "She's weak, having just recovered from a grave illness."

The preacher appeared hardly convinced. "Nevertheless, she's not herself. I cannot be a party to this."

"My dear sir," Jack said, striving to hold on to his temper. Weeks of anxiety combined with tonight's tension had taken their toll, and it was by pure will alone that he suffered this fool. "On this night we will set out on an ocean voyage. This woman and I will share a cabin, a bed, as man and wife. I'd prefer deflowering her with God's blessings, but I tell you, sir, it will be done with or without the words spoken."

The preacher was aghast that a gentleman could think

to do such a thing. His first thought was to run for help, for he didn't for a second doubt the man's words. Lord, he should have known something was wrong. Being called upon to marry someone on a ship in the middle of the night was hardly an everyday occurrence.

The preacher took a step back, but a glance at the hard-faced, grizzled men standing to his left and right instantly dissuaded him of further movement. It was then that Reverend James Chester decided the woman would be better off married to the scoundrel than forced to live in sin. He began the service.

Jack had to shake Lizzie each time a response was needed. "Say 'I do,' Lizzie."

"I do, Lizzie," came the sleepy reply.

Jack smiled and thought that seemed easy enough. Only it wasn't half so easy when it came time to say the vows. "I, Elizabeth Matthews," he whispered, and was relieved as she repeated the words.

". . . take John Black."

"Where?"

James Chester shook his head. "She doesn't know what she's saying. This isn't legal."

"It's legal. I'll tell her what she said tomorrow. Now finish it."

One of the three seamen who made up their circle grunted in agreement. It was then that the preacher noticed two others fingering knives, each long, each apparently sharp, judging by the gleaming blades. The preacher decided the sooner he finished with this business, the better.

A pen was held in Lizzie's hand and she was told to write her name. Somehow she managed.

Jack breathed a sigh of relief as the marriage certificate was secured in his pocket. He paid the preacher, lifted Lizzie into his arms, and moved toward his cabin.

He had hardly closed the door behind him when the call was sounded for the ship to leave port.

In his cabin, all had been readied for their arrival, for their wedding night. Jack looked around the room at the flowers, the candles, the sparkling glasses, the wine and food, the tub filled with warm, scented water.

He'd planned everything down to the last detail, even to the silk robe lying across the bed. He'd thought tonight, they would manage to get to the bed without shoes.

Jack watched her sleep, his heart squeezing with tender emotion, knowing there would be other nights. He eased her out of her clothes and helped her slide under the coverlet. Then, as Lizzie slept, he took a bath. With a towel wrapped around his waist, he sat and ate his wedding-night dinner alone.

Lizzie felt the ship's rocking and sighed as it lulled her back to sleep. The bed dipped at her side and she heard a familiar voice. "Are you going to sleep forever?"

Lizzie sighed, "Not if you keep talking to me. What time is it?"

"Almost six o'clock."

"Are you mad? Six o'clock in the morning?" She rolled to her back. Jack was in her room. She looked momentarily confused. This wasn't her room. "Where are we?"

"On my ship. And it's six o'clock at night."

Lizzie frowned. "At night?" And then she nodded, remembering. "The laudanum. I shouldn't have taken so much."

"Do you remember last night?"

Her gaze softened with love. "I remember that you got me out of that dreadful place."

"Do you remember what happened after that?"

"You put me in a coffin. It's going to take a while before I forget that."

"I know, and I'm sorry that had to happen. But what

I meant was, do you remember what happened after you boarded my ship?''

"No. I think I fell asleep. What happened?"

Jack reached for the cup of tea on a nearby table. "We got married."

Lizzie smiled. "We did? How odd. I would have thought I'd remember something like that."

Jack shrugged. "It took a little prodding, but you answered the questions."

Lizzie chuckled and came to a sitting position. The covers slipped to her lap and she pulled them up. She held them under her arms and took the offered cup from his hand. "Suppose I said I don't believe you."

Jack's body instantly responded to the glimpse of naked breasts. He found he had to clear his throat twice before saying, "I have the paper."

Lizzie shot him a look that mingled laughter with suspicion. "Have you? I'm sure you wouldn't mind showing it to me then."

Jack moved to his trunk. For the first time she noticed he was wearing only a robe. He brought a paper back to her and held it just out of her reach.

It looked to be a marriage certificate, all right, and something that resembled her signature was scrawled at the bottom. She reached for it. He pulled it away.

Her eyes widened. "Am I not allowed to touch it?"

"I'm not sure if I trust you. It took a lot of effort to get this."

Lizzie laughed again. "It's a forgery."

"It will hold up in any court."

Her eyes were bright with laughter. "So if we're married, why aren't you in bed with me?"

His dark gaze moved slowly from her laughing eyes to the wild curls fallen over creamy shoulders and the definite outline of feminine charms. "The thought crossed my mind, but I had a notion you'd enjoy dinner first."

Lizzie glanced around the room, her gaze taking in the slightly wilted flowers, the lit candles, the bottle of wine, the shimmering glasses and dinner plates ready to be filled. And then she saw the tub. Jack had made sure she had enough water to wash while in prison, but she hadn't had a real bath in weeks. "Oh, Jack, a tub! Did you do this for me?"

"For us. Are you strong enough to get up?"

Lizzie only grinned and, without saying another word, stripped aside her covers. If she heard his sudden intake of breath, she gave no notice as she came from the bed. "Oh," she said, reaching out for the wall. "I'm dizzy."

"You're still weak from the fever," he said, his arms circling her waist, steadying her slight form against him. "Tomorrow you'll be stronger. Perhaps we should wait."

"No. I moved too fast, is all. I'm fine." She turned in his arms, watching as he studied her face. "Truly."

Jack lifted her then and walked the few feet to the tub. Gently he lowered her into the warm water.

"Oh Lord, this feels lovely," she sighed, slipping down until her shoulders were covered, most of her hair wet. She slipped under the water and came up sputtering. "Simply lovely."

Jack moved a small table near the tub. On it he placed toweling and soap as well as two glasses of wine.

Lizzie's eyes closed as every fiber of her being absorbed the luxury of warm, scented water.

A moment later she was nudged forward. "Give me some room."

Lizzie smiled as Jack squeezed in behind her, his legs surrounding hers, his arms pulling her back to lean against his chest. Lizzie sighed. "I can't imagine what I ever saw wrong in the aristocracy."

"Liar," he whispered near her ear.

Lizzie laughed softly. "It's the tub. It's woven a magical web over me, making me say things I don't mean."

She turned a bit so her lips could brush his chest. "Or perhaps it's just the magic of you."

"Am I making you say things you don't mean?"

"I mean it when I say I love you."

"You can't leave it there. Tell me why," he said, his voice husky and warm, his arms tightening around her waist.

"Because you're wonderful."

"More," he urged.

"You chanced everything for me."

"I had no choice. Nothing means anything without you. What else?"

"You're brave. You could have sent someone to get me out, but you did it yourself."

"You're wrong there, Lizzie. I would have gone mad not knowing what was happening. I had to do it my-self."

"I love you."

He breathed a deep sigh, knowing he'd never tire of hearing it. "Good."

Lizzie waited for him to go on, to add his love words to the tender moment, but heard only, "Can you reach the soap?"

Lizzie took the bar from the table and turned to face him. The water came to just below her breasts, and Jack took full advantage of the luscious view. "Haven't you got anything to say?" she asked.

"Yes. Taste this wine. It's delicious."

Lizzie sipped at her drink and then sipped again. "It is good." And then, "I just told you I love you. Aren't you supposed to say something in return?"

Jack grinned. Taking the soap from her hand, he teased, "Well, I could say, my men are going to give me some strange looks. This soap smells like French perfume."

"Jack." Her gaze narrowed with warning.

He laughed and then, replacing both glasses on the

table, pulled her against him and buried his face in her neck. "I love you, too. But you already knew that."

"Tell me why."

"That's the problem. I haven't the foggiest notion why."

"Wretch," she said, slapping his shoulder and trying to wiggle free of his arms.

Jack laughed, ignored her attempts, and adjusted their bodies so that her silken legs wrapped around his hips, his arms around her waist. "All right, let's see, why do I love you?" There was a moment of silence and then he said, "It couldn't be just because you're beautiful. I've known a lot of beautiful women and never loved a one."

Lizzie watched his expression.

"It couldn't be because you smoke a pipe, drink brandy, ride a horse astride, or force me to make love to you until I'm damn near dead."

Lizzie frowned and muttered, "Force?"

Jack ignored her response and shook his head. "No, it has to be something else.

"You didn't know how to kiss. At least you didn't at first, so that can't be it."

Lizzie frowned. "You don't love someone because they can kiss."

"But you can because they can't." He thought for another few seconds before saying, "You were a nasty wench, insolent, impudent, and brazen." Jack raised and lowered his eyebrows in rapid succession. "I was intrigued. Perhaps that was it."

"I wasn't a wench at all," she corrected. "I was a lady."

Jack strangled on a laugh, which he wisely turned into a cough.

Lizzie pretended not to notice. "And I was only nasty because I was afraid of you."

"You were not," he scoffed in total disbelief.

Lizzie nodded. "It took a while, but I finally figured it out. I knew instinctively that you were dangerous. I knew you'd complicate my life."

"Did I?"

"You were trying to find the reason why you love me. Don't change the subject."

"All right, how about this for a start? I love you because you let the baby crawl all over you and never complain that she wrinkles your dress or musses your hair. I love you because you love Alice, most of all."

Lizzie's eyes grew suddenly sad.

"What's the matter?"

"She won't remember me by the time I get back."

"She'll remember, I promise."

Lizzie shook her head, tears misting her eyes. "She won't. Babies forget so fast." Lizzie surprised them both with a sudden sob.

Jack's arms brought her tight against him. "No tears. Promise me you won't cry."

"I won't," she said even as she sobbed again and began to cry in earnest. But Lizzie didn't cry only for Steven, who would believe she had deserted him; for Alice, who wouldn't understand where her mommy went; for Joey, who would probably eat himself into twenty extra pounds. She cried for her sister and mother, for a dear grandfather she might never see again. She cried because of the fear and anxiety so recently suffered, for the horror of prison, for the fool she'd been in not giving more thought to the consequences of her actions.

"The war should be over in a few months," Jack soothed as he ran his hands down her back. "Lizzie, don't cry, please," he said, never feeling more helpless. "And as soon as it's over, we'll send for the children."

Lizzie's tears eased to an occasional sob. She wiped her eyes with the back of her hands. "Do you mean they'll come? All of them?"

"All the children, their nurse, and probably Mercy. We might have to wait a bit before seeing the rest."

"How long, do you think?"

"As soon as your grandfather clears your name."

Lizzie sighed. "Suppose he never does. What then?"

"He will. Have you forgotten his influence?"

Jack waited for her smile before continuing, "Now, where was I?"

"You were telling me why you love me."

"Oh yes, now I remember. I love you because you roll in the grass, careless of the stains to your gowns. And even though they're far too big, you give the boys rides on your back. I love you because you're brave, because you had the courage to go with your beliefs and spy for your country. Damn it, Lizzie, it makes me crazy to think of that."

"Then think of something else."

Jack took a deep, calming breath and forced his mind to other avenues. "I love you because you care for the orphans. I love you because your name is Lizzie and I've always fancied a woman with that name."

She frowned. "What?"

Jack laughed. "I love you for your laughter, your spirit, your smiles, your glaring looks that twist at my heart, for the way you answer me back, for all of it, because of it, or in spite of it, I'm not sure." One hand left her waist and a finger ran a wet trail over damp skin from her shoulder to one plump breast. "But I love you especially because you once shook my hand when you were naked."

"I think that made more of an impression than I'd intended."

His eyes darkened and his voice grew low and husky. "If you moved closer, I could make an impression of my own."

Lizzie's smile was purely wicked. "Closer than this? I'm already sitting on your lap."

"I dropped the soap in the water. Help me find it."

*   *   *

"Are you happy?" Jack asked this after they had dinner and taken their time making sweet, languorous love.

Lizzie turned in his arms. Leaning against him, her eyes closed, she laughed softly. "You might say that.

"You never told me where we're going."

"The West Indies."

Lizzie frowned. The West Indies could hardly be considered safe. The English and French as well as the Spanish battled constantly over control of the islands and their rich ports of trade. "Are you sure it's safe?"

"I'm sure. France seized Dominica two years ago. I have a place there." He shrugged. "Besides, the fleets quit the West Indies during hurricane season."

"Hurricane season? Do you mean real hurricanes?"

Jack grinned. "We shouldn't have trouble. It's almost November. By the time we reach port, the season will be long over."

Lizzie's smile looked slightly sick. "I hope you're right."

Chapter 18

"**L**and ho," was called from above, and Lizzie moved from the shade of a sail to the railing. Moments later a faint, hazy line of green touched upon the horizon.

Lizzie asked a passing seaman, "Have you seen Lord Black?"

"No, ma'am."

Lizzie entered the cabin. Jack was working at his desk and looked up at her entrance. "I know. I heard."

"Is it Dominica?"

"It should be. Mark Lessor is an excellent navigator. I checked with him this morning and he said we were on course."

Lizzie glanced at the table. "Is it teatime already?"

Jack's gaze dropped to her bodice. Her watch was gone. Now that he thought on it, he hadn't seen it since she was arrested. "What happened to your watch?"

"Oh, I meant to tell you."

"You lost it?"

"No. I gave it away."

"Did you?" Jack was obviously unhappy at the thought. "You mean it meant so little to you that—"

"No!" she said, cutting him off. "I don't mean that at all. It was a beautiful watch and I loved it."

Jack frowned. "You loved it, but you gave it away?"

"There was a woman in prison. She was there because of debts owed. Jack, she had nothing and I had everything."

Jack smiled as he came from behind the desk, took her into his arms, and rocked her against him. "Do you have everything?"

"Almost." Lizzie snuggled close and reached a hand between their bodies. Her smile turned wicked as she found him hard and most eager to accommodate her every wish. "There is something you could give me."

His hips moved forward and Jack's eyes darkened with hunger, delighting in her bold investigation. "And I'd be most willing to give it," came his sultry response. "Tell me what it is you want."

Her eyes shone a brilliant blue. Despite the fact that she'd kept mostly to the shade, these last weeks had darkened her skin and brought a healthy pink glow to her cheeks. She was well again and as strong as ever. Her happiness was obvious and would have been complete had she not missed her children. Still, thanks to Jack, she had every confidence that they'd be together again, and soon.

In the meantime Jack mostly kept her mind from her temporary loss. He loved her so much, it almost hurt.

"Another watch," Lizzie teased.

"You little wretch."

Lizzie laughed, a low, sultry sound, as her hand continued its wicked study of his ever-hardening body. "I think you've hidden one in here. There's something hard and I'm sure I heard ticking."

"Aye. Open my trousers and you may have it."

Lizzie slipped out of his arms with a laugh. "God, you're a terrible liar."

"Unlike some"—he managed to shake off his passions for a moment and give her a pointed look—"I've found no need to perfect the art."

Lizzie only laughed again. "It wasn't as difficult as you might imagine. Most people want to believe a woman to be an empty-headed piece of fluff and incapable of anything but warming a man's bed."

"Speaking of beds, I know one that needs warming."

Lizzie smiled as she poured their tea and then glanced toward the object in question. "You mean it's cool already, after what happened this morning?"

Jack thought they might never come closer than they had this morning to setting the bed on fire. He'd never seen her more bold, more daringly seductive. He'd never grown hotter than when lost in the sweetness of her mouth and tongue. He'd fallen completely under her spell. In truth he should feel drained and totally replete, but it took only her touch to call for a repeat performance. "I'm afraid it is. Poor thing."

Lizzie chuckled as she added sugar to his tea and handed him the cup. "You're being very silly. If you want to make love, why not say so?"

"I want to make love," he dutifully returned.

"I can't. We'll be docking soon and I have clothes to pack."

"We won't be docking for hours yet."

Lizzie's blue eyes darkened with interest. "Hours? Are you sure?"

Jack nodded and then sighed with pleasure as he watched her reach for the buttons of her dress. Lizzie's gaze moved toward the bed. "Now that you mention it, the poor thing does look a bit lonely. Sort of cold and pathetic, wouldn't you say?"

"We could make it feel better."

Lizzie pushed both dress and chemise down her hips. "We could try."

Jack watched generous breasts bounce and shiver with her movement as she pulled away her drawers, and knew they wouldn't have to try hard.

The *Black Gold* slipped around the southern portion of the island, just outside the coral reef. Beyond the sky blue water breaking in gentle waves along a pure white sandy shore stood greenery the depth of color Lizzie had never imagined. A perfectly manicured lawn came into view, and at its center, a huge white house. It was three floors high and had six pillars that went all the way to its red roof. A balcony ran along the second floor, and Lizzie could see dark green French doors leading to rooms beyond. Potted flowers dotted the second floor, but a profusion of color bloomed along the neat drive, at each side of the front steps, and up the walls of the house.

"Do you like it?" Jack asked, coming up behind her, wrapping his arms around her waist.

"What? The house? It's beautiful. Do you know the people who live there?"

"I have a nodding acquaintance with the owner, but I know his wife intimately."

Lizzie turned in shock at his statement. Jack grinned. "She's a sweet piece of arse, I don't mind telling you. Hard for any man to resist."

Lizzie only blinked, unable to believe him capable of so insidious an act. And then she saw the twinkle in his eyes and the smile that teased the corners of his mouth. "Do you intend to see her again?"

"I'd bloody well better. The woman has stolen my heart."

Lizzie smiled. "I'd wager it must be difficult to go on without a heart. You should ask for it back."

"Nay, she can have it, all right, as long as she promises to take care with it."

Lizzie chuckled softly just before she punched him in the stomach.

Jack gasped and then crushed her against him.

"You beast. You almost had me fooled."

Jack gentled his hold and shot her a heart-stopping grin. "What do you mean, almost? I did fool you."

Lizzie's smile held a promise of retaliation before she returned her gaze to the house and snuggled her back to his chest.

"I love you, Lizzie. I'm always going to love you. After all the trouble I went to to get you, do you think I'd even look at another woman?"

"I know you love me. Still, I'm afraid you'll have to pay for that," she said as if she had no control of the matter.

Jack laughed and snuggled his face near her ear. "I'm not afraid of you."

Lizzie ignored his statement, knowing, of course, he never would have said it if he weren't. "You do have a penchant for big houses, don't you?"

"I told you, my uncle left it to me. All I've done was fix it up a bit." And then, "What are you going to do to me?"

Lizzie ignored the question. "You said it was a plantation and that you grow fruit. What kind?"

"Bananas and copra, but mostly limes. We make rum. And I've been thinking lately of marketing some timber. The mountains in the background are unbelievably thick with trees." And then, "Lizzie, what are you going to do?"

Lizzie shook her head. "Nothing."

"Should I believe you?"

"That's up to you, I suppose." Which told Jack just what she wanted him to know. Nothing.

Lizzie could see the hazy outline of green mountains

in the far distance. "Does your property go back to the mountains?"

Jack nodded. "It's a volcanic island and dotted with hot springs. Boiling Lake is up there." He pointed to the mountains. "Water shoots three feet into the air there."

Lizzie's gaze glowed with pleasure as she turned to face him again. "I can't wait to see it," she breathed. "I'm going to love it here."

"But you'll always love me more, am I right?"

Lizzie's only response was a laugh.

An hour later the *Black Gold* docked in Roseau, the island's capital. The island was small, its capital a tiny metropolis that excelled in trade. The narrow streets were jammed to a standstill with carriages and horses, while people, some black, others different shades of brown, walked to and from the docks. Most of the native women balanced huge baskets, filled with fruit or meat or bread, on their heads. Vendors hawked their wares, creating bottlenecks in the snail-paced traffic as elegant women shopped from the luxury of their carriages.

Almost everyone, even servants, held parasols. Those who didn't wore wide-brimmed straw hats. Lizzie laughed at the sight of a man on horseback shading himself with a parasol. Most of the frilly lace lay torn and hanging sadly over the edge like bedraggled ribbons.

A moment later a carriage went by. The driver, dressed all in white, sported a parasol that matched his female passenger's.

The dock below was a beehive of activity. Ships loaded into their holds barrels of rum, crates of copra and limes. And even more barrels of lime juice, while other ships unloaded foodstuffs, tobacco, tea, boxes of machinery and parts, as well as bolt after bolt of material.

The place was a riot of color. From a distance Lizzie had thought the color came from flowers. On closer inspection she found her assumption only partly correct, for much of it was the dresses and scarves worn by the natives. She thought she'd never seen more brilliant color in one place.

Jack wore white. As usual he sported no ruffles at his throat or cuff. His black hair was tied neatly back, and the sun gleamed off his dark head. She'd never seen him so startlingly attractive. "Are you ready?" Jack asked, reaching for her hand. Lizzie smiled and allowed him to lead the way.

A carriage and two wagons waited just beyond the gangplank. Their driver was black. Lizzie had, coming from the colonies, seen black men before. But house servants had never been so stiff and formal, so obviously learned in manners, nor had she ever known one with a French accent. His name was Valoir, and Lizzie watched, fascinated, as he ordered, with great authority, laborers to load up the wagons. Jack helped Lizzie into a carriage, while men hurried to secure baggage in the wagons behind them.

Soon the small caravan was squeezing through the narrow streets on their way south toward Jack's home. Once the city was left behind, Lizzie saw the trees formed a canopy over the road, allowing them cool shade. Jack was right when he'd said her clothes would be too heavy for the island's climate. Lizzie thought she'd have a few dresses made right away.

"Are you tired?"

"No. Why?"

"Hot?"

"Some."

"I'll send for a seamstress as soon as we get to the house."

"Thank you."

Lizzie didn't recognize the fruit of some of the trees they passed. Jack ordered the driver to stop at the edge of a field where they sampled tart refreshing limes, sweet oranges, and mangoes.

Once again in the carriage, they continued the two-hour ride that would bring them home.

Lizzie had thought the house beautiful from a distance, but found it breathtaking on closer inspection. Each large room boasted of high ceilings and great doors that led to shaded terraces. The second-floor terrace was edged with elaborate ironwork.

After a quick walk through the main rooms, Lizzie entered the large, airy suite she and Jack would share. She moved to the balcony door and sighed as a gentle breeze came off the ocean. It soothed her heated skin. She turned then, her gaze taking in the simple white furnishings. The floor shone, the wood a soft polished brown, while the rest of the room was white. She touched the white coverlet and allowed her hand to drift over the ruffled edges of silk pillows. It was a beautiful room, a beautiful home, and Lizzie thought if her family were here with her, she might never feel the need to leave this place.

"What do you think?" Jack asked. Stepping into the room, he'd watched her gaze touch upon the bed, the lounge chair, the chest of drawers, and the mirror above it. The sheer drapes that hung beside the doors, the fresh flowers that sat on nearly every surface.

"I think you have excellent taste. Did you do this yourself?"

Jack shrugged. "I'm not much when it comes to combining colors, so I thought if I used one per room, I'd do all right."

Lizzie smiled. "White is usually used for a woman's bedroom."

Jack sat on the bed, testing its softness with a bounce or two. "Is it? Good, because now it belongs to a woman."

"You mean we will have separate rooms?"

"Who? Us?" Jack asked with a puzzled frown. "Do you want separate rooms?"

"You said once that we would."

Jack smiled as he took off his boots and gathered pillows behind him. "Was I drunk?"

"No, you were tired."

Jack chuckled, "Tired enough to talk nonsense, I think. Are you hungry?"

Lizzie shook her head. "Show me the house."

"It's the hottest part of the day and everyone is resting."

"But I'm not the least bit tired."

"Good. Come over here," he said while patting the bed at his side.

The next morning, just after a breakfast of fruit cut into mouth-size pieces, tea, fried bread with butter and cinnamon, and a light cream pudding, the seamstress came. Mrs. Withers took Lizzie's measurements and promised to return on the morrow with at least one dress suited for the island's warm climate.

After her fitting, Lizzie found Jack waiting for her on the terrace just outside the breakfast room. He had led her through a few more rooms last night, but Lizzie had been more tired than she was willing to admit. He promised a closer look today. "Are you ready?" she asked.

"Would it be all right if I showed you the house tomorrow? I thought we'd take a ride."

"Where are we going?"

"It's a surprise and we have to hurry. I don't want to be caught there after dark."

"After dark? It's only ten o'clock in the morning."

Jack grinned. "Not nearly enough time for what I have in mind."

"I've only known you to have one thing in mind. And that doesn't take ten hours."

Jack only took her arm and guided her toward the stables.

He used a path that cut through the thick woods. Lizzie followed close behind. The sun was brilliant, but in these wooded mountains, only the barest dapple of light managed to show between the thickly branched trees. "Are you sure you know where you're going? It's almost black in here."

"We're almost there," he said.

Hardly had he said the words when the horses moved into a small, bright meadow. At its center stood a pool about five feet across spouting hot water straight up in the air every thirty seconds or so. Jack dismounted and left his horse to graze on the tall meadow grass. "Hurry up, we only have about nine hours left."

Just then steam belched from the ground near Lizzie's foot. She moved quickly from the spot. "Hurry up and what?" Lizzie was having visions of the ground collapsing, drawing her into a bottomless pit, or erupting, throwing her high into the sky with a million pounds of boiling lava. Neither thought thrilled.

"Take your clothes off." As he spoke, Jack was following his own suggestion.

"Are you sure it's safe to be here?"

Jack placed his gun on the rocky edge of the pool. "It's safe." And then, noticing the direction of her gaze, he said, "That's just a volcanic vent. The island is full of them. Nothing to be afraid of."

He was naked, and she hadn't begun to undress. "Jack, I don't think this is a good idea. We're standing on a volcano. Suppose it explodes."

"The whole island is a volcano and it hasn't exploded yet. I've been coming here for years," he said while sliding into the pool. "I promise you, it's safe."

"Perhaps I shouldn't," Lizzie said, still unconvinced. The bubbling water and smell of sulfur hardly went far toward easing her mind.

Jack said nothing. His look of ecstasy said it all.

Lizzie reconsidered. "Perhaps I'll just dip my feet."

Jack smiled as she took off her shoes and stockings. "Take off your drawers, too."

"Why?"

"You don't want them to get wet, do you?"

Lizzie did as he asked and then sat at the water's edge and slipped one foot beneath the surface. "Oh, that feels lovely, doesn't it? How deep is it?"

"I'm standing." The water came to the middle of his chest.

"Lift up your dress and I'll bathe your legs."

Lizzie did as he asked, but found her dress was never high enough as he lapped water over her legs and thighs. "Are you sure you want to wet only my legs?"

"Of course." Jack laughed at his lie. "Does that feel good?"

"It feels wonderful."

"Are you sure you won't come in?" he teased.

"The water doesn't feel too warm."

"It's very warm," he said, "but you'll get used to it."

Lizzie stood and pulled her dress and chemise over her head. Naked and beautiful, she looked like a goddess, Jack thought, absorbing the sun, reveling in it.

A thudding sound came from the woods behind them. "There's no one around here, is there?"

"No. Just that group of men working the field to your right."

Lizzie gasped and reached for her clothes again just as Jack came from the pool and took her against him.

"I'm teasing. No one is here but you and me. The thudding came from some animal."

Again in the pool he slowly eased her down the length of his body. "Hold on to my shoulders. I want to show you something."

His hands moved to her thighs and brought her legs to circle his hips. A moment later Lizzie smiled as his aroused body slid smoothly into her warmth. "You could have showed me this in our bedroom."

"I could have showed you something *like* this. Not this.

"Here, lean your back against the edge of the pool. I want to show you something else."

"You want to show me a lot of things. Like this?"

"Aye. Exactly like that," he said as their bodies separated from the waist up and his hands moved to cup her breasts. "Now, isn't this better?"

"It's not better than cream pudding, but it is better than strawberry tarts," Lizzie teased, closing her eyes.

"Is this better than cream pudding?" he asked as one hand moved beneath the water to tease her passions.

"Mmm," Lizzie said, arching into the pleasure. "That's even better than licking cream from Mrs. Molston's bowls."

"Do you do that?"

"I had to," Lizzie said in all innocence. "Who else would show the children how?"

Jack grinned at the thought of a grown woman licking a bowl clean. "You'll get fat."

"I fully intend to, one day. Nothing is uglier than a skinny old lady, except perhaps a skinny old man."

Jack chuckled.

"Mmm," she moaned. "Jack, this is absolutely heaven."

"What?"

"Everything. You, what you're doing, this water."

"Are you enjoying your honeymoon, Mrs. Black?"

Lizzie gasped helplessly as he moved more deeply into her tight warmth. "It's the Countess of Dover, if you don't mind."

Chapter 19

"What are you doing?" Lizzie asked Jack as the woman behind the counter went to measure a dozen yards of white lace.

"I've asked Mrs. Withers to make you a proper wedding dress."

Lizzie frowned. "You said we were married."

"And we are. Only I want you to say the words while fully awake this time."

"Meaning what? The marriage isn't legal, is it?"

"It's legal. Would you rather not marry me again?"

Lizzie could see this was important to him. "I'd love to marry you again. And I want the dress. But do you think we could renew our vows when my family is present? My mother would so like to be involved. And Gran, he'd want to be there."

"All right. We'll have the dress made, but we'll wait to say the words again."

The carriage was piled with packages as it moved out of town. Jack drove and Lizzie sat at his side, protecting them both from the sun with her parasol. "This has to stop, you know. I've been here four months and you're still buying me clothes. There aren't enough days in a year to wear them all.''

His hand reached around her waist and brought her closer to his side. ''You'll be needing a whole new wardrobe soon.''

Lizzie thought he was talking about when they returned to England. She grinned, relishing her sweet secret. ''Will I? You mean we might be going home soon?''

''Aye, but probably not before the baby comes.''

There was a moment of silence before Lizzie admonished, ''Jack! I was waiting for the perfect moment to tell you. Now you've ruined everything.''

''You've had two months of perfect moments to tell me. When were you going to do it?''

''I was waiting for our next visit to the pool. How did you know?''

''Well, two months with no sign of your monthly time was an obvious clue. And there was the occasional morning when your stomach emptied itself the instant you came awake. But what really convinced me, I think, was watching your eyes fill with tears at a sunset.''

Lizzie laughed. ''Didn't you notice I stopped smoking my pipe?''

''Aye. Do you think smoking is bad for the baby?''

''I don't know. It makes me dreadfully ill, and still I never stop wanting it.''

Jack grinned. ''After the baby comes, you can start again.''

''I wish my mother were here,'' she said with a touch of melancholy, wishing not only for her mother but all her family.

''Why don't we send for her? She should be with you, especially when the baby comes.''

Every day they expected to hear that peace had been signed. Lizzie wondered how much longer she'd have to wait. She desperately needed to see the children and all her family again. But mostly, especially during this time of her life, she wanted her mother. "Do you know that I love you?"

Jack kissed her long and hard, and then moaned into her neck, "Let's go home and you can show me how much."

Andrew Thomas was summoned to Lord North's office. He'd been there often enough of late, but this was the first time he'd actually been invited.

"Here," the prime minister said, the moment greetings were exchanged and Andrew sat. "You might like to read this."

Andrew smiled as he read the morning paper. Obviously a war-weary nation, having long since called for peace, had finally seen the fruition of their hopes. Commons had yesterday declared, "It would consider as enemies to His Majesty and England all those who should advise or attempt the further prosecution of offensive war on the Continent of North America."

"My ministry is finished, of course," Lord North said on a weary sigh. "But before I resign, as a favor to an old friend, I thought you might be interested in this."

He handed Andrew a document that clearly exonerated Lizzie of any wrongdoing and proclaimed her a citizen of England, in good standing.

Andrew smiled and then, looking up from the document, he asked, "A citizen?"

"You didn't think I was taken in by accounts of her early demise, did you?"

"Why not? Everyone else was."

Lord North grinned. "But everyone else doesn't know you like I do." He shrugged. "Besides, your stepson didn't wait for the funeral before disappearing, a highly unlikely bit of circumstance, since he obviously loved the girl." Lord North shook his head. "By the way, you might tell Margaret I thought her tears most convincing."

Andrew laughed and wondered how many others they had not convinced.

Lord North nodded toward the document still in Andrew's hands. "I assume you have no objections if I sign that?"

"None at all, sir. But what about Summitt? Was he convinced?"

"I'm not sure. Still, he's finally seen reason. His wife's threat to leave him if he didn't put aside his obsession obviously did the trick."

Andrew grinned and, for the first time in months, breathed easy.

Jack and Lizzie had breakfast almost every day on the balcony of their room. Lizzie was enjoying a bowl of fruit, something she couldn't seem to get enough of of late, while Jack drank coffee and looked through his mail.

Suddenly Jack jumped from his chair and laughed as he waved a letter almost in Lizzie's face. "It's finished!" He grabbed her up and swung her around. "It's finally over."

"The war? Do you mean peace was signed?"

"I mean, peace was signed and North cleared your name, all at the same time."

"Does that mean we can go back?"

Jack laughed. "We can go anywhere you like." And then he asked, "I thought you loved it here."

"I do. It will always be a special place. We had the most perfect lazy honeymoon here. But the boys will be sent off to school soon, and I'd rather not be an ocean away. Besides, I miss my family terribly."

"And you'd rather live in England?"

Lizzie smiled. "You did buy that castle. It really shouldn't go to waste."

"What about the colonies?"

"My feelings for the colonies will never change. But everyone I love is in England."

"And the one you love most of all?"

Lizzie smiled, for Jack never tired of hearing himself put first in her life. "Oh, you mean that earl fellow?" She snuggled closer and reached on tiptoe to kiss his jaw. "He was despicable at first, don't you think?"

"I don't know. I thought he was a decent sort."

"As it turned out, he wasn't so bad. Keeps asking me if I love him, though."

Jack growled. "You little wretch."

Lizzie laughed as she spun out of his arms. "There's only one way to convince him, I think."

"And that is?"

To Jack's absolute delight, Lizzie tore away her clothes, sending them flying every which way. And as she did she backed into their room. She didn't stop until she stood in only her stockings and shoes. "He told me on more than one occasion that he particularly enjoys shaking my hand."

"He does," Jack returned, particularly enjoying everything about this woman.

Lizzie took two steps toward him and offered him her hand. "How do you do?" she said. "I'm the Countess of Dover."

It was hours before Jack stopped grinning.